THE MUSIC OF SOUND

By

Ian Jarvis

Paperback ISBN 978-1-78705-138-6
ePub ISBN 978-1-78705-139-3
PDF ISBN 978-1-78705-140-9

Published in the UK by MX Publishing
335 Princess Park Manor, Royal Drive,
London, N11 3GX
www.mxpublishing.co.uk

Cover design by Brian Belanger

Chapter 1

1912

Stained glass began to rattle in the decorative mahogany screen behind Bernard Quist and he twisted in his chair to look around the wood-panelled smoking room. The other clientele had paused mid-conversation, most turning to watch the crystal decanters tinkle noisily against one another on their shelves behind the bar.

'Intriguing,' said Quist, as the vibrations ceased. Settling back into the leather seat, he drew on his cigar and frowned curiously. 'What on earth could that have been?'

Lenny Logan sat opposite Quist at the table. He'd placed his whisky too close to the edge and the tremors sent the glass tumbling over. The wiry Scotsman caught the drink and raised it to show that nothing had spilled. Logan belched and took a gulp. 'How about that?' He laughed loudly. 'Lucky Lenny, they call me. Lucky, lucky, lucky.'

Several nearby aristocrats turned to scowl, appalled at the coarse sound of his voice. These people weren't used to hearing drunken Glaswegian accents.

Sir Ronald Norberton sat beside Quist, eyeing Logan in a manner that couldn't have held more contempt had the Scotsman been a negro. Norberton was proud of the British class structure; it was the finest in the world. He'd been stationed as an army officer in India and, although their caste system seemed to work, it was organised over five complex levels. England had a straightforward *three*: the cream, the pen-pushing middle class and the scum.

The lower classes were a necessary evil, needed to man factories, dig coal and keep the streets clear of shit, but Norberton never had cause to speak with these horrendous people and they knew their place. That *place* would soon be following the orders of their *betters* and marching towards German machine guns. These people were oiks and Norberton prided himself on his ability to smell them. You could bathe an oik, spray it with expensive cologne and clothe it in finery, but the seedy stench would remain. He glared again at the drunken Glaswegian. There were higher chances of women being allowed to vote than an oik getting into this first class lounge, and yet Logan appeared to have somehow managed it.

Norberton turned to the middle-aged man beside him. Bernard Quist's large aquiline nose and dark wavy hair reminded him of the early portraits of the Duke of Wellington. Quist was cultured, intelligent and highly knowledgeable, but try as he might, Norberton couldn't figure him out. His eloquent English voice was right and his clothes were right, but Quist simply didn't *feel* right. Somehow he seemed *classless*, which, of course, was impossible.

'We're hundreds of miles from the coast,' said Quist, looking around again. The smoking room had been constructed to resemble an exclusive gentleman's club and a blue tobacco haze shrouded the ornate ceiling. 'So what could have caused that shuddering? Has something happened down in the engine room? Perhaps a minor explosion?'

'I very much doubt it,' said Norberton. 'Everyone knows this ship is the finest in the world. I'm sure you're worrying unnecessarily.'

'Ah, who cares?' said Logan, leaning across the table to the two men. 'I don't know you chaps, but here's a question for you both. What do you think of me? Be honest.'

Norberton's rude grunt suggested he didn't think much.

Quist was more diplomatic. He sat back in the leather chair and drew on his cigar. 'What do you mean?' he asked.

'When you look at me, what do you think?' The Scotsman gave an inebriated grin. 'How much do you reckon I'm worth? Come on. Take a guess.'

Disgusted, Norberton raised his eyebrows. A gentleman would never dream of asking such things. Logan's watch chain was gold and his clothes were certainly expensive, but his suit was the only one in the room that wasn't handmade. It was the sort of thing a gambler might wear and far too flash for his discerning tastes.

'I can't imagine,' said Quist. 'That really isn't for us to comment on.'

'Yes, well…' Copious amounts of whisky had loosened Logan's tongue. 'You wouldn't believe me if I told you. There's a lot of weird things you fine, upstanding chaps wouldn't believe.'

Quist puffed his cigar and smiled. 'Oh, you'd be surprised at the weird things *I* believe, Mister Logan.'

'How about magic? Do you believe in *that*?' The Scotsman took out a pack of cards and placed three face-down on the table. He lifted one to show it was the Queen of Diamonds, then briskly moved them around. 'Where is she now? Where's the Queen?'

'For God's sake,' growled Norberton. He'd heard about this stupid trick, but had never witnessed it before. Apparently, it was something the oiks wasted money on in taverns – a grubby gambling diversion for the weak-minded. He'd been watching carefully and tutted as he tapped the central card. 'It's that one, obviously.'

'Really?' Logan turned it to show the Two of Hearts and flipped over the one beside it. 'No, the Queen's there. Hey, it's a good thing you didn't bet a shilling on that.'

'Indeed,' said Quist. 'Although, seeing as this gentleman owns most of Hampshire, I doubt such monetary losses would be cause for concern.'

Logan laughed loudly. 'Find the Lady. Do you know how much that little trick has made me? How much it *will* make me?' He reached over and produced a palmed shilling from behind Norberton's ear. 'I'm going to be the richest man in America.'

'What on earth are you talking about?' Norberton peered at

3

the Glaswegian as though he were mad. 'I know certain types practise such twaddle and I'm aware you can coerce idiot gamblers into parting with petty cash on street corners, but you'll never make any *real* money. That stupid conjuring nonsense with the coin isn't going to impress anyone.'

'I only need to impress *one* person: Sarah.' He pulled another shilling from Quist's ear. 'Sarah is fascinated by Find the Lady and my little feats of magic.'

'Oh, yes, your travelling companion,' snorted Norberton, disdainfully. 'Your rather attractive and very young *niece.*'

Logan answered with an earthy chuckle which confirmed his suspicion – this sleazy character was most definitely *not* the girl's uncle.

'Sarah?' Quist tapped his cigar in the ashtray and sat forward, suddenly interested. 'Yes, I saw her with you at dinner. It's approaching midnight. I assume she's retired?'

Logan nodded. 'She's catching up on her beauty sleep, not that she needs it. Quite a looker, isn't she?'

Quist nodded slowly. From the little he'd seen of this petite blonde, she appeared rather naïve and *Uncle* Lenny was doubtless enjoying bedtime fun and games in his cabin. Sarah hadn't been aware of Quist until this evening, but after noticing him from a nearby dining table, she'd shown a great deal of interest. It didn't seem to be romantic interest, but several times he'd caught her staring inquisitively and he was curious as to why.

'I don't suppose I'm making much sense,' said Logan. 'The card trick itself isn't going to make money and neither is my sleight of hand magic, but they entertain…' He hesitated, then decided against explanations. 'Here's to Sarah.' He raised his glass instead. 'The very best *niece* any man could wish for.'

The Scotsman gulped the whisky, hoping that Sarah really *was* asleep in their suite. *She'd spent much of the voyage on a quiet area of the deck gazing at the ocean. The last thing he needed was for her to be washed overboard by some freak wave. Then again, that was hardly likely as he was lucky, lucky, lucky.* Logan smiled to himself. *He'd certainly been lucky the night he met Sarah shivering on the Glasgow docks. She'd stowed away on a boat from somewhere and he'd been the one to find her.* The girl had made Logan a fortune in Scotland, but his gambling habit had forced him to flee. He was now able to pay his debts many times over, but he'd made too many enemies, the kind who didn't like card cheats and were willing to write off lost cash for the pleasure of slicing him into pieces. He'd taken Sarah south by train and booked their sea passage to America, his new-found wealth ensuring they travelled first class. He finished his drink and smirked. *New York would be a lucrative place to begin afresh. The east coast was filled with rich people who could easily be relieved of their money.*

'Excuse me.' Quist gestured to a passing steward. 'What was the shudder we felt a short while ago?'

The young man smiled politely. 'Nothing to be concerned about, Sir,' he said. 'We almost collided with an iceberg.'

'Almost?' said Norberton. 'But the jolt…'

'It only scraped us, Sir. Fortunately the lookout spotted it and we were able to turn.'

'I see.' Quist drew on his cigar. 'So there's no damage?'

'Well…' The steward shrugged. 'We sustained inconsequential scarring along the starboard hull, but certainly nothing to worry about.' He gave a smile of reassurance. 'This is Titanic, Sir, not some rusty old freighter.'

'There you go,' laughed Logan. 'We *almost* hit an iceberg. Like I told you, I'm lucky, lucky, lucky.'

* * * *

The steward had probably been mistaken in his damage estimation, decided Quist, and Lenny Logan was certainly wrong about being lucky. It was now two and a half hours since their *inconsequential* encounter with the iceberg and Titanic had

5

virtually disappeared. Only the stern remained visible and Quist stared in horror at the nightmarish sight. There were no storms, huge waves or blazing fires – the destructive things one might associate with maritime disasters – just a luxury liner slowly and bizarrely vanishing into the calm ocean, the star-encrusted sky reflecting on the mirrored surface around it.

Quist floated in the freezing water, attempting to keep his head up without kicking his legs. People could only survive for around fifteen minutes in these conditions and exertion would shorten that time; the more energy he used, the quicker he'd lose heat. The body cools faster in water than in air and *this* water was way below zero; the sort of temperature found in British swimming pools. His shivering had stopped and his teeth were no longer performing a frantic castanet melody. His breathing had slowed too and so had his heartbeat. These weren't good signs. Hypothermia had set in, his core temperature was falling and he knew he'd soon slip into unconsciousness.

Quist had given his lifejacket to a child and he wondered if it had helped. Probably not, he decided woefully. Bodies floated all around him, some writhing, but the majority now motionless, turning the tranquil Atlantic into a surreal soup of the dying and the dead. Most of the lifeboats had rowed away, fearful of being sucked down in the vortex created by the sinking vessel or, more probably, because of the danger of being swamped and capsized by panicking survivors. Turning, he saw that one boat was still close enough to reach and, forcing his sluggish legs to work, he slowly swam towards it.

A young woman floated on her back just ahead. Her piled coiffure had fallen apart and the soaking golden hair covered her face, but he recognised the striped dress from earlier at dinner. It was Logan's niece Sarah. Swimming to her, Quist lifted her head and searched with numb fingers for a pulse in her neck. It was there, thankfully, but feeble and slow. The girl's body mass was

6

smaller than his and she'd cool much faster. If he didn't get her out of this icy water in the next couple of minutes, she'd be dead.

'Wake up, Sarah,' slurred Quist, cupping her chin and swimming backwards towards the lifeboat. 'Stay awake.'

'Water,' mumbled the girl, consciousness returning. 'I'm in water.'

'Yes, but you're going to be alright.' Quist looked around for Logan, but he was nowhere to be seen amongst the floating bodies. With the amount of whisky he'd drunk, he was probably asleep in his cabin. 'Just try to stay awake.'

Some thirty feet in length, the lifeboat had been built to carry sixty-five people, but held forty and most of the empty seats were filled with expensive suitcases and hat boxes. The steward in charge stood up, watching their arrival dubiously. Reaching the side, Quist held onto the hanging grabline and lifted the girl as high as possible.

'Help her,' he slurred. 'Take her.'

The steward appeared indecisive, but several arms reached out and hoisted Sarah to safety.

'The little lamb's frozen,' said an American woman, wrapping a blanket around her. 'Squeeze up to her with me and use your bodies to warm her.'

Several aristocrats glanced at each other, shocked at the disgusting suggestion.

'Is she first class?' asked one of the ladies, her luxurious leather trunk taking up the three seats beside her. Wrapped in the skinned corpses of rare felines, her face reminded Quist of a painted ferret. 'We already have two girls from steerage in here. I may as well be sharing the boat with prostitutes.'

Quist hauled on the grabline, attempting to raise himself.

'Sorry, mate,' said the steward, holding up a hand. 'No room for you.'

'Are you serious?' gasped the American. 'Pull him in, you

7

fool.'

The sailor glared at Molly Brown. He was tired of this mouthy Yank and it was time to assert his authority, even if it meant someone dying. 'I'm in charge here,' he snapped. 'Your lives are in my hands and it's my job to make the critical decisions. I'm sorry, but sometimes you have to be cruel to be kind.'

'Help him,' said Sarah, finding her voice. 'You must help him.'

'The boat can't take any more, Miss.' The steward shook his head and picked up the oars. 'We're already too full. A big wave could sink us.'

'A wave?' Molly Brown glanced incredulously at the mirror-like ocean. 'No, you have to let him in. Just throw out some of these jewellery boxes and you'll have more than enough room to...'

Her words were drowned by a deafening rumble and a cacophony of horrendous screams. Titanic had broken in two and the stern thundered as it vanished beneath the surface in a creamy eruption of bubbling foam.

The terrified steward began to row. 'Shut up,' he snarled. 'The boat's full.'

'Don't worry, Sarah,' mumbled Quist, releasing the grabline. 'It will be alright.'

Watching the lifeboat row away through white clouds of breath, he tried moving his legs, but he no longer had any feeling from the waist down. A piece of planking floated nearby, too small to clamber onto, but ideal for what he had in mind. Quist knew the hypothermia wouldn't kill him, but he was close to blacking out and had to work fast. With dead fingers, he clumsily fumbled off his trouser belt, tethering it tightly around his left wrist and securing the loose end to the wood. This would keep his body afloat and ensure he was found. Consciousness began to fade and, finally allowing his eyes to close, Quist's head slipped slowly beneath the surface.

Somewhere below him, Lenny Logan lay drunkenly comatose on his bed, blissfully unaware of the porthole cracking under pressure and that his first class suite was on a two-mile journey to the ocean floor. The unimaginable horrors of the past few hours had completely passed him by.

Perhaps he *was* lucky after all.

* * * *

Chapter 2

Present Day

Torrential rain poured from the night sky onto the vast expanse of Dartmoor, the rugged terrain drinking it in like a greedy black sponge. The armoured van motored south through the darkness, heading along the lonely lane from Princetown to connect with the main road in the Devon town of Yelverton. Phil Turner sat with his prisoner in the rear, peering dourly through the tiny barred window and listening to the deluge hammering on the roof. This sort of weather was normally only seen on British bank holidays, or when the television forecasters predicted sunshine.

Turner had never understood why the tourists and walkers viewed Dartmoor as beautiful; he hated this desolate wasteland of bleak heather, sucking mires and rocky outcrops. Folklore told of Hell hounds that supposedly roamed this wilderness after dark, bounding out from Wistman's Wood to hunt down unwary travellers. He grunted scornfully. Any devil dog with a modicum of sense would take one look at this miserable place and piss off somewhere else. *Anywhere* else. He hated the countless eerie legends and romantic myths of the moor. He hated the cheery descriptions of the area in the Devon travel brochures. Above all, however, he hated the way his prison transfer request appeared to have been *misplaced* in favour of more suitable officers.

Turner had been stationed at Dartmoor Prison for six years and most inmates referred to him as *Turner the Screw*, although only the bent solicitors and other more literate prisoners understood the jokey reference to the writer Henry James. Despite its formidable appearance, the centuries old jail had been downgraded to Category C and now housed white-collar criminals and sex offenders. The guard turned from the window to stare at the slender prisoner sitting opposite. Sebastian Moran was definitely not

Category C. Psychiatric experts and most normal people would argue that he deserved a category all of his own

'You don't like me, do you?' asked Moran. He flexed his wrists in the handcuffs. A chain tethered the security belt around his waist to an anchor point on the side of the vehicle and kept him a safe distance from Turner. 'I've noticed how you always look at me in a certain way.'

'Yeah, that *certain way* is loathing.' Turner let out a dry laugh. 'I didn't like you when we thought you were a nonce, but since they discovered the truth and found out what you *really* are…' He grinned sarcastically. 'No, Sebastian, I don't like you one bit.'

The police had arrested the forty-year old Moran in one of their Internet paedophile operations and prosecuted him for the horrific images of young boys on his computer. He'd been sentenced to two years in Dartmoor, but things quickly changed when the new people who purchased his rented property decided upon an extension. A gruesome surprise awaited them under the dining room floorboards and, following a hasty judicial rethink, Moran was now on his way to Broadmoor Mental Hospital to await trial for multiple murder.

'You'll like your new home,' said Turner. 'They have special padded wallpaper and you'll get a smart new coat that fastens at the back. Won't that be lovely?'

Moran smiled thinly. 'I can't wait.'

'I hear you could be there a while; your solicitor is arguing that you're insane.'

'I don't doubt it. People with alternate tastes are often described that way by the unenlightened.'

'I'm sure they are. I have to admit, I'm no authority on psychopaths, but sane people don't tend to store half-eaten male prostitutes under their floor in plastic bags.' Turner laughed again. 'You'll have to speak to the loony bin about their dinner menu.

11

Maybe they can cater for your *alternate tastes* if you ask nicely and…'

The bang wasn't particularly loud, but the small explosion destroyed the front left wheel causing the prison van to brake hard and lurch sickeningly. Turner was thrown to the floor as the out-of-control vehicle left the moorland lane and careered down a banking. The van bounced twice, rolled completely and, incredibly, came to rest upright on its three remaining wheels.

'Shit!' snarled the guard, tumbling at Moran's feet. 'What the fuck was…'

The prisoner instinctively attacked. Seizing the opportunity to wrap his legs around Turner's neck, he ignored the scratching fingers, clamped tightly and contracted his thigh muscles. He swiftly choked the guard into unconsciousness, then relaxed the strangle hold to heave the comatose body closer and search the pockets for the restraint keys.

What was that explosion? Moran glanced at the rear door. *What could have happened? Had a tyre burst, or did the engine blow up?*

He unlocked the waist belt and quickly released himself from the handcuffs, all the time listening for movement. Rain hammered on the metal roof of the van, but there were no other sounds coming from up front or outside. *Hopefully the driver and the other guard were unconscious too, or maybe dead. If he could just open the rear door he'd be free. Turner should have the key on him.*

He rummaged and found another set in the uniform pockets, one of which looked right. Realising he'd need food if he had to hide on the moors for any length of time, he snatched Turner's arm and twisted, feeling the bone crunch in the shoulder socket. The guard screamed himself awake.

'You might not like me,' said Moran, 'but I'm sure I'll like *you*. I prefer younger meat, but once I manage to wrench it off, this arm should be delicious.'

Moran punched down hard to stun Turner, then turned angrily as the security door behind him swung wide. He was expecting the other prison officer from the cab, but a huge black-garbed man appeared in the opening, his bald head glistening in the torrential rain.

'Time to go, Mister Moran.' The gruff voice had an East European accent. 'Come on out.'

Moran eyed him warily, stiffening to hear the whining sound of an aircraft engine starting up. He couldn't see the helicopter in the inky darkness; its navigation and internal lights were obviously switched off.

'This prison transport is fitted with GPS trackers,' snapped the bald man. From the clothing, the webbing belts and machine pistol slung over his shoulder, this muscular character was probably military. 'The authorities will know you've just made an unscheduled stop. We don't have much time.'

'What is this?' shouted Moran, above the roar of the helicopter rotors. 'Who are you?'

'Sergeant Gruner.' Rain lashing his shoulders, the soldier produced a taser from one of his belt pouches. 'Explanations can wait. Get out here now, or we'll drag you out.'

'Why should I trust you? Where are you taking me?'

A fat man with a small moustache appeared from the darkness to join Gruner.

'Good Lord!' Moran's eyes widened. 'You look just like...'

The words *Oliver Hardy* turned into a hiss through clenched teeth as Gruner fired the taser and Moran fell unconscious to the floor. The fat man flexed his right wrist and a thin blade shot out from his jacket cuff.

'Retract that,' snarled Gruner. 'You don't need your knife here. In fact, you don't ever use that thing unless I tell you to. Do you understand?'

His accomplice stared coldly.

'*Do* you understand?'

'Yeah, whatever.' He twisted his wrist and a mechanical snap sounded as the blade vanished back into the concealed housing on his forearm.

'Now help me carry him to the chopper.' The Sergeant smiled and gestured to the unconscious prisoner. 'Mister Hardy, meet your new partner, Mister Laurel.'

* * * *

Chapter 3

365 taverns trade in the ancient city of York; one for every day of the year. This was a legend related by the university students. Financial recessions, or probably a more sober count-up, have lowered the figure, but over 200 can still be found. Ye Olde Starre Inne lies off Stonegate – one of the oldest streets – hidden down a *snickleway*, as these narrow pedestrian passages are known here. A beautiful tavern of white-painted stone, flower baskets and lanterns, many assume the twee name must be a recent creation to attract tourists, but the place was christened in the early sixteen-hundreds.

It was seven-thirty, that relatively quiet interval between the daytime crowds and the night clientele. The April evening was cool and three men sat beside the stone fireplace. An attractive black youth of nineteen, John Watson wore jeans and a denim shirt and tapped the pub table in time to the song playing quietly on the bar hi-fi. His short curly hair was hidden by the long mane and wrinkled brow of a Klingon wig and, acutely aware of his bizarre appearance, he glanced over his shoulder to check if anyone was staring. A handful of customers sat around the room, but none seemed to care that he resembled a *Star Trek* character. Sighing, he reached in his shirt and slipped on a pair of sunglasses in case anyone he knew should walk in.

Watson peered disdainfully through the shades at the beamed ceiling, the polished floorboards and oak-panelled bar. He preferred bright modern pubs, with music four times louder than this, and a large selection of scantily-clad girls. This archaic décor depressed him, but he knew someone who absolutely adored it. The man he worked for sat beside him and had a real love for historical buildings and this old-fashioned crap. Then again, although he appeared to be in his forties, Bernard Quist had been around for a *very* long time.

Watson glanced at his employer and the Starfleet badge on his black leather overcoat. Quist's floppy dark hair framed a pleasant face, with tawny eyes and devilish eyebrows, but the youth had always been more interested in the size of his aquiline nose. He smirked as Quist took a drink of beer, the nose vanishing into the pint glass and emerging with froth on the tip. *If this man ever swam the backstroke*, decided Watson, *it should be accompanied by the shark theme from Jaws.*

The youth turned to the third man sitting with them at the inn table. Overweight and shaven-headed, Charlie Milverton guzzled lager and grinned at his new acquaintances.

'I love this song,' said Milverton, nodding to the hi-fi speaker. He unzipped the shoulder bag on his lap and Watson saw it was crammed with discs. 'If you're interested, I have pirate copies of the album.'

'I wish I'd bumped into you before tonight's meeting,' said Watson. 'No, I bought this on the morning it came out.'

'I think everyone did,' agreed Milverton, shrugging. 'It ruined my sales figures.'

Quist fingered his Star Trek badge. 'It seems a somewhat random way to make a living,' he said, in his clipped English accent. 'Surely you can never foresee how many DVDs and CDs you'll sell in a week?'

'I sell more than enough,' said Milverton, grinning. 'I've got pirates of all the latest cinema releases. *Kes* has just come in.'

'*Kes*?' Quist frowned. 'The boy with the falcon? That's decades old, isn't it?'

'Don't be daft,' chuckled Watson. 'He means the remake.'

'You're joking?' said Quist. 'You're telling me they've remade that Ken Loach classic?'

'About time too,' said Milverton. 'Remakes are always better than the old original rubbish. Just look at *Alfie*, *Psycho*, *Get Carter*, *Total Recall*, and *Robocop*. I watched *Kes* this afternoon to

16

make sure it's a good copy. It was filmed in a cinema by someone pointing a phone at the screen and my customers don't like to see too many people getting up for a piss and blocking the camera.'

'How unreasonable,' drawled Quist. 'I'm sure some folk just enjoy grumbling.'

'I hear it's a brilliant film,' said Watson, brushing back the long Klingon hair and leaning forward excitedly. 'A black crack addict called Billy doesn't fit in with the street gangs. He's a loner and he steals a falcon to sell for a fix.'

Quist listened in disbelief.

'That's right,' said Milverton. 'The bird's CGI, but you can't tell. Billy decides not to sell it, and bonding with it gets him off the drugs. It's a sad ending though. His own brother kills the falcon in a drive-by shooting.'

Quist nodded slowly. 'Is it still set in Yorkshire?'

'Of course not,' said Watson. 'This one's in Los Angeles.'

'Actually, I was being sarcastic.'

'I'll get you a copy,' said Milverton. 'The ones in my bag are spoken for, but I'll be seeing you again at next week's counselling session. Speaking of which, you two were pretty quiet there. Most of the time you just sat listening to everyone else.' He ran his eyes over Quist's Star Trek badge. 'I've been meaning to ask. What are you supposed to be?'

'Well, I'm a Klingon, obviously,' said Watson. He jerked a thumb at his companion. 'He's a werewolf.'

Quist choked on a mouthful of beer and turned aghast to the teenager.

Watson grinned. 'Yeah, I know I'm supposed to keep it quiet, but Charlie's okay.'

'I love it,' laughed Milverton. 'So you eat people and stuff?'

Watson laughed too. 'No, he's what you might call a *good* werewolf. He's never killed anyone, so he can control it and he doesn't feel the blood lust.'

'Oh, that's brilliant.' Milverton gulped more lager, 'It's the full moon soon, so he'll be changing, I expect?'

'It doesn't work like that,' said the youth. 'He can change any time during the hours of darkness.'

'Nice one!' Milverton turned to the shocked Quist. 'So will I become a werewolf too if you bite me?'

'That's right.' Watson nodded. 'He bit a guy last Christmas and he's one now.'

'Unbelievable,' muttered Quist, massaging the bridge of his large nose. He watched disdainfully as the teenager opened a crisp packet with a black pocket knife. 'Hey, it's a good thing you carry that,' he said, sarcastically. 'It's almost impossible to get into a pub snack without a special forces knife. Just look at all those different tools. What's the spike with the hole in it used for? Removing Boy Scouts from horse hooves?'

'It's for mending sails,' said Watson, missing the sarcasm by a mile.

'Right. That'll get plenty of use then.'

The pub music ended and Quist cringed as the barmaid pressed the hi-fi replay button. He was aware of this mediocre female artist, the music world's current flavour-of-the-month, and he was tired of hearing her second-rate songs. This wonderful old tavern should be playing Vivaldi.

'This wouldn't harm him.' Watson showed Milverton his knife blade. 'Only silver and fire can kill him. Oh, and chopping his head off would probably do the trick. You should hear him yelp if you touch him with something silver.'

Milverton chuckled knowingly. 'But only when the Social are around, eh?'

'That's right,' said Quist, glaring at Watson. 'This nonsense is all for the Social Services.'

'I'll give you a tip.' Milverton lowered his voice. 'Don't go

18

too far with that. The therapist who hosted our counselling meeting isn't stupid. He can spot if you're faking and he'll get your benefits stopped. I'm supposed to have been clinically depressed and a little crazy for three years and no one realises it's bullshit because I keep it low-key. I've pretended to take an overdose, but that's as far as I've pushed it. The trick is not to appear *too* crazy because you might get yourself sectioned.'

'Good advice,' said Watson, winking at Quist. 'You need to stop that howling at the moon bollocks. A straightjacket wouldn't suit you.'

Milverton swigged down his lager. 'Anyway, thanks for the drink, but I have to unload these DVDs down at the club and then I'm off to the airport. I'm working as a taxi in the free car the Social gave me for being *disabled* with depression.' He smirked at Quist and patted his shoulder bag. 'Do you fancy a film before I go? Maybe something risqué like *Debbie Does Crufts*? Sizzling doggy action is ideal for you werewolves, or how about *Anal Albanians*? Lovely economic migrants fresh from the back of the smuggler's lorry.'

The barmaid overheard and gave the trio a dubious look as she pulled a pint. *The clientele appeared to have gone downhill since Guy Fawkes drank in Ye Olde Starre Inn, and despite his fame, Fawkes was technically a terrorist.*

'Tempting, but no.' Quist smiled tightly. 'I'm watching a documentary about Stravinsky tonight.'

'Oh well.' Milverton headed for the door. 'Have fun on the full moon and I'll see you at the next meeting.'

'What a creature,' said Quist, watching him leave and shaking his head. 'It will be a real pleasure to see him prosecuted.'

'Yeah,' agreed Watson, 'but what a brilliant way to screw the system. Pretend you're depressed and a bit bonkers. You don't have to fake a limp or wear a surgical neck brace. All you need do is talk crazy when you speak to someone in authority.'

19

'Speaking of which, what the hell was all that?' snarled Quist. 'You told Milverton everything about me.'

'Yeah, like he believed me,' snorted Watson. 'As if *anyone* would believe it. You're supposed to be scamming the Social, pretending to be loony like me.'

The private detective unclipped the Star Trek badge from his lapel, removed the tiny microphone on the rear and took out his concealed recorder, rewinding the conversation to the point before werewolves were mentioned. 'I was supposed to be a starship captain and you think you're a Klingon. If you intend to change the plan, you could at least warn me.'

The teenager laughed. 'Yeah, sorry about that, Guv.'

'And remove those sunglasses. You look ridiculous in here.'

'You mean this shit *doesn't*?' Watson pulled off the Klingon wig. 'These designer shades are brilliant. Rex gave me them, along with the special forces knife.'

'Yes, and you look just as stupid as *he* does when he wears them indoors.' Quist erased the wolf talk, pocketed the recorder and picked up the black pocket knife to examine it. Their friend Rex Grant had given it away when he abandoned the ridiculous idea of joining the SAS. 'You *are* aware that this isn't special forces issue? Some company made it to cash in on the weirder elements of society. The sort who drool over *Soldier of Fortune* magazine.'

'Yeah, it's great, isn't it?' Once again, Watson missed the irony. 'And how can anyone look stupid wearing Jo Milan designer sunglasses outdoors *or* in? They cost Rex the best part of a grand.'

'You even mentioned Rex, for God's sake.'

'I didn't mention his name; just that you bit him. Speaking of which, how's it going with him and the werewolf thing?'

'*Watson*,' hissed the detective, 'I wonder if you keep your voice down? If it isn't too much trouble, of course?'

'You're scared someone might overhear that you're a wolf

and over two-hundred years old? We're a couple of mental cases, remember?'

'I prefer discretion, said Quist. 'The fewer people who are aware of my lycanthropy, the better. Come along. Let's get some fresh air. After listening to Milverton, I need it.'

'Fresh air and a cigarette too, I imagine?' said Watson.

* * * *

Chapter 4

Some of the faces were ferocious, some looked comical, but the majority were demonic and frightening. Bernard Quist drew on his cigarette and peered up at York Minster, knowing he could gaze at these ornamental stone heads every day and still find one he'd never noticed. Most people referred to them all by the same name, but only the ones that formed rainwater spouts were gargoyles. The others were known as grotesques, and Quist never tired of studying these ancient carvings on the medieval cathedral.

'Beautiful beyond words,' murmured the private investigator, or *consultant detective*, as he insisted upon referring to himself. 'How incongruous that this architectural masterpiece was created by the same species who manufactured those abysmal DVDs – the horrendous films sold by that benefit cheat.'

Watson smirked at how flowery this sounded. He'd been working as the detective's assistant for six months, but sometimes he still found Quist's genteel English accent and cultured mannerisms comical. He had to concede, *for a terrifying supernatural monster, his boss was quite urbane and eloquent.*

'Yeah, whatever,' he said, checking his phone texts. 'It's a big church.'

'I suppose some might describe Europe's largest Gothic cathedral in that way.' Quist nodded. 'Some idiots, at any rate.'

Bathed by golden floodlights, the ethereal limestone bulk soared over two-hundred feet above the surrounding rooftops. White and gleaming by day, the twin western towers could be seen for over forty miles, rising from the Plain of York like a gigantic fairy-tale palace. Quist had paused with Watson in Precentor's Court, the expanse of cobblestones at the western end of the Minster nave. Spring had been pleasant so far and the trees in the square were covered in a froth of creamy blossom.

The detective loved this ancient city and the wealth of

physical history that had been left behind by the Romans, the Vikings, the Elizabethans and the countless others who had called this their home. They had just walked along the street named Stonegate and only a few feet beneath the cobbles ran the Via Praetoria, the original Roman road that led to the basilica in the Roman fortress. Both Severus and Constantine travelled this route with the Sixth Legion, most of the soldiers wishing they could leave the freezing rains of northern England and return to the Italian warmth to reacquaint themselves with their testicles. Quist smiled to himself and raised his eyes above the Minster towers as the silvery clouds parted and a familiar yellow globe appeared.

'The full moon,' said Watson, grinning. 'I'd better watch myself, eh?'

'You've nothing to worry about, as you well know,' said Quist. 'Besides, it isn't quite full until tomorrow.'

A shooting star zipped across the sky and Watson toyed with the idea of making a wish. Stuffing his hands in his jeans pockets, he wished he hadn't left his jacket in his employer's car.

'Rex Grant, however, is another matter entirely,' said Quist. He inhaled cigarette smoke and gazed at the Minster's Great West Window. The central stained glass was held in place by stone tracery in the shape of an enormous heart: the *Heart of Yorkshire*, as it was traditionally known. 'Although I can shapeshift any time between sunset and sunrise, I never transform at this time of the month if I can help it. I've advised Rex to do the same. It's easier for me, as I've had so long to get used to the dark urges.'

'1790, wasn't it?'

'Indeed it was. The bestial impulses are still very new and alien to Rex.'

'So how's it going with him?'

'As you're aware, I've made sure I'm always with him during this lunar phase. I watch and monitor his behaviour and I'll continue until I'm certain he can cope with the impulses. He tends

23

to get a little irrational and hot-headed, but nothing too bad. I point out any mood swings and help him to calm himself.'

The youth nodded. 'I can sympathise. I live with my mum and she goes a little crackers every month too. The trick is to get out of the house, or walk on eggshells and not point out how loopy women are when...'

'Your understanding and compassion are to be commended, Watson, but Rex's condition is somewhat more dangerous. That's the main reason we're going to London for his birthday this Thursday.'

'*Main* reason? You're obviously forgetting the free booze and all those models and minor celebrities he'll invite to the party. I don't do too badly with the girls, but Rex is something else. He has a constant string of top birds lining up to jump into his bed.'

'The lycanthropy will attract them,' said Quist. 'Females subliminally sense the wolf. The aura of supernatural darkness adds to his charisma, but as I understand it, he was very much the playboy before this. The girls he goes for all tend to be the same, however: quite beautiful, but amazingly thick.'

'Exactly. What more could you want?'

'Wouldn't you prefer someone you could converse with after sex?'

'Why?' Watson looked puzzled. 'So you don't regret what you did, Guv?'

'Biting him was the only way to save his life,' said Quist. 'Rex may appear superficial, conceited and thoughtless, but he's a good person at heart. As with many similar people, the loud arrogance, open chauvinism and glibness are a subconscious attempt to conceal their lack of intelligence.'

'I have news for him – it doesn't work.'

'The thing is, I'm now responsible for Rex.' Wrapping the lengthy leather overcoat around himself, the detective turned to stroll along High Petergate, a medieval thoroughfare of Tudor buildings that leads to Bootham Bar. 'I've never done this before and we're learning together. Like me, he's on a vegan diet and I've taught him a few helpful techniques. I've also given him a series of exercises and meditations to settle his mind and keep him, shall we say *human.*'

With its portcullis and arrow-slit windows, Bootham Bar was the oldest of the fortified gateways that allowed passage into the city through the perimeter wall. Taking its name from this fourteenth-century tower, and once the primary route to Scotland, the tree-lined street of Bootham runs north from the barbican. They followed it a short way to where the group therapy meeting had taken place earlier. Owned by the York Social Services, the office was situated on the second floor of a large house, above a girl who practised homeopathic *medicine* in her incense-fogged *surgery*. Quist knew plenty about alternative medicine and also that treating ailments with tap water didn't work.

'It's good to hear that Rex is handling this okay,' said Watson, heading for Quist's car. 'So you're driving us to London on Thursday and we're staying over after the birthday party at his place in Hampstead?'

'Yes, he gets back from Edinburgh tomorrow.' Quist winced slightly. 'I shudder to speculate what a Rex Grant party will be like.'

Watson smiled to himself. Quist had never been one for the party scene, but since employing his teenage assistant, he'd emerged from his introverted shell a little. *It would be interesting to see him in the company of the kind of girls Rex fooled around with. It would be even more interesting to be in their company himself.*

He watched Quist unlock the car, a metallic grey Ford. Watson had often laughed about the detective's boring motors, but Quist claimed nondescript vehicles were essential in private investigations. The youth had to grudgingly admit he was probably right. The kind of souped-up monstrosity he'd have chosen might

25

not be ideal for discreetly following people.

'That mobile phone you bought…' Watson jumped into the passenger seat and gestured to the night sky through the windscreen. 'Did you know you can get a free App? It tells you all the phases of the moon and when it's going to be full.'

Quist gave a dry laugh. 'I'm the last person to need that. The lupine urges tell me exactly when it's due. The full moon lasts three days and, during that phase, the impulses come and go in daylight too. The vegan diet and yoga exercises keep things in check. I've also perfected a mental technique that can be used in times of high stress. I concentrate on *The Young Prince and The Young Princess* from *Scheherazade*.'

Watson stared as if he'd begun to speak Japanese.

'A beautiful piece of music by Rimsky-Korsakov. I banish all thoughts and fixate instead upon the melody in my head.'

'Have you taught Rex the trick? Do you have him concentrate on this Sherry Hazard tune…'

'The secret is to use music that's personal to you.' Quist started the car. 'His is somewhat different. It's special to him, from a time in his youth when he felt happy and content.'

'What is it?'

Quist looked evasive. 'It's unusual, but it appears to work.'

'So what is it?'

'No. It's personal and you'd mock him. You trade insults and bicker like childish idiots when you're together.'

'Ah, it sounds to me like he's picked a really crap song.' Watson smirked. 'Okay, it's obvious you see this as some doctor and patient confidentiality thing, so you don't have to actually tell me. I'll list some shit and you cough if I get it. *Agadoo* by Black Lace. *Itsy Bitsy Teeny Weeny Yellow…*'

'I'm not going to tell you,' sighed the detective. 'His peculiar choice doesn't surprise me. As we know, he's a rather odd character and…'

'Thick as pigshit?'

'You have the subtle vocabulary of a diplomat. I was about to say mildly eccentric. Rex is still wearing black clothing and sunglasses all the time. He seems to like his er, change in circumstances a little too much and that concerns me.'

'What do you mean?'

'He was frightened and hated the lycanthropy to begin with.' Quist pulled away from the kerb and drove along Bootham. 'Once he grew accustomed to the reality of his new life, he began to embrace it. Rather too much, if I'm being honest. It isn't normal.'

'Brilliant, Guv.' Watson laughed. 'You're talking about him being a werewolf and you use the word *normal*.'

* * * *

Chapter 5

Normal wasn't a word that sprang to mind when acquaintances were describing Rex Grant. His behaviour had always been unconventional, even *before* he became a supernatural creature of the night.

Not the brightest of young men, Rex exuded the extrovert self-assurance seen in many dim people who are fortunate to have both striking good looks and a shit load of money. The knowledge that only silver, fire and decapitation could harm him had boosted this genial arrogance. April was colder in Scotland than London and he wore a black leather jacket, black jeans and a black silk shirt, all bearing overpriced designer labels that fashion slaves would kill to possess. He'd taken to dressing in chic black clothes during his futile attempt to join the SAS, inexplicably believing this image would help. It was eight o'clock in the evening, but the dark didn't prevent Rex from completing his outfit with a pair of expensive sunglasses, which instantly transformed his appearance from fairly cool to farcical.

The special forces pipedream had ended abruptly last Christmas when Bernard Quist saved his mortally wounded friend with a supernatural wolf bite. Rex had to admit, he enjoyed unexpected gifts, but as surprise Christmas presents went, this would take some beating. Over the months, his original fear and misgivings at becoming a werewolf had gradually turned to acceptance and then excitement. His toned twenty-five year old body was stronger, his senses had been augmented and his recuperative powers were truly phenomenal. Sniffly colds, tummy bugs and other ailments no longer affected him, and he could drive fast cars like an idiot, safe in the knowledge that a steering column through the torso would ultimately be as harmful as a bee sting. He'd continued with the stylish black attire and the sunglasses, now believing this to be the ideal look for someone with a cool

28

paranormal secret.

Rex sat in the passenger seat of Charlotte Michie's Mini Clubman, gazing at the brightly-lit buildings of the Scottish capital as the young redhead drove along Princes Street. The city was busy for a Tuesday evening and he peered up at the Balmoral where he was staying. The palatial neo-Gothic hotel dominated this main thoroughfare.

'I have to admit, I really like Edinburgh,' he said. 'What do you Scots call it? Bald Freaky?'

'Auld Reekie,' laughed Charlotte, pulling up at the traffic lights. 'It means *Old Smoky*. Balmoral means *majestic dwelling* and your hotel certainly lives up to the name, doesn't it? The Victorians built it as a railway hotel in the Scottish baronial style. The huge clock on the tower up there was always set three minutes fast so guests didn't miss their train. You used to be able to take a lift from the platform in Waverley Station straight up into your hotel lobby.'

'Hey, you know your stuff, don't you?'

'That'll be why Gordon picked me to be your guide.'

Rex had flown up from London to finalise a deal with the McNulty Caledonian building company and, rather than hire a car, Charlotte, one of the assistants, had been given the job of chauffeuring him around. They'd driven to the Leith waterfront, where Grant Homes were to build their housing development, and then to McNulty's offices to sort out the paperwork. The business was now complete and this evening city tour had been Charlotte's idea. Rex might be brash, chauvinistic and a little dumb, but he was a likeable character with an infectious sense of fun. His short black hair, blue eyes and white teeth reminded her of a young Tom Cruise and a couple of times she'd found herself absentmindedly humming the *Top Gun* movie theme.

'So, you're flying home in the morning,' she said. 'I expect we'll be seeing more of you when Grant Homes expands north?'

'I imagine so,' said Rex. 'My father plans to build in

29

Edinburgh and Glasgow before branching out to other towns.'

'How long have you known my boss Gordon?'

'Gordon McNulty's a family friend; he's been hunting with my Uncle Rupert for years. I hear Gordon has electric radiators, Wi-Fi and music installed in the shooting butts on his grouse moors. Apparently, they shoot the birds to Wagner's *Ride of the Valkyrie*.'

'Yes, Gordon loves his hunting and shooting.' Charlotte laughed. 'You millionaires are all alike. You all seem to get off on golf and killing animals.'

'Well, I dislike both and technically I'm not a millionaire. The family wealth comes from the housing company, plus various investments over the decades, but I can't just dip into the accounts. I have to live on a monthly allowance. If I want a Ferrari or something, I have to go cap-in-hand to my father.'

'Poor you. No one should have to live in such harsh conditions.'

'Mind you, the allowance is pretty generous.' He gave a sexy wink. 'I'm still very much the eligible bachelor.'

'Eligible to some. For me, your gender gets in the way.'

'Whatever.' Rex smirked. Charlotte claimed to be gay, but he'd decided he might cure her of that nonsense before the night was over. In *Goldfinger*, 007 had cured Pussy Galore with a few judo throws and a manly kiss, so it shouldn't be too difficult. He pointed to the illuminated baroque tower soaring two-hundred feet above them. 'Hey, what's this thing? It looks like a stone rocket.'

'That's our famous Scott Monument.'

'Oh right. Terry Scott, the first guy to make it to the North Pole. You lot must be proud that a Scotsman beat that German Anderson.'

'Er...' Charlotte glanced at him, wondering if this was a joke, but apparently it wasn't. 'No, Sir Walter Scott, the writer. You know - *Ivanhoe* and all the old classics.'

'Ugh! Books.' Rex pulled a face. 'I'm not really into books and especially not classics like *Withering Heights* and *Pride and Pregnancy*.'

'You told me you studied at Cambridge. I take it you didn't major in English?'

'To be honest, I didn't major in anything. When you have millionaire parents and that huge allowance I mentioned, you don't need to study too hard.'

Rex and his brother Raoul were the heirs to Grant Homes, but Rex had never wanted anything to do with the family company. He'd prolonged university to avoid this, his main interests being young women, fast cars and nightlife, and he'd only begun working for his father very recently, after his ludicrous dreams of joining the military fell through.

Charlotte drove past the Royal Scottish Academy and Rex saw the vast expanse of Princes Street Gardens appearing on their left. He looked across the parkland to Edinburgh Castle, an illuminated cluster of granite ramparts and sixteenth-century buildings seated atop a huge volcanic plug. *It was difficult to distinguish where the black crag ended and the fortifications began; the stronghold appeared to be growing from the basalt.* Swirls of silvery cloud framed the castle and a large yellow moon was rising, beginning its slow ascent over the Palace of Holyrood to add to the fairy tale tableau. The moon would be full tomorrow and Rex recalled Bernie Quist's warnings about this time of the month, almost as if lycanthropic tampons were necessary. Over the next three days, the dark bestial urges were supposedly difficult to control and the private detective had made a point of baby-sitting him on every full moon since his transformation. *Yeah, like he couldn't handle such things by himself.* Quist even claimed the impulses affected werewolf behaviour during daylight too, which was obviously nonsense.

Charlotte turned left up Lothian Road and left again along

31

King's Stables Road, the route winding around the base of the castle crag and into Edinburgh's atmospheric Old Town. She gestured to a statue of a little dog sitting on a roadside plinth.

'Look,' she said. 'Another of our famous sights for you. There's Greyfriars Bobby.'

'Oh right.' Rex gave a dry laugh. 'The dog who's famous just because his geriatric owner died.'

'I see I'm chauffering a sensitive soul.' Charlotte cruised along George IV Bridge. 'And here we have the Royal Mile,' she announced, jokingly adopting the voice of a tour guide. 'This was once the busiest street in Europe. The gentry lived here before the eighteen-hundreds, but once the New Town was built north of Princes Street, they abandoned these tenements to decay into an overcrowded slum. It's changed quite a bit, as you can see. The visitors love it.'

Lined with granite tenements, churches and taverns, the Royal Mile followed the crest of the volcanic hill from the castle parade ground down to Holyrood Palace. Rex saw the lower parts of many buildings had been opened as ornate tourist shops, their windows packed with Scottish souvenirs, Highland paintings and the ubiquitous tartan tins of shortbread. In place of the beggars and body-snatchers, international holidaymakers now filled the route.

The moon reappeared above the buildings, once again reminding Rex of the lycanthropy and the staggering way in which his life had changed. Unbelievably, he'd remain twenty-five forever, looking exactly as he did now, so it was a good thing Quist had bitten him when he did. He couldn't imagine the nightmare of going through the centuries with unfashionable hair or an unsightly paunch, but thankfully he had a great physique, much of his university time having been spent in a health spa. Quist had covered this age *problem* in one of his stupid lectures. He'd warned how acquaintances become suspicious of an unchanging appearance and swapping identities was necessary, but perhaps this wouldn't be such a dilemma in the twenty-first century. With modern surgery and chemical aids, Rex knew millionaire socialites with faces that hadn't altered in decades. Then again, those faces *did* resemble weird plastic dolls.

Charlotte had turned the car down so many of the Old Town streets, Rex felt lost. Lost, thirsty and in need of a smoke. 'These lovely old inns look amazing,' he said. 'Why don't we get a drink somewhere?'

'Sounds like a sensible idea,' said Charlotte.

He lowered the sunglasses and smiled. 'Maybe somewhere romantic and cosy?'

'You *are* aware that you're not exactly my type?'

'You never know. I tend to grow on most young ladies.'

'I doubt you'll grow on *this* one. Maybe if you were more feminine and had a different set of genitalia.'

'Ah, I love it when girls talk dirty.'

'Yeah, right.' Charlotte laughed and ran a hand through her ginger hair. She drove into Cowgate, a narrow street with tall buildings on either side. 'Anyway, aren't you dating the model from that reality show? *I'll literally eat shit for money*, or some such rubbish? I read about it in the gossip columns.'

'Andromeda? Not any longer. We broke up weeks ago.'

'Too intellectual for you?'

'No, to be honest, she was pretty stupid.' Like Quist's assistant, there were times when Rex wouldn't recognise sarcasm if it walked up and kicked him between the legs. He spotted a nightclub on Brodie Street, a cul-de-sac leading off Cowgate. 'Hey, stop and back up, would you? What do we have here?'

'Club 69.' Charlotte reversed and grimaced. 'No, you don't want to go in there. It's a real shithole.'

'Someone doesn't think so.' He nodded to the four Bentleys parked outside. 'Come on. Let's take a look.'

Shrugging, Charlotte turned in and parked her Mini behind

the upmarket vehicles.

Rex climbed out and lit a cigarette. 'Do you smoke?' he asked, offering her the pack. He held out his lighter, making sure she saw the cool wolf's head engraving.

'No thanks. It's one of the few bad habits I don't have.' She gestured to the Bentley rear windows. 'Ah, I might have known; these cars are rented. Do you see the discreet stickers? It's a local company called Tartan Prestige, but I've never seen so many together.'

Rex puffed on the tobacco and stared up at the ancient canopy of wrought iron and coloured glass that extended over the pavement offering shelter to queuing customers. It probably sported the original name of the building, but this was hidden with a tacky *Club 69* neon sign and various posters advertising *Happy Hour* and other drinking promotions. From what he'd heard about the Scots, they wouldn't need much incentive to get pissed. He half-smoked his cigarette before paying the entrance fees, taking Charlotte's arm and strolling into the dimly-lit club.

'Hey, this was once a fancy old place,' said Rex, looking around and raising his voice above the throbbing music. He recognised the track as *Born Slippy*, the old hit by the group *Underworld*. 'What did it used to be?'

'I'm not sure,' said Charlotte. 'A theatre, I guess.'

The huge room had two rows of fluted Greek columns, their Corinthian capitals supporting a lofty ceiling richly painted with cherubs playing instruments. The ornate décor had long since passed its best. Decades of cigarette smoke had left these celestial musicians with olive brown faces and Rex felt they'd now look more at home selling kebabs than strumming lyres. The pair made their way through the crowd to a counter where they caught the eye of a young barman.

'What can I get you?' Rex asked Charlotte.

'Oh, I'm cheap to take out.' She nodded to one of the

34

pumps. 'Just a half of McEwan's, please.'

'A half for the lady,' said Rex. 'I'll have a Lobo.' He turned to the girl and smiled smugly. 'That means *wolf* in Latin.'

The barman looked puzzled. 'Don't you mean Spanish?'

Rex gave a contemptuous grunt. 'So the barmen here are experts in Latin and Spanish, huh?'

'Some of them are.' The youth nodded. 'The language students, like myself, who work here part-time are. So what exactly is a *Lobo*?'

'A cocktail.'

'A Lobo cocktail? Er...'

'One part whisky,' sighed Rex. 'Two parts vermouth over ice.'

'Isn't that a Manhattan?'

He grimaced. 'Okay, so put in three parts vermouth. There... *that's* a Lobo.'

Rex and Charlotte turned to watch the dance floor as the barman busied himself with the drinks. Several dozen young people were moving to the pulsating electronic music, but a natural gap had formed around two petite girls in the centre of the throng. Both wore identical black mini dresses and appeared to be the focus of everyone's attention. The girl facing Rex had an elfin face with short silvery hair, and he caught his breath as her companion turned.

'*What*?' he gasped. 'That can't possibly be who I think it is?'

'It can and it *is*.' Charlotte's mouth fell open. 'Oh my God, that's Ligeia.'

* * * *

35

Chapter 6

Rex paid the nightclub barman for the drinks and turned to stare at the two young women on the dancefloor. 'Wow, this is unexpected, to say the least,' he said, lowering his sunglasses to see better in the dim, blue-tinted lighting. 'Ligeia is the biggest star in the music world right now. Do they often get singers like her in here?'

'Take a look around this dump,' said Charlotte. 'Then take a wild guess.'

'So what the hell...'

'I can't believe it either.' Charlotte shook her head in amazement, unable to take her eyes off the tiny girl. Ligeia's female companion was dancing slowly behind her, caressing the singer's waist and kissing her naked shoulders and throat. 'She gave a concert at the Murrayfield Stadium last night; that's why she's in Edinburgh. I tried to get tickets online, but they sold out within minutes of going on sale.'

'I'm guessing the Bentleys outside must belong to her entourage.'

'Definitely, but what on earth is she doing in *this* hole? Of all the places to go clubbing in the city, she came *here*?'

Rex watched the girls gyrating sensually to the hypnotic *Born Slippy* music track. Ligeia looked to be around five feet tall in her stilettoes, with short, glossy black hair and chocolate-tanned skin, her silk mini dress exposing her entire back and smooth naked legs. Her companion was the same petite size, with similar elfin features and silvery hair. He stared wide-eyed as Ligeia gave her girlfriend a lingering kiss on the mouth, before slowly sinking into a squat and rising to repeat the kiss, the erotic dance move almost revealing her buttocks. Rex swallowed awkwardly and sipped the Lobo cocktail to moisten his dry mouth. Peering at their identical black attire, he saw there were no tell-tale signs of underwear beneath the tight designer silk. Enhanced lycanthropic vision certainly came in useful on occasions.

He cleared his throat and leant close to Charlotte. 'They're both absolute stunners,' he said. 'I just wish Ligeia's voice matched her looks.'

'*What*?' The girl's mouth fell open. 'You *are* joking?'

'No, I don't rate her as a singer. To be honest, I wouldn't go to see her if you gave me a free ticket.'

'Incredible,' laughed Charlotte. 'You have to be the only person I've ever met who has no musical taste.'

'Each to their own.' Rex watched the sensuous dance. 'But she really is gorgeous and I love the name Ligeia, like Princess Ligeia in *Star Trek*. I think I'll set my sex appeal phaser to *stun* and beam myself over there.'

'I think you mean Princess Leiah, not Ligeia. And she was in *Star Wars*, not *Star Trek*.'

'Never argue with a movie expert.' Rex gave a condescending smile. 'I know which franchise is which. Captain Kirk was in *Star Trek*. Jean Luc Picard was in *Star Wars*.'

'Er…' Charlotte hesitated. 'Yeah, whatever.'

'Not only a movie expert, but a gentleman too.' Rex downed his cocktail and handed her the empty glass. 'It would be ungentlemanly and downright rude to leave Ligeia dancing with some girl. Why dance with a girl when there are guys like me around?'

'Yeah, right,' laughed Charlotte. 'She's clearly having an awful time with her friend there. You'd better go save her.'

Winking and adjusting his sunglasses, Rex strolled onto the dance floor and moved through the crowd to the girls. Two large men in suits immediately appeared on either side of him and grabbed his arms tightly. *From their vice-like grip and threatening demeanour, they probably weren't hoping for a smooch.* He gave Ligeia a beaming white smile and raised his eyebrows above the shades.

'I was thinking we might have a dance,' he shouted over the electronic beat. 'But these guys don't seem keen on the idea. I take it they're with you?'

'Let him go,' said Ligeia, smiling sweetly at the two giants. Her foreign accent was difficult to place. 'I like him.'

'Well, you obviously have great taste,' said Rex. He waited until the bodyguards had left before moving closer and dancing with the petite girls. Ligeia's silver-haired companion eyed him sexily. 'I thought they were going to wrestle me to the floor.'

'They probably would have done,' admitted Ligeia, giggling childishly. 'They're my manager's friends. They watch me all the time.'

'Visits to the bathroom must be interesting.'

Rex saw her two security personnel take up a vantage position at the edge of the dancefloor next to an attractive middle-aged woman. Smartly-dressed in a sophisticated suit, she wore a black patch over her left eye and stood chatting to a large muscular man with a shaven head. A slender black character stood beside the pair, staring intently at Rex in a way that left him slightly uncomfortable.

'Which one of the Three Amigos is your manager?' he asked. 'Larry, Moe or Curly?'

Ligeia gestured to the one-eyed woman with the sleek dark hair. 'Irana is my manager. The others are her friends: Mister Lafont and Sergeant Gruner.'

'To be truthful, they don't concern me,' said Rex. Now aware of her bodyguards, he spotted another five obvious types stationed at intervals around the dancing crowd. 'Nothing concerns me when I'm with the two most beautiful little ladies in Edinburgh.'

Cringe-making as the chat-up line was, Rex wasn't exaggerating; close-up, these girls really *were* incredible. He'd assumed Ligeia was tanned, but now saw it was her natural dusky skin colouring. This, coupled with her sexy accent and jet black hair had him wondering if she was Mediterranean. Her friend had the same flawless skin and both were the same height and stature, with sparkling pale blue eyes and striking elfin features. They could easily be sisters.

'This is my very best friend Elva.' Ligeia twirled around, then leant forward and kissed her silver-haired companion slowly and deeply. 'I'm Ligeia.'

'Er, yes…' he mumbled, a little dazed from watching their tongues entwine. Hopefully, they *weren't* sisters. 'Actually, I knew that. Rex is my name. Rex Grant.'

'Hello, Rex.' Ligeia threw her arms around him. 'I like you and I can see Elva likes you too. Would you like to buy us both a drink?

'Let me think about that.' He stroked his chin in sham deliberation. 'Yes, I would.'

Taking both girls by their hands, Rex led them through the crowd to the open-mouthed Charlotte at the bar. He honestly couldn't believe his luck; he'd just been dancing with the most famous young woman in show business and now he appeared to have *pulled* her. The Rex Grant sex appeal was legendary, but this was quite something and a real notch up from the models and minor celebrities he usually dated. Rex frowned slightly. *The most famous young woman in show business in a run-down Scottish nightclub? What was she doing in here?*

'This is Elva,' he said, smiling at Charlotte. 'And I think you might know Ligeia here. Ladies, I'd like you to meet my friend Charlotte. She's a big fan of yours, Ligeia.'

'Isn't *everyone* a fan?' stammered Charlotte, her face turning crimson. 'I can't believe you're here. This is amazing. I really can't believe I'm actually speaking to you.'

'Hello, Charlotte.' Ligeia slipped an arm around the girl's

waist and kissed her cheek. 'Mmh, I like your smell. I think it's really nice that you enjoy my music.'

'*Enjoy* your music?' spluttered Charlotte, her words tripping over each other as she rambled self-consciously. 'I absolutely love it. I know you don't do interviews, so I've never heard you speak before. That cool accent of yours is great. Where are you from?'

'I don't know.' Ligeia shrugged slightly. 'Everywhere.'

'That sounds like a nice place,' said Rex, grinning. 'I'll have to go there one day.' He noticed how two of the bodyguards had followed him and had positioned themselves at the bar some six feet away. He winked at Elva. 'Hey, you don't say much, do you?'

Elva smiled and shook her head, her blue eyes twinkling in the dim light.

'I was hoping to see you last night,' said Charlotte, 'but there were no concert tickets left when I tried to...'

'I wish I'd known.' Ligeia squeezed her hand. 'I could have invited you as my guest. I'm singing again soon. Would you like to come and listen to me as my guest?'

'*What?*' Charlotte choked on her drink. 'Are you serious?'

'Of course I am. I'll tell my manager to give you the very best tickets.'

'You have no idea how much that would mean to me.' Charlotte laughed nervously. 'I'll cancel whatever I have in my diary: work, weddings, funerals, surgical operations... When is it and where's the venue?'

'I don't know.'

Elva touched Ligeia's arm to get her attention and began using sign language.

'Friday in London,' said Ligeia. 'I'm at a place called the O2.'

Rex was puzzled. *Had she never heard of the London Dome?* 'What's wrong with Elva?' he asked. 'What's this waving

40

thing she's doing?'

'She's vocally impaired,' said Charlotte. 'She's signing.'

'Oh, right.' Rex shrugged. 'She was waving her hands like she was deaf and dumb.' He saw that Ligeia's people were watching him. The manager with the eye patch was talking to her black companion and it was obvious that Rex was the topic of conversation. 'I see Captain Morgan, your manager, has her *eye* on me. I guess it'll be easy for her to get you on pirate radio?'

Ligeia and Elva looked baffled.

'Pirate radio? You know? Pirates like Captain Morgan had eye-patches and...'

'Irana is a Colonel,' said Ligeia. 'Not a pirate.'

'Er, okay.' Rex had no idea what the hell this might mean, but his brilliant joke had fallen flatter than a motorway hedgehog. 'Right, let me get you girls a Lobo. It's a rather tasty cocktail I devised myself, Lobo being the *Spanish* word for wolf.' He glanced sarcastically at the bartender, but needn't have bothered. The man was captivated by Ligeia and oblivious to the cynical look. 'There was a Klingon called Lieutenant Wolf in *Star Wars*, you know.'

'You're funny,' laughed Ligeia.

'*Funny*?' Rex was slightly crestfallen. Attractive and alluring, yes, but *funny*? Hard as it was to believe, maybe she wasn't interested in him sexually. 'Well, yes, I have a great sense of humour and...'

'I'd really like to have sex with you,' broke in Ligeia.

'What?' said Rex. Maybe she *was* interested.

'Do you like to have sex?'

'Er, you could say that.' *The childish way she phrased the question made her sound a little simple, but how could she be? This was Ligeia, for goodness sake.* 'On my list of favourite pastimes, sex *does* rank higher than trainspotting. I'm at the Balmoral Hotel. We could maybe have a few drinks and then...'

'We're staying there too,' said Ligeia. 'I don't think I want

41

a drink anymore. I feel very close to you, Rex. Instead of drinking, we could go and have sex right now.' She glanced at Elva and her face lit up. 'Perhaps you'd like to have sex with both of us? Men like doing that.'

He stared for several seconds, his jaw slowly dropping. 'Are you joking?' Rex turned to Elva. 'Is she joking?' He felt a little stupid asking a mute girl.

Elva laughed silently and shook her head.

'Of course I'm not joking, you big silly.' Ligeia stood on tiptoes to kiss him slowly. 'The three of us.'

Charlotte cleared her throat. 'Three, or possibly more,' she said, hopefully.

'I'm sorry.' Ligeia smiled sweetly. 'Would you like to join us?'

Charlotte almost fainted. 'Let me think about it,' she stuttered, trembling and debating whether to pinch herself. 'I'm going to say yes.'

'I'd like that,' said Ligeia. 'Yes, it would be lovely if you came too.' She turned back to Rex and kissed him again. 'I feel very close to you, Rex.'

* * * *

The rooms and suites in the Balmoral Hotel were arranged around a central quadrangle, with some facing inwards and the more opulent looking out over the Edinburgh sights. Colonel Irana Adler had rented an entire corner of the building on the fourth floor, installing herself and her security people on either side of the suite occupied by Ligeia and Elva. She walked through her own suite and joined Lafont at one of the open windows. The thin black man didn't turn or acknowledge her.

'A beautiful night,' said Adler, peering across the Princes Street Gardens to the floodlit castle on its crag. Almost full, the moon shone down on the panorama and her single grey eye twinkled in its silver light. 'What are you looking at, Padre?'

As usual, Lafont smiled at the nickname. 'The stars,' he murmured. His native tongue was Haitian Creole, but even when speaking English like this, the French accent was noticeable in his deep voice. 'You can learn a great deal from the stars.'

'So you're always telling me.' The woman laughed quietly and slipped her hands into the pockets of her expensive Italian suit. 'Will I be meeting a tall, dark stranger? Perhaps I'm going on a journey? I have air tickets to America that seem to confirm the latter.'

'Who are they?' asked Lafont. 'The couple with Ligeia?'

'No one to be concerned about.' Adler shrugged. 'I don't know who the girl is, but the man's name is Rex Grant. I had his hotel booking hacked and ran the usual detail checks. He's part of some southern housing company and they're planning to build in Edinburgh. According to the reports, he's a stupid London playboy.'

'Is Ligeia with them now?'

'Yes, she and her dumb friend are screwing them. Grant has a room on this floor, but on the opposite side of the building. He's harmless enough and I have security posted in the corridor. Ligeia can't come to any harm. As we're both fully aware, when she says *no*, it definitely means *no*.'

'I was drawn to that man in the club,' said Lafont. 'There was something about him and I couldn't take my eyes off him.'

'You surprise me, Padre. I thought you preferred women?'

Lafont chuckled at the joke, but couldn't shake the feeling of foreboding. There was something ominous in the air, like when the electrically-charged atmosphere told him a storm was approaching, long before the first grumble of thunder broke the silence. 'Tell me,' he said, 'why did Ligeia want to go to that place tonight? That particular nightclub?'

'I have no idea. It was a real dive, but as long as such things keep her happy, I don't particularly care.'

'You *should* care.' Lafont stared at the night sky for a long moment. 'I noticed how she was drawn to that club, and she was instantly drawn to this man Grant too. I don't know why, and not knowing makes me uneasy. Understanding such whims will help you to control her.'

'I suppose you're right, but there's nothing to worry about.'

'Probably not.' Lafont shook his head slowly. 'This *stupid playboy* as you refer to him, like I said, there's something about him.'

'Something?'

'I don't know.' He narrowed his eyes. '*Something.*'

* * * *

44

Chapter 7

Rex squinted in the morning sunlight as he peered at Calton Hill through the hotel room window. The flat-topped bulk loomed above the Edinburgh rooftops and, laying on the bed with arms folded behind his head, he could see the summit parkland and its surreal collection of buildings. A Georgian astronomical observatory rubbed sandstone shoulders with a commemorative tower to Nelson, an Egyptian obelisk and, perhaps most incongruous of all, a replicated section of the Athenian Parthenon. The façade of columns would have been extended to duplicate the Greek original, had the city not embarrassingly run out of cash in the eighteen-hundreds. The view of the hill from this high floor of the Balmoral was amazing, but Rex looked down at the naked girls curled around his body. Ligeia and Elva slept with their heads on his stomach and Charlotte was using his thigh as a pillow, her mane of red hair covering his genitals. Yes, Calton Hill looked great, but all things considered, he much preferred this closer view.

'Ah, it's great being me,' he murmured, grinning smugly.

His phone lay on the bedside cabinet and he checked the time – it was eight o'clock on Wednesday. *What a pity this wasn't Thursday morning. How fantastic would it be to wake with three stunning girls on his birthday tomorrow, one of them being the most famous music star in the world? That would definitely be a birthday to remember.* He toyed with the idea of taking a phone picture and sending it to some of his friends, but decided against it. This laddish prank was pretty low, even for *him,* and in today's politically correct world it would doubtless be considered sexist and inappropriate.

Tonight was the full moon and Rex wondered if the lunar phase was influencing him during daylight as Bernie Quist claimed it would. He dismissed the notion as ridiculous. The detective insisted upon monitoring him over these three-day periods, pointing out what he considered to be irrational behaviour, but Rex didn't need some stupid babysitter telling him what to do. The idiot clearly saw himself as Rex's private physician; not exactly a conventional doctor as he'd advised him to continue smoking. As Quist pointed out, cigarettes could no longer harm him and anything that appeared to settle the nerves – despite there being no medical basis – could only be a good thing. He'd even given him one of his old pipes, a ridiculous curved calabash that looked as if it should be part of the ornate plumbing beneath a Victorian sink. Apparently, the therapeutic ritual of flaking tobacco, filling the pipe and tamping it down could settle the mind, but Rex hadn't bothered with it. Quist had warned him never to transform during the full moon, but he'd tried for a few moments last month and hadn't felt like ripping anyone apart.

Hah! What did Quist know? Rex just felt elated and very much *alive* during these times and he wished his self-appointed nanny would leave him alone and not stick his big nose in.

'Big nose,' he chuckled. 'That's a good one.'

His quiet laughter roused the girls and they began to squirm slowly on the dishevelled cotton and stretch like cats in the sun. Ligeia wriggled up his chest to kiss him, her pale blue eyes sparkling. *This was amazing. He'd actually pulled the world's most famous star. Ah, you couldn't beat the good old Rex Grant charm.*

Thinking about it, he realised charm hadn't played any part in this. Ligeia had been the one to suggest they went back to the hotel for sex and she'd invited the other two girls, although that probably wouldn't be the case when he related the story. Ligeia had taken full control, the lovemaking had lasted most of the night and it had been beyond belief – truly sensual, almost feral, and like nothing he'd ever known. Ligeia and Elva had been incredible, and although he'd never admit it to anyone, he and Charlotte had felt like sexual novices beside them.

'Good morning, ladies,' he said, stroking the nape of

46

Ligeia's neck. 'I'd ask how you slept, but we didn't do *much* sleeping, did we?'

'I still can't believe this,' said Charlotte. Laughing nervously, she ran a trembling hand through her hair, her face reddening. 'I keep thinking I must be dreaming. It all feels like some amazing dream.'

'Maybe you'd like me to pinch you?' asked Rex, winking. 'It'll pay you back for scratching my back open last night.'

'Er, yeah, sorry about that.' Charlotte smiled sheepishly, unaware that the fingernail gouges had healed within seconds. 'I haven't been with a guy since I was fifteen and confused. I genuinely have no idea why I screwed you and enjoyed it.'

'Well...' Rex shrugged. 'It isn't exactly difficult to understand.'

'No, last night was just crazy.' Charlotte shook her head. 'For a while, I really wasn't myself, and here in the morning light it feels so surreal. I honestly can't imagine what got into me.'

Rex was about to say *he'd* gotten into her, then realised she wasn't being literal. At some point in their marathon orgy, Ligeia had said she wanted to watch Charlotte with Rex and Charlotte had eagerly complied. Like many sexist idiots, he'd always secretly believed that lesbians were just straight women who hadn't met the right guy yet, but out of the several he'd propositioned, this was the first time the girl hadn't laughed in his face.

'Ligeia,' whispered Charlotte, stroking the singer's short hair. 'I love that name. Elva is a nice name too.'

Elva kissed Charlotte and signed to her friend.

'She says thank you,' translated Ligeia. 'She says she's had many names.'

'Really?' said Rex, unsure of what this could mean. He'd never known anyone who couldn't speak, although the models he dated weren't overly talkative; most of them stared silently at their phones, sometimes during sex. 'Well, Elva is lovely. You're petite and elfin, so Elva suits you. I should stick with it.'

Charlotte gave Rex an embarrassed smile. 'Speaking of Elves, this is like a being in some fantasy world, isn't it?'

'Oh, I don't know.' Laughing quietly, he wrapped his arms around Elva and Ligeia. 'Last night was just your typical Rex Grant evening.'

Ligeia laughed too, a sweet tinkling sound. 'We ought to go,' she said, running her fingers down Rex's cheek and blinking her large blue eyes. 'My manager will be wanting me back.'

'Yes, it's a shame, but I have to get ready too.' Rex checked the time. 'I fly back to London at eleven. My gorgeous personal taxi driver here is taking me.'

'Speaking of which...' Charlotte rummaged in the pile of clothes beside the bed and pulled out her phone to check the messages. 'I'd better ring the office.'

'I'm singing soon,' said Ligeia. 'You said you'd like to listen to me.'

'You bet.' Charlotte sat beside her on the bed, nodding eagerly and opening her phone calendar. 'More than ever. Where did you say the concert was?'

Ligeia giggled. 'I don't remember things like that.'

Rex frowned slightly. The sensual eroticism had vanished and Ligeia now seemed simple and childlike again, just as she'd been in the nightclub. It was almost as if there were two people. Charlotte glanced at him, obviously thinking something similar.

Elva signed and Ligeia nodded. 'She says it's in London on Friday night at a place called the O2. I'll get the tickets from my manager and you must come too, Rex.'

'I will,' he said. *Most artists would be aware of their upcoming venues, but obviously not Ligeia. Apparently she'd never even heard of the London Dome either.* 'Yeah, the O2 at Greenwich. You told us last night, but it slipped my mind. One or two things have happened since then. Charlotte, you can stay at my place if you're travelling down for this concert.'

'After I sing there, we're going to a place called America,' said Ligeia, excitedly. 'It's all the way across the sea.'

'Er, yes...' murmured Rex, astonished. He exchanged another dubious glance with Charlotte. *Perhaps she really was a little simple in the head, or whatever today's politically correct term might be: probably loopy, or a bit crackers.* 'So I've heard.'

'I have a nice idea,' said Ligeia. 'Come with me.'

He laughed. 'Yes, that's a *very* nice idea, but impossible.'

'What do you mean?' Ligeia frowned. 'Come with me and Elva. We'd like that, wouldn't we?'

Elva nodded excitedly.

'Well, I can't, obviously,' said Rex. 'I'm right in the middle of two building transactions. One here in Scotland and...'

Ligeia's frown deepened, her lower lip protruding like a sulky toddler. Elva wrapped a comforting arm around her and kissed her cheek. She signed again, her hands moving fast.

'No, the Colonel won't mind,' answered Ligeia. 'She won't be angry that I asked. I want Rex to come to America. I like him.'

'Ligeia, I've told you it's impossible...' began Rex.

'Make him,' said Ligeia, pouting at Charlotte. 'Tell him to come.'

'Why don't you want to go with her?' demanded Charlotte, irately. 'You can see that you're making her unhappy. You should go if she wants you...'

'What are you talking about?' Rex shook his head, confused. 'You know I can't.'

'Go with her to America,' insisted Charlotte. 'It's what she wants.'

'Is this a joke?' Rex laughed nervously. 'Charlotte, you're acting crazy.'

'I don't understand this,' snapped Ligeia. 'Why won't you do as I ask?' She gave another infantile pout, jumped off the bed and began to pull on her black mini dress. 'I have to go to my room. Come, Elva.'

Elva swiftly dressed too and kissed Rex and Charlotte before following her friend.

'Well, that all went weird pretty fucking quickly,' muttered Rex. He sat on the bed, watching as the door closed behind them, before turning to Charlotte aghast. 'What the *fuck*? Go *with* her to the States? What on earth were you thinking?'

'I don't know,' admitted Charlotte, confused. 'I honestly don't know. I realise the suggestion was totally irrational, but it seemed like a good idea and...' She shook her head and headed for the bathroom with her phone. 'This whole experience has kind of thrown me. I still feel like I'm dreaming.'

Rex nodded, his eyes wide. 'I know women can't get enough of me, but wow!'

He followed the naked girl and then paused at the closed bathroom door. He could hear Charlotte chatting to the office on her mobile, along with trickling toilet sounds. Despite their intimate experiences together, he decided to let her have some privacy.

'Weird,' he muttered, replaying Ligeia's childish outburst in his head. 'Really weird.'

Pulling on the hotel complimentary robe, Rex strolled to the window, noticing the pages of drawings on the table. Quist had compiled this yoga routine and advised him to perform it every morning, especially during the full moon. Rex smirked and shoved the papers in his bag. He'd taken more than enough exercise for one day.

A knock sounded on the bedroom door and Rex opened it to find a middle-aged lady in a very expensive blue suit. Attractive and elegant, with shoulder-length dark hair, she smiled warmly. He recognised her from the Edinburgh nightclub, the black silk eye patch being something of a giveaway.

'Good morning, she said. 'I'm Ligeia's manager, Colonel

Adler.'

'Oh, right. Hi there.' *As a rule, Rex didn't sleep with girls over the age of thirty, but this one could get lucky if she played her cards right.* He frowned slightly. 'Colonel, you say? A lady Colonel?'

Adler glanced down at her small pert breasts, her smile widening. 'Apparently.'

'Well, you could certainly *bring me to attention* any time.' He gave her an exaggerated wink and immediately wished he hadn't; she might think he was mocking her one eye. Despite Ligeia's odd departure, he still felt giddy and elated from the incredible night. 'Nice to meet you, but if you're looking for her, she left a few minutes ago and...'

'Yes, I've just spoken to her and she's upset. Ligeia tells me she asked you to accompany her to America and you refused.' Adler regarded him thoughtfully. 'How is that possible, Mister Grant?'

'Huh? What do you mean?'

'No matter. We can discuss it later. We're leaving shortly, so I don't have time to string this out. As Ligeia told you, she wants you to come with us.'

'This is to be expected.' Rex nodded his understanding. 'I don't blame the poor kid for being infatuated with me; she's only human. I'd still like to see her before she leaves for the States, so I'll give her my number and I'll get in touch when I...'

'I'm not making myself clear,' broke in Adler. 'Ligeia has a concert in London this Friday and then we're heading for Miami. She'd very much like you to join her.'

He peered at the eye patch and resisted the juvenile urge to make a pirate *Arrhhh* noise. 'I don't understand.'

'There isn't much *to* understand. Ligeia wants you to accompany her to America and so do I.'

'But that's ridiculous. I'm heading back to London this

51

morning and I'd like to see her O2 concert, but I can't possibly...'

Rex shook his head. 'Just a minute. Do you have any idea how ridiculous that request sounds?'

'Does one-hundred thousand pounds make it sound less ridiculous? That's tax-free cash paid into the account of your choosing.'

'Is this a joke?'

'I'm not one for joking, Mister Grant. Come with us to America and I guarantee it will be worth your while.'

Rex laughed. 'What the hell *is* this? Do you think I'm some sort of gigolo?'

'No,' said Adler. 'You build and sell houses – Grant Homes. You've been sleeping with my girl and I've had all night to run a full series of background checks on you.'

'Yeah, well I don't like the sound of that. Goodbye, Blackbeard.' Rex slammed the door in her face, turned angrily, and had taken five steps when another knock sounded. 'Jesus!' he muttered. 'How many times do I have to tell this stupid woman?'

He opened the door and his eyes widened in disbelief. 'What on earth...'

Oliver Hardy smiled at him, his bulky body filling the doorway. There was no bowler hat and the grey suit was modern, but the small tuft of moustache, the greased-down hairstyle and chubby face were unmistakable.

'*Oliver*...' began Rex.

Adler appeared from behind the fat man, taking advantage of Rex's shock to swiftly press a small stun gun to the side of his neck. The electrical prongs crackled brightly and he crumpled to the carpet as 150,000 volts sizzled through his nervous system.

'Blackbeard?' said Adler. 'I assume that was some sort of pirate joke mocking my eye patch? How comical.'

'*Hardy*,' croaked Rex, blacking out.

* * * *

52

Chapter 8

It's easy to understand why over seven million international tourists descend upon York each year with eyes wide and cameras flashing. Two thousand years ago, the Romans constructed their huge northern outpost of Eboracum on the River Ouse there. Later it was held for over a century by the Norse invaders, who rechristened the city Jorvik, and the winding thoroughfares still bear the same Viking names suffixed by *gate*, their word for *street*. Both civilisations left a wealth of archaeological remains which were added to by the Norman conquerors and following inhabitants, most notably the Elizabethans, Georgians and Victorians. York has the enormous Gothic Minster, the celebrated street known as the Shambles, many Roman ruins and masses of stunning Tudor architecture, all enclosed by miles of picturesque medieval wall, fortified gateways and ramparts. All of these wonders had one thing in common – they didn't interest Watson in the slightest.

The teenager's boss Bernie Quist was continuously waffling about the historic delights of York and how the small city rivalled Prague, Siena and other European gems for scenic splendour. Watson lived in a less splendid area: the rundown Grimpen council estate in the suburb of Acomb, but there were many aspects of York he *did* like: the countless lively pubs and the two breweries that stood just down the road in Tadcaster, both producing excellent ales. He liked the comedy clubs, the nightlife and the hordes of foreign females, both the tourists and the students at the university. He also liked the way gullible American girls had a thing for good-looking black guys with *quaint* Yorkshire accents. The dimmer ones were fascinated by the stories of his father being in both the Rolling Stones and Led Zeppelin, despite neither band ever having a black member.

Watson also liked his job at the private investigation agency where he'd been Bernard Quist's assistant for six months.

Most of the *consultant* detective work involved run-of-the-mill surveillance and divorces, but there were exciting interludes and he enjoyed how no two days were ever the same. It was also pretty damn cool having a real-life werewolf for a boss, even though he could never mention this to anyone. The majority of people were now more tolerant of ethnics, gays and folk who were somehow *different*, but they'd soon revert to the old ways and begin forming lynch mobs if they ever became aware of supernatural creatures living amongst them. Especially big furry supernatural creatures who could eat them in four or five bites. Manufacturers of burning torches and silver bullets would have a field day.

The corner building that housed their small agency stood just outside the city wall on the junction of Fishergate and Baker Avenue, with a kitchen showroom below and a debt collection firm next door. Returning with the Wednesday lunchtime sandwiches, Watson climbed the stairs and closed the office door behind him. He smirked to see Quist sitting at the desk, scratching his large nose and staring at his computer monitor with a puzzled frown. As usual, there would be some technical challenge here for Watson to solve; something perplexing, like switching the machine on or getting the cursor to move. The private detective had never been a fan of technology, but at Watson's insistence, he'd recently and reluctantly invested in his first computer and mobile phone. The teenager had set them both up and taught Quist the operational basics, but he still had to help with problems on a daily basis.

'Salad with margarine instead of butter for the weird vegan,' said Watson, handing over a bag. 'I've got myself bacon and egg with extra brown sauce.'

'Delightful,' murmured Quist, deep in thought and still scratching absent-mindedly at his nose. 'Please don't splatter the desk when you bite into it.'

Watson smirked again, picturing his boss sunbathing on a beach with that nose sticking up in the air. What a laugh it would be to draw numerals in the sand around his head and turn him into a living sundial. 'Doesn't it ever bother you, not being able to eat meat?' he asked.

Quist gave a lopsided smile, a movement of his mouth corner that Watson had always found a little odd. 'It's been so long, I've forgotten the taste of flesh. I can't eat any animal products, as you know. It's difficult, as many food items are produced using eggs, milk, or whatever.' He held up his sandwich. 'Even margarine can contain traces of whey. I avoid these things as best I can, but miniscule quantities aren't too worrying. If I were to consume a substantial amount, the beast within would begin to stir.'

'The beast within,' laughed Watson, through a mouthful of sandwich. 'A bit dramatic, aren't we?'

'I give in,' said Quist, with a frustrated sigh. He sat back in the chair and gestured to the monitor. 'How do I attach this report to my email?'

'Yeah, I knew you were stuck.' The youth stooped over the desk and tapped at the keyboard. 'I reckon this is the main reason you employ me. Well, this and my gusset-moistening good looks.'

'This and your resourcefulness, resilience, and the fact that you're far more intelligent than you know. You have a tremendous IQ, but you're too unsophisticated to realise.'

'Thanks for the compliment. Er, *was* it a compliment?'

'You also instantly adapt to any crisis and hazardous situation, which is an exceptional character trait. Just look how you accepted my lycanthropy.'

'The way things happened that night, I didn't have much choice.' Watson nodded to the screen. 'I take it this Charlie Milverton's report for the Social?'

'As Milverton is currently our only case, I can hardly compliment you on your powers of deduction. We do, however, have an email from the Social Services about a similar gentleman: someone who claims full disability, but plays football every weekend. They want us to investigate and supply video footage. It looks as if this could be regular work.'

'Same old crap, eh? Divorces, dickheads and benefit scroungers. After the last *real* adventure, I thought things might pick up around here and get more exciting.'

'You mean the *real* adventure where you spent the entire time on the verge of soiling yourself?'

'A brave black guy like me?' The teenager chomped his sandwich. 'You're confusing me with someone else, Guv.'

'Anyway, it might be boring…' Quist gave a lopsided smile. 'But it keeps the wolf from the door.'

'Oh, very good. Maybe you should pack in private investigations and try stand-up comedy.'

The stark contrast in personalities and accents often bemused people on meeting Watson and his cultured employer, but Quist had chosen his assistant *because* of their dissimilarities. The consultant detective lived alone on the outskirts of Askham Richard village, some five miles to the west of York. Constantly changing identities and striving to remain unnoticed, he'd lived alone for many years, relationships and lasting friendships being tricky for someone with his bizarre supernatural secret. Feeling isolated and despondent, he'd decided he needed someone to help reconnect him to humanity and the real world; someone with a lively modern outlook, and this streetwise nineteen-year old was ideal.

'Amazing,' said Watson, reading Milverton's report on the screen. 'I can't believe it took you so long to buy a computer and a phone. I don't understand how you got through life without them.'

'I managed admirably,' said Quist. 'Believe it or not, the human race managed for several years before computers appeared.'

'That's what I can't work out. You must have been around when the first one was invented by Charles Cabbage, or whatever he was called. I thought you'd have had dozens of different models as they progressed over the decades.'

'Babbage invented the *Difference Engine*, as he christened it, a sort of early mechanical calculator. I blame Alan Turing for today's computers.'

'*Blame*?'

'Sorry.' Quist lit a cigarette. 'Yes, I know that's the wrong word, but from their first appearance, I could envisage the technological nightmare that was heading my way; a nightmare for all creatures such as myself. Changing identities was relatively easy before the second world war, but that all changed as information began to be collected and collated in databases. As computing advanced and the Internet took over the world, it became virtually impossible to vanish and reappear as someone else in a new town.'

'But you still manage it.'

'With great difficulty, and I haven't attempted the process for over thirty years, so who knows how the next identity change will go.' Quist drew on his cigarette and grimaced. 'My initial aversion to the technology became an intense dislike.'

'I see what you mean.' Watson took another mouthful of sandwich, spraying brown sauce onto the monitor. 'Do you have to send Milverton's report right now? You're sure you can't wait until he gets me a pirate copy of the *Kes* film?'

'You have the finesse of an Albanian pimp,' said Quist, wiping the screen. He tapped *enter* and submitted the email. 'You'll have to watch it the conventional way, by visiting the cinema or waiting for the official DVD release. Anyway, it sounds terrible. Just like those television programmes you love.'

'All old folk say that.'

'Old?'

'You're over two-hundred, Guv. That *is* knocking on a bit.'

'Point taken, but what's that rubbish you watch? *Love Thy Neighbour, the Next Generation*? It's horrendous. And those awful reality shows...' Quist shuddered. 'What kind of warped mind came up with the idea of getting three nuns from a convent to change places for a month with Manchester prostitutes?'

'*God Swap* is brilliant. Did you see the last episode when Sister Brigitte had to learn the reverse cowgirl position and tromboning? It was hilarious.'

'Tromboning?' The detective stared blankly. 'No. I can't imagine how, but I must have missed that particular episode.'

'It's repeated this Saturday.'

'I've attempted to instruct you in elementary deduction, but I really must teach you how to spot sarcasm.' Quist picked up the office phone. 'Rex's birthday is tomorrow. I'd better ring his hotel and find out what time he wants us to arrive in London.'

'Unbelievable.' Watson watched him consult a scrap of paper and key in the number. 'You've finally bought a mobile phone, but you haven't grasped the technology. You don't ring hotels anymore and ask to be put through; that ended about a hundred years ago. You ring Rex himself, mobile to mobile.'

'As we've established, I'm quite old and...' The Hotel picked up. 'Ah, hello. I understand you have a Mister Rex Grant staying there. I wonder if you could put me through to him, please?'

'Er...' The receptionist hesitated, her voice unsure. 'Mister Grant, you say? Just a moment, please.'

A Bach concerto took over as Quist was placed on hold. 'I'm sorry...' He turned to Watson as he waited. 'I've attempted to fight the urge, but it's no use and I have to ask. I'm aware of the sexual position known as *reverse cowgirl*, but what the hell is *tromboning*?'

'Hello.' The music ended and an authoritative male voice spoke. 'Who is this, please?'

'Bernard Quist. Unless you've recently developed a Scottish accent, I'd say you're not Rex Grant.'

'How astute of you, Sir. You're speaking to Detective Inspector MacKinnon. May I ask what you want with Mister Grant?'

58

'A private matter. Er, is everything alright? Is he there?'

'What's wrong?' mouthed Watson.

'No,' said the policeman. 'As a matter of fact he *isn't* here. We don't know where he is and we'd like to speak to him urgently. Do you have any idea of his whereabouts?'

'I'm afraid I can't help you, Inspector,' said Quist. 'I haven't seen him for a while. What does this concern?'

'I can't divulge that information.'

'Well I'm afraid I don't know where he might be. Sorry.' Quist thumbed off the phone and turned quickly to his desk computer. He brought up the BBC News website and clicked on Scotland. 'Oh God!'

'*Oh God*?' Watson raised an eyebrow. '*Oh God* doesn't sound good.'

Quist turned the monitor to show his assistant the headline: *Gruesome Murder in Edinburgh Hotel*.

'Shit!' whispered Watson. He shook his head. 'Hey, wait a minute, Guv. You don't know that this is connected to Rex.'

'According to the police, he's vanished.' Quist bowed his head, slowly rubbing his eyes. 'The moon is full, someone has been murdered in his hotel, and the police are looking for Rex. You realise what this could mean?'

Watson laughed uneasily. 'It probably means the birthday party's off.'

Quist walked to the office filing cabinet and took a bottle of single malt from the bottom drawer. He half-filled a glass and stared silently through the window.

'Come on, Guv,' said Watson. 'Okay, someone's been killed, but it doesn't mean Rex is to blame.'

Quist knocked back the whisky and turned to gaze at him.

'Shit, Guv.' The teenager gulped. 'What the fuck are we going to do?'

* * * *

Chapter 9

Quist and Watson climbed the steps from Edinburgh's Waverley Station to emerge on the crowded central thoroughfare of Princes Street. The Wednesday afternoon train had taken less than three hours from York, but twilight had already descended on the city; the *gloaming*, as the more romantic Scots still referred to this time of day. The teenager wore a denim jacket against the cool April air and turned to look across the parkland that separated the old and new towns. The Scottish capital shimmered in a golden glow, the castle, soaring towers, Gothic spires and countless monuments basking in the radiance of a thousand floodlights. He lowered his sunglasses and peered up at the Scott Monument rising above him like some Gothic spaceship designed by Jules Verne.

'Wow!' said Watson. 'I've never been to Scotland before. Where are all the kilts?'

'They're mostly in the tourist shops,' said Quist, buttoning his long leather overcoat. 'Keep your eyes peeled and I dare say you'll spot one, along with one or two tartan shortbread tins.'

The detective carried the small overnight case that he always kept ready in the office, with binoculars, cameras, toothbrushes and other bits and bats, including clean underwear and socks that would fit them both. The indispensable *grab bag* was taken if they ever needed to leave hurriedly on a case like this with no time to call home. He still couldn't believe how quickly the day had changed. A tedious Wednesday morning compiling benefit fraud reports had suddenly turned into an investigation into murder; a murder that seemingly involved their friend. Quist had been ringing Rex's mobile every ten minutes and, knowing it would be a waste of time, he tried the number again.

'His phone is still switched off,' he said, glancing up at the full moon and grimacing before setting off towards the Balmoral Hotel. 'Come on. We really need to find out what happened here.'

'Hey, look at this, Guv.' Watson pointed to a huge poster taking up the entire side of a bus shelter. 'Ligeia.'

'Who?'

'Watson looked aghast. '*Who*?'

'I just said that.'

'Ligeia. Only the biggest thing in the music world right now. This is the advert for her concert here a couple of nights ago.'

'Forget about stupid pop concerts.' Quist increased his pace. 'Right now we have far more important things to concern us. If Rex has anything to do with this death, I hold myself fully accountable.'

'This guilt trip is screwing with those amazing powers of deduction you're supposed to have. I keep telling you, the murder and Rex's disappearance could be a coincidence. Why not find out first before you start with all the...'

'*Coincidence*? *Guilt trip*? Do you realise how serious this is?' The detective sighed. 'Yes, I suppose you're right, but it's the full moon and I have a very bad feeling.'

'Let's just see what happened first.' Watson knew there was a good chance that Rex was responsible, but he was trying his best to ease the tension and worry. He peered over his sunglasses at the sumptuous neo-Gothic hotel on the corner of Princes Street and North Bridge. Soaring two-hundred feet above them, the ornate bulk of the clock tower dominated the twilight skyline. 'Wow! Is that the Balmoral? Big fancy place, isn't it?'

'Yes, it is.' Quist ran his eyes over the building architecture, calculating the distance between the upper windows and the rooftops. *The multitude of baroque ledges and decorative balconies could prove useful later.* 'Take off your sunglasses before we go inside. It's evening and you're starting to look ridiculous as usual.'

'Modern fashion says you can wear shades anywhere at any time.' He slipped the glasses into his jacket pocket. 'You *are* aware that these are Jo Milan? Like I told you before, these cost Rex over nine-hundred quid.'

'They must cost around ten pounds to produce. How on earth do they justify charging nine-hundred pounds for two pieces of coloured plastic and a little bent wire?'

'They have the name Jo Milan etched on one of the lenses.'

'Well, why didn't you say so? Money well spent.'

'Exactly.'

'Once again, I was being sarcastic. One day you'll pick up on it.'

Watson was pleased to find the Balmoral's traditional doorman wearing a kilt. The concierge held the door wide and they entered the elegant reception. The teenager's wide eyes drifted from the polished marble floors and sparkling brass to the chandeliers and ornate splendour of the ceiling plasterwork. Quist gave one of his peculiar lopsided smiles and walked to the reception desk.

'Hello there,' he said, unbuttoning his overcoat. 'We'd like a twin room, please.'

'Certainly.' The girl checked her computer. 'We have external twin rooms with truly amazing views, or internal facing onto our central courtyard.'

'External, please, and a high one. I suffer from terrarphobia.'

The receptionist looked blank.

'A fear of the ground,' explained Quist.

The girl peered at his feet

'Er, yes.' He shrugged. 'It comes and goes.'

'Top floor it is then,' she said, sliding a registration card across the desk.

Quist signed and watched as his credit card was swiped before picking up a complimentary evening newspaper. A teenage bellboy appeared, grabbed the detective's bag and showed them through a gleaming brass door into the elevator.

'Welcome to the Balmoral, gentlemen.' The young man beamed from ear to ear. 'My name's Scott. That's my Christian name, not my surname. I'm no relation to our famous author.' Scott laughed quietly. He'd cracked this joke to dozens of guests and it was still as clever and funny as the day he'd thought of it.

Watson nudged Quist. 'What author?' he whispered.

Quist ignored the question. 'Hello, Scott,' he said. 'This is a lovely place, but I understand you had some unpleasantness last night?' He held out the newspaper he'd taken and gestured to the headline. 'A murder?'

'Oh, it's best not to dwell on such things, Sir,' said Scott. 'You're right; this is a wonderful hotel. We have everyone staying here. Royalty, ex-Presidents, Prime Ministers and countless film stars. Ligeia is our latest celebrity.'

'*Ligeia*?' gasped Watson. 'You mean she's here now? In *this* hotel?'

'No, she left this morning. She gave a concert at the Murrayfield Stadium which I hear was quite something.'

'Yes,' broke in Quist, 'but I was wondering about that awful murder?'

'I'm afraid we're not allowed to speak about it, Sir.' Scott gave a sympathetic shrug as the doors opened and he led them out into a corridor. 'We have to be very discreet. I'm sure you understand?'

Quist pulled out three banknotes.

'It was a young lady,' whispered Scott, glancing around and swiftly pocketing the money. 'She wasn't a hotel guest, so I don't know her name and the police haven't released it. The cleaning staff found her body this morning in the room of a guest named Rex Grant.'

'She was killed in his *room*?' Quist felt his stomach lurch and closed his eyes. '*Oh, dear God.*'

'Yes, he appears to have brought her back for sex and she

63

stayed the night. The police aren't telling us much. They must think we'll shoot our mouths off.'

Watson raised an eyebrow. 'Perish the thought.'

Scott snorted. 'Mica behind reception thinks I'm a big mouth, but she's no room to talk. She's into threesomes and tells her friends all about it on Facebook.'

'Wow!' said Watson. 'Really?'

'Oh, yeah, there are some real perverts here. That other bellboy Lance is into married couples.'

'Anyone into tromboning?' asked Watson.

'Rex Grant's room,' broke in Quist, testily. 'You say that's where the murder happened? Where is that?'

'On the fourth floor; the floor below yours. The police have the area sealed off.'

'Tell me…' Quist swallowed dryly, dreading the answer to his next question. 'How was the girl killed? What state was the body in?'

'I don't know.' Scott gave him a peculiar look. 'Apparently, there was blood, but I haven't been able to speak to the cleaner who found her and, as I say, the police haven't given away any details.' He opened a door with a key card. 'Here we are.'

'Did you meet this guest Rex Grant?' asked Quist.

'Yes, he seemed like a cool guy; he wore sunglasses indoors.' Scott shook his head. 'Who would ever have thought he was some murderer? And to think he screwed Ligeia too.'

'What?' gasped Watson, his mouth wide.

'Yeah, she spent the night with him too, but as I say, I can't tell you too much. We have to be very discreet.'

'Of course, Scott.' Quist gazed blankly. 'Discretion is clearly your middle name.'

* * * *

Watson walked into the hotel room stunned. 'Rex actually shagged Ligeia,' he muttered. 'That's incredible.'

'Incredible?' snapped Quist, tossing his bag onto one of the beds. 'What's incredible is how you're more concerned with *that* than the fact that this killing took place in Rex's room. A girl was actually killed *in* his room on the full moon. This just gets worse.' He gestured to the television. 'Turn that music off, would you?'

As in many upmarket hotels, the screen was displaying a welcome message and showing the guest facilities and restaurants to a backing of traditional Scottish tunes. Watson pressed the remote control, but instead of switching off, the set changed to a music channel. *Well, talk about coincidence?* Ligeia was performing in a concert. He decided against mentioning this to the anxious detective and, rather than switching off, he muted the sound and gazed enviously at the tiny singer. *Unbelievable! Rex had actually shagged Ligeia?*

'This is terrible,' muttered Quist, skimming through the report in the newspaper. 'The murder has made it into this evening edition, but it's far too early for the police to release any real information. I need to see where the killing happened and then take a look at this girl's body.'

Watson gulped. 'You want to break into the morgue and check to see if she's ripped up and half-eaten?'

'I need to discover the truth, however horrific.' Throwing down the paper, he shrugged off his overcoat to reveal a brown corduroy jacket. 'The first thing is to investigate Rex's room. According to our friend Scott the discreet bellboy, it's on the floor below us.'

Quist opened the bedroom window to peer down at the Waverley Station rooftops and the busy North Bridge away to his left.

Watson joined him and stuck out his head. 'Why didn't you ask for a room near Rex's?'

'Ask the receptionist to put us close to the murder room? Was that a serious question? It's safe to say they'll be putting their guests as far away from there as possible.'

'That's right. The bellboy said the police have sealed off the area.'

'Come along.' Quist strode to the door and held it wide. 'Let's find out.'

'Hey, this is more like it, Guv.' Watson grinned. 'Real detective stuff again instead of those divorces and benefit cheats.'

The detective sighed. 'I honestly wish I could share your excitement. Right now, all I feel is an ominous foreboding.'

They walked to the elevator and descended one level. The doors opened and a uniformed policeman quickly approached.

'I'm sorry,' said the officer, holding up a hand. 'This section is temporarily restricted. It's just this northern side of the fourth floor. You can still access the opposite sides of the building using the other lift. I'm afraid it's a police matter.'

'I wouldn't have guessed.' Quist gestured to the police cordon tape and the forensic people milling about. The Scenes of Crime Officer and his team appeared to be leaving one of the rooms and he noted the door number before closing the elevator. 'Good night, officer.'

* * * *

Chapter 10

'There's only one way to do this,' said Quist. Slipping off his corduroy jacket and hanging it over a chair, he leant through the open bedroom window and looked left and right to get his bearings. The vast rooftops of Waverley Station stretched out below, and theatres, galleries and museums glowed with amber floodlight. 'I don't like to transform when the moon is full, but I don't have any choice.'

Watson wasn't listening and stared instead at the muted television that he'd left on. The Ligeia concert was still playing and the petite singer gyrated silently on stage. 'Isn't she incredible?' he said. 'I think this is the NEC concert from a couple of months back.'

'Ligeia?' Quist glanced at the screen and rolled his eyes. 'She wouldn't be my first choice if I wanted to relax with a little music. I don't know much about her, but I presume she picked her name from Poe.'

'Winnie the...'

'Edgar Alan,' sighed Quist. 'Ligeia is a character in the *Tomb of Ligeia*. A classic.'

'Oh right. She doesn't have a surname, which is pretty cool, you've got to admit. Have you heard her hits?'

'It's pretty much impossible to avoid them. They constantly play her music on the radio, and every other car that drives past seems to have her album blaring from the window. They were playing the album over and over in the pub yesterday when we were with the benefit cheat.'

Watson nodded and turned up the volume.

'The public never cease to amaze me,' said Quist, watching the singer. 'I suppose it's all to do with clever marketing and media promotion. They go crazy over this girl, yet she sounds so average.'

'*What*?' Watson turned to him, shocked. 'Her album *Water*

Music has broken all previous sales. It's officially the biggest seller of all time. You don't think she's the most wonderful thing you've ever heard?'

'Oh, come on, Watson. It's all marketing hype and you've allowed yourself to be wooed by it. She reminds me of those karaoke singers on the television talent shows. Pleasant enough in an amateur sort of way, but decidedly mediocre.'

'I can't believe you. Talk about having no taste? Her new album is out next week – the *Music of Sound*. Her voice actually speaks to your soul.'

'Good lord! I can't believe you just said that.'

'Just listen to the lyrics.' Watson closed his eyes, repeating the words as she sang. '*The months go by, my music keeps me sane, my love*. Whoo, yeah, I'm going out to buy this right now.'

'Well, I think it's safe to say you're a bit of a fan.' Quist shook his head, incredulous. 'Don't you already have this first album *Water Music*?'

'Um, yes, but…' Watson gave a puzzled shrug and laughed. 'Yeah, you're right. Why would I buy it again?'

Quist regarded him curiously, then dismissed his thoughts. 'Anyway, to far more important things.' He leant out through the window again. The moon shone brightly above Arthur's Seat, the extinct volcano that looms over Holyrood. 'We're on the top floor overlooking North Bridge and Rex's room is on the floor below, but on the other side of the hotel facing Princes Street.'

Watson was still staring at Ligeia. 'She's gorgeous,' he murmured. 'I can't help getting horny whenever I see her.' He turned from the television and saw that Quist had quickly undressed and was pulling down his underpants. He peered blankly at the naked man. 'But sometimes the horny feeling doesn't last very long.'

Removing his signet ring and wristwatch, Quist handed them to his assistant for safekeeping. The youth looked at the RQ initials; the letters had been engraved in the 1780s, back when his employer had been the human Richard Quist.

'Oh, fuck,' groaned Watson, beginning to tremble. 'Here we go.'

Taking a deep breath, the detective clenched his teeth, shuddered and bent double, a mass of thick dark fur sprouting to cover his expanding back. He shook his head, pointed ears emerging and his face elongating into a large hairy muzzle. Watson stepped back, wincing to hear the sickening sound of bones snapping and crunching as they changed and lengthened. The room temperature dropped alarmingly as Quist grew in furry bulk and height, until finally the human had vanished and a huge black wolf stood on two legs in his place.

'Shit, I'll never get used to seeing that,' croaked Watson, his throat and mouth dry. He gaped at the enormous creature with its glowing amber eyes and, despite the heating, he saw his breath cloud on the air. 'You say it sucks up energy or something when you change?'

'Yes,' growled Quist. 'The lupine transformation drains the natural energy from the surrounding atmosphere. Corporeal energy is transformed into esoteric, ethereal energy.'

'Well, there's my science lesson for tonight. Thanks for that and the free laxative.'

The wolf wagged his tail and grinned, the yellow eyes sparkling and razor teeth glinting in the wide mouth.

'No, don't smile like that, Guv. It doesn't exactly help.' Watson stared warily, unable to prevent himself shivering. 'I thought you don't like to transform when the moon's full?'

'With the police keeping everyone away, I can't access Rex's room by conventional means. That's why I requested a high bedroom. I'm black, so no one should see me climbing over the roof. I'm much faster and stronger in this form too. I can leap further if needs be.'

'You're hoping to get in from the outside?'

The wolf nodded. 'The SOCO team were leaving the crime scene when we called down there. Hopefully they've finished their work and it will be empty.'

'Are you sure about this? The outside of the building's lit by floodlights.'

'Which cause dark shadows.' Quist shoved his large furry head through the open window and checked that no one was watching from North Bridge down to his left. 'Now is as good a time as any; the moon is behind cloud.'

'Good luck, Guv.'

Switching off the bedroom light, the wolf held up his front paws, the bones crackling as taloned fingers sprouted. He climbed out and quickly scaled the ornate façade, snatching hold of ledges and sinking his claws into crevices between the sandstone blocks.

Watson leant out to watch in disbelief. 'Fuck!' he whispered. 'You look like Spider-man in a mink coat.'

Quist reached the roof with its hotchpotch of pitches, dormers and chimney stacks, and dropping low, he bounded across on all fours, jumping ventilation ducts, lantern lights and pipework. The Balmoral clock tower soared two-hundred feet above Princes Street and arriving at the base, he crouched like a shaggy gargoyle to look around. His eyesight was enhanced in lupine form and from here he could see over Leith and Portobello to the Firth of Forth, the wide estuary that opens into the North Sea. He watched the melancholy winking of the lighthouses and gazed thoughtfully at the twinkling streetlamps of Abedour in distant Fife.

He should never have bitten Rex and passed on the lycanthropy. Yes, the bite had saved his life, but because of his actions, another life had been lost. An innocent girl had died and he was responsible.

Quist shook himself. He needed to stop agonising, concentrate on what he was doing here and not be seen. The moon emerged from behind the cloud and he moved back into the shadows of a dormer window. A night breeze ruffled his fur and he lifted his muzzle to sniff the air, all the time fighting the powerful lunar urge to throw back his head and howl.

The huge creature looked down as vehicle horns began honking in the busy traffic below. A van had pulled out of a side street and a texting girl in a car had run into it. Quist heard a volley of foul language and smiled, knowing all eyes would be on the minor collision and this was the ideal moment to make his move. He glanced over the edge, checking where the ledges and balconies were situated, then bounded swiftly along from the clock tower, counting the dormers as he passed. It was fortunate that the hotel exterior was an elaborate mass of baroque décor – the fancy protrusions were ideal for pigeons, roosting starlings and climbing werewolves.

'Three, four, five,' he growled. 'Here we are.'

The wolf dropped over the side, grabbing one of the ledges below and clambering onto it. He peered through the closest window to ensure it was the correct room and winced; the blood on the carpet was something of a giveaway.

Wait a moment. Quist raised a bushy lupine eyebrow. As far as he could make out, there didn't seem to be *much* blood. This was a good sign.

Thankfully the room was empty, but the window was locked and he turned before breaking in to check that he hadn't been seen leaping from the roof. No one on the street appeared to be looking up, save for one wide-eyed child staring in utter amazement. Before he could stop himself, Quist had given a little wave, then grinned guiltily and leant back into the shadow of a balcony. The frightened boy tugged at his mother's coat, yelling something about a werewolf, and was rewarded with a smack across his head for being a lying brat.

Pushing up the sash with supernatural strength, Quist

71

snapped the lock, jumped in and quietly closed it. Switching on the lights was unnecessary; the street lamps outside provided adequate illumination and these dim conditions were no problem with his nocturnal vision. With eyes glowing yellow, he padded around on all fours, sniffing carefully and checking the entire room. No other wolf scents were present, which came as a huge relief, and so did the single pool of blood. Quist had seen grisly werewolf kills before and they certainly didn't look like this. No one had been torn apart here – there were no arterial splatters or visceral mess, just a few gravitational droplets in the carpet fibres and a small congealed pool where the corpse must have lain. He snuffled around, picking up the scent of the female cadaver.

The wolf glanced to his right and spotted another tiny patch of blood on the floor near the bedroom door. He padded over, sniffed and studied the unusual spray; it looked to have been blown through a straw. *Had someone wiped a knife clean as they left, casting off the blood in this peculiar little jet pattern*? The urge to taste it suddenly overwhelmed him and his hungry wolf tongue snaked out.

'No,' he snarled, twisting away. 'No.'

Quist fought the compulsion, concentrating on his calming *Scheherazade* melody. The urges faded and he stood upright, taking a few deep breaths to fully compose himself. No, he was more than satisfied. This definitely wasn't a werewolf kill. This had been a simple murder with a conventional weapon like a knife, if the awful act of murder could ever be referred to as *simple*.

He turned to the dishevelled bed; the police had obviously instructed the hotel staff to leave everything as it was. He sniffed the pillows and sheets, picking up the scent of Rex Grant in human form and someone else. No, *three* other people, all female. The wolf raised what passed for eyebrows. *Rex had obviously been a busy boy*. Much perspiring and sexual activity had taken place and the scents were strong, one of them belonging to the dead girl who had lain on the floor.

What could have happened here and why had Rex fled the scene?

Quist twisted sharply, hearing the muted sound of footsteps outside the room. The door lock clicked and he sprang over the bed, darting into the bathroom as two forensic personnel walked in and switched on the light. He silently eased up the toilet window and climbed out onto the ledge, closing it behind him. Checking Princes Street below for observers, the wolf leapt from balcony to balcony, negotiated the ledge around the corner of the building and bounded over further balconies, counting the windows he passed until he was sure he'd left the police cordoned area.

Finding a dark empty bedroom, he pushed up the window, breaking the catch, and climbed inside. Black fur and fangs fell out and turned to dust as he grunted and crackled, his huge lupine body shrinking and transforming painfully back into a panting naked man. Quist raided the wardrobe for the complimentary dressing gown, slipped it on and let himself out. He glanced up and down the hotel corridor to ensure there was no police activity, then hurried along to the lift and ascended to his floor.

Watson answered the knock and grinned to see him. 'Well, that's a bit less dramatic than your exit, Guv. Did you manage to get in?'

'I did.' Quist closed the door. 'There's no need to visit the morgue and check the body. I don't know what took place down there, but I *do* know that young woman wasn't killed by a wolf. The signs indicate a stabbing.'

'That's brilliant news.'

'Brilliant? Not for the poor girl.'

'True.' Watson grimaced. 'Sorry.'

'But the fact remains that she was killed in Rex's room and he's vanished.'

'Yeah, do you think he had anything to do with it?'

'Knowing Rex, that's highly unlikely, but disappearing will doubtless have made him the police prime suspect.' Quist shook his head. 'Why on earth would he do that?'

'God knows.' Watson shrugged. 'But you have to remember, he *is* a bit of a twat.'

* * * *

Chapter 11

The genteel Edinburgh development named the New Town was built in the mid-eighteenth century when the medieval streets and wynds of the Old Town around the castle became too cramped for the gentry. Quist gazed at the Georgian architecture from the taxi cab, noticing the way the Thursday morning sunlight reflected on the granite. He loved these regal avenues, squares and crescents, and could certainly understand why this had been designated a World Heritage Site. He'd managed a few hours of sleep at the hotel, between periods of worried deliberation and reading the Internet on his phone. Sleep hadn't been a problem for Watson. After a couple of lagers in the Balmoral bar, he'd happily snored the night away, filling the twin room with a low, droning purr.

'All very grey, isn't it?' said Watson, peering out of the cab window.

The detective frowned. 'Grey?'

'Yeah, the buildings and shit.'

'Open your eyes,' said Quist. 'Edinburgh is mostly constructed using Scottish granite and sandstone, but if you *really* look, especially at the architecture in the Old Town, you'll notice the beautiful shades of pink, blue, buff…'

'And grey.'

'This is a wonderful old city.' Quist lowered his voice so the driver wouldn't hear. 'I lived here once. I was a doctor at the infirmary in the eighteen-seventies.'

'A doctor?' The teenager whistled. 'Hey, that's pretty cool, but it's a bit of a come down to a consultant detective, isn't it?'

'I really don't look upon it in that way; I've held various professional positions over the years. Yes, it was an interesting few years and I had some good friends here back then. Joseph Bell and a young fellow named Arthur. The three of us used early forensic science to assist the police with one or two crimes. I've always had something of an insatiable curiosity and a compulsion to solve mysteries.'

'Well, we certainly have one now that needs solving, don't we? It sounds like you're feeling a bit better.'

'A little, now that my primary concern has been lain to rest. Rex didn't kill in wolf form, which is a huge relief.'

The problem was, a girl had been murdered in Rex's hotel room and, for some unexplained reason, their friend had vanished. They needed to find out what had happened and quickly. It was unthinkable that Rex could be involved, but why on earth had he fled the scene? Quist had rung McNulty Caledonian, the company Rex was dealing with, as soon as the offices opened and a part of the mystery was immediately solved. The dead girl was called Charlotte Michie and she worked there as a personal assistant to the director.

The taxi turned down Lothian Road and onto the bustling thoroughfare of Morrison Street.

'This area is as close as Edinburgh gets to a financial district,' said Quist, looking at the banks, insurance companies and law firms that lined the route. 'The place should be just down here.'

McNulty Caledonian stood half way along near the International Conference Centre, one of the many modern buildings of green-tinted glass and chrome that rub shoulders with the sandstone tenement offices. Quist checked his watch as he climbed from the taxi and paid the fare. It was nine-thirty.

'Nice place,' said Watson. 'So this is the housing company that Rex is dealing with? They don't look to be short of money.'

'McNulty is a multi-millionaire,' said Quist. He lit a cigarette and slipped his free hand into the pocket of his lengthy overcoat. 'I looked him up on the internet while you were snoring. The Leith waterfront down on the Firth of Forth used to be a rundown mess of derelict warehouses and pubs, and he bought land at rock-bottom prices. He anticipated such areas becoming *the* place to live and he was right. It was the same in every city; the elite all wanted flats in renovated factories and other properties on the river.' Quist drew on the tobacco smoke. 'Instead of rats, drunks and prostitutes, the apartment blocks on McNulty's land are now filled with surgeons, solicitors and footballers.'

'I imagine prostitutes still visit,' said Watson. 'But these days they'll look like movie stars, the prices will have gone up, and they'll no longer leave customers feeling as if they're pissing barbed wire.'

'Eloquent as ever.' Quist took a final few puffs and died out the half-smoked cigarette underfoot. 'Anyway, that's his story. He made a killing.'

Watson glanced at him.

'Ah, yes.' Quist smiled ruefully as he mounted the steps, leather coat flapping like a cloak. 'Perhaps that wasn't the best choice of phrase today.'

A chubby blonde girl sat at the reception desk and smiled at the two visitors.

'Good morning,' said Quist. 'I rang a short while ago and it was probably you I spoke to. We're here to see Mister McNulty.'

'Yes, it was me. I'm Katrina.' Realising they weren't clients and knowing the reason behind their visit, the receptionist let her polite mask drop. 'This is a terrible business, isn't it?' she said, tears welling in her eyes. 'Really awful.'

Terrible? Watson looked around, puzzled. Form the size of the premises and furnishings, it was obviously quite a *successful* business.

'Charlotte Michie,' said Katrina. 'As I told you, Charlotte was one of Gordon's assistants and she was a friend of mine. We were all her friends and now she's been murdered. Can you believe it?'

'It's tragic,' agreed Quist. 'It's difficult to know what to say. I'm so sorry about Charlotte. Can you think of anyone who might have wanted to harm her?'

'Are you serious?' she snapped, unable to conceal her grief and anger. 'Yeah, I can think of someone: that mad bastard she was taking to the airport. You said on the phone you were looking for him.'

'Er, yes, we're trying to find Rex Grant, but the police haven't actually confirmed that he was the one who...'

'Well, it's obvious that he did it. She was killed in his bedroom and he's disappeared. He packed his bag and vanished without paying the bill or going through the hotel lobby.'

'I have to admit, that does sound suspicious.' Quist spotted a large stuffed bird in a glass case by the nearby water dispenser and attempted to change the subject. 'Isn't that a sea eagle?'

'Yes.' Katrina nodded, sniffing and wiping her eyes. 'Gordon shot it on the Isle of Mull a couple of years back.'

Quist looked bemused. 'I thought they were well-protected.'

A dry laugh sounded and Watson turned to find an elderly red-haired Scotsman behind them. McNulty wore a smart grey suit and sported a thick moustache of tight ginger bristle that looked as if it could be used for scrubbing potatoes. He'd overheard the exchange.

'*Well-protected*?' said McNulty. 'Don't you city folk know *anything* about wildlife? A rhino is well-protected; virtually armour-plated. You have to use a bullet the size of a corona cigar to bring those bastards down. All your eagles have is a layer of feathers. A simple twelve bore cartridge will knock them out of the sky.'

'Er...' Quist opened his mouth, but thought better of it and held out a hand. 'Mister McNulty?'

'Call me Gordon.' McNulty shook hands. 'You'll be Bernard Quist. Katrina said you'd rung. Rex has told me about you. You're the private eye from Yorkshire.'

'Consultant detective,' said Quist.

'What's the difference?'

'Not much,' said Watson. 'But certain members of our firm believe *consultant detective* sounds more upmarket and gives a discreet image.'

McNulty turned to shake hands with the teenager. 'I take it you're Watson? I'm sorry, but Rex never mentioned your first name.'

'Yeah.' Watson nodded. 'I don't think he knows I have one. As your receptionist will have mentioned, we're trying to find Rex.'

'Lovely,' muttered Katrina to herself. She busied herself with the desk paperwork. 'It's nice that we're on first name terms with Charlotte's murderer.'

'We're all trying to find him,' said McNulty. He led them away from the girl and poured himself a water from the dispenser. 'Some people seem to have already found him guilty.'

'Natural, I suppose,' said Quist. 'Considering.'

McNulty nodded. 'No one has heard from him, and the police say his phone isn't just turned off. It's been deactivated, which means they can't track him.'

'Is that so?' Quist raised an eyebrow. 'As I say, it's natural that some would view such things as a sign of guilt.'

'Some?' repeated McNulty. 'But not you?'

'I know him well. He isn't a murderer.'

'My thoughts exactly. I've known Rex since he was a kid. He was here to finalise a housing deal between myself and Grant Homes. I'm a good friend of his father and an even better friend of his Uncle Rupert. We hunt together.'

'Rex told me,' said Quist. Apparently, McNulty and Uncle Rupert were huge advocators of reintroducing wolves and bears into the wilder areas of Scotland. Mostly so they could shoot them.

'How long has he been missing now?' asked Watson.

'Since yesterday morning,' said McNulty. 'Sometime between eight-thirty and ten. He was booked on a return flight to London at eleven, but never turned up for it.'

'The police have state-of-the-art technology,' said Quist. 'Yet they're unable to locate him with the CCTV cameras everywhere, their facial recognition software and credit card alerts? Your receptionist told us he didn't leave the hotel through the lobby.'

'No, the police checked the reception camera footage. They checked *all* the footage.'

Quist frowned. 'So presumably he used a staff or fire exit. I wonder why? I noticed the street cameras all around the hotel. It would be practically impossible to leave the vicinity without being filmed.'

'Well, he somehow managed it.' McNulty looked around the reception. 'We need to speak privately and people are always in and out of my office. Do you two smoke by any chance?'

'I don't.' Watson rolled his eyes. 'But the boss here *has* been known to have the occasional one or two.'

'I could certainly use one. Come this way.' McNulty led them to the elevator. 'It's stupid, I know, but I'm blaming myself for Charlotte's death. Rex flew up from London and I suggested that, rather than rent a car or use taxis, my assistant could ferry him around. Charlotte spent Tuesday afternoon with Rex and then apparently spent the night with him at the hotel.' The lift doors opened and, ushering them in, he pressed *Roof*.

Quist sighed. 'As you say, you can't blame yourself for giving Charlotte the job. Only one person is responsible for this and that's the killer. I asked your girl Katrina, but can *you* think of anyone who might have wanted to harm her? Perhaps a jealous boyfriend who found out she'd slept with Rex, or...'

'Well, she was gay, but no, there was no one permanent in her life at the moment. I've been racking my brains to help the police, but I can't think of any reason for this.'

'I can't understand why Rex would run,' said Watson.

'That makes two of us,' said McNulty. 'Fleeing the murder scene has made him very much a *person of interest*, as the police like to say.' The elevator opened into a glass rooftop structure and he led them out through a revolving door onto a terrace. 'Charlotte was fine when she rang me from his hotel at eight-thirty and the cleaning staff discovered her dead at the guest check-out time of ten o'clock. Rex was nowhere to be seen.'

'Am I missing something here?' asked Watson. 'If Charlotte was gay, why was she spending the night with Rex?'

'They were...' McNulty groped for the correct word. '*Partying*, I believe is the modern term. Rex and Charlotte ran into two young women at a club and took them back to the hotel. These girls left around eight-thirty and they were the last people to see him.'

'Two?' gasped Watson. 'Ligeia...'

'Yes, the singer and her friend. The police have interviewed them, but they were no help. They say Charlotte was alive and Rex was acting quite normally when they left, with no sign of any...'

'*Three* girls?' Watson almost fainted. 'Rex had sex with Ligeia and two other girls?'

McNulty smiled at the dazed teenager. 'No one can hear us out here,' he said, leaning on the handrail that ran around the edge of the roof. 'From what Rex has told me about you two, I believe I can trust you not to repeat anything I tell you?'

'Don't worry,' said Quist, taking out his cigarettes. 'You can tell us anything.'

Watson nodded in agreement. Still stunned, he peered over the handrail at the International Conference Centre just along the way and the bustle of traffic on Morrison Street below. *This murder was one thing, but Rex had been in a threesome with Ligeia. A foursome, if there was such a word.*

'So he's their prime suspect?' said Quist, handing a cigarette to McNulty and taking one himself. 'The police will believe these girls left, then Rex killed Charlotte for some unexplained reason, panicked and ran.'

'There's more to it than that,' said McNulty. 'My brother is a high-ranking officer in the Edinburgh police. He's part of my Masonic lodge and a good grouse shooter. Through his police Masonic connections, he assisted Rex with that er... unpleasantness last Christmas. The murders and the fire and everything. You two were involved and helped him too, didn't you?

'We did indeed.' Quist had helped by biting the dying man, but prudently decided against mentioning this. 'Ah, the good old Masons.'

'The thing is, the police are looking for Rex because they're sure he's involved, but they're not fully convinced he killed Charlotte.'

Quist lit the two cigarettes and narrowed his eyes. 'Why?'

'This goes no further.'

'It won't, I assure you.'

'Have you heard of Alistair Ramson?'

'You mean the psychopath?' asked Quist, puzzled. 'The tabloids called him the Hounslow Ripper.'

McNulty nodded. 'He killed at least four people and fled the country last year. They caught him in France two months ago. The thing is, Ramson always slashed a letter R into the chests of his victims with some weapon they never found. They know it's a thin stiletto blade made of titanium.'

'Wait a moment...' Quist raised his eyebrows. 'Am I correct in assuming Charlotte Michie had the R on her chest.'

'Yes, and her puncture wound was identical. Forensics rushed the analysis through and there were microscopic traces of titanium present. They also found a blood spray in the room consistent with Ramson's other killings. They believe he wipes the blade clean in a particular way which leaves the pattern. Like the letter R, they view it as a signature.'

'Intriguing,' murmured Quist. He recalled seeing the peculiar blood spray on the bedroom carpet. 'Do they have any CCTV footage of Ramson entering the hotel?'

'No. It's crazy, but they're entertaining the possibility that Rex may have killed Charlotte in some copycat fashion. The forensic evidence on Ramson and these signatures were never released to the press, but they think it's possible Rex might have found out somehow, then got hold of a similar titanium blade and copied the trademark letter and cleaning manoeuvre.'

'Rex wasn't filmed as he left,' said Quist. 'So there has to be a blind spot in the street CCTV coverage. This Ramson could have entered and left the Balmoral the same way.'

'Hang about,' said Watson. 'You say they caught this serial killer in France, so how come...'

'He escaped,' said McNulty. 'The police were transporting him back to Britain when a masked team sprang him at Calais. A very professional job apparently. They jammed the police van radio signal, boxed in the vehicle, tasered the officers and got him out in seconds. He hasn't been seen since, and he was a pretty big chap so it must be hard for him to hide.'

'Intriguing,' repeated Quist. 'Yes, I recall the newspaper photographs. Ramson was obese and he'd certainly stand out.' He stroked thoughtfully at his large nose. 'Why would anyone go to the trouble of engineering this killer's escape? What did they want with him, and if Ramson escaped in France, what was he doing in Edinburgh?'

'More to the point,' said Watson, 'what was he doing in Rex's bedroom? I can't believe Rex has anything to do with this, but it's also hard to accept that some escaped killer would randomly appear in his hotel room at eight-thirty in the morning.'

'True,' agreed Quist. 'If Ramson is now in Edinburgh and

he wanted to kill someone for sadistic enjoyment, he could find a far more appropriate and secretive location.'

'So if Ramson killed her, why would Rex vanish?' asked Watson. 'Maybe he saw too much.'

The detective drew on his cigarette. If that was the case, he felt pretty sure Rex would have contacted him. With their unique bond, Rex knew he could be sure of understanding and help. One thing was for certain, this Alistair Ramson couldn't harm Rex. Titanium blades had no effect on werewolves and he was strong enough to fight off any attack. *So where the hell was he and what was going on here?*

'You say Rex's phone was deactivated?' said Quist. 'Do you happen to know where?'

'Yes, the police can track mobiles by triangulating the phone masts. I don't know how that works, but the last time Rex used the phone, it was in the Balmoral and they were just mundane calls to Charlotte and myself. He didn't ring anyone else and didn't receive any other calls. The signal was switched off there yesterday morning.'

'Interesting.' Quist stroked his nose thoughtfully. 'So a girl was killed and Rex immediately vanishes, but not before he's removed his phone battery and Sim card? If he wasn't involved, why would he do that?'

'He's not the sharpest tool in the box,' said Watson. 'Would he think to do that, especially if he was in a panic?'

'Something that's puzzling me,' said Quist. 'You say this singer and her friend left Rex's room at eight-thirty and they were the last people to see him? I remember our hotel bellboy saying Ligeia left the Balmoral with her people that same day. Are you telling me the police interviewed the girls and simply believed everything they said? We only have their word that they didn't have anything to do with Charlotte's death. I can't believe the police would allow her to return to London so quickly.'

84

'It's Ligeia,' pointed out Watson. 'She's a VIP with important things to do.'

'I wonder if your policeman brother could let you have a transcript of their statements?' asked Quist. 'I'd like to know if Rex said anything relevant to them.'

'I'll ring and get them,' said McNulty.

'I need to check Rex's movements too. Everywhere he went and the people he spoke to from his arrival in Edinburgh. The police will have checked the route of Charlotte's car with the city CCTV and the number plate recognition system. Your brother could perhaps supply that information too?'

McNulty nodded. 'Again, that'll be no problem.'

'Thank you,' said Quist. 'I'd also like to know where Rex met this singer Ligeia.'

* * * *

Chapter 12

Quist paid the fare and watched the taxi drive away down the narrow cul-de-sac of Brodie Street in Edinburgh's Old Town. He turned to look up at the ornate brick facade and wrought iron canopy of the Club 69 nightclub.

'So this is where Rex and Charlotte met Ligeia,' said Quist, lighting a cigarette. 'It's a wonderful old Victorian building. I wonder what it used to be?'

Watson had more pressing things on his mind, things that totally eclipsed architecture. 'Group sex with three girls,' he gasped. 'One of them was Ligeia, for God's sake. Can you believe that lucky bastard?'

The detective nodded. 'Yes, I detected Rex's scent in the hotel bed and three others, all female.'

'You were sniffing his bedsheets?' The youth eyed him curiously. 'Oh, right. You never said.'

'Strangely enough, it wasn't something I felt like talking about.'

'I imagine not.' Watson guessed it wouldn't be too hard to pick up scents with *that* nose. 'Do you get up to, er anything else like that and not tell me?'

Quist gave a lopsided smile and puffed his cigarette. 'What do you make of this Alistair Ramson angle?'

'The Hounslow Ripper who escaped in France? Weird, don't you reckon?'

'Very weird, if you believe this obese character showed up from nowhere at eight-thirty in the morning, murdered a girl in Rex's room and then vanished into thin air. One thing's for sure, if this man *did* kill Charlotte Michie, it wasn't a random act.'

'I'd agree with that.'

'Oh, well. Come along.' Quist stamped on his half-smoked cigarette. 'Let's take a look at this place.'

The door was unlocked and the pair strolled in, Quist marvelling at the painted ceiling and the Grecian columns. Cleaners were busily picking up broken glass and other garbage, and a middle-aged tubby man with long white hair and a kilt was auditioning a female group on the stage. Watson winced. The four pouting teenagers had bare midriffs, identical purple hair and an abysmal screeching act, their voices reminiscent of a deranged Evangelist attempting to baptise cats.

'There you go,' said Quist. 'I imagine this *music* will be right up your street. Maybe they'll sell you a CD.'

The youth shot him a sarcastic glance. He'd never seen a nightclub with the main lights on and the bright electric bulbs didn't do this place any favours. Watson had to agree with Quist about the Victorian exterior looking good, but coming inside was similar to turning over an attractive garden ornament to find a sickening mess of slugs below. He looked around at the filthy décor and trash, wondering why the cleaners weren't wearing those fire service protective suits used at chemical spills.

'Hello,' said Quist, strolling over to the kilted man. He raised his voice to be heard above the female squawking. 'I hope you don't mind us walking in, but your front doors were unlocked. I wonder if you can help us?'

'Andy McLeish,' said the man, holding out a hand. 'What can I do for you? Are you musical talent scouts?'

'Bernard Quist.' He shook with McLeish. 'This is Watson. We're actually conducting a private investigation into the disappearance of someone who was in here on Tuesday evening.'

'Wow, you're private eyes? Like Sam Spade?'

'Consultant detectives. Are you the manager?'

'I own Club 69.' McLeish ran a hand through his mane of white hair. 'They call me the Scottish Stringfellow.'

'Club 69,' said Quist, hiding his derision. 'Unusual name. I suppose the sexual innuendo will attract a certain juvenile clientele.

However did you think of such a clever name?'

'This is 69 Brodie Street.'

'Ah!'

'I see you're eyeing my kilt.' McLeish grinned at Watson and shook hands. 'I wear it for local colour; the punters love it. You say you're looking for someone?'

The teenager nodded. 'A guy named Rex Grant who...'

'Oh, the murderer? Yeah, the police have been here. Hang on a moment...' He turned to the stage. 'You're too fucking loud. Turn your amp down, you silly bitches, or you'll deafen everyone.'

'Who are they?' asked Watson.

'An Edinburgh act,' said McLeish. 'They're called *Daddy Issues*.'

The youth peered dubiously at the girls. 'Are these typical of your bands?'

'Fuck, no. These tarts aren't that bad. We get a few semi-famous bands like *Glaswegian Queef* playing here and...'

'But none as famous as Ligeia?' broke in Watson.

'You heard about that, eh?' McLeish nodded. 'No one was more surprised than me. We don't get many famous faces in here. I think *the Proclaimers* were the last celebrities.'

'The Scottish duo?' said Watson, amazed. 'I like their stuff.'

'Yes. Well, we had one of them in anyway, and to be honest, it was just an emergency visit to use our toilet.' McLeish led them away from the stage to a quieter spot near the bar. 'Aye, Tuesday was a good night. Ligeia's entourage had hired Bentleys. People saw them parked outside here and knew someone big must be in. It really drew the punters.'

'With all due respect,' said Quist, 'I can't believe one of the richest pop stars in the world would come here.'

'You and me both,' admitted McLeish. 'But Ligeia was fascinated with the place. She kept walking around and showing her friend things.'

'Her friend? Rex Grant?'

'No, some dumb bird she had with her.'

'Dumb as in stupid…' began Watson.

'As in she couldn't speak,' laughed McLeish. 'Not *thick* dumb. Normally we wouldn't let any weirdos like that in here. They might creep out our clientele, but hey, anyone who a top star wants to bring in...'

The detective hid his disgust.

'Ligeia could have brought in a wheelchair if she wanted,' continued McLeish. 'The doormen have orders to keep out gimps, retards and suchlike, along with the fatties and ugly birds…'

'Naturally,' said Quist, deciding he'd better interject before he punched the man. 'So you're aware that Grant was here? Do you remember how long he stayed and who he might have spoken to?'

'I don't recall seeing him on the night. I was too busy watching Ligeia, but since finding out we had a killer in, I've watched his visit from the moment he walked in. We filmed everything on our CCTV.'

'Splendid,' said Quist. 'Everyone has cameras installed these days which simplifies investigations for people like us. Could we see the footage?'

'You could if the police hadn't taken it.'

'Not so simple then,' said Watson.

McLeish shrugged. 'You didn't miss much. He arrived with that redheaded dyke who was killed, danced for a few minutes with Ligeia and her dumb pal, then took them to the bar for a drink. A Lobo cocktail, according to my barman.'

Quist closed his eyes momentarily, cringing inwardly.

'The barman and Ligeia are the only people he spoke to. I hear he took all three back to his hotel to rattle them and then killed the lezzer the following morning. I wonder why he didn't kill Ligeia and the dumb bird too?'

The detective shuddered. 'You say Ligeia was showing her friend things?'

'Memorabilia from the old days.' McLeish nodded to a sepia-tinted print. 'That, for example. There's the place at the turn of the last century, back when it was the music hall.'

'Ah.' Quist nodded. 'This was the famed Edinburgh Apollo?'

'Yeah, I've wanted to rip out the columns and that painted ceiling, but it's a listed building. They won't let me change the structure or the décor up there.'

'Really?' Quist smiled derisively. 'Yes, the authorities have some strange ideas.'

Watson felt his feet sticking to the floor. *Presumably there was a carpet down there, but it was concealed by years of spilled drinks, dried vomit and chewing gum.* He decided this twat ought to forget about changing the structure and perhaps think about changing his cleaners.

'Hey, is that weed?' shouted McLeish, pointing to two of the girls who were lighting up on stage. 'What the fuck have I told you? No drugs in here, you silly slags. You do your drugs around the back with the bouncers.'

He marched away to reprimand the group and Quist turned to Watson.

'Delightful man,' he said. 'He really is charm personified.'

'He's wasted running this place,' agreed the teenager. 'He ought to work as a therapist for the disabled and depressed.'

'I see you've noticed the carpet?' said the detective, watching as his assistant moved his feet. 'The furnishings aren't much better. They're filthy, threadbare and ripped with knives. Look at the barman smoking as he cleans the glasses.'

'Yeah, it's hardly the Ritz.'

'Exactly. Her singing leaves me cold, but Ligeia is undoubtedly the biggest thing in the music world. What on earth was she doing in this rundown toilet of a club?' He walked over to the old posters pointed out by McLeish, now framed in armoured glass to protect from thrown beer glasses. 'The Edinburgh Apollo Music Hall. So she was showing these to her friend? Why do you suppose they interested her?'

Shrugging, Watson looked at the drawings and read the text. They advertised acts from a century ago.

Billy Doyle. A Silly Song and Laughter.

Sally Songbird. The Scottish Nightingale.

Flinty Flanders and his Musical Dog. Never a Dull Moment.

'Hey, I bet you used to watch this stuff back in the day?' drawled the teenager, grinning at the illustrations, especially the old man with a howling spaniel on his lap. He couldn't have sounded more sarcastic had he tried. 'Fuck me! That's what you called entertainment and you have the nerve to say today's television shows are crap.'

* * * *

Sitting on a bench in Waverley Station, Quist stared at his phone and looked up to see Watson returning with a cheeseburger and a carrier bag of crisps and sweets for the journey.

'Our train's due any minute now, Guv,' said the youth. 'Any luck?'

'Not really.' Quist pocketed his mobile. 'I rang McNulty for the phone numbers of Rex's family. I've spoken to them all and no one has any idea where he is.'

'Right.' Watson sat beside him. 'And we know it's pointless trying his phone again if he's deactivated it. I really don't understand what's going on. If he had nothing to do with this murder, why did he run? Why didn't he talk to the cops?'

'Why indeed?' murmured Quist.

'I thought he might have rung you by now. He knows he can trust you.'

'I suspect he can't ring. I also don't believe he ran.' The detective took out his cigarettes and lit one. 'My initial concern was that Rex had succumbed to his lupine urges and killed that girl in wolf form. The worry didn't allow me to think straight, but I'm now satisfied that he didn't, and we both know there'd be no other reason for him to harm anyone.'

'True. He's a bit of a dickhead, but he wouldn't hurt a fly.'

'The forensic evidence is interesting, isn't it? The letter R cut into Charlotte Michie's chest and the titanium blade point to this escaped murderer Alistair Ramson, the Hounslow Ripper. McNulty said the police think Rex may have been a warped fan. He might have read about the Ramson murders and copied his methods...'

'Which we know is absolute bollocks.'

'Exactly. I find this story of Ramson's escape in France highly intriguing; I've just been reading the old news reports on my phone and McNulty was correct. A professional group freed him from police custody. They sound like a police SWAT team or a military outfit. If this Ramson character was in Edinburgh and killed the girl, perhaps he took Rex for some reason and he was the one who deactivated the phone.'

'You mean Rex saw the murder and...' Watson frowned. 'But if the killer wanted to get rid of a witness, he'd have killed Rex, not kidnapped him.'

'Killing Rex isn't so easy these days, but you're right. Why would he take him?'

'How about a sweet to help you think?' Watson chomped his cheeseburger and rustled his bag under Quist's nose. 'Or a vegetarian crisp?'

Quist shook his head. 'As I pointed out to McNulty, Alistair Ramson escaped two months ago. If he wanted to kill for pleasure, he could do it anywhere: behind a pub or down some back alley. He wouldn't enter a hotel at that early hour and murder someone in a stranger's bedroom. If he *was* the murderer, he must have known Charlotte spent the night there and he killed her for some specific reason.'

'Maybe, but again, why take Rex?'

'I don't know, but there's another peculiar fact. The girls who spent the night in his room were the last people to see Rex and the victim, apart from presumably the killer. I asked McNulty to contact his policeman brother and find out about the interviews with Ligeia and her friend. I was hoping they might contain relevant information. He sent me their statements as an attachment.'

Watson smiled. *Attachment – it had taken a while, but his boss was finally picking up the technological jargon.* 'Her friend's statement can't have been very long,' he laughed. 'She was mute.'

'It was conducted through a signer and no, it wasn't long. Neither was Ligeia's. Believe it or not, the interview Ligeia gave before leaving for London lasted just four minutes.'

'That's a bit short, isn't it?'

'An understatement. The police would never let key witnesses go like that and yet they did. These girls could easily have been involved with either the killing or Rex's disappearance and apparently they weren't even checked for trace evidence.'

'Maybe Ligeia's in the Freemasons?'

Quist laughed dryly. 'I can't understand it. I rang her press office to ask about this, but they were no help.'

'Wow, you rang Ligeia's people?'

'These are normal people and you need to stop with the blind hero worship.' Quist stood up as their train pulled into the station. 'This girl is a mediocre singer, not a Goddess.'

'Mediocre?' Watson laughed and followed him. 'You're amazing, Guv.'

'What's happened to him?' muttered Quist. 'Where on earth could Rex be?'

* * * *

93

Chapter 13

Rex Grant woke with a cotton sheet covering his naked body. His mouth was chalk dry and, groaning, he rubbed his crusty eyes. As far as he remembered, this was how it felt after a night of heavy partying. There were several drawbacks to being a werewolf, but one of the benefits was he never suffered from hangovers. He sat up groggily and looked around, realising he'd been laying on a collapsible camp bed. The small white-painted room had no windows, carpet or furniture. There was a single dim ceiling light and two doors, one of which was metal-lined. The last time he'd woken, it had been in a palatial bedroom with three stunning girls wrapped around him. He knew which scenario he preferred.

What had happened and where was he? Was this the basement of the Balmoral? Why would he be down in the hotel cellar?

Rex frowned, suddenly recalling how Ligeia's manager had visited him, zapped him with a stun gun and stuck a syringe of something into his neck. It must have been hallucinogenic, as nothing after that made any sense. He'd seen the old movie comedian Oliver Hardy and a pirate. *No, wait, the pirate was the singer's one-eyed manager, but...* Rex shook his head to clear it. *Had he really seen Oliver Hardy, or did that happen after the injection?* The images were too jumbled, but one thing was certain – he was sitting on a camp bed in a windowless storeroom and *this* wasn't a dream. Wide awake now, he felt confused and frightened, then realised there was no need for fear. Wherever he was and whatever had happened, he couldn't be hurt. Not unless there were silver bullets flying around and fortunately that didn't happen too often.

Why had that bitch with the eye patch drugged him and why was he here?

He climbed unsteadily to his feet and checked the two

doors. The sturdy, steel-lined one was locked from the outside; the other opened into a walk-in cupboard with a sink. The bucket with a toilet roll beside it told him this was his en-suite bathroom.

'Oh, how thoughtful of someone,' he mumbled, caustically.

The lycanthropy had heightened Rex's sense of smell, but anyone would have picked up the strong bleach aroma. This was almost certainly a cleaning storeroom. Mops, buckets, floor buffers and suchlike would normally be kept here, but by providing a bed for him, the place had been turned into a makeshift cell. His small suitcase stood against the wall and, opening it, he found someone had considerately packed everything he'd taken to Scotland. Even his Rolex watch and wallet filled with cash were there, but not his mobile phone. Snapping the watch bracelet onto his wrist, he saw it was twelve o'clock, but was that twelve noon or midnight? Without windows, it was impossible to tell.

Rex pulled on a black shirt and jeans, made use of the "en-suite" and washed his face with cold water in the sink, the icy splashes clearing his drug-induced wooziness and bringing back a jumble of memories. *Yes, that's right. Charlotte had walked out of the Balmoral Hotel bathroom. I thought he was alone, someone had said.*

'What the hell...' muttered Rex, rubbing his eyes and concentrating.

Yes, Charlotte was shocked. She'd started asking angry questions. Did that really happen? The images of Oliver Hardy felt starkly real, but his being there was obviously impossible; the returning memories were insane. A blade shot out from the film star's sleeve and Charlotte fell. 'No,' someone had shouted. 'You didn't have to do that, you fool.' The fat man bent over the naked girl, quickly doing something to her before the knife vanished back into his jacket, the retraction wiping it clean by spraying out a coating of blood. 'He's still awake,' Hardy had said. 'Look, his eyes are half-open and I think he saw that.'

95

The stinging needle had jabbed into Rex's neck again and inky darkness had fallen. *Were these actual memories or just madness from a drugged nightmare?* If it *was* a dream, it was weirder than the ones he usually had: the ones where he was back at school, he'd forgotten his trousers and Miss Williams had spotted his wolf tail. Even as a twelve-year-old, he'd fancied his geography teacher Miss Williams. He shook his head irately. *Why the fuck was he pondering this rubbish when Charlotte could be injured? When she could even be dead.*

The lock clicked and the door opened. Ligeia walked in wearing a thin black sweater, tight jeans and a concerned frown.

'*Here* you are,' she said, running to him and wrapping her arms around his chest. 'Why are you here?'

Rex stepped back. 'You're asking *me*?'

'I mean why are you in this room, you big silly?'

'Er...' He didn't know how to answer. 'Is this part of the Balmoral Hotel?'

'No, it's a nice place with a river.'

'Er, *right...*'

Rex moved further back and gazed at her. *This answer didn't exactly help. It was the kind of thing he'd have expected from a woman with thirty cats.* Ligeia's childlike persona was no longer sweet and endearing and her sensual accent failed to arouse him. In light of recent events, she just appeared crazy. Dangerously fucking crazy.

'Rex?' she giggled. 'Why are you looking at me like that? Are you alright?'

'You know what...' He laughed too, but the noise was manic. 'As a matter of fact, I'm *not*.' He circled her slowly, backing away towards the open door. 'You remember my friend Charlotte? Do you know what happened to her?'

'Mmmh, Charlotte was nice.' Ligeia looked over his shoulder. 'Hello, Irana.'

Rex turned and stiffened to see the singer's manager standing in the doorway.

'Ligeia?' Colonel Adler smiled sweetly. 'Who unlocked the door and let you in here?'

'One of your nice friends,' she said. 'He's called Billy.'

'Billy?' Adler frowned. 'Ah, that'll be William Baxter. He's one of the house security. He isn't part of my team.' She nodded and gestured to the passage outside. 'My dear, I wonder if you could leave Rex and I alone for a while? We need to chat.'

'Too fucking right we do.' Rex visibly shook with anger. He looked the woman over, taking in the black eye patch, the casual suit and expensive shoes. He recalled finding her attractive when she called at his hotel room, but she'd almost certainly ruined her chances of sleeping with him now. 'What have you done?'

'Language, please,' said Adler. 'There are ladies present. You're here as our guest.'

'I'm locked in what amounts to a cell and I've just taken a shit in a plastic bucket. Maybe you should think about reviewing your guest policy?'

'Irana, I don't want to go.' Ligeia took the Colonel's hand and squeezed. 'I want to be with Rex.'

'You will be, my dear,' said Adler, kissing the singer's forehead. 'In a very short while, but first I need to speak with him.'

'Alright.' Ligeia looked around and pouted. 'But I don't like this nasty room. I don't want him to be in here.'

'Guess what?' snapped Rex. 'That makes two of us.'

The Colonel laughed. 'Why don't you run along to the river and I'll bring him down there to you?'

'The river?' Ligeia's face brightened. 'Yes, I'll see you there, Rex.'

Rex watched her leave and turned back to Adler, trembling with fury. 'What the fuck did you do to me? Where am I?'

'Oh, Mister Grant...' The woman sighed and folded her

arms. 'Why didn't you just take the money I offered and come with us when I asked? Everything would have been so much simpler. Instead, I had to take alternative measures and do it this way.'

'You *had* to?'

'I never take no for an answer. Not when something important is at stake.'

'So you kidnapped me.'

'You're here as our guest,' repeated Adler.

'I know you used a stun gun and a syringe of something, but everything feels weird. My memory is playing tricks…'

'You were injected with a South American drug. Four doses were administered at intervals to ensure you had a good sleep. I don't know why it's banned in the west; it works admirably.'

'I saw Oliver Hardy and all kinds of weird shit in my hotel room.' Rex ran a hand through his short black hair. 'What about Charlotte Michie? What happened to her?'

'Was that her name? Yes, a young lady *did* leave your bathroom and storm out.'

'It looked like she was stabbed…'

'It sounds to me as if you're right. Your memory *is* playing tricks.'

'So what's going on? What did you say your name was?'

'Colonel Irana Adler.'

'You're serious? A female Colonel?' Rex laughed dryly. 'So Ligeia has a Colonel for a manager, like Elvis Presley?'

'As far as I recall, Colonel Tom Parker was actually a private, discharged from the army due to mental problems. My military rank is genuine. I served with the German army before moving into the private sector.'

'Hey, but talk about coincidence? You share similar mental problems.'

'You're quite a comedian, aren't you, Rex? Pirate jokes

about my one eye yesterday and now quips about my sanity. Do you really think goading me is wise when I'm currently in charge of your well-being?'

'*Yesterday*?' Rex checked his watch. 'How long have you had me here?'

'It's now Thursday afternoon. Who's Quist?'

Rex was jolted by the unexpected question. '*What*?'

'Someone named Bernard Quist rang Ligeia's press office asking about you.' Adler took three sheets of paper from her jacket. 'He also appears to have drawn these pictures on personalised office stationery. His name and the address of his York office are printed as a letterhead at the top. He's a private investigator.'

'My yoga exercises?'

'That's right. Why would this man be looking for you?'

'This is ridiculous,' snarled Rex. 'I don't have to answer your questions. I'm leaving.'

A large man in a black uniform appeared in the doorway behind Adler. He'd obviously been waiting in the passage.

'I'm sorry, but that isn't possible,' said the Colonel. 'I need you here for a little while.'

A surge of rage filled Rex and he fought down the urge to punch the pair unconscious and run. This wasn't like him and he wondered if the full moon was to blame. *Hitting women was generally frowned upon, but did this apply when they'd kidnapped you? Then again, he had no idea where he was or if there were other locked doors out in the passage. No, it was best to discover where he was being held and establish what was going on.*

'Thursday?' Taking a deep breath, he calmed himself. 'Unbelievable. This is my birthday.'

'Well many happy returns.' Adler held the door wide. 'Ligeia was right; you shouldn't be cooped up in here. Come through into the house and we can celebrate.'

* * * *

Chapter 14

Ligeia's manager really *did* need to review her guest policy, decided Rex, seething as he climbed a flight of stone steps behind her. His *bedroom*, he'd just discovered, had been a basement ablutions store next to a wine cellar. He followed the Colonel along a corridor, past a series of oak-panelled rooms, all brimming with exquisite furnishings and antiques, to arrive in a hall filled with chandeliers and oil paintings. Adler had used the word *house*, but this was something of an understatement. The British royals often referred to Buckingham Palace as *the house*, or *ice* as they inexplicably pronounced it, and this place rivalled any palace for splendour.

'Thank you, Prescott.' Adler turned to the large uniformed character who had followed them. 'You can leave us alone now.'

Still bristling with anger, Rex watched the man disappear.

'To be honest, I didn't really need a bodyguard shadowing us,' said Adler. 'I have black belts in four separate martial arts. I'd say that was more than enough to handle any house guest.'

Rex gave a derisive smile. *She'd need those fucking belts to prevent her intestines falling out if he clawed open her stomach with his lupine strength and talons.* Realising Quist might be right and the moon may be affecting him, he shook himself and looked around the hall. These mansions were built in a time when a certain strata of society were wealthy enough to have homes with dozens of enormous rooms: sitting rooms, drawing rooms, and reception rooms, with some devoted to pursuits such as needlework, billiards and reading. Most seemed to have a *blue room*, which Rex assumed was for when the owners were feeling down.

'Very nice place,' he said, sarcastically. 'So where are we?'

'Charlington Hall,' said Adler, leading him into a spacious room with French doors opening onto a terrace. Sunshine lit the cream décor and glinted on gilt fixtures. 'Lovely, isn't it? This used to be Lord Cantlemere's place and we bought it fully furnished six months ago. Welcome to the morning room.'

'I'm no wiser,' snapped Rex. 'Where is this?'

'Happy birthday.' Adler opened a cabinet and poured two whiskies, handing one to him. 'We're on the Thames near Richmond.'

'London? But I was in Scotland.'

'We flew down to the City Airport yesterday and came here by helicopter. I had to buy a leather travelling trunk in Edinburgh to transport you, but don't worry; I won't be billing you for the cost.'

'You packed me in a fucking trunk?' snarled Rex, knocking back the drink in one gulp. 'This is getting weirder, if that's even possible.'

'I'm sure you'll be missing these,' said Adler. Reaching into her jacket, she brought out Rex's cigarettes and wolf head lighter. I held onto them until I was sure you were fully conscious. I didn't want you accidentally setting fire to your bed down there.'

'How considerate.' Rex snatched them. 'Where's my phone?'

'I appear to have misplaced it. Sorry, but you'll have to do without it for the time being.' Adler sipped her drink. 'Charlington Hall is extremely private and secure and it's been an ideal base. The grounds cover five acres, so it's compact enough for my team to protect Ligeia and keep the fans and Paparazzi away. It also has certain unique features which she enjoys. I do everything I can to keep her happy.'

'Including providing her with boyfriends?' Rex lit a cigarette and stowed the pack in the rear pocket of his jeans. 'Surely that can't be why you abducted me?'

'It's one of the reasons.'

'Are you crazy? Anyway, now that I'm out of the locked room, what's to stop me leaving?'

101

'Why would you want to leave Ligeia and this wonderful place?'

'Oh, let me think.' Rex sucked angrily on his cigarette, pondering in mock deliberation. 'Maybe because I don't like being a prisoner.'

'You're my guest, not a prisoner, but I really would advise against trying to leave.' Adler gestured through the French doors. 'Those gentlemen strolling around out there are my team and they're all armed.'

Rex joined her at the doors and saw four men in black military outfits positioned at strategic points around the grounds. 'Shit!' he gasped. 'Two of them are carrying machine pistols. This place is like one of those drug baron's mansions in Columbia.'

'Yes, we sleep quite safely here. Security fences protect the perimeter, secreted radar units and alarm systems warn of intruders in the grounds and scanners detect any wireless signals. Our radio mast jams everything apart from our modified phones and communication sets. Of course, my men wouldn't need their guns to prevent you leaving. They could easily stop you with their bare hands.'

I wouldn't bet on that, thought Rex. *The lycanthropy made him faster and stronger than humans. Even so, with the fences and other security measures here, the best plan would be to wait until nightfall and then secretly transform to escape. Quist had warned him never to shapeshift during the full moon, but it would only be for a few minutes and it wouldn't matter. Besides, waiting until dusk would give him time to learn why the hell he'd been abducted.*

A wide terrace of gravel and stone urns extended along the front of the building and, beyond this, lawns dotted with fountains led down to the River Thames. Rex couldn't see the water, as a huge marquee tent had been erected on the lower area of parkland blocking the view.

'I see the circus is in town,' he sneered.

102

'We're ready for the garden party tomorrow,' said Adler. 'Ligeia is releasing her new album, *the Music of Sound*, and the newspapers and music press are all attending.'

A large man appeared outside the glass doors and was obviously guarding the front terrace. He wore a black uniform similar to the other guards and Rex recognised him from the Edinburgh nightclub. He'd be difficult to forget. Six feet, five inches in height, his head was shaved and his arm muscles looked as if they belonged on his upper legs.

'That's Sergeant Gruner,' said Adler. 'He's Serbian and rather strong. He's been charged with watching you. If you try anything unwise, he's the one you'll be dealing with. Good luck.'

'Has he taken his steroids today?'

'Come along.' The Colonel opened the glass doors and stepped out. 'I'll show you around and explain the situation.'

Rex walked by Gruner, giving the man a sardonic smile. Adler paused to speak quietly with her Sergeant and then followed. The terrace was edged with a stone balustrade and wide steps led down from the front doors of the house to a lily-covered moat, a stone bridge providing access to the gardens.

'Oh, lovely,' said Rex, looking back at the Georgian mansion. 'You live in Downton Abbey and you have your very own moat.'

'Yes, it's quite deep,' said Adler. The house is effectively an island, which I suppose is the entire purpose of a moat. The rear walls and those on the eastern and western sides rise straight out of the water.'

'Really?' Rex flicked cigarette ash. 'The damp treatments must cost a fortune.'

'Thanks to Ligeia, money isn't a problem. We have fifteen staff working in the house, the kitchens and the gardens, along with our own resident doctor and my Entertainment Director. Then there's the security. My core team of twelve have been with me for years, but an extra twenty have been hired to police the grounds here and oversee the security at the British concerts.'

'Thirty-two paid security?'

'As I say, money isn't a problem, but it *was* for Lord Cantlemere. He died owing millions and his son attempted to pay the debt by turning this place into a tourist attraction. It's in a good spot, between Richmond and Kingston-upon-Thames, but his plans didn't work and eventually he was glad to sell relatively cheaply. What he did, however, made it perfect for Ligeia.'

They walked over the bridge, where Elva sat on the wall smiling at Rex, her cross-legged pose and elfin appearance reminiscent of a pixie on a toadstool.

'Hello again,' he snorted, tossing his cigarette stub into the moat. 'Hey, thanks for the other night. First you fucked me and then you *really* fucked me. How does it feel to be part of a kidnapping, you sick little shit?'

Confused and distressed at his tone, the girl jumped down from her perch and headed for the house.

'Oh, dear, you've upset her,' said Adler, leading Rex across the lawn. 'We found our mute friend in Prague when Ligeia was performing there. She was probably some Irish backpacker who did too many drugs and ended up living rough. At any rate, she was begging in the street and Ligeia spotted her from the car and made us stop. For some reason, she took an instant shine to her and wanted Elva to live with us. I made a similar proposal to the one I gave you, but she turned down the money and came anyway.' The Colonel nodded to the house. 'Who can blame her? This place is preferable to sleeping in shop doorways.'

'How do you know she's Irish? Was her accent *that* obvious?'

'You really are quite the comedian.' Adler walked him around a high rhododendron hedge. 'Ligeia communicates with her. Elva taught her signing and she learnt surprisingly quickly.'

104

Rex jumped at the sound of screeching birds. A row of aviaries and cages stood behind the high shrubs.

'The private menagerie,' said the Colonel. 'Young Lord Cantlemere hired out Charlington Hall for weddings and functions, but his idea was to attract the paying public with a small zoo and funfair.' She motioned past the parrots and cockatoos to the larger enclosures ahead and the big tiger in one of the cages. 'Cantlemere sold the few animals he had, but we've bought one of our own.'

Alarmed at Rex's appearance, the birds shrank away from him and even the tiger edged warily back, its lip curling in a rumbling growl.

'Ligeia loves tigers,' said Adler. 'We acquired this one for her and she's named him Mister Tigsy.' A building ran along the rear of the cages and the cat vanished through a hatch into its indoor quarters. The Colonel eyed Rex inquisitively. 'He didn't seem to like you, did he? Neither do the birds; just listen to them going wild. I wonder why?'

Rex ignored the question. Animals sensed his supernatural aura and wouldn't come anywhere near him since he'd become a wolf. 'You actually bought her a pet tiger?'

'We give Ligeia anything she wants; anything to keep her content. Since the first album went on sale, money isn't an issue.'

'Anything she wants? Like me, you mean?'

'Exactly.'

'You're out of your mind. Just playing the devil's avocado, if I'd taken up your offer and come along with her, what was I supposed to do here?'

'Simply keep her happy.' Adler grinned at him. 'This is a very important time and everything is unbelievably hectic. Tomorrow we're holding the press conference and then we have the O2 concert tomorrow night. We have a flight from there to a concert in Miami, and then on to California where we're relocating. Ligeia then goes straight into her American tour.'

'Ooh, busy, busy, busy.'

'Indeed. Then suddenly, immediately before all that, she met you. She wanted you and came to me sobbing when you turned her down. She fixated upon you, Rex, and that's one of the reasons I brought you here.'

'You kidnapped me to keep your singer happy?' Rex laughed harshly. 'But this is completely *insane*. Music star or not, you don't have to pander to her every childish whim.'

'Actually I *do*. She wants you here and I'm making sure she has you for now. I really do *not* want her upsetting at this critical moment in her schedule.'

'I honestly can't believe this. You said keeping her happy was *one* of the reasons you brought me here?'

'Yes.' Adler narrowed her eyes. 'Why did she fixate upon *you* in particular? She's never done this with a man before and there were plenty of other good-looking idiots in that sleazy club.'

'Well, I *am* pretty unique. The Rex Grant charm and sex appeal are both legendary in the London clubs where I…'

'The crucial point is you're able to resist her. She asked you to come with her and you refused. How are you able to resist Ligeia?'

'*What*?' Rex shook his head. 'What the hell are you talking about?'

'Well, there we have the main reason for you being our guest. I need to understand how and if you genuinely don't know, I'm sure the Padre will be able to tell me soon enough.'

'Who's he? Your chaplain or something?

'*Padre* is a private joke. A nickname for Mister Lafont who supplies a form of spiritual assistance.'

'Are you really a female Colonel, as you claim, or is that some nickname too?'

'I'm a Colonel and Gruner really is a Sergeant. He's been with me for many years, as have my team.' Adler gestured again to the large men positioned around the grounds. 'They're my military unit from the days when we operated as *Red Globe Security*.'

'Mercenaries?'

'An unpalatable term, but my extra security staff are indeed all mercenaries. We're dispensing with them tomorrow before we leave for America. It won't be difficult to find new guards for the California estate. My core team of twelve were freelance military advisors who provided private security and assistance overseas. That's all in the past, however, and we've since moved into the music business. The name is now *Red Globe Management*.'

'Seriously?' laughed Rex. 'You're telling me there are female mercenaries?'

'Not many, but yes. Believe me, some are extremely proficient.'

'But your bunch have gone from being mercenaries to managing pop stars?'

'Just *one* star. All my life I've been able to spot opportunities and I always take them. Where other people deliberate, I simply snatch the moment and Ligeia was most definitely one of those moments.'

Bewildered, Rex slowly rubbed his eyes. 'This all sounds so crazy.'

Adler nodded. 'I believe we've established your feelings.'

The rhododendron hedge ran around the menagerie, screening it from neighbouring properties and river boats, and walking through an archway in the tall shrubs, they arrived at a similarly concealed funfair. A carousel stood next to a bright red Chinese pagoda and a larger fairground building with fake spiders climbing an exterior painted with garish monsters. Ligeia sat on one of the carousel horses, spinning to the sound of jolly organ music.

'*This* was the beginnings of Lord Cantlemere's tourist dream?' Adler laughed. 'Those cages back there and these few old rides from a travelling fairground. He hoped to buy adjoining land

and build something grander, but huge pay-outs to the right people were needed to gain planning permission and after that his money ran out. It isn't much; just a hall of mirrors, a ghost train and a merry-go-round, but Ligeia likes it as you can see. She loves this and the river. Being near water makes her happy.'

'And you do everything it takes to keep her happy,' muttered Rex, watching the girl.

The Colonel turned to the huge Serbian who had been following them. 'Sergeant Gruner. I believe you've met our friend Mister Grant?'

'I feel close.' The bald man grinned. 'I organised his guest accommodation in the cellar yesterday, undressed him and put him to bed.'

'I don't think we need you,' said Adler. 'There's no reason to shadow our guest so closely with the team around. I wonder if you'd take care of that business I mentioned back there on the terrace?'

Rex watched Gruner head back to the menagerie building. *So this twat organised his "bedroom", did he? He obviously hadn't been trained by the Balmoral Hotel staff. He didn't leave any chocolates on the pillow.*

* * * *

Chapter 15

Few men in the Parachute Regiment had liked Corporal William Baxter, or *Bastard Baxter* as he'd been known. The soldiers had also christened him *Bastard Billy*, *Billy the Bastard* and several other names, all with a common theme – they had *bastard* in the wording. This wasn't in any way connected to his parents being unmarried, but because the Corporal was an absolute bastard.

Leaving the army had come as a relief to Baxter. He'd hated the military progression into the twenty-first century, the enlightened views that had crept in and the new attitude to human rights. The Corporal despised all Muslims, but this gradually became unacceptable and investigations were held every time he shot some Afghan or Iraqi civilian he didn't like the look of. Baxter had moved straight from the Paras into the lucrative private sector, where "military advisors" could kill without red tape and for a lot more cash than the British government paid. For the last three years his skills had been put to use in Africa and it was refreshing to wipe out villages on the orders of dictators without BBC journalists and hesitant, career-conscious officers breathing down his neck. Derogatory *bastard* nicknames were still occasionally invented by some of the other mercenaries, but they didn't stick for long. About as long as it took for him to hear of it and take out his gun.

Some six months ago, Sergeant Gruner had recruited a squad of twenty mercenaries, including Baxter, as private protection at Charlington Hall. Compared to the Corporal's usual contracts, it was mundane security work, but the pay was triple. Unfortunately, it was a temporary arrangement and the squad were receiving their final payment tomorrow when their employer relocated to America. Colonel Adler had headed *Red Globe Security*, a famous name in Baxter's world, but a year ago she'd bizarrely and inexplicably moved into the music business. To begin with, the Corporal had disliked the idea of working for a woman. In his opinion, tarts had no place in the military, but he'd grown to respect her professional skills and cold efficiency. Baxter had decided to speak with Gruner and try for a permanent position on Adler's team, now known as *Red Globe Management,* and as luck would have it, the Sergeant had just asked to see him. *This would be the ideal time to enquire.*

The concrete menagerie building was single-storey and eighty feet in length. Baxter walked along the rear corridor, wondering why he'd been told to meet here. A sequence of doors split the passage into compartments, presumably to contain any animals which might escape from their indoor quarters. Metal doors on his right provided access to these chambers, but all were empty. The corridor terminated in a large tiled workroom, which also housed the tiger's indoor cage, and he saw Gruner busy at the bars with a lengthy cattle prod.

'It's Corporal Baxter,' he said. 'You wanted to see me, Sergeant?'

'Come in, Corporal,' said Gruner, without turning.

The sliding exit to the outdoor pen had been bolted shut and the Sergeant poked the pacing cat, herding it into a small tiger-sized cage that was clamped onto the door of the enclosure. The electric prod crackled on its flank, the tiger hissed and bolted inside and Gruner dropped the door.

'Got you,' he chuckled. Unclamping the cage, he pulled it away from the door, turned it on tiny wheels and rolled it into the centre of the room. The angry cat tried lashing out, but the space was cramped and the bars were too narrow for its paws. 'Ligeia calls him Mister Tigsy. Have you been this close before, Corporal?'

'I can't say I have,' said Baxter. He saw there were electric motors on one side of the cage linked to pistons. 'I've always fancied an Indian safari shooting these things. I reckon it'd be good fun.'

Gruner nodded. 'This device is called a *crush*,' he said, producing a remote control similar to the ones used for televisions. 'Vets use them to squeeze large animals into a tight space and prevent them moving. They can then make examinations and work on them while they're awake, taking rectal temperatures, administering injections, treating small wounds and suchlike.' He pressed the remote, the motors hummed and the pistons slowly pressed in the side of the cage trapping the cat against the opposite bars. 'It's always best to keep them awake. Every time you tranquilise an animal, you run the risk of killing it, as estimating the weight and getting the right dose is tricky.'

'What are you planning on doing with it, Sergeant?'

'You'll see.' Gruner studied the Corporal for a few moments and smiled. 'As a child in Serbia I used to enjoy hurting animals. I'd pour petrol over the village dogs, light them up and watch them run. How does that make you feel?'

'Er…'

It sounded like a bloody good laugh, but Baxter shook his head, unsure of how to react. If Gruner now regretted his childhood behaviour, showing approval could be wrong. If Baxter was hoping to join *Red Globe*, he needed to get his answers correct. Who knew what kind of personality they were looking for in their recruits?

'My father used to beat me for this,' continued Gruner. 'He said these were the actions of a psychopath, but he was wrong. I've since discovered it's sociopathic behaviour, which is quite different. As I grew older and larger, I discovered I much preferred hurting people.'

'That makes two of us,' said Baxter, grinning.

'Very good.' Gruner laughed quietly. 'You were in the Parachute regiment, I believe? When you left, I imagine you were delighted to find dictatorships who were prepared to pay you for hurting people. I know I was.'

'Absolutely.' The Corporal nodded. 'I'd say we think alike,

111

Sergeant.'

'Occasionally I still indulge myself with an animal like this. Call me a nostalgic fool, but it takes me back to my childhood.'

'Great.' Baxter eyed the huge cat with malevolence. 'Are you going to fry it a little with that cattle prod?'

'No.' Gruner unzipped his trousers and positioned himself behind the struggling tiger. Unable to move, Mister Tigsy hissed viciously as he pushed forward through the bars. 'I've found this doesn't hurt it too much physically, but it's an excellent form of mental torture. The hatred builds, but the beast is unable to do anything about it. This ferocious killing machine is completely subservient.'

'Er, right…'

Baxter watched with wide eyes. He'd seen many weird sights during his time as a mercenary, but none quite so weird as this. He was no stranger to rape, but his victims had usually been female and invariably human.

'I can best any man in a fight,' said Gruner, thrusting. 'But obviously I'd be unable to beat the tiger if it were free. This way, I'm the master. Animals need to understand who is in charge and learn subservience. We both know our friend here is faster, fiercer and more powerful, but I have the brain and the technology to allow me to do this whenever I wish.' The furious tiger let out a deafening snarl. 'Oh, yes, he knows who's in charge,'

The Sergeant withdrew and fastened his trousers. Baxter was aware that Gruner hadn't climaxed, but realised this bizarre episode hadn't been in any way sexual. It was a basic masculine display of crude power.

'We're leaving this place tomorrow night,' said Gruner, operating the crush wall and allowing the enraged tiger to move at last. Its head whipped around, glaring at the men with ears pressed flat, and its claws raked the bars. 'People are calling on Saturday morning to transfer the cat to a zoo. A pity, as I've come to enjoy these little interludes.' He turned to the Corporal. 'But enough of that. You'll be wondering why I asked to see you.'

'What? Er, yes, that's right.' Baxter had forgotten he'd been requested. Strangely enough, the violation of the tiger had pushed it from his mind. 'Is there a problem, Sergeant?'

'I understand you allowed Ligeia to see the prisoner in the cellar earlier?'

'That's right.'

'This was after the Colonel gave orders that no one should go near him?'

'She asked me to unlock the door.'

'*What*? Why would you disobey a direct order?'

'I don't know. At the time it seemed…' Baxter frowned. 'I don't know.'

'Wait a moment.' Gruner sighed as realisation dawned. 'Where are your audio implants?'

'Well, I'm wearing them, of course.'

'I'll ask once more, and I really would advise against lying. Where are they?'

Baxter swallowed uneasily. 'The right one is fine; it's in my ear.' He reached in his pocket and produced a tiny device wrapped in tissue. 'I had to temporarily remove this left one yesterday night. I have a minor infection which…'

'But you didn't think to mention this.' Gruner shook his head and walked to the corridor door. 'As a soldier, you know that orders are always given for a reason.'

'I apologise, Sergeant. I think my ear reacted to the implant being fitted so deep.' Baxter grimaced as Gruner opened the door to leave. *This didn't look good. Had he ruined his chances of joining Red Globe Management*? 'I know I should have told you, but…'

'Do you know what time it is?' asked Gruner.

Baxter looked at his watch. 'Er…'

Pressing the remote control, the Sergeant opened the crush

allowing the furious tiger to burst out. 'It's Mister Tigsy's feeding time,' he said, closing the door on the screams.

* * * *

Chapter 16

Sullen and resigned now to spending the next few hours captive at Charlington Hall, Rex sat astride a grinning wooden horse on the funfair carousel. He hadn't ridden one of these since the age of six and now he remembered why – they were utter crap. Tediously twirling to an organ waltz probably felt like an action-packed extravaganza to Victorian kids, but he couldn't imagine what modern children would think. Today's youngsters were used to *real* entertainment involving video games, go-carts, virtual reality and laser battles. He glanced at the horse beside him and saw that the merry-go-round *was* entertaining one child.

Ligeia held on tightly, gasping with delight. 'Isn't it wonderful?' she giggled.

'Amazing,' he sighed. 'I've never known such fun.'

The singer had pleaded with him to join her on the carousel and Rex had grudgingly obliged. Four of Adler's guards stood a discreet distance away on the edges of the funfair, all maintaining a low profile and quietly watching the young couple. Rex had been kidnapped, drugged, transported in a trunk and dumped in a madhouse, but he didn't have to put up with it for much longer. From what Adler had told him about the security, it would be best to wait until nightfall before escaping and sunset would arrive soon enough. The rides had been constructed near the river at the lower end of the lawns, but the tall screen of shrubbery blocked his view. He'd been told the grounds covered five acres, which roughly equated to five soccer pitches. Rex attempted to get his bearings for later, although working out the topography would be a lot easier were he not spinning in circles.

Elva appeared through the tree arch and Ligeia jumped nimbly from the moving steed to excitedly embrace her. Rex watched the petite girls kissing and hugging as if they hadn't seen each other for ages. *They were lovers, but their bond must be incredibly strong if they carried on like this all the time.*

'Best friends, eh?' he said, leaping from the horse as the ride passed them. He misjudged the jump, but his lupine senses kicked in and he landed on all fours. 'Well, that wouldn't have won the Olympic gold.'

'That was funny.' Ligeia clapped happily until Elva began signing to her. 'Rex, I don't understand. Elva says you spoke nasty to her and made her feel bad. She says she thought you came because you wanted to be here.'

Rex sighed and rubbed his eyes. These girls would register off the scale on any psychiatrist's fruitcake meter. They obviously had no understanding of his abduction and being angry with them was as pointless as booting puppy dogs for the crime of looking cute. 'Yes, and I'm sorry,' he said. 'I was annoyed on the bridge earlier and I wrongly took it out on Elva. I'm really sorry, Elva.'

Elva reached out and stroked his face, her eyes filled with remorse. She signed again.

'She's sorry too,' said Ligeia. 'Elva says she didn't know anything about the kidnap.' She looked puzzled. 'What *is* kidnap?'

'*What*?' Rex shook his head, astounded. 'Er, it's like ketchup,' he muttered. 'Only it doesn't taste as nice.'

'You make me laugh.' Ligeia pulled at his arm and headed towards the Chinese pagoda. 'Come on. You have to see the rest of the funfair.'

'Sure,' he said. 'Oh, I honestly can't wait.'

The red pagoda turned out to be an antiquated hall of mirrors, its wooden walls covered in gilt frames of curved glass. Rex had seen these places in old movies and they looked to be as much *fun* as the merry-go-round. Whoever sold Lord Cantlemere this crap must have been rubbing their hands with glee to get rid of it. The girls held each other and laughed at their distorted reflections.

'Look at Elva in this one,' giggled Ligeia. 'Look how silly

she looks.'

'Yes, that's hilarious,' drawled Rex. He watched Elva laughing silently and narrowed his eyes at a sudden thought. They were temporarily out of sight of the guards, and if these girls were as mental as they appeared, this idea would work. 'Hey, I've just remembered,' he said. 'I have some lovely fluffy kittens at home and I forgot to ask my friend to feed them. I'd better ring him now. Could I borrow your mobile for a moment?'

'My what?' asked Ligeia.

'Your mobile phone.' Rex spoke slowly. 'To ring my friend about the fluffy kittens. Elva, if you can't speak, I imagine you use one to text.'

Elva signed that she didn't, and Ligeia shook her head. 'I'm sorry,' she said. 'We've never had one of those.'

He nodded resignedly. Two gorgeous young girls without phones. Had Rex heard this before today, he'd probably have fainted, but here in the riverside asylum of Bedlam-on-Thames, it sounded perfectly normal and didn't surprise him one bit.

'This way now,' said Ligeia. Pulling Rex past the mirrors, the girls took him to the larger building next door. 'Come on, hurry. I know you're going to love this.'

'A ghost train?' he said, grimacing. 'I'm shivering with fear already.'

'Look, this is how we turn it on.' Ligeia threw a master switch on the wall by the redundant ticket desk and the ride burst into raucous life, with strobe lights, scary music and recorded howls of fear. 'The Colonel showed me how to work this and the merry-go-round so I could play on them anytime.'

Rex saw the large cards taped on either side of the switch with GHOST TRAIN ON and GHOST TRAIN OFF printed on them. Adler obviously understood the intelligence level she was dealing with. He quickly checked behind the ticket counter for a phone, but found nothing.

There was only one ghost train car, a stylised skull where the riders sat in the gaping mouth, and he watched it trundle through the swing doors into the dark tunnel beyond. Adapted to run without personnel, Rex assumed it simply travelled around and around until the master switch was thrown back. Two of the guards followed them in to keep an eye on things.

'Get ready.' Ligeia kissed Rex and gripped his hand. 'It doesn't stop, so you have to be quick.' The swing doors burst open, the car reappeared, and she jumped into the seat with Elva, pulling Rex beside them. 'It's really scary, so you'll need to hold us both very tight.'

'No problem,' sighed Rex.

It was a typical ghost train, with pitch-black tunnels filled with sharp twists and turns. Fake cobwebs trailed over their faces, huge hairy spiders wobbled overhead, jiggling skeletons lit up in corners and luminous plastic monsters wailed. Elva and Ligeia shrieked like terrified children, but Rex had seen far scarier things – mostly in his apartment mirror when he transformed. The skull car pushed through the exit doors and he attempted to stand, but Ligeia pulled him back down.

'Again,' she giggled. 'We need to go again.'

Rex had already decided that Ligeia and Elva were as mad as March hares, but after six more rattling trips through the tunnels with the pair screaming in his ears, he was ready to stake his life on it. 'I'd really like to see your river now,' he said, as the exit doors burst open once again. 'You know? The lovely water.'

Her face beaming, Ligeia leapt up and pulled him from the slow-moving car. Elva switched off the ride and ran out of the ghost train into the sunlight behind them. They passed through one of the floral archways in the shrubbery screen and Rex found himself on the grassy riverbank.

'I love the water, said Ligeia, sitting on a rock and snuggling up to Elva. 'I like to sit by the moat and sing, but the river is much more beautiful.'

'Yes it is,' agreed Rex, standing behind them and looking around to digest the topography of the area.

According to Adler, he was somewhere between Richmond and Kingston, and the Thames here was unrecognisable as London's famous waterway. Some 300 feet across, the river was far more genteel, with lush banks, tree-covered islands, swans and pleasure craft. Large multi-million pound houses stood between clumps of woodland with their extensive gardens leading down to the water. Rex spotted boathouses and jetties, including one to his left that jutted out from the Charlington Hall parkland. *Ah, this might come in useful later.* His smile faded as he realised it would only be useful if there were boats tied up and this jetty was empty.

He turned to the two girls as Ligeia began to unexpectedly sing one of her slow love ballads. Anyone rowing past would be getting a free concert from the world's biggest star, but her mundane voice did nothing for Rex. Lighting a cigarette, he glanced over his shoulder as two guards from the funfair followed them through the trees. Bushes blocked his view to the right, but looking left along the sparkling river, he saw a security fence running down into the water a couple of hundred feet away. This had obviously been constructed along the western edge of the grounds and he knew an identical barrier would protect the eastern perimeter. The mesh looked to be high-tensile steel and around ten feet in height with razor wire curled around the top.

He'd been right to wait for darkness; these fences wouldn't pose a problem in wolf form. He could leap over or tear the mesh, and if it came to it, he could easily swim this river. It was April and the sun would be setting around seven-thirty. Yes, a few more hours of this craziness and he'd be away.

Ligeia stopped singing and gasped as a bright blue kingfisher shot past. 'Did you see that? Look at the water and those ripples on the surface. Aren't they beautiful?'

Rex noticed Ligeia's manager had appeared on the jetty. Adler was speaking with the thin black man from the Edinburgh nightclub.

'Yes, the river's wonderful,' said Rex. 'But these people aren't.' He nodded to the small pier. 'The people you're living with don't seem very nice to me.'

'No, they're lovely people,' said Ligeia. 'They're my friends. Irana gives me presents all the time and I like her. I like you better though, Rex. You're special and I *really* like you.' She giggled playfully. 'I know. Shall we have sex?'

'*What*?' said Rex.

'Here by the water.' She kissed Elva. 'It's lovely and sunny. Isn't that a nice idea?'

The nearby guards raised their eyebrows and smirked at one another.

'What?' repeated Rex. 'No, actually it's a very bad idea.'

'But you liked it so much the last time.' Ligeia looked puzzled. 'Look, Elva wants to.'

Nodding enthusiastically, Elva jumped up from the rock and began to unfasten her jeans.

'No, don't,' said Rex, grabbing her wrist. He couldn't believe he was turning them down, but sex was the last thing on his mind and he definitely wasn't going to treat a one-eyed mad woman and her cronies to a live show. 'No, this is all wrong.'

The disappointed guards sagged slightly.

'The mood isn't right,' said Rex. 'I don't know why, but men with machine guns have always been a real turn-off.'

* * * *

Standing on the pier with Lafont, Colonel Adler watched the young trio further along the bank. She turned as her Sergeant joined them. 'What did Corporal Baxter have to say for himself?' she asked.

'The idiot removed one of his audio implants,' said Gruner.

'Ah, I guessed as much. Some of our additional security are fairly stupid, but the salary ensures they don't ask questions and they do as ordered.'

'This one didn't,' said Lafont. 'Will Baxter cause any more problems?'

'I shouldn't think so,' said Gruner. 'As we speak, Ligeia's tiger is explaining the importance of obedience.'

'Not to worry.' Adler smiled. 'We're dispensing with the extra security before we leave tomorrow. Now we have one less to pay.'

'If anyone is going to be a problem, it's *this* man.' Gruner gestured to the distant Rex. 'Why are we keeping him? I know Ligeia wanted him, but she'll soon grow tired and she has her mute lover there to entertain her, not to mention Ramson and Moran.'

Lafont peered curiously at the Sergeant. 'He's able to resist her,' he said. 'We need to know how this is possible before we consider getting rid of him. She said she wanted him to come with her and he refused. I knew there was something strange about him and I need to discover what.'

'Exactly,' said Adler. 'We need to know in case this ever happens again.'

Rex drew angrily on his cigarette, glaring at the Colonel as she walked with the two men along the water's edge to join him.

Adler peered at Ligeia. 'You appear troubled,' she said.

'It's Rex.' The girl sat on the rock, pouting. 'He won't have sex with me.'

'I shouldn't worry,' said Gruner, smirking. 'These problems aren't uncommon with some men when they're stressed.'

'*What?*' snarled Rex, this suggestion taking priority over his abduction. *No one was going to pity his sexual prowess.* 'Hey, let's get something clear, pal...'

'Ligeia,' broke in the Colonel, 'I've asked the chef to make chocolate ice creams for you and Elva. Why don't you run along

121

and enjoy them while I speak with your new friend.'

'Ice cream,' enthused Ligeia, pulling at Elva. 'Chocolate.'

'What the hell?' gasped Rex. He watched the pair skip away hand-in-hand. 'You know she isn't right in the head, don't you? I'm no doctor, but I can tell you they're both several pawns short of a chess set. In medical terminology, they're fucking crackers.'

'Such things are subjective,' said Adler. 'Ligeia is a very happy girl and the billions she's generated make me a very happy Colonel.'

Lafont gazed intently at the young man.

'What's with the staring?' snapped Rex. 'I saw you in the Edinburgh nightclub and you were staring at me then.'

'This is our Padre, Mister Lafont,' said Adler. 'He's a native of Haiti. My security company were employed to assist in certain political troubles out there. It's where I lost my eye. His unique skills impressed me and he agreed to work for me.'

'Helping you look for the eye?' asked Rex, sarcastically.

'I help in other ways.' Lafont took Rex's hand and squeezed, peering at him and muttering.

'What the hell is this?' Rex snatched his hand away.

'You took the words out of my mouth, Mister Grant.' Lafont gazed suspiciously. 'What *is* this? I touched you when you were drugged and I sensed something wasn't right with you, but now you're awake and your esoteric energy is flowing, the feeling is so much stronger. What *are* you?'

'What the fuck? You touched me when I was asleep?'

'I did more than that,' said Lafont. 'I took hair and some of your blood in a syringe. Tonight the moon is full and I can go to work on them. My blood ritual should reveal what you're hiding.'

'Our Padre is an accomplished practitioner of the occult,' said Adler. 'He used to be what they call a Houngan, a priest of voodoo, but he long ago surpassed that rudimentary level. His

122

rituals are a powerful blend of Haitian and western traditional magic and very shortly he'll perform a working to discover your secrets. That's probably difficult for you to believe?'

Rex peered warily at Lafont. After some of the things he'd experienced in the last few months, especially the occasions when he turned into a huge wolf, some twat performing voodoo wasn't at *all* hard to accept. *So his kidnappers had a real-life witchdoctor working for them? This shit just got weirder and weirder.*

Adler glanced over Rex's shoulder. 'Ah, I think it's now time to come clean with you.'

Rex turned, his mouth falling open to see two men crossing the lawn. One was fat, one was thin, and both wore grey suits, bow ties and bowler hats. The Colonel's voodoo priest suddenly seemed fairly unremarkable next to Oliver Hardy and Stan Laurel.

'Well,' said Hardy, chuckling. 'Here's another nice mess you've gotten yourself into.'

'*What the...*' whispered Rex. He stared at them for several seconds. 'You have to be fucking joking? Laurel and Hardy?'

'Laurel and Hardy,' confirmed Adler.

'Impossible.' Rex shook his head slowly. 'This is totally...'

'Totally real,' said Adler. 'Please feel free to touch them.'

'So he *was* there in the hotel. I didn't know if I was hallucinating when you drugged me, but I *did* see Oliver Hardy.'

'Yes, everything you remember really happened.'

'Charlotte was hurt...'

'She's dead, Rex.' The Colonel shrugged apologetically. 'When I called on you, you appeared to be alone and I wrongly assumed she'd left. Unfortunately, Miss Michie emerged from the bathroom as we were injecting you.'

'Dead?' stammered Rex. 'You killed her?'

'Ollie did,' said Adler. 'Her body was left in your hotel room and I'm afraid you're the prime suspect. The police interviewed us and asked if we knew anything of your whereabouts, but we couldn't help them.'

'They're searching for you,' said Hardy. 'But you appear to have vanished off the face of the earth.'

'Oliver Hardy,' gasped Rex, stunned. He tore his eyes away from the fat man to gape at Lafont. 'Is this something to do with your voodoo magic, or is it like *Jurassic Park*? You're cloning old movie stars?'

The Colonel laughed. 'I offered you money to be with Ligeia and that offer still stands. I'll triple the cash if you stay with us and the police will never find you.'

'I was right; you *are* insane.' Rex felt fury building inside and knew the moon was partly to blame, but he was past caring. 'You killed Charlotte,' he snarled, glaring at Hardy. 'You stabbed her, you bastard.'

'*Jurassic Park*?' Hardy fussed with his bow tie and turned to Laurel. 'Ligeia has a thing about him, Stanley? I take it she must like mental cases.'

'I guess so, Ollie,' chuckled Laurel. 'This one's an idiot.'

Rex leapt on Hardy, slamming his bulk to the ground and punching him. Gruner rushed at the grappling pair, but Hardy twisted his wrist, snapping out the concealed blade and stabbing it upwards into his assailant's chest before the Sergeant could wrestle him off.

'You stabbed him in the heart,' yelled Gruner. 'You crazy bastard. What have I told you about using that knife contraption?'

'It's an instinctive thing,' said Hardy. 'He was the one who attacked…'

'*Instinctive*?' hissed Adler. 'I went to all the bother of bringing him here for Ligeia and now he's dead. Thank God she didn't see this. It would have upset her.'

Upset Ligeia? thought Rex, sinking into blackness. *I'm not too happy about this myself.*

* * * *

124

Chapter 17

Quist and Watson left the Edinburgh train and walked through the entrance hall of York Station. A huge Victorian complex, the platforms and halls were constructed of ornate ironwork and a honey-coloured brick that always left Watson thinking of cinder toffee. The railway buildings provided quite a contrast to the white limestone of the fortified city wall which ran along the grassy embankment opposite.

The detective's mobile rang. He answered it and looked puzzled.

'Who was that?' asked Watson.

'Probably a wrong number.' Quist slipped it back into his overcoat pocket and walked past the busy rank of taxis. 'They heard my voice and rang off. I was hoping it might be Rex calling, or someone to say he'd turned up.'

'I've been telling you to get a mobile phone for months and you've finally listened to me. Pretty useful, aren't they?'

'I've never disputed the advantages of these amazing devices, but to many people they're like heroin. Look around you at these crowds. Look anywhere, for that matter, even in the passing vehicles. Some live their lives through their phones, permanently glued to them with their mouths hanging slackly open. To some, their phone *is* their life.'

'Whatever,' drawled the teenager, realising this described a good few of his friends. 'I suppose you prefer to stick your nose in a book.' He glanced at Quist's aquiline beak and cleared his throat. He could have chosen his words more prudently.

Lighting a cigarette, the detective headed into the Queen Street car park where his Ford saloon had been left during their overnight trip.

'You smoke like a fish,' said Watson.

'Fortunately cigarettes can't harm me. Surely the

expression is *drink like a fish*?'

'You haven't seen my mum frying them.'

'Ligeia,' said Quist. 'The more thought I give to this singer, the more she intrigues me.'

His assistant grinned. 'That makes two of us, Guv.'

'I suspect I find her interesting for quite different reasons. She and her mute friend were the last people to see Rex and the murder victim. It's very possible they may have seen other things too.'

'If they did, they didn't tell the police.'

Quist gave a short laugh. 'From the length of time they were interviewed, they wouldn't have been able to say *anything*. I'm actually starting to wonder if they were involved in some way, so why aren't the police entertaining the same possibility? Those girls were present in the crime scene with the victim and the prime suspect just before the murder took place. We only have their word that they weren't there *when* it happened. They could easily have been complicit and yet the police allowed them to go after a few minutes of rudimentary questioning and without conducting any forensic tests on them for trace evidence. I can't believe they would act so blasé and unprofessional.'

'Are you thinking they were bribed or something?'

'I doubt it, but I want to question the two girls myself. The people in Ligeia's press office were no help when I rang. They appeared hostile and kept asking why I was so interested in Rex. We need to speak to Ligeia in person. At the very least, Rex may have said something relevant to her and provided clues as to where he might be.'

'Actually speak with Ligeia.' Watson grinned excitedly. 'It'd be amazing if we could. I've read she lives in a big mansion somewhere down south, but I can't remember where.'

'An internet search will remedy that,' said Quist. 'Yes, you keep up with the pop music scene, don't you? What do you know about Ligeia? Is she British?'

The teenager shrugged. 'I guess it sounds a bit crap coming from a fan, but I don't know *what* she is. Ligeia never gives interviews and the papers never tell you her history, probably because they don't know. I think she likes to keep an air of mystery.'

'That's more likely to be a managerial ploy. It will help the sales.'

'The sales don't need much help; she's the biggest selling artist of all time. The few times I've seen her speak on TV, she sounds foreign. Like those gorgeous birds in films about Russian gangsters, only sexier.'

'Really?' The detective nodded. 'So perhaps East European?

'Who knows? She just appeared out of nowhere last year and took the music world by storm. Her concerts always sell out immediately. I know she's playing the O2 Arena in London on Friday night and then she's going to live in America.'

'In that case, we'd better hurry if we intend to question her.'

'Speaking of singers and songs, what is it?' Watson smirked. 'The shit song that Rex uses to stop him eating Little Red Riding Hood?'

'I've already told you, it's pointless asking. The melody is personal and confidential and I have no intention of divulging...'

'Oh. Come on, Guv...'

'Hello there,' called out a gruff voice from behind. 'Bernard Quist?'

The pair turned to see two large men following them across the station car park. Both had short-cropped military hairstyles and pumped-up muscles bulging beneath dark suits and overcoats.

'Gentlemen.' Quist nodded politely. 'You have me at a disadvantage. I don't believe we've met.'

127

'We've met now.' The larger of the two grinned. 'We'd like to talk to you.'

'Really?' Quist ran an eye over them. The big man who'd spoken was over six feet in height and his shorter, stockier companion sported a knife scar down his face. From their size and intimidating appearance, they probably weren't Jehovah's Witnesses wanting to talk about the Bible. 'I'm all ears.'

More like all nose, thought Watson, but he decided the atmosphere wasn't conducive to jokes.

'Not here.' The scarred man gestured to the southern side of the car park. 'We have a vehicle over by the wall. We'll talk there.'

'Talk about what?' asked Quist.

'You'll find out. Move – now.'

'You know something?' said the detective, stamping out his cigarette. 'All things considered, I don't feel particularly talkative.'

The larger character grabbed Watson's arm, brought his free hand from his pocket and showed them the small device he held. The teenage gulped uneasily. It resembled an electric shaver, but the blue crackle of electricity dancing between the prongs told him this wouldn't be much use for a stubbly chin.

'A stun gun?' said Quist. 'Aren't they illegal in Britain?'

'If you say so.' The man laughed. 'Now do as you're told and get moving to our van.'

* * * *

128

Chapter 18

Spasming violently, Rex awoke on a steel table and sucked in air as his senses returned. A fluorescent strip light glared above, a zoo smell filled his nostrils and a deep rumbling growl sounded to his right.

'Amazing.' Colonel Adler leant over him, smiling excitedly. 'Well, I think it's safe to say you have remarkable powers of recuperation.'

Sitting up, Rex realised he had to be in the menagerie building. This tiled room was obviously behind the tiger enclosure and the growling was coming from Mister Tigsy. The big cat paced restlessly in its cage and Lafont stood beside the metal table with Laurel and Hardy, the trio curiously watching Rex.

An elderly man stood with Adler and looked decidedly nervous. 'No, this is impossible,' he gasped. The stunned voice was a whisper, but Rex still picked up on the American accent. 'He was dead when I examined him. I honestly can't believe this.'

'This is Griffin Roylott,' said Adler. 'He's our resident doctor. We didn't know how badly wounded you were, so I had him rush down from the house to tend to you.'

'Impossible,' repeated Roylott, fingering Rex's chest. 'I assure you he wasn't wounded. He was…'

Rex smacked the old man's hand away.

'Griffin had a wasted journey,' said Adler. 'Firstly, because my Sergeant was correct; Ollie's blade pierced your heart and you were indeed dead. Secondly, because your *fatal wound* healed almost immediately and you began to breathe again.'

Sergeant Gruner stood at the end of the table holding a pistol. 'Rather than carry you to the house, we brought you in here,' he said. 'We didn't want Ligeia to see your body and become distressed, but we needn't have bothered. You're fine.'

'What are you?' asked Lafont.

'Yes, what are you?' echoed Adler.

Rex felt his chest through the bloody shirt, but Adler was right – there was no sign of a stab wound.

'Sorry about your shirt,' said the Colonel. 'It's a real mess. I hope you have another in your bag, but if not, I'm sure we can find something that will fit.'

Rex jumped off the table and Gruner gripped the gun tighter.

'Hardy shouldn't have stabbed you,' said the Sergeant. 'But sometimes he loses it and he's difficult to control. The same thing happened with your girlfriend in Edinburgh. To be honest, he's something of a liability.'

'Hey, you can hurt a person's feelings,' laughed Hardy. He turned to Rex. 'I suppose I *should* exercise more restraint. I should think before I lash out, but it doesn't seem to matter this time.'

'Ollie uses a spring blade in a rather clever concealed device,' said Adler. 'It's usually fixed to his arm, but luckily he didn't have it with him when he was arrested. We retrieved the weapon from one of his hideouts after I liberated him. He likes to constantly wear it, but as my Sergeant says, it does occasionally cause problems.'

'Liberated?' Rex gaped at the woman. 'From where? Some nuthouse where he believed himself to be Oliver Hardy?'

Stan Laurel chuckled and played with his bow tie.

'From a police escort,' said Adler. 'But he *was* heading for what the authorities politely refer to as *secure mental accommodation.*'

'You set him free?' shouted Rex. 'You freed this lunatic and now he's killing people like Charlotte?'

'I didn't kill you, did I?' said Hardy, defensively. 'You took my blade through your heart and you lived.'

'I'll ask again,' said Lafont, moving close to Rex. 'What *are* you? I knew there was something different about you.'

130

'Different?' laughed the American doctor. 'You don't say.'

'That's why Ligeia was drawn to you,' continued Lafont, his voice low and his French accent menacing. 'She could sense it too. The energy is strong and exceedingly dark.'

'Our Padre understands this kind of thing,' said Adler. 'As I mentioned, he's an occultist. He's shown me many strange things, so this biblical resurrection doesn't faze me. I need to know your secret, Rex.'

'What are you?' repeated Lafont. 'And who is Bernard Quist?'

Rex swallowed uncomfortably and didn't answer. Turning away to watch the pacing tiger, he hoped his face remained deadpan, but wouldn't have bet money on it.

'I asked earlier about this man Quist,' said the Colonel. 'The Padre handled those pages of yoga exercises that were in your bag – the ones drawn by Mister Quist.'

'I picked up vibrations from the paper,' said Lafont. 'Vague supernatural vibrations left by the artist; the same dark feelings I get from you. I believe the tiger can sense you too. There are six other people in this room, but his eyes remain permanently fixed upon you and look how alarmed he appears.'

'Ooh, spooky,' sneered Rex.

'The Padre has psychic abilities,' said Adler. 'I trust his feelings, so that makes this Bernard Quist very interesting.'

'Wow, your own American doctor and a personal psychic too?' Rex laughed dryly. 'Guess what? I'm clairvoyant myself and I'm picking up a spirit voice; it's giving me a message for you. I'm making out the words... *fuck off.*' He watched as the tiger began to hiss, its nervous eyes still fixed on him. His own eyes suddenly widened in shock. He hadn't noticed it before, but a blood-drenched human leg lay in the corner of the enclosure. '*What...*' He pointed shakily. 'What the fuck is *that*? *Who* the fuck is that?'

Adler ignored the babbled question. 'The yoga instructions

are on office paper printed with Quist's letterhead. The telephone number on the letterhead is in your mobile.'

Rex tore his eyes from the grisly limb. 'How did you get into my mobile without the password?'

'Don't be absurd.' The Colonel laughed. 'Passwords are simple enough to overcome. When this man rang our press office asking about you, I had the number identified. I need to know why this detective is interested in your disappearance. More importantly, why is the Padre picking up these psychic sensations from the pictures he drew?'

'I've no idea,' said Rex. 'He's my yoga instructor and that's all. As for these *sensations*, maybe your pal's voodoo radar is screwed.'

'Maybe.' Adler laughed. 'No matter. I've sent someone to interview Mister Quist so everything will be explained soon enough. When the sun goes down, the Padre will also be working on the blood and hair that he took from you. I wonder what he'll discover?'

'Yeah, I wonder,' said Rex, turning to glare angrily at Hardy. 'You know what, there's an elephant in the room and I'm not talking about this fat bastard's size. Who the hell are Laurel and Hardy?'

'I wondered when you'd ask,' said Adler. 'A remarkable likeness, don't you think?'

'They look real,' admitted Rex.

'These two gentlemen vaguely resembled the old comedians and my doctor here worked his magic on them. Not *real* magic like the Padre's, of course, but medical wizardry. They were both eager to disappear and jumped at my offer to join us and live in luxury. This is Alistair Ramson and Sebastian Moran.'

'No, you have to be joking?' said Rex, astounded. 'You mean the serial killers? I remember Ramson from the news; they called him the *Hounslow Ripper*. I read about Moran too. This twat actually eats people.' He stared closely at the two smirking men. 'So I assume you used plastic surgery?'

Adler shook her head. 'My doctor uses something a little more advanced. Ligeia likes the old Laurel and Hardy comedies. We play them for her in the private cinema, but I decided to give her the real thing and she was overjoyed.'

'That doesn't surprise me.' Rex rubbed his eyes resignedly. 'I've heard that spoilt pop stars can make ludicrous demands, but this is quite a step up from insisting all the blue sweets are removed from their bowl of Smarties.'

A loud hiss came from the tiger cage. Mister Tigsy was getting more agitated over Rex's lupine presence.

'You're distressing the cat,' said the Colonel. 'This place isn't conducive to chatting, is it? Come along, let's go back to the house and we'll see about finding you that shirt.'

'Yeah, let's,' snapped Rex. 'I'd like something in Kevlar.'

* * * *

133

Chapter 19

A large white van stood at the furthest end of the Queen Street car park in York. Adler's two thugs had parked in the corner, with the rear doors facing the high wall behind. Quist and Watson were marched across the tarmac to it, the larger man gripping the teenager's arm and virtually dragging him.

'You say you want to talk to us?' said Watson, nervously. 'Er, why can't we just chat out here in the open?'

'I don't think so.' The big man glanced over his shoulder, checking for witnesses. There were fewer vehicles here, most people having parked closer to the railway station entrance. 'We've picked a nice private spot for this.'

His scar-faced accomplice opened the rear doors of the van and invited Quist to climb into the windowless interior with a jerk of his thumb.

'Yes, no one can see us here,' said the detective, ignoring the gesture and dropping his overnight bag on the ground. 'I'm curious. How did you recognise us and how did you know where we'd be?'

'Our employer is interested in you,' said the larger thug. 'She tracked your phone. We knew you were on the train from Edinburgh and I rang your number when the crowd left the station.'

'Ah, the silent phone call.' Quist nodded. 'Who's your employer?'

Both heavies laughed dryly, the sardonic noise suggesting this question wouldn't be answered.

'Tracking phones isn't an easy task,' said the detective. 'I know the police can do it, but you must have excellent resources.'

'Shut up,' snarled the scarred man. 'Get inside.'

'I much prefer the fresh air out here. Tell me, what does this concern?'

The big man held up his stun gun, crackling the electric

prongs inches from Watson's frightened face. 'You rang the press office for the artist Ligeia earlier today,' he said. 'You were enquiring about a man named Rex Grant. You're going to tell us why you're so interested in his disappearance and everything you know about him.'

'Well, that shouldn't pose any problems,' said Quist, thoughtfully stroking his chin. 'Let's see. What can I tell you? He's rather good-looking. Some say he resembles Tom Cruise in his younger *Top Gun* days, and he enjoys…'

The scar-faced character smashed a fist into the detective's face. 'I don't like insolence,' he growled menacingly. 'And I don't like flippant bastards.'

'Is that so?' said Quist, fingering his cheekbone and wincing. 'You certainly won't like Watson then.'

'And you certainly won't like *this*.' The larger thug released the trembling youth, grabbed the detective and lifted him from his feet to throw him inside the vehicle. 'You were asked nicely, but you chose to be…'

Quist slammed an elbow into the man's stomach and brought his fist up beneath his chin. A loud crack sounded as the lower jaw fractured in two places and he crumpled into an unconscious heap. His accomplice reached quickly into a pocket for his stun gun, but the detective snatched his arm and twisted sharply, snapping a bone. The man screeched and Quist slapped a hand over his mouth to silence him, glancing around the car park to ensure no one had seen or heard anything.

'Bloody hell, Guv,' stammered Watson, stepping back. 'Nice work.'

'Right,' said Quist, shoving the wounded man against the van. 'Now it's time for *you* to answer a few questions. Why do you want to know about Rex Grant and, more to the point, where is he?'

'Fuck you,' hissed the heavy.

'I told you I didn't feel talkative,' said Quist. 'I don't feel

135

fuckable either. Where's Grant and who's your employer?'

Watson winced to hear a crackling sound as the detective squeezed the fractured arm.

'Where is he?' repeated Quist. 'What happened to him in Edinburgh?' He squeezed the arm again, then twisted it, tutting irritably as the man passed out and collapsed.

'*Shit!*' said Watson. 'You're amazing, Guv. You look like my boring old geography teacher from school and then you fight like Muhammad Ali on cocaine. They never expect it and that gives you the edge. Mind you, I suppose having werewolf strength doesn't harm.'

'Fortunately they're unconscious and didn't hear that,' snarled Quist. 'Anyway, as I've pointed out on many occasions, violence is nothing to be proud of.'

'Er, yeah.' Watson eyed the comatose heavies. The larger one's fractured jaw hung loosely open and three teeth had fallen out. His accomplice's arm was bent into the horrific shape of a letter N. 'Yeah, whatever you say.'

'Interesting.' Quist gazed thoughtfully at the pair. 'The pain must have been unbearable when I twisted his arm.'

'Hey, really? Have you had medical training?'

'The point is he still wouldn't talk. He's obviously been trained to resist torture.' Quist removed the man's watch. 'I'd say they're both military, or ex-military.'

'Are you robbing him?' asked Watson.

'Don't be ridiculous.' The detective pointed to the small tattoo that had been obscured by the watch. 'His blood group is on his wrist; it's a common practise in the armed forces.' Tugging off the coat and ripping the man's shirt to check his arms, he found a regimental tattoo on the right bicep. 'Ah, there you go; our scarred friend here was in the Royal Marines.' He began to go through his pockets. 'Take a look in the van, would you? See if you can find any clue as to who they are.'

Watson rummaged through the cab as Quist searched both unconscious thugs. Neither carried identification, but both had a mobile phone.

'Nothing in there, Guv,' said Watson, climbing out. 'No paperwork or anything. It's as clean as a whistle.'

Quist held up the two phones. 'These are both locked, but they could tell us something if we could get into the data. I wonder if your computer genius friend Gareth Lestrade could help?'

'Gazza?' The youth nodded. 'They'll be no problem for him.'

Quist stared at the heavies. 'So someone tracked my phone after I rang Ligeia's press office and sent characters like this to ask questions about Rex? I presume the idea was to beat information out of us. One thing is now crystal clear – if Rex is involved with characters like *this*, then he's really in trouble.'

'They said their employer wanted the information,' said Watson. 'They said *she*, so it sounds like it could be a woman.'

'Your deductive powers are obviously improving.'

'I'm guessing you're thinking the same as me? This *employer* might have Rex?'

'That would be a very safe bet, Watson. Speaking of phones...' Quist took out his mobile and using lupine strength, crushed it in his fist. 'As I say, someone is tracking this one.' He tossed the mess of circuitry over the nearby wall. 'Incredible! I shied away from those things for years and, the first time I purchase one, our adversaries use it against me.'

* * * *

Chapter 20

A redbrick building at the end of York's celebrated Shambles, Granary Court stood on St. Andrewgate and had once, unsurprisingly, been a Victorian granary. Back in the nineties, when wealthy people decided old rundown warehouses and factories were the perfect place to reside, it was attractively converted into apartments and Watson's friend Gareth Lestrade lived on the top floor overlooking the nearby Minster. Surrounded by *Star Trek* memorabilia, Quist and his assistant sat in the lounge, sipping tins of beer and watching as the young man worked at his desk of computer equipment. Gazza, as everyone referred to the techno-genius Gareth, had plugged the mobile phones into one of his three terminals and unlocking them had been a rudimentary task.

'Hey,' whispered Watson, nudging Quist. He nodded to the hi-fi where, ironically, Ligeia's album *Water Music* was playing. 'How about that for a coincidence?'

'Indeed,' said Quist, with the sort of enthusiasm parents exhibit when changing a full nappy. '*Lovely* music, isn't it?'

The teenager smirked. *It went without saying that Gazza was a fan of Ligeia; so was everyone Watson had ever met with the exception of Cyrano de Bergerac here, the consultant detective who was educated and cultured, but who clearly had zero musical taste.*

'These are fairly new phones,' said Lestrade, scrolling through the data. 'There's no real information on them apart from a list of telephone numbers and call records. No address books, photographs, or anything.'

'They rang one number lots of times,' said Watson, pointing at the monitor. 'Can you find who it is?'

'I'll need to hack the records,' said Lestrade, changing screens and typing. 'Here we go; someone called Irana Adler.'

Quist raised his eyebrows, impressed by Lestrade's speed. Fortunately, Watson's friend didn't bother himself with things like regulations and data protection laws. 'Can you discover who the phones are registered to?' he asked. 'That would be helpful.'

'Not a problem.' Lestrade nodded. 'Let me take a look.'

The detective leant closer to the screen as the young man typed at the keyboard, going through several menus to arrive at the correct website. A few seconds later he'd hacked into a secure databank.

'They appear to be company phones,' said Lestrade. 'Both numbers are registered to a firm called *Red Globe Management*.'

'Who are they?' asked Quist.

'Let's check the register of companies.' Lestrade typed again, his fingers a blur. 'I remember the last time you asked for my help like this. I accessed police post mortem reports for you. I take it this is another of those detective cases you can't talk about?'

'Yeah.' Watson grinned. 'We have a real mystery for a change. It certainly beats the wayward husbands and scumbag benefit cheats.'

'Here they are,' said Lestrade. 'Apparently *Red Globe* are music management. Ah, and the company is owned by Irana Adler.'

'The woman they kept phoning,' said Watson, nodding.

Lestrade read through the information. *'Red Globe Management* only have one client.' He turned excitedly. 'Wow, you'll never guess who it is.'

'Ooh...' Quist gazed at the ceiling in mock deliberation. 'Let me take a wild shot in the dark, Gazza. Would it be Ligeia?'

'That's right.' Lestrade gestured to his music speakers where the singer warbled. 'Incredible, eh?'

'Bloody hell,' gasped Watson. 'How about that, Guv? Is the company address there?'

Lestrade clicked on the name. 'Charlington Hall in Richmond...'

'That's it,' said Watson. 'I remember now. That's the mansion where Ligeia lives.'

'Why am I not surprised?' said Quist. He stroked his chin thoughtfully. 'Leaving aside these two phones for a moment, I wonder if your exceptional talents extend to accessing the footage from closed circuit television cameras?'

'CCTV?' Lestrade shrugged. 'It depends. The clue is in the name *closed circuit*. I probably can't if the camera is on someone's private house, but if it's connected to an internet-linked computer and the recordings are stored as files, then yes. I can get into most street camera footage.'

'I was thinking about the cameras at Edinburgh airport?'

'I see.' The young man nodded slowly. 'Well, as you can imagine, with all this terrorism, they really tightened the security on airport computers. It could take a while to break in there.'

'Shit,' sighed Watson. 'How long?'

'Two or three minutes.'

The detective and his assistant exchanged dumbfounded looks and then sat back to observe as he hurriedly went to work. Watson knew that Quist felt decidedly uncomfortable about paying Gazza money and encouraging his illegal hacking like this, but Rex was almost certainly in danger and their options were limited.

'Bingo,' said Lestrade, eventually. 'I'm in.'

'Unbelievable,' said Quist. 'It's reassuring to see how well-protected the system is. It took you almost five minutes, not two or three.'

'Er, yeah.' Lestrade gave a guilty grin. 'They have cameras everywhere. Are you interested in a particular one?'

'The units covering departing aircraft,' said Quist. 'Could you show me yesterday's runway footage for around noon, or possibly early afternoon?'

'Ligeia's plane?' said Watson. 'Yeah, we'll be able to see who boarded it.'

'Exactly. It will most probably be a private flight.'

Lestrade flicked through the camera feeds and found a host

of passengers queuing to climb the steps to a large jet.'

'That appears to be a normal plane,' said Quist. 'What else do we have?'

The film footage was fast-forwarded until a smaller aircraft taxied into view.

'A Gulfstream.' Quist sat forward. 'This could be it. These are luxurious executive jets with seating for around fifteen or so.'

'Fifteen?' Watson grinned. 'Any commercial charter airline would soon cram in another fifty or so economy seats with zero legroom. Can you zoom in on the door, Gazza?'

'Sure.' Lestrade adjusted the settings and whistled as cars drew up beside the plane and Ligeia climbed out. 'Oh, wow, there she is. Isn't she gorgeous? What wouldn't I give for twenty minutes alone with that girl and a bottle of warm baby oil?'

'Absolutely,' whispered Watson. He watched the singer board the jet with another petite young girl. An older woman accompanied them, along with a slender black man and a huge character who resembled a bald gorilla. 'No sign of Rex, Guv.'

'Wait a moment,' murmured Quist. 'What's this?'

Towed behind an electronic buggy, two trolleys laden with luggage arrived. The airport staff lifted over a dozen cases on board, along with a large traveller's trunk.

'A trunk?' Watson turned to the detective. 'They used to bury treasure in those things, but who uses them these days?'

'Who indeed?' said Quist. 'I presume you share my suspicions?'

'That Rex is inside? Yeah, maybe.'

'Who's Rex?' asked Lestrade. 'You think Ligeia packed her pet dog in a trunk?'

'A dog?' Watson smirked. 'Actually, you're closer to the truth there than you know.'

* * * *

Chapter 21

The chapel at Charlington Hall stood to the west of the house moat. Constructed of sandstone and surrounded by iron railings and yew trees, the small, unassuming building was twenty feet in length. Colonel Adler smiled to herself as she closed the door behind her. Many British aristocrats had private churches like this built in the grounds of their stately homes. Family funerals, weddings and Christmas services would be conducted in them and the crypt below stored their dead. Thanks to Ligeia, Adler had more than enough cash to build her own cathedral.

The Cantlemere family, the original owners, probably wouldn't recognise the chapel interior now and Adler felt certain they wouldn't approve. Black candles flickered in candelabras on either side of the short aisle, their beeswax aroma mingling with an incense fog that spewed from upright thurible stands. Human skulls from the crypt hung from the ceiling beams, animal bones dangled beside them, and a bizarre collection of magical paraphernalia and statuettes covered the altar. A red silk tapestry hung behind, the glossy backdrop embroidered with voodoo symbols around a golden pentagram. Lafont wore a purple robe and stood at the altar, busily working with Rex's bloodstained shirt and three black cockerels.

'Those chickens have seen better days,' said Adler, laughing quietly. They wouldn't be seeing anything else, for they no longer possessed heads. 'We're fortunate the RSPCA don't carry out surprise visits on voodoo temples. Tell me again what you call this place?'

'A Hounfour,' said Lafont, wiping his grisly hands on the robe and turning to his visitor. 'It is a voodoo temple of the spirits, but as you know, it is a long time since I was a simple Houngan. The term is actually incorrect, as my occult practises go way beyond the elementary Caribbean magic, but it will suffice and it serves to remind me of my former life in Haiti.'

'Yes, most folk have photographs as a reminder, but a voodoo temple is better.' The Colonel chuckled at her witticism, then peered curiously at the dishes of blood on the altar and the small model Lafont had constructed: a crude representation of Charlington Hall with a wide circle of red ash around it. 'So, Padre, how did Grant take a blade through the heart and live? How could the wound vanish? Do you have answers for me yet?'

'I do.' Lafont shook his head in annoyance. 'How many times have I told you to listen to me when I experience sensations and channel vibrations?'

'I always listen. You know I trust your powers.'

'But evidently not enough. I knew there was something wrong with Grant, just like I knew about Ligeia's mute friend. Their vibrations are wrong.'

'Wrong?'

'I've tried to tell you before; Elva's psychic vibrations are very similar to Ligeia's.' Lafont grimaced, groping for the right words. 'They're actually the same, yet they're different.'

'Well, that's as clear as mud,' snorted Adler. 'What a pity she can't sing. We could market her too.'

'This is a serious matter,' snapped Lafont. 'These feelings are a warning. If she feels wrong to me, then she *is* wrong and a danger to us.'

'I'm sorry, Padre, but I disagree. You didn't like Elva and you warned me not to bring her to Charlington Hall, but the girl has caused us no problems. On the contrary, she's been very beneficial to Ligeia and keeps her content. You fail to understand that this is a business I'm running. A highly lucrative business and I have dozens of daily problems to deal with. You get these psychic *feelings* constantly and I can't act upon every one of them.'

'As you wish,' said Lafont. 'But you must definitely act upon Rex Grant.'

'I'm listening,' said Adler, crossing her arms. 'I take it you've discovered something from the samples of blood and hair you took?'

'My rituals told me what we needed to know.' Lafont slid a ring from his finger. 'Watch this.' He placed the ring in one of the saucers of blood on the altar. 'This is Grant's blood. It has been infused with my magic to temporarily give it life.'

The Colonel stared curiously at the congealing liquid. Nothing happened for several seconds and then the saucer rattled as the contents began to bubble, the blood instantly evaporating in a violent hiss of crimson smoke.

'What the hell...' muttered Adler, stepping back. She noticed the temperature had fallen and her breath was visible. 'What did I just witness?'

'This ring is silver.' Lafont replaced it on his finger. 'Grant's blood was unable to tolerate it because he is loup-garou.'

'*What*?'

'Grant is a supernatural creature, Colonel. He returned from death because he isn't alive in the way that you and I are. You saw for yourself how the fatal wound healed. My moon ritual on his blood revealed the truth in esoteric visions and the silver test confirms it. He is loup-garou.'

'Seriously?' Adler shook her head and laughed. 'Loup-garou means werewolf in your language, doesn't it? Are you seriously talking about wolf men from horror films?'

'I'm talking about the real thing: lupine shapeshifters.'

'Amazing! You've opened my eyes to many strange things, but *this*...' Adler laughed again, a nervous reaction as she attempted to process the unbelievable information. 'I had no idea that werewolves were genuine. Are you certain about this?'

'Absolutely. You witnessed his resurrection. You saw the silver reaction, and the magic does not lie.'

'This is what you could sense when you saw him in

Edinburgh?'

Lafont shrugged. 'I could sense something wrong with him; something supernatural, but I didn't know what. I could also sense danger. In Haiti, we were well aware of the wolf spirit that can possess certain humans.'

'So you're saying at the full moon…'

'Some change, yes, but most loup-garou can control the change. They master the wolf spirit and are able to transform any time during the dark hours.'

'Incredible. Truly incredible.' Adler stood thinking for several moments, her heart pounding. 'These supernatural feelings you picked up from him – are they the same feelings you get from Ligeia and Elva?'

'No, fortunately he isn't like your girls.'

'Evidently not. We haven't seen either of them howling at the moon.'

'Please don't be flippant about this. I've never liked Elva. As I keep telling you, she doesn't feel right.'

'You win,' sighed Adler. 'If it makes you feel better, I'll find Ligeia another playmate and get rid of her as soon as we reach America.'

'That's good, but Grant is our most pressing problem. In light of what we now know, you need to eliminate him immediately.'

'Oh, no, Padre.' The Colonel smiled. 'If this is true, I don't view him as a problem at all. I see Mister Grant as something else entirely.' Her eyes were drawn to the model of the house on the altar with the circle of ash around it. 'I have to ask, what *is* that?'

'Something I constructed the moment I discovered the truth about Grant. I've mixed his blood with the ash.'

'Very nice. What for?'

Lafont smiled. 'Allow me to explain.'

* * * *

Chapter 22

Rex stood peering through the French doors in the Charlington Hall library, gritting his teeth and attempting to quell the surges of feral anger that rose and subsided with increasing regularity. A vast corner room, the glass doors provided an excellent view of the terrace and gardens and a side window overlooked the moat. Dusk had fallen and a bright full moon shone down illuminating the trees and shrubbery with its cold silver rays. Rex knew this had to be the cause of his erratic mood swings, although being kidnapped and stabbed in the heart by a bunch of lunatics didn't help matters.

Childishly oblivious to his feelings, Ligeia sprawled on a lengthy couch behind him with the American doctor and a blonde-haired man who sat reading a computer tablet. Adler poured whisky at a drinks cabinet and Sergeant Gruner stood quietly watching by one of the bookcases, his brawny arms folded and his expression wary. Rex took a deep breath to control his anger, deciding this had to rank as his weirdest birthday ever. The whole thing was beyond belief and utterly crazy. *He was being held captive by mercenaries, apparently to amuse a singer who had obvious mental health problems. Colonel Adler didn't appear particularly sane herself, what with her pandering to such abnormal whims. She also employed a voodoo witchdoctor and had pet serial killers strolling around in the guise of Laurel and Hardy.*

The thought of Charlotte Michie being murdered by Hardy, or Alistair Ramson as he really was, brought on another rush of fury. Rex closed his eyes and tried concentrating on his personal song, as Quist had taught him, but it only served to make him feel foolish which generated even more anger.

'Please...' Adler strolled over with two glasses of whisky and handed one to Rex. 'Come and sit with us. We really ought to talk about your future on my team.'

'*Future*?' Rex snatched the drink and gulped down half. He remained standing, but turned from staring at the moonlit grounds. 'Believe me, there isn't going to be any future with you.'

'I assure you, being a part of my team would be highly lucrative and agreeable. These gentlemen accepted my offer and have never had cause to look back.' Adler settled herself in an armchair and gestured to the elderly doctor on the library couch. 'You met Griffin in the tiger house. Doctor Griffin Roylott was a celebrated Beverley Hills surgeon, but he was forced into early retirement a couple of years ago by allegations of misconduct.'

'Spurious allegations,' said Roylott, quickly. 'I never touched any of them, despite that girl waking from the anaesthetic with her pants on back to front. My nurses lied on oath that they'd witnessed me with my trousers around my...'

'Oh, absolutely,' interrupted Adler, smirking. 'But Griffin retired under something of a cloud. I approached him and he now works exclusively for *Red Globe Management*. He tends to my men and he's constantly on call if Ligeia should fall ill.'

'Good idea,' grunted Rex. 'Yeah, you wouldn't want any medical problems preventing your goose from laying her golden eggs.'

'Indeed,' said Adler. She crossed his legs and smiled at the doctor. 'His skills are indispensable. As I explained, Griffin is responsible for the faces of the two comical gentlemen you met earlier.'

Rex sipped his drink, realising the Colonel was keeping the talk cryptic so Ligeia wouldn't understand. From what he'd seen of the singer so far, he guessed she didn't understand very much.

'He's quite the maestro,' said Adler. 'He views skin and facial bone structure as an artist's canvas. He chose the right two people from dozens of possible candidates and I provided the medical means to accomplish the amazing end result. The transformations you witnessed are the result of unique pharmacological serums, not surgery; a permanent and rather advanced version of Botox, you might say. My parents researched and synthesised the drugs using rare South American toxins.'

'Really?' Having seen Laurel and Hardy, Rex was impressed, but he'd no intention of admitting it to this character. 'So Mummy and Daddy are doctors, are they?'

'Were.' Adler nodded proudly. 'They're both dead, but my father was a true genius.'

'It's a shame he wasn't a doctor of psychiatry,' said Rex. 'You might have turned out a bit more stable.'

Doctor Roylott smiled warmly and squeezed Ligeia's arm. 'Do you like the actor Tom Cruise?' he asked. He turned to Adler. 'I've been studying Mister Grant's features. With your drugs, I could create a masterpiece there. He'd be an ideal addition to your celebrity collection.'

'I don't know who Tom Cruise is,' said Ligeia. 'But I really like Rex.'

Fury raged inside Rex. *How dare these bastards discuss altering his face in such a casual manner? Night had now fallen and, if he transformed and got to work with his wolf claws, he'd show them how to REALLY alter faces.* Once again he tried concentrating upon his personal melody, mentally playing it in his head, but it was a waste of time.

Rex cleared his dry throat. 'How did you end up as Ligeia's manager?' he asked. *Perhaps talking about something more conventional would help calm him down.* 'She appeared out of nowhere last year. Where did you meet her?'

'One of those small countries in the Balkans,' said Adler. 'Most people have heard the names on the news, but few can point to them on a map. My security firm were assisting in some unpleasantness there.'

'So a gun-for-hire became the manager of a pop star? Overnight, you went from shooting people and helping to overthrow regimes to booking concerts and selling records?'

'Pretty much.' The Colonel laughed. 'I knew nothing about music when I met Ligeia, of course. As you rightly point out, my talents lay in other very different areas. That's why I employ Shane here as my Entertainment Director.' She gestured to the blonde middle-aged man sipping wine and reading his computer tablet. 'Shane Guevara knows everything about the entertainment world.'

'*Shane Guevara*?' repeated Rex, deadpan. 'Shane *fucking* Guevara?'

Guevara looked up from his digital pad. 'I changed my name by deed poll,' he said, defensively. 'In my business, a cool name opens doors.'

'You changed to Shane?'

'How stupid are you? No, my name *is* Shane. I changed my surname to Guevara.'

'Shane helps me organise the venues,' said Adler. 'He arranges the meetings with the recording industries and all the general details. He managed many acts in the past and I rely on his knowledge and advice. He knows not to disappoint me.'

'Yeah.' Rex nodded, bristling at being called stupid. 'I'll bet.'

Adler looked around the ornate library. 'In many ways I'll be sorry to leave Charlington Hall,' she said. 'I'm selling the place fully furnished through an agency and the majority of our personal effects have already been packed and sent ahead to California. Zoo people are calling in the morning to take the tiger and the birds to another collection. Still, onwards and upwards, as they say.'

'Hey, you've made all the newspapers,' said Guevara. He smiled at Rex and held up his tablet. 'I've just been scrolling through the front pages. They're saying you're highly dangerous and warning the public not to approach you.'

Rex clenched his teeth, seething uncontrollably. *So thanks to these crazy bastards everyone believed him to be a murderer?*

His parents and all his friends were thinking he'd stabbed a girl to death in his Edinburgh hotel? The whisky glass shattered in his hand as he unconsciously squeezed. 'I've had enough of this insanity,' he snarled, viciously. 'I'm leaving.'

'I don't think so,' said Adler. 'I need you to remain here for the time being and I have a little supernatural surprise to ensure you do.'

'Yea, whatever,' said Rex, opening the French doors.

'Sergeant.' Adler nodded to Gruner. 'Stop him, would you?'

The huge Serbian darted across the library, grabbed the young man and then bent double as Rex punched him hard in the gut.

'Don't be ridiculous,' laughed Rex. The feral anger taking over, he lashed out, launching Gruner through the air with a backhand swipe of his arm. 'Believe me, those newspapers are right when they say I'm dangerous.'

'Wonderful,' gasped Adler. 'Now *that* was impressive.'

'You're silly.' Ligeia began to giggle, watching as the Sergeant rolled on the carpet winded. 'That was so funny.'

'Make the most of it,' said Rex, vanishing through the door. 'There won't be a repeat performance because you won't be seeing me again.'

'Excellent.' The Colonel jumped up gleefully from her armchair to watch Rex race across the terrace. 'I was hoping he'd run.'

'Are you sure about this, Ma'am?' groaned Gruner. 'You could have just drugged him as I advised.'

'I wanted to see his power.' Adler brought out the tranquiliser dart gun that had been concealed beneath the chair cushion and walked over to help the groggy Sergeant to his feet. 'I had a feeling something like this would happen when I told you to stop him. Yes, that was very impressive.'

* * * *

Rex ran down the front steps from the terrace and crossed the moat bridge. A guard turned, unslinging his machine pistol, then fell to the ground unconscious as his head snapped back from a punch. He ran faster, following the gravel driveway to his right, which he guessed would lead to the main gate of Charlington Hall. *If it looked to be too heavily guarded, he'd dodge into the trees, transform out of sight and escape over the boundary fence he'd seen earlier. In lupine form, he could probably rip the steel security mesh and create a hole to get through.*

The driveway curled into a small copse of beech trees, the overhead foliage creating a dark arboreal tunnel, and the young man slowed down, coming to an abrupt halt halfway through. Something felt wrong – *very* wrong. The hair stood up on the back of his neck, goosebumps covered his spine and he began to pant in short, shallow gasps. Rex looked around guardedly, wondering what could be causing this weird sensation, then realised the problem lay right in front of him. He moved forward and quickly stepped back. He'd no idea why, but for some inexplicable reason he couldn't proceed.

What the hell was this?

He tried again, but *something* was definitely preventing him. His legs simply refused to carry him any further forward than this point. Retracing his steps several feet, he rushed and stopped again. *This was insane; it was almost as if an invisible wall blocked his path.*

'Oh, come on,' muttered Rex, nervously. 'What *is* this?'

Glancing over his shoulder to ascertain no one was following, he saw the curve in the drive shielded him from the house. He felt the air with his hands, knowing he must look like one of those mime acts running their palms over a non-existent pane of glass, then hurried left and right and found it was the same. He dropped onto hands and knees to try crawling instead, but it was no use.

'Oh, shit. This is just crazy.'

Fixing his gaze on a patch of gravel three feet ahead, Rex concentrated, forcing himself to crawl to it. He began to tremble and perspire and knew he couldn't do it.

Was this the supernatural surprise Adler had mentioned? Had that creepy voodoo guy of hers done something? If it was supernatural, he could probably overcome the magic in his wolf form. Yes, they didn't know about the lycanthropy and certainly wouldn't have considered that. He could fight supernatural with supernatural.

Rex looked back again to ensure he was alone, then shuddered and arched his spine. He growled as his features extended and his body swiftly crackled and twisted through the lupine transformation, the shirt and trousers splitting at the seams and falling away as a sleek black wolf appeared from the torn garments. The change complete, he moved forward on all fours, but found he still couldn't breach the invisible barrier.

'Oh, no, you have to be joking,' snarled the wolf. 'This is just…'

A dart smacked into his furry buttock and he twisted around to see Adler and four armed men quietly appearing from the shadows of the trees behind him.

'Incredible,' said the Colonel, lowering her silenced rifle. 'Truly incredible. I believed the Padre, but I still had to see it for myself. You're a genuine werewolf.'

His head swimming dizzily from the drugged dart, Rex groaned and collapsed. He attempted to stand, scratching at the gravel with his front paws.

'You're wasting your time,' said Gruner, grinning tightly as he approached. 'The tranquiliser is quite strong. We sometimes use it on the tiger.'

The bravado and forced smile concealed the Sergeant's

amazement and fear. Adler had told him what to expect, but he hadn't fully believed and he trembled to see the huge black creature. His life in the Serbian military and his later mercenary career had exposed him to many strange and frightening sights, but none quite so strange as this.

'Two-hundred feet from the house,' said Adler. 'The occult barrier is exactly where the Padre said. Excellent.'

The perspiring wolf concentrated and began to crawl, but once again came to a halt. Adler stooped to pick up a Rolex wristwatch, then walked past Rex and squat a few yards in front of him.

'You can't reach me, can you?' she said. 'I goaded you into running because I wanted to see if the Padre's magic would work. Mostly though, I was hoping you'd transform. I wanted to see the wolf and you didn't disappoint me.'

Rex exposed his razor teeth and snarled loudly.

'Ooh, scary,' chuckled the Colonel. 'When the Padre discovered what you were, he used your blood and hair to construct this supernatural barrier and contain you. If it didn't work, the guards at the gate were ordered to shoot you with tranquiliser, but it *did* work.' She gazed in admiration at the creature. 'Good Lord, Rex, you truly are remarkable.'

Rex bared his teeth again. He wanted to tear into these men and especially their boss, this grinning bastard woman. *Was it his situation or the full moon making him feel so violent and murderous? Who cared?* He lunged at the Colonel, snapping his jaws, but it was no use.

Gruner pointed his gun, but Adler gestured to hold fire.

'I'm afraid you broke your expensive watch.' She held up the Rolex. 'You obviously forgot you were wearing it when you transformed. These steel bracelets are very strong, but your snapped it when your wrist changed into a paw. Your strength impresses me, Rex. Your recuperative powers impressed me; you survived a mortal wound.' Adler laughed quietly. 'Everything about you impresses me.'

'Just let me go,' said Rex, growling and panting. 'I swear I'll kill you all if you don't let me go.'

'I don't think so,' said Adler. 'Originally, I wanted you to keep Ligeia happy, but now I see other benefits and opportunities. Do you recall me telling you how I never allow opportunities to escape me? The Padre calls you loup-garou, but I call you *true power*. Oh, I'm so glad I met you, Rex.'

She signalled to Gruner who raised his rifle and fired another dart into Rex's flank. The wolf yelped and squirmed on its belly, the second dose of tranquiliser surging through its system. The black fur fell away as the drugged creature shrank in size and shapeshifted back into the form of a naked trembling man.

The Sergeant had finally regained his composure. Squatting beside Rex, he drew back his muscular arm. 'Here's a little something for tossing me across the room back there and making me look bad.' He smashed his fist into the young man's face, breaking his jaw and dislodging three teeth.

Happy fucking birthday, thought Rex, sinking into unconsciousness.

* * * *

Chapter 23

The iconic Tower Bridge often springs to mind when the majority of people picture London; Tower Bridge, the Houses of Parliament, or perhaps the colourful bustle and neon of Piccadilly Circus. Few think of the pastoral landscapes of woodland and leafy lanes surrounding Richmond and Kingston-upon-Thames. This is understandable, as both are remote from the metropolis and only became London boroughs after being poached from Surrey following the boundary changes in the sixties. Quist had located Charlington Hall on an internet map, complete with satellite views, and saw that it lay between these two small towns on the eastern bank of the meandering river. He'd lived in the capital several times over the years and had never looked upon London as a city, viewing it instead as a sprawling southern county made up of many towns and villages. Some of these he didn't much care for, but he had a real fondness for the likes of Westminster, Highgate and Hampstead. Richmond and Kingston-upon-Thames were definitely high on his list of favourites.

It had taken almost four hours to drive the 212 miles from York, with a brief service station stop to buy Watson a brunch of burger, crisps and sweets. It was now noon, the weather was bright and Quist had dressed in a casual tweed coat, shirt and tie, appearing quite smart next to his assistant who wore a denim jacket, jeans and sunglasses.

'Real detective work again,' enthused Watson, peering through the windscreen at the tree-lined Richmond lane. 'We have the murder in Edinburgh, the mystery of Rex's disappearance and big nutters threatening us at York station. Best of all, though, if everything goes well here, we might actually get to meet Ligeia.'

'You need to reign in the excitement and concentrate upon the risk,' warned Quist. The entrance to Charlington Hall was set back from the lane and, turning onto a semi-circle of gravel, he pulled up outside the gates. 'Those *nutters*, as you refer to them, were ex-military. That means there could be danger here and we need to be careful.'

'It's only the other day you were saying I adapt instantly to hazardous situations.'

'Well, let's try not to put that to the test if we can help it.'

The black iron gates hung between stone pillars and were operated electronically by a modern gatehouse. Two cars waited in front of Quist's Ford and Watson watched as security personnel in tuxedos checked paperwork before allowing the visitors onto the driveway beyond.

'It looks as if something is going on today,' said the youth.

'Indeed.' Quist lowered his side window, straining to hear the exchange between the security and the closest vehicle. 'They're saying something about a garden party and a press conference.'

The car drove through the gates allowing Quist to pull up beside the booth. 'Good afternoon,' he said. 'We're from *Music Today* magazine.'

'Afternoon, Sir.' The guard nodded curtly and held out a hand. 'You'll have the necessary documentation?'

'*Music Today*,' repeated the detective. 'Are you telling me you aren't aware of the situation? The paperwork never arrived and I understood you'd been notified.'

'The passes were sent out three weeks ago, Sir.' The large man smiled tightly. 'Without a pass, you don't get in.'

'There's obviously been a communication breakdown.' Quist tutted with irritation. 'I'm sorry, but I was informed this had been rectified over the phone. My editor contacted your employer, who said we'd be admitted. If you'll just allow us to…'

'Look, I'll make it simple, pal,' broke in the guard. He leant down, sticking his square jaw through the window. 'Without a pass, you don't get in. You turn this car around and fuck off right now. Do you understand?'

'I don't know,' said Quist, sarcastically. 'Perhaps you could be a little clearer?'

'We don't have a pass, Guv,' explained Watson, helpfully. 'He won't let us in without…'

Shaking his head, Quist slammed the car into reverse and pulled away from the gate.

* * * *

From the internet satellite views Quist had studied, he knew the grounds of Charlington Hall extended down to the Thames. After leaving the front gate, he'd driven to nearby Richmond and called at one of the small companies who rent motor launches. Entering from the road was clearly out of the question and, short of parachuting in, this appeared to be the only option. Sleek and white, with a windscreen, four seats and a steering wheel connected to a rear outboard, their boat purred along the river, cruising past huge houses and gardens.

'How much do these places cost?' muttered Watson, sprawling in the passenger seat. 'Fifteen million? Twenty million? Who the hell lives in them?'

'Who knows?' said Quist. Puffing on a cigarette, he steered around a small island, scaring two screeching coots into the reeds. 'Probably bankers and hedge fund managers. Maybe footballers and elderly rock stars. These days, it could even be rappers and teenage software tycoons.'

The teenager laughed. 'There's supposed to be some sort of recession, but no one seems to have told these bastards.'

'It's a beautiful part of the world to live,' said Quist.

'I suppose,' snorted Watson. 'If you're into trees and water.'

'Not enough loud pubs and clubs for you?' The detective glanced at him. 'The area is steeped in history. Hampton Court Palace is just upriver from here.'

'Are you trying to get me giddy and overexcited? Yeah,

157

remind me to add that to my *must visit* list. Speaking of what's upriver, do you know how fast this thing can go? There's a bit of a clue in the name *speed boat*.'

'It's actually a motor boat.'

'It'll still *motor* along much faster than this.'

'We don't want to get ourselves noticed by speeding. We're just two chaps out for an afternoon jaunt on the water. A garden party for the press means Charlington Hall will be filled with strangers. If we can only manage to sneak in from the river, we should be able to blend with the crowds and look around.'

'And hopefully find Rex if he's there.'

'Exactly.' Quist tossed his cigarette stub into the water. 'Those guards on the gate reminded me of the thugs at the railway station; they looked to be ex-military types. After my phone was tracked and they were sent to question us in York, I knew the kind of people we'd probably be dealing with. To be honest, I wasn't sure about bringing you along.'

'Hey, I can look after myself. I'm a big boy.' Watson grinned. 'Some girls say *very* big. Anyway, the garden party comes in handy again, doesn't it? No one is going to do anything to us with a load of journalists and television news people there.'

'That's true,' admitted Quist.

The river curled past a small wood and the grounds of Charlington Hall appeared on their left. A rhododendron thicket grew along the banking with a white marquee beyond this. Recalling the satellite view, Quist decided the tall row of shrubbery had been planted to screen buildings of some sort from the water. Luckily there was a jetty near the huge tent with steps leading up to the lawns and, luckier still, there were no security staff or other people watching. Killing the motor and drifting up to the pier, Quist jumped out and had just finished tethering the boat to a post when two large characters in tuxedos hurried down the steps.

'Shit,' whispered Watson. 'We've got a welcoming

committee.'

'What the fuck do you think you're doing?' demanded one of the men.

Quist sighed. 'I'm tying up my boat,' he said. 'I believe *mooring* is the correct nautical term.'

'This is private property,' snarled the security guard. The pair marched along the jetty and loomed aggressively over him. 'Get back in, turn around and fuck off right now. Do you understand?'

'Your colleague on the front gate imparted almost identical advice.' The detective nodded. 'You obviously attended the same etiquette class.' Stretching out his arms in an exaggerated yawn, he snatched both their heads and swiftly cracked them together. The unconscious pair crumpled into an untidy heap on the wooden boards.

'Bloody hell,' hissed Watson, shocked. He lowered his sunglasses, looking around to ensure no one had seen, then watched as the men were quickly dragged along the pier and dumped out of sight beneath a weeping willow.

'I shouldn't feel too sorry for them,' said Quist opening their jackets. 'From the slight bulging in the material beneath their left armpits, I deduced they were armed.' He tossed two Glock automatics into the river. 'They can't have known handguns are illegal in Britain.'

'Yeah.' His assistant grinned nervously. 'The authorities ought to tell people these things.'

'No need for these either.' Both guards sported communication earpieces and, tugging them out, Quist threw their radio sets into the water, before shrugging his tweed jacket straight, adjusting his tie and climbing the steps to the lawn. 'Come on. Try not to appear furtive. We're members of the press, remember, and we're here by invite.'

Watson followed, nervous excitement quickening his

heartrate as he saw the small groups of people chatting, smoking and drinking champagne on the lawn. The majority, he guessed were inside the large marquee. He strolled casually between them with Quist, gazing at the tent. Any bigger, he decided, and he'd expect to find trapeze artists and lion tamers inside. Charlington Hall stood beyond the marquee, larger and much grander than the houses he'd seen along the river.

'Wow, just look at that,' he whispered. 'I'm betting the owners of this place will be no strangers to croquet, butlers and offshore tax havens.'

'Very true,' said Quist. 'But it would appear the press conference is being held in the tent.'

'Let's check it out,' said Watson. They headed for the marquee entrance, then spotted the security personnel and stopped. 'Shit! They have metal detectors.'

'Unfortunately, they do,' murmured Quist. He watched the burly men running handheld scanners over the entrants, then glanced down as his assistant pretended to fasten his trainer. 'What are you doing?'

'Hiding my SAS knife down my sock,' whispered Watson, winking. 'They won't find it there.'

'You brought that stupid thing?' Quist sighed and shook his head. 'Metal detectors are the least of our worries. The guards on the front gate mentioned security passes and all the people going into the tent have them hanging around their necks.'

'Ladies and gentlemen,' called out one of the staff. 'The press conference is about to begin. If you'd all like to make your way inside, please.'

'So what do we do?' asked Watson.

'We do *this*.' He led Watson around the side of the tent, pressed his ear to the fabric at various points and listened. 'The sound is muffled here,' he said, quietly.

'Which means?'

'There's evidently something between this section of canvas and the crowd inside. Make a peephole so I can check, would you?'

'With what?'

'With what?' Quist closed his eyes. 'How about the SAS knife?'

'Oh, suddenly it's not so stupid, eh?' Smirking, Watson cut a two-inch slit and waited as the detective peered through.

'I was right,' said Quist. 'Slice it open right here so we can get through.'

Watson cut a waist-high slit and returned the knife to his sock as Quist wriggled through the opening. The pair appeared in the tent behind a stand of tall display boards, erected to show advertising stills for the new Ligeia album. They shuffled along the rear of them, emerged around the side of the exhibit and quickly mingled with the crowd, the teenager slipping off his sunglasses.

A stage had been erected at the end of the tent with a vast blow-up photograph of the new album behind. Shane Guevara, *Red Globe's* Entertainment Director, sat on this raised platform with Colonel Adler, but Watson only had eyes for the petite girl in the sparkly white mini dress who sat between them. His mouth became dry, he trembled with nervous excitement and his heart raced. *He was in a tent with Ligeia. He was in a fucking tent with Ligeia, standing a mere twenty feet from her.*

'Do me a favour, Watson,' murmured Quist, glancing at him and hearing his panting. 'Try not to faint.'

* * * *

161

Chapter 24

'Yes, *the Music of Sound* is the new album,' said Shane Guevara. Gesturing to the enormous photograph of Ligeia that served as a stage backdrop, he smiled excitedly at the marquee tent audience. 'We can see the cover right here and it's a stunning picture, isn't it? Audio specialists claim that all sound contains a form of music if we listen hard enough, but with Ligeia's voice we don't need to listen *too* hard.'

The nodding crowd laughed, but Watson didn't hear it. He didn't hear the Entertainment Director, he hadn't heard the short welcoming speech or the first three press questions; he was too busy staring open-mouthed at Ligeia to hear *anything*. Cross-legged, relaxed and smiling sweetly, the petite singer sat on her white leather chair beneath the bright stage lighting. Quist was more interested in the two people seated behind the microphones on either side of her: Guevara and the attractive dark-haired woman on the right. Ligeia's manager wore a smart indigo suit and black satin patch over her left eye. *So this was Irana Adler, the person who sent the two heavies to question him in York?*

'Ligeia, are you looking forward to the American tour?' enquired a journalist in the crowd.

'Absolutely,' said Adler. 'The first concert is in Miami and then Ligeia flies to San Francisco. The launch party for the new album will be in Los Angeles next Saturday. America excites her greatly and she'll be living there from now on.'

'Where in the States?' asked a voice.

'Near the ocean in Los Angeles,' said Adler. 'Ligeia loves the ocean.'

Quist looked around with bemused interest. The press obviously didn't mind the girl's manager giving banal answers to their questions. They seemed thrilled just to have Ligeia sitting close like this for their flashing cameras. *Maybe her silence was supposed to add to her mystique.*

'Your British fans will be so sorry to see you go,' called out another reporter. 'We like to feel you belong here, like the Beatles and the Stones. When are you leaving us?'

'As you know, Ligeia plays the O2 at ten o'clock tonight,' said Adler. 'We fly to Miami immediately afterwards. She can't wait to perform there and meet all her American fans.'

'Don't go,' shouted a female journalist. 'We love you, Ligeia.'

Adler laughed and nodded. 'Ligeia loves you too. Could we have another question about the new album, please?'

Quist raised a hand and Adler gestured in his direction. 'Ligeia, you're a wonderful artist,' he said. 'Everyone is fascinated by your amazing voice.'

The singer peered at him, frowning slightly.

'We'd all love to hear you answer these questions yourself. How do you feel about someone constantly speaking for you as if you're their puppet?'

'Oh, dear!' Adler nodded to one of her security, who moved quickly through the crowd towards the detective. 'The term *gutter press* springs to mind,' she said. 'I wonder if we could have a more *relevant* question about the *Music of Sound*?'

Ligeia's eyes narrowed as she searched her memory. 'Hello again,' she said, smiling warmly at Quist.

A large man in a tuxedo appeared behind the detective and snatched his arm. 'You're leaving,' he grunted. 'Now.' He noticed there was no security pass around Quist's neck. The black youth beside him also lacked identification and he grabbed his denim jacket. 'Come on, both of you.'

'But I didn't say anything,' pleaded Watson. *This character appeared to have been hired from the same Rent-a-Thug agency as the huge men policing the front gate and the ones on the pier.* 'Can't I just stay here and watch Ligeia?'

The pair were brusquely marched to the exit as Adler continued to answer press questions. Quist glanced back to see the Colonel staring at him as she spoke.

'Where are your passes?' snapped the security guard. He pushed them both out of the tent and poked the detective's chest. 'They're supposed to be hung around your neck.'

'We've already been through this,' sighed Quist. 'We're from *Music Today* magazine and our passes didn't arrive. We brought all the other documentation and showed it to your colleagues on the front entrance.'

'So show *me* this paperwork.'

'It's still at the front gate, along with our identification.'

The guard scowled. 'That doesn't sound right.'

'Well, I'm obviously unfamiliar with the rules here,' said Quist, 'but how else would we have been allowed in?'

'I need to check this.' The man turned to leave. 'Wait here.'

'Oh, well done, Guv,' whispered Watson, glaring. 'Yeah, brilliant work. There I was, less than twenty feet from my all-time favourite pop star and you managed to get us thrown out in the first five minutes.'

Quist took two glasses of champagne from the tray of a passing waitress and handed one to Watson. 'Here you go,' he said, sipping the drink. 'Mmh, it's rather good, but I'm afraid it isn't lager.' He lit a cigarette and frowned thoughtfully. '*Hello again*? What did Ligeia mean by that?'

'Well, I'm no brilliant consultant detective like some I could mention, but it sounds to me as if she's met you before.'

'But she hasn't.' Quist drew slowly on the smoke. 'Having said that, close and devoid of make-up, her face did seem vaguely familiar just now. I've seen her on the television, of course, but I've never taken much interest. Whenever she appears, I switch channels.'

The teenager shook his head. 'Weirdo.'

'She looks to be in her early twenties, so if we *have* met, it must have been in the past few years, but I simply can't place her.'

A girl appeared by the detective's side. Very attractive with short silvery hair, she wore a blue mini dress and looked him over with open interest.

'Good afternoon,' he said. 'Can I help you, young lady? Are you with the press?'

Shaking her head, she touched her mouth and signed something. Quist was amazed to see Watson tuck his champagne glass under his left arm and sign back to her.

'Good Lord!' said Quist, watching them silently chat. 'So you know sign language?'

'Well, it's easy to see why you became a detective,' said the youth. 'You're a natural with the deduction shit. Yeah, I grew up with a cousin who's deaf and I once had a deaf girlfriend. Believe me, I know some pretty juicy phrases…'

'Let's not go there.' Quist puffed his cigarette. 'What is she saying?'

'Her name's Elva. She's a friend of Ligeia's and she's pleased that someone else can understand her at last.'

'Good afternoon.' Quist smiled pleasantly and shook her hand. 'I assume you're the young lady who was in the Edinburgh club with Ligeia?'

Elva nodded.

'You met someone named Rex Grant there? He's a good friend of ours. You wouldn't happen to know where he is?'

The girl spoke with Watson and he turned back to Quist. 'Good news, Guv. She says he's here.'

'Splendid,' said Quist. 'We'd very much like to see him.'

'I'm amazed,' said Watson. 'You can't sign?'

'Evidently not.'

'Cool.' The teenager smirked. 'What with your age, I thought you knew everything and now you're telling me there's something I can do that you can't?'

'Oh, I'm sure there are lots of things.' Quist took a drink of champagne and smiled sarcastically. 'You once told me you can do 'wheelies' on a motorcycle and double back-flips on a skateboard.'

Elva laughed silently, tugged at Watson's arm and signed again.

'She says she likes you and she's sure Ligeia will too. She says you're funny...' He raised his eyebrows. 'Er, but she also likes you because you're the same as Rex.'

'What?' Quist cleared his throat. 'What does that mean?'

'Well, she can't mean you look like a young movie star. She can't mean you're as thick as a builder's sandwich, so that only leaves...'

'Good afternoon, gentlemen.' Colonel Adler strolled from the marquee tent with two men. 'I understand there's a problem with your security passes? I'm the director of *Red Globe Management.*'

Quist turned and raised a curious eyebrow. 'Yes, I was listening to you on the stage. Are you telling me they've sent Ligeia's manager to handle a minor security problem?'

'I'm establishing if it *is* minor.' She smiled and held out a hand. 'Colonel Irana Adler.'

'Pleased to meet you,' said Quist. He shook hands, eyeing the muscular men behind her. This pair appeared quite different to the guard who'd quizzed them over the missing passes and the other security personnel they'd met here. Black uniforms instead of tuxedos and a professional demeanour suggested they were trained military. 'I'm Bernard Quist and this is...'

'Ah, so *you're* Mister Quist,' said Adler. 'You rang my press office enquiring over the whereabouts of Rex Grant.'

'That's right.'

The Colonel turned to Elva. 'I need to speak to these gentlemen, my dear, so why don't you run along and watch

Ligeia?'

The young girl signed goodbye to Watson and vanished into the tent.

'I ran checks on you,' said Adler. 'It seems you're a private investigator based in the northern city of York.'

'Consultant detective,' corrected Quist, finishing his drink.

'Indeed?' Adler smiled at the teenager. 'And according to my information, this must be John Watson, your sole employee.'

He grinned. 'Yeah, that must be me.'

'You ran checks on me?' Quist dropped his cigarette and died it out underfoot. 'I feel honoured that someone should show such an interest. Speaking of employees, two of your people were good enough to meet us from the train in York yesterday afternoon. They wanted to know why I'd phoned your press office.'

'Yes, I understand they're in hospital.' Adler frowned with sham concern. 'They obviously met with some accident after leaving you.'

Quist nodded. 'Obviously.'

'I sent them to speak with you because I was curious as to your interest in Rex. According to my press office, you claimed you were searching for him. I'm now even *more* curious about Ligeia's interest in you. Where have you met before?'

'We haven't,' said Quist.

'That's odd, isn't it? Because she said *hello again*, which would suggest otherwise.'

'She's clearly mistaken.'

The Colonel answered her vibrating phone. 'I see,' she said, slipping it back into her pocket. 'So you're looking for Rex, are you?' Politely taking their empty champagne glasses, she handed them to a nearby waitress. 'I can't imagine how you entered this place without security clearance, but your search is over. He's staying here with us for a few days.'

'You make that sound like the most natural thing in the

world,' said Quist. 'The thing is, we both know that isn't so.'

Yeah,' said Watson. 'The cops are after him and, for once, it has nothing to do with him speeding.'

'Yes, a stupid misunderstanding,' said Adler. 'One that will soon be resolved. Come along. We'll go speak with him.'

Quist and Watson followed the woman across the lawn, the detective glancing over his shoulder to see the two men walking behind them.

'What exactly is going on?' asked Watson. 'Do the cops know Rex is here?'

'They soon will,' said Adler. 'Unfortunately, Rex has found himself implicated in that terrible Edinburgh murder, but very shortly he'll be able to prove his innocence. I'll let him explain it all to you.'

'Are you really a woman Colonel?' asked the youth.

She smiled. 'Funnily enough, our mutual friend Rex asked me the same thing. Yes, I was a Colonel in the German army.'

'Interesting,' said Quist, gesturing to the uniformed pair behind him. 'Would I be correct in assuming these men are also military?'

'Almost correct,' said Adler. 'All my men are ex-military.'

'Hey, you've got a zoo,' said Watson, rounding the rhododendron hedge and seeing the row of cages. He looked closer. 'Er, but apart from a few parrots, a completely *empty* zoo, apparently. Yeah, that's useful.'

'Swings and roundabouts, as they say,' laughed Adler. 'No animals, but no feeding bills either.' She led them to the long menagerie building that ran behind the enclosures and opened the door to the rear corridor. 'This way, please.'

Quist looked inside. The passage ran the full length of the building, broken into short sections by internal doors. This first section had two metal doors on the left, both with small barred widows. He deduced these were the indoor quarters which animals could access from their outside pens.

'You're telling me Rex is in here?' he asked.

'The menagerie isn't completely empty,' said Adler, ushering them in. 'We have a tiger and Rex is helping the vet with him.'

The detective smiled grimly and strolled in. This sounded like nonsense, but he decided to play along. Hopefully this woman would drop the genteel act once inside and reveal her true intentions. They were now out of sight of the press conference guests, but he could easily overcome Adler and her henchmen if necessary.

'As I said, I have to check all security breaches.' Adler closed the door behind them. 'You have no entry passes and I need to be certain about anyone who is allowed near Ligeia.'

'You could let us *really* near,' said Watson, hopefully. 'Anyone can see we're nice guys, especially me.'

'Really? I understand you were questioned by the police several months ago in relation to certain deaths in York.'

'We assisted with their enquiries,' said Quist, suspiciously. 'We weren't charged with anything, but how could you know this?'

'Friends in the police has access to all the data. By the way, that phone call I just answered was my Sergeant informing me that someone has attacked two security personnel on the riverbank.' Adler turned to her men. 'Code six.'

The pair instantly whipped out automatic pistols and trained them on Quist and Watson.

'Code six?' repeated the teenager, gulping. He backed up against the passage door and eyed the guns nervously. 'I don't like the sound of *code six*. Don't you have any friendlier codes?'

'I expected something like this,' said Quist, moving in front of his assistant and tensing his muscles. *He could protect Watson with his body. Being shot would be painful, but it wouldn't harm him.* 'So now you've shown your true self, perhaps you'd like to tell us what you've done with Rex and what happened in Edinburgh? Where is he?'

'All in good time,' said Adler. 'You interest my Padre, Mister Quist, and that means you interest me.'

'You have a Padre?' Quist raised his eyebrows. 'How strange that I should interest someone I've never met.'

'He has certain supernatural abilities and he's able to sense things. He handled something of yours and picked up your esoteric vibrations.'

'You mean a clairvoyant?' asked Watson, laughing uneasily. Slowly slipping a hand behind his back, he tried the passage door handle, but it was locked. 'You've been listening to some fucking psychic and now you have blokes waving guns about?'

'What is it about you, Mister Quist?' The Colonel gazed at him. 'What can the Padre sense? Are you like Rex Grant?'

Watson glanced at the detective. 'Like Rex? You mean an arsehole?'

Adler chuckled. 'I think Mister Quist knows exactly what I mean.'

'Oh?' The detective eyed her coldly, working out the best way to tackle these three. 'And what do you *think* you know?'

'I know enough to plan ahead and cover all possibilities. I bought Charlington Hall fully-furnished and that included a small silver collection. Being military, we have the equipment to manufacture ammunition and last night I had my armourer melt part of the collection and produce several dozen bullets.'

'Really?' murmured Quist, stiffening.

'Yes, really. These weapons contain silver bullets.' Adler nodded to one of her men. 'Search them and empty their pockets.'

The pair were swiftly patted down and Watson's phone was taken.

'Sorry to be so brusque and impolite,' said Adler. 'I'm

170

rather busy with the press at the moment, as you've seen. We'll have a chat later to establish what you know, and more to the point, who and *what* you really are.'

The metal doors off the corridor had keys in their locks and the Colonel opened the closest. The large empty chamber was obviously designed as indoor accommodation for an animal. The door had a barred inspection hatch, the concrete floor sloped imperceptibly to a small drainage grating, and a sliding metal gate provided access to the outdoor cage enclosure. Quist noticed the heavy padlock securing it.

'I'm told a bear once lived in here,' said Adler. 'It's now been refurbished as the guest accommodation and you're the first guests. Enjoy your stay.'

'Thanks,' said Watson. 'How do we call room service?'

* * * *

Chapter 25

Rex had spent most of the night unconscious in a menagerie enclosure identical to Quist and Watson's *guest accommodation*, but his system was now clear of tranquiliser. His chamber had been tastefully furnished with an inflatable mattress and a plastic patio chair on which he sat brooding. The central floor grate was obviously intended for incontinent animals, but he'd discovered it worked equally well for humans. Plastic water bottles and cigarettes had been provided and a guard had called earlier with a lunch tray of sandwiches and, bizarrely, a flute of champagne. Rex wore a black shirt and trousers provided by the security staff, his own clothes having been ripped apart when he transformed. The more he thought about it, the more he wanted to rip his captors apart – Lafont, Gruner, but most of all that one-eyed bitch Adler.

The silence was broken by the sound of the Colonel's voice. 'How ironic that this was originally constructed to house a pair of wolves.'

Rex looked up from his chair to see her peering through the barred panel in the door. He glared, but didn't answer.

'You really impressed me last night,' said Adler. 'Sorry about my Sergeant punching you.'

'Don't worry about it,' said Rex, tartly. He lit a cigarette and blew smoke through a gritted smile. 'My broken jaw healed and, as you can see, my teeth grew back.'

'So chewing your lunch was no problem?' Adler nodded to the empty plate. 'I had them bring you a selection of smoked salmon, cucumber and ham from the garden party, along with a glass of Bollinger. How was it?'

'I've had worse.'

Rex had removed the meat and tasted the bread to ensure the kitchen used margarine, not butter. He knew not to eat animal products, but had risked the fish. Rightly or wrongly, mostly

172

wrongly, he'd never viewed fish as animals.

'Let's open this so we can speak better.' Adler tugged back a bolt and lowered the small panel of metal bars. 'The garden party is over and you'll be pleased to know it was a success. The media have now left and they're raving over Ligeia's new album.'

'Whoopee!'

The Colonel laughed. 'Your private detective friends Quist and Watson called looking for you a couple of hours ago and...'

Rex stood up. 'Do they know I'm here? Where are they?'

'They're currently in a room just like this one further along the passage, but it's pointless shouting to them. You're separated by two soundproof corridor doors. They're an unusual pair, aren't they?'

'If you say so.'

'Not as unusual as *you* though.' Adler gazed admiringly at the young man. 'A genuine werewolf; how incredible. Until last night I honestly believed such creatures were the stuff of legend.'

'Yeah, you know what I am.' Rex drew angrily on his cigarette. 'You must also know now that I won't be going along with your crazy plans. I won't be coming to America as Ligeia's paid boyfriend, so why don't you just let me go and fuck off there after your concert tonight? You forget you saw me transform and I'll forget all about you kidnapping me.'

'Oh, Rex, you know that's impossible. Besides, although you might forgive me for bringing you here, I doubt you'd ever forgive me for Charlotte Michie's unfortunate death. Despite the fact that it was Ollie who killed her, I feel you still hold me responsible.'

Rex bristled with fury at the thought of Charlotte, unconsciously crushing the cigarette in his fingers.

'I've had all night to debate upon this and I've altered my *crazy plans* somewhat. Apart from the traditional mythology, I don't know much about lycanthropy, so the Padre has filled me in

173

with a few facts. I now have several weapons loaded with silver bullets. This one for example.'

Rex stepped back as a handgun appeared in the hatchway, the muzzle trained on his crotch.

'I need answers,' said Adler. 'I'm sorry, but if you don't tell me what I want to know, I'll shoot you. I won't aim for your heart or head, just your legs. I haven't a clue what will happen. The silver may kill you, or the wound may heal; I honestly don't know. Do we really want to find out, or are you going to be sensible and talk to me?'

Rex stood his ground and silently lit another cigarette. He knew he should be scared, but all he felt was mounting anger. He also knew the full moon was rising. Even indoors, at this time of the month he could sense when the sun was low on the horizon and the moon was appearing.

'I'm far from naive,' said Adler. 'I've always known that Ligeia wasn't a normal human. This uncanny ability she has to charm people with her voice is obviously supernatural. The Padre explained this to me, but he's never been able to understand her power. He doesn't know why people slavishly buy her music and obey her when she speaks in a certain way. Doctor Roylott fitted my team with specialised audio implants in their ears for protection, but you don't need such devices. Now I know how you're able to resist her; you're a werewolf. It seems other supernatural creatures such as yourself aren't affected.'

Rex nodded slowly. That certainly explained a few things.

'The police interviewed us after the Edinburgh murder, but Ligeia asked them to let us leave. She told them the brief statement she'd given was enough and they accepted that. A wonderful talent, don't you think?'

'Yeah, wonderful,' drawled Rex. 'She must be great for getting rid of salesmen and religious nutters when they knock at your door.'

174

'Absolutely.' Adler laughed. 'But I'm here to talk about *you*, not Ligeia. Your strength impressed me last night. You threw Gruner across the room as though he were nothing. I like that strength and I like your power. Tell me, can you change any time you feel like it?'

Rex snorted and smoked his cigarette.

'You *will* answer and you'll answer truthfully. I'm remarkably adept at spotting deception. If I believe you're lying, I'll shoot you in the kneecap.' The Colonel aimed her gun. 'There will be no second warning. Now can you change at any time?'

'Yes,' hissed Rex. 'Any time between sunset and sunrise.'

'Do you control the wolf, or does it control you?'

'It's my mind in a wolf's body; it isn't like those horror films. I don't go running wildly around villages eating peasants, if that's what you mean.'

'Good to know.' Adler smiled. 'Well, if *you* can control the beast, it can't be too difficult.'

Rex pulled a sarcastic face at the insult as the Colonel took out her phone and thumbed a number.

'Bring her in, would you?' said Adler. Pocketing the mobile, she turned back to her captive. 'I've witnessed your amazing recuperative powers. Ollie's blade had no effect, but what *does* harm you?'

'Silver doesn't do me any favours.' Rex gestured to the gun. 'But you seem to have worked that out for yourself.'

He heard the corridor door open as Gruner arrived with Elva.

'Ah, there you are, my dear.' The Colonel took the tiny girl's hand and drew her to the enclosure door where Rex could see her through the hatch. She gestured for the Sergeant to leave and smiled warmly. 'Do you know how I'm so successful, Rex? If I see an opportunity, I always take it. No debating. I take it and deliberate later.'

175

'You've told me this already.' Rex eyed Elva warily, wondering why Adler had asked for her. 'You obviously spout that same shit whenever you can.'

'You answered my questions when I threatened you with the gun. Call me intuitive, but I didn't think you'd comply with my next instruction without additional motivation.' Adler rolled up her left sleeve and pulled Elva close to her. The girl's face contorted in silent pain.

'What are you doing?' Spitting out his cigarette and rushing to the hatch, Rex shoved his face through to see Elva's arm being twisted up her back. 'Let her go, you mad bitch.'

'An arm for an arm.' Adler shoved her free hand through the aperture. 'Bite mine, or I'll break hers.'

'Are you insane?' shouted Rex. 'I can't do that.'

'Do it,' snarled Adler. She twisted cruelly and Elva bent forward in agony, silently sobbing. 'Do it now, or I swear I'll tear this bone from the socket. Do it *now*.'

Rex snatched the offered arm and sank his teeth into the flesh. The Colonel grunted at the pain and swiftly withdrew it.

'Thank you.' She released Elva, who ran out weeping. 'There, we'll see how that goes. If it doesn't work, nothing ventured, nothing gained, eh?'

Rex ran to snatch his water bottle, his mind spinning at the enormity of what had just taken place. Not wishing to accidentally swallow any blood, he spat out several mouthfuls of water and made a huge effort to quell the anger and think straight. *The bite probably wouldn't work while he was in human form. Then again, why didn't he bite her entire fucking arm clean off? If he'd had the time to transform, he would have done. He hated this woman.*

'You have no idea how to handle this,' he whispered, furiously. 'You just did it?'

'I've had all night to think about it.' Adler inspected the bloody marks in her flesh. 'Mmmh, nice, neat bite. I see you have good, expensive dentistry to go with those male model looks. As I said, if I see an opportunity, I take it. It's made me one of the wealthiest women in the world.'

'You don't know what you've done.'

'Of course I do,' hissed Adler. 'I know exactly what I've done. If this works, I've gained your strength, your power and those amazing recuperative abilities. Will my eye grow back?'

'Bad luck,' growled Rex. 'If it works at all, you'll remain as you are at the time of the bite. In your case, a one-eyed fucking lunatic.'

'Thank you.' Adler laughed loudly, slammed the barred panel shut and bolted it. 'Thank you for your help, Rex.'

* * * *

Further along the menagerie building, Quist sat on the concrete floor in a lotus position with his back against the wall and legs crossed beneath him. Concentrating upon his Scheherazade melody, he regulated his deep breathing, but Watson's profanities and grunts of frustration made it difficult. The detective turned to watch as his assistant squatted by the door, pushing one of his knife tools into the keyhole and turning again and again. Watson had tried moving the barred hatch, but it was bolted from the outside. A padlock secured the metal gate from this chamber into the outdoor animal enclosure, but it too seemed impervious to cheap SAS knives that were made in China

'I thought I had it then,' muttered the youth, twisting and pulling. 'It wouldn't hurt for you to help me instead of sitting on your arse like Buddha.'

'The yoga and breathing exercises control my emotions,' sighed the detective. 'I can feel the full moon rising and you wouldn't want to be locked in with an angry werewolf, would you? I honestly believed I had the advantage earlier. I allowed that woman to lead us into this building in the hope that she'd show her hand and explain about Rex. I never, for one second, expected her

177

to be armed with silver bullets. I can only deduce that she's discovered his secret.'

'Instead of sulking over it, why not try and deduce a way out of here?'

'You're wasting your time with that knife. That's an advanced security lock and I saw a bolt on the outside too.'

'What if they didn't use the bolt? Maybe they're not as clever as they think. I hid the knife down my sock and they never looked there when they frisked us. Besides, trying to pick the lock takes my mind off this and stops me crapping myself. It's better than just chucking in the towel.'

'You're confusing patience with surrender,' said Quist, climbing to his feet. 'I'm awaiting darkness. During this lunar phase, I can always sense when the sun is setting and that's when I'll get us out. I noticed the keys to these enclosures are left in the doors. If I can bend those bars in that hatch, I should be able to reach out and unlock it.'

The teenager leapt away startled as the hatch in question suddenly slid down with a clang. He looked up, his eyes widening to see two men in bowler hats and bow ties peering through the aperture. The fat one sported a tuft of moustache and both smiled amiably. Sometimes visual information is too confusing for the brain to process and the mind momentarily locks up. Watson's head felt numb as he stared blankly at Laurel and Hardy. Quist had seen many strange things over the centuries, but even *his* mouth fell open.

'Mmmh, just the kind of young black guy I like to eat,' said Laurel, licking his lips and somewhat ruining the illusion.

'What the *fuck*...' whispered Watson. Whoever these men were, they were identical to the celebrated movie comedians. 'What in the name of...'

'Hello,' said Quist, warily.

'Good afternoon,' said Hardy. The visitors politely tipped

their hats. 'So you're the Colonel's new guests?'

'Is it me?' asked Watson, staring blankly. 'Or has this just got really weird?'

'Very nice to meet you,' said Hardy. 'I'm sure we'll be seeing more of one another.'

'I'd like to see a little *more* of the kid,' said Laurel, running an appreciative eye over Watson's trim body. 'He looks delicious.'

'Stan and Ollie?' Quist moved to the hatch for a closer look. 'So what are you two doing here? Moving a piano? Selling fish? I've seen all your movies and I have to admit, I'm a bit of a fan.'

'Well, that's good to know,' said Hardy. 'It's always nice to meet admirers.'

'Why not come in for a chat?'

'No, I don't think so.' Laurel slammed the barred window shut. 'We just wanted to see you. We'll be getting acquainted soon enough.'

The pair headed away down the passage laughing.

'I don't believe what I just saw,' stammered Watson. 'Who the fuck were they?'

'I saw the size of Oliver Hardy,' said Quist. 'I don't know how they did it, but something tells me we just met the killer Alistair Ramson.'

* * * *

Chapter 26

The Colonel strolled into Charlington Hall fingering the antiseptic dressing on her forearm. The pain seemed to be receding, which was an excellent sign. If this bite healed as quickly as she anticipated, it meant her impulsive gamble had paid off.

Guevara hurried out of the library. 'Gruner has paid off your extra security,' he said. 'They've packed and they're leaving.'

'Good.' Adler nodded. 'We're finished with Charlington. We won't be returning after tonight's concert.'

'There could be a problem with that. Ligeia's in there and she's upset that your team won't allow her to see Grant.'

'Really?' Adler smiled thinly. 'She doesn't know it yet, but she won't be seeing him again.' *As soon as it was certain this wolf bite had worked, Grant would be getting the double treat of a silver bullet in the head and an evening swim in the Thames. Alternate lovers could soon be found for Ligeia: young men who would relish the chance to sleep with her and who would have far less baggage and no unpredictable lupine streak.*

'She keeps asking about the other guy who gate-crashed the garden party,' said Guevara. 'We have the concert in a few hours and she's unhappy.'

'Don't worry. We have plenty of time to lighten her mood. The helicopter is picking us up at nine and taking us directly to the O2 at Greenwich.'

'Can't you let her see this private eye? That will cheer her up.'

The Colonel snorted. 'I don't believe that would be wise right now. I have a little surprise for her instead.'

'If her mood doesn't improve, cancelation is always an option. We can say she's ill.'

'Where's your professional pride, Shane?' chuckled Adler. 'The final sell-out gig in Britain? I really don't think so. Those tickets retailed at obscene prices and I've no intention of reimbursing anyone.'

Guevara shook his head. 'The sales from *Water Music* could buy a country. *The Music of Sound* is the most anticipated album in history and it will sell even more. It's ready to launch so it won't matter if she misses *one* concert. Do you know how unbelievably wealthy we are? These inflated concert tickets are bringing in…'

'You say *we*.' Adler stared icily. 'I made you a multi-millionaire, Shane, but I'm looking towards a great deal more. I intend to be one of the most powerful and wealthiest women on the planet. Go make the final preparations and leave this to me.' Adopting a wide grin, she opened the library door and strolled in to see Ligeia sitting on one of the couches.

The singer looked up with a sullen pout. 'Your friends won't let me see Rex.'

'I'm sorry, my dear.' The Colonel sat beside her and wrapped a motherly arm around Ligeia's shoulders. 'He's already left for your concert and he's really excited. There isn't going to be room in the helicopter so he's driving there instead.'

'I don't understand why he had to stay in the zoo building. Why wasn't he here in the house with me? I wanted to sleep with him last night.'

'He said he had a bad headache and besides, he loved it in there. I think he likes Mister Tigsy.'

'I wanted to see him before he left.' Ligeia frowned. 'Where's the nice man from the tent? I want to see him too.'

'Ah, Bernard Quist? Yes, he *is* a nice man, isn't he? How do you know him?'

Ligeia folded her arms, her sullen pout suggesting she didn't want to answer questions.

'I'll see to it, I promise you,' said the Colonel, standing up. 'But first I've organised something for you. A little treat.'

Ligeia watched moodily as she opened the library door and gestured for Laurel and Hardy to enter.

'Time to start earning your keep.' Adler leant close to Hardy's ear, her voice a threatening whisper. 'Have you mastered it? Tell me you watched the recording and you know this.'

'Don't worry.' Laurel tried an American accent and lifted his bowler hat to scratch his head. 'We know it just fine, Miss Colonel, Ma'am.'

Adler returned to the unhappy girl, grinning widely. 'Surely you must trust me?' she said, squeezing her tiny shoulders again. 'You must know that everything I do has your best interests at heart. I've done so much for you, my dear. Look at this lovely house with its funfair and the wonderful river. I bought you Mister Tigsy, your beautiful tiger, and I arranged for your favourite silly men Laurel and Hardy to stay with us. Now, I'd like you to enjoy *this*.'

Ligeia watched curiously as the pair stood side by side in front of her.

Hardy began to sing. 'In the Blue Ridge Mountains of Virginia…'

'Oh yes.' Ligeia's face lit up. 'I love this so much. They sing it in that film.'

'That's right,' said Adler, holding her hand and smiling sweetly as Laurel joined in with the melody. 'Why don't we go to see the Blue Ridge Mountains when we live in America? There'll be rivers and lakes there and huge waterfalls.'

'And the ocean,' enthused Ligeia. 'You said we'd live by the ocean.'

'Yes, we will.' Adler glared at the two killers and nodded to their feet, reminding them to dance as they sang. 'We're going to be in a place called California with thundering waves right outside and sunsets over the sea.'

'It sounds lovely,' said Ligeia, listening to the song.

'It does, doesn't it?' Adler cuddled her. 'So do you think we'll have a lovely concert tonight?' she asked quietly.

'Yes, of course we will.'

'That's a good girl.' The Colonel kissed her cheek. 'We'll soon be having an exciting ride in a helicopter.'

'Again,' laughed Ligeia, as Laurel and Hardy came to the end of their dance routine.

'I'll leave you to enjoy this,' said Adler. Standing, she glanced meaningfully at the killers. 'Trust me. They'll sing and dance as many times as your little heart desires.'

Oblivious to her leaving, Ligeia watched the two men singing, clapping her hands joyfully. Elva slipped in from the hall, glancing behind and hurrying to the couch.

'She hurt me,' signed Elva. 'The Colonel really hurt me.'

'What?' Ligeia gasped. 'I'm sure it was a mistake.'

'No, she almost broke my arm.' Elva rubbed the tenderness and glanced at Laurel and Hardy. 'Ask them to go.'

'Will you leave us, please?' said Ligeia.

Thankful to stop dancing, the pair tipped their bowler hats and gave a forced smile before heading for the door.

'But I don't understand,' said Ligeia. 'Why would the Colonel hurt you? She's a nice lady. She gives us both nice things.'

'I don't believe she *is* a nice lady,' signed Elva. 'Not any more. She twisted my arm and she's keeping Rex locked up.'

'What do you mean? The Colonel said he'd left to see my concert.'

'No, she lied. I don't know why, but Rex is in a locked room in the menagerie. Those men who came to the tent are locked up there too.'

'Then we'll let them out,' said Ligeia. 'Come on. Let's go now.'

Elva shook her head. 'The Colonel and her friends wouldn't like that and they'd stop us,' she signed. 'You stay and I'll get Rex out. They don't bother to watch me.'

'And the other man too,' said Ligeia. 'The nice man from the boat.'

Elva frowned slightly. 'What boat?'

* * * *

Chapter 27

'Great plan, Guv,' said Watson, still attempting to pick the door lock with his knife. 'We sail into Charlington Hall, *literally* sail in, introduce ourselves and get shoved in a fucking cell. Yeah, as plans go, I can't see how we could have come up with anything better.'

Quist sat on the floor of the menagerie enclosure behind him, pondering over Laurel and Hardy and Ligeia's intriguing greeting. '*Sail in*?' he muttered, thoughtfully.

'They're obviously ahead of us.' The youth knelt on the tiles, twisting his can opener blade in the keyhole. 'The one-eyed bird was ready with silver bullets, so she obviously knows what she's dealing with. We came to help Rex. Hah! That's a laugh. These people have him and now they have us, so I'd say that ship has sailed. Do you think he's okay or...' Watson noticed the detective's stunned expression. 'Hey, what's wrong?'

'*Sailing in*?' repeated Quist. '*Ship*?' He smacked the palm of his hand to his brow. 'Good heavens, I don't believe this.'

Watson stood up. 'What?'

'Of course. I *have* met her before.'

'Ligeia? Seriously? You met the biggest pop star in the world and you managed to forget about it?'

'It was so long ago and such a brief *meeting*.' Quist rubbed his eyes and climbed to his feet. 'Remembering her face was the last thing on my mind that night. Her hair was blonde, as I recall, and very different; she wore it piled up as the fashion dictated back then.'

'Er...' Watson looked puzzled. 'The fashion back when?'

'1912. We were on the Titanic together.'

'Okay.' The teenager stared for several seconds. 'You *are* joking!'

'Do I look as if I'm joking?'

Watson continued his blank stare.

'She was in the restaurant.' Quist gazed at the floor, straining to remember the details. 'Later I helped her in the water.'

'Titanic?'

'I don't think she knew my name.'

'Er, right. Okay, right.' Watson cleared his throat. 'Would that matter? I thought you keep changing your name?'

'I do, but I rotate identities. I was Bernard Quist at that time too.'

'So you were on the Titanic and you survived?' The stunned youth allowed it to sink in and grinned nervously. 'What did you do? The doggy paddle?'

Quist smiled tightly. 'That horrific night was nothing to joke about, Watson. I knew the cold water wouldn't kill me, but it closed down my system and I appeared lifeless. I managed to lash myself to driftwood before I passed out and it kept me afloat until the rescue ship Carpathia found me.'

'Bloody hell, Guv. This is unbelievable.'

'I eventually woke in their makeshift morgue on the way to New York. Ligeia must have been aboard the Carpathia too, but I never saw her again.'

'You're telling me Ligeia was on the fucking Titanic? So that means...' He shook his head. 'She looks about twenty, but it must make her...'

'Well over one-hundred years old. Yes, she's obviously a supernatural creature of some sort.'

'Maybe a werewolf?'

'No, I don't think so,' murmured Quist. 'I remember now, she was travelling with some Scotsman who bragged about making a fortune from her. He was probably exploiting her singing talents, just as this Adler woman is now doing.'

'Ligeia was on the Titanic,' repeated Watson, still attempting to process the information. 'Jesus!'

'The man was taking her to America from Scotland. If he'd been profiting from her on the stages up there…' Quist thought for a moment. 'Is that why she wanted to go to that awful Edinburgh nightclub? Did she perform there when it was the old music hall?'

'Unbelievable,' muttered Watson, shaking himself and returning to fiddle with the lock. 'I honestly can't get my head around this.'

'Stand back, said Quist. 'The sun has now set. If I transform, I should be able to bend those bars.'

'No need.' Watson's face lit up as the lock clicked and the door opened slightly. 'How about that? I did it.'

Elva opened the door further.

'Oh!' Watson sagged. '*You* did it.'

'Thank you, Elva,' whispered Quist, hurrying into the corridor and looking around. 'Are you alone? Why did you let us out?'

The girl signed to Watson.

'She says these are bad people.' He laughed quietly. 'Hey, who'd have guessed that, Guv? She says Ligeia wanted her to let us out and told her to get Rex out too.'

'Do they know you're here?' asked Quist. 'Did anyone see you come here?'

She shook her head.

'Where is he?' asked Watson. 'Where's Rex?'

Elva pulled at the teenager's arm and led them through the doors to the other makeshift cell further down the menagerie corridor. Alerted by the sound of footsteps, Rex stood looking through the hatch and grinned to see them.

'We've had a word with the governor,' whispered Watson through the bars. 'Good news – your parole has come through.'

'Am I glad to see you.' Rex laughed nervously. 'I take it you've been looking for me?'

'Yeah. Everyone thinks you killed someone, but we knew

that was crap.' The teenager unlocked the door. 'We realised you had to be in trouble.'

'I had nothing to do with that murder is Scotland,' said Rex, hurrying out. 'Ligeia's manager is responsible for all this. The people here are absolutely crazy.'

'But evidently not *this* young lady,' said Quist. 'You have Elva to thank for your freedom. She released us from another animal enclosure further along the passage.'

Rex smiled at her, running an eye over her blue mini dress and recalling their night in Edinburgh. The current situation was desperate, but old habits were difficult to supress. 'I've been their prisoner for three days,' he said. 'Have you met Colonel Adler? That one-eyed lunatic will do anything to keep Ligeia happy, including kidnapping me. She even has Laurel and Hardy here because Ligeia likes them.'

'Yeah, they called on us,' said Watson, following Quist to the external door. 'They're identical to the real thing. How's that possible?'

'Adler and her doctor can alter faces with drugs of some sort. By the way, Hardy was the one who killed Charlotte in Edinburgh. He has a knife contraption up his sleeve and...' He recalled it sinking into his heart. 'It's pretty lethal.'

'I'd already deduced that,' whispered Quist, opening the door slightly and checking for guards in the darkening grounds outside. He turned to Elva. 'Why would the Colonel do that? Why did she kidnap Rex and why does she want Laurel and Hardy here?'

She signed to Watson.

'They make Ligeia happy,' said Watson. 'She only sings when she's happy and content. When she's sad, there's no magic in her voice and no one listens to her.'

'Magic in her voice?' Quist peeped through the door crack again, sniffing the twilight air. 'I see. Add that to her longevity and this is beginning to make sense. Unfortunately, we don't have the time to discuss such things. The most important thing right now is to get away from this place.'

Elva quickly signed again.

'She won't leave Ligeia,' said Watson. 'She says she doesn't like the Colonel anymore and she won't leave Ligeia with her. She says Rex can't go either. What do you mean, Elva?'

The girl signed and pointed to the door.

'Apparently, the Colonel has done something to stop him leaving.' Watson shrugged. 'She heard them talking about it and she'll show us.'

'Lead the way,' murmured Quist, opening the door. 'But please be very cautious.'

Elva spoke to Watson and he nodded. 'She says they're leaving Charlington Hall after the concert. Most of the Colonel's men have now gone and only her main team of twelve are left.'

'Good,' said Rex, swallowing uncomfortably. 'But twelve are still too many. Adler's loaded some of their guns with silver bullets, so we need to watch ourselves.'

'Indeed,' said Quist. 'We also need to discuss that particular point the moment we're safe. Come on, let's go.'

Mellow twilight illuminated the gardens and, utilising his lupine senses, the detective listened and watched for security personnel as Elva led them swiftly past the rhododendron hedge and through a thicket of trees. They neared the mansion moat and cut through a small gravel car park with a dozen black vehicles. Three were upmarket saloons, but the majority were Range Rovers, Land Rovers and Hummers. Glancing through one of the windows, Quist noticed keys in the ignition. With potential thieves unable to gain access to the grounds, the chances of anyone stealing these were nil.

Seeing Elva drop to her knees, the detective grabbed Watson and Rex by the shoulders, silently pushing them down behind a car as one of Adler's armed guards walked past on patrol.

Quist had picked up the approaching footsteps, but evidently this girl had acute hearing too. Elva turned as the man disappeared behind the bushes, smiled nervously and waved them on. Beyond the vehicles stood another copse of trees and the small chapel. Rex eased open the door and found it was empty.

'Incredible,' stammered Watson, seeing the occult temple with the pentagram banner and skulls. 'This is straight out of a Hammer horror film.' The dash across the gardens had left his heart racing. It wasn't so much the burst of exertion, as the knowledge that, at any moment, machine guns might be fired in his direction. 'Is this shit for real?'

'Yeah, this must be Lafont's place,' said Rex, quietly closing the door behind them. 'He's Adler's very own voodoo witchdoctor. She calls him the Padre.'

'Don't switch on any lights,' warned Quist. 'We still have enough daylight shining through the windows.'

Elva took them along the short aisle to point at the altar.

'*This*?' asked the detective, astounded. He peered closely at the model of Charlington Hall with the circle of blood-soaked ash surrounding it. 'You're saying *this* is preventing Rex from leaving?'

She nodded.

He leant close and sniffed. 'This is your blood, Rex,' he said. 'I know the scent.'

'You should,' said Watson, uneasily. 'You once tasted it.'

'This chapel has been turned into an occult temple,' said Quist, gazing around at the bones and paraphernalia. 'From the little I know about such matters, this model house looks to be part of some occult ritual. If Adler has a practitioner of voodoo working for her, as you say, I assume he's performed a ritual to construct a supernatural barrier. This is crude, but it's built to scale and the blood circle will represent an invisible wall that prevents you leaving the grounds.'

'Piss off,' laughed Watson. 'That's impossible, Guv.'

'Oh, no, it's possible,' growled Rex. 'And it works too. No matter what I tried last night, I couldn't cross the thing.'

'Amazing.' Watson turned to Quist. 'Elva claims Ligeia has magic in her voice. Is the Colonel using voodoo to make her so successful?'

'I don't believe so.' The detective shook his head. 'No, that doesn't explain her being over a century old, or how she had power in her voice back then.'

'What the hell do you mean?' asked Rex, confused.

Elva signed with Watson.

'She says no, Guv. Ligeia is Lamarai.'

'What?' Quist searched his memory. 'I know the name Lamarai. Why do I know that name?'

'We don't have time for word puzzles,' said Rex. 'What about this supernatural force field shit? Do you have any ideas?'

'I have *one*.' Quist smashed the model and wiped away the blood with the altar cloth. 'My knowledge of such things is limited, but destroying the ritual model should end the magic and allow you to leave. One of those Range Rovers back there had the keys inside, but just to be on the safe side, I'll drive through the barrier and...' He paused for several seconds. 'Of course – Lamarai. Suddenly, this begins to make sense.'

Watson frowned. 'What are you talking about, Guv?'

'But the danger...' gasped Quist. He turned to Elva. 'Ligeia is Lamarai? You're certain about this?'

The girl nodded timidly.

'Does the Colonel or her occultist know?'

She shook her head.

'I can't allow this to continue,' he muttered, irately. 'From what I recall, the risks are unthinkable.' The detective hesitated, quickly deliberating and reaching a decision. 'I need you three out of harm's way right now, but I'm not coming with you.'

'What?' snapped Watson. 'Why not?'

'I have to speak to Adler. She's doesn't know what she's dealing with, but I have to enlighten her. Ligeia can't be left with her; it's far too dangerous. I know what Lamarai means.'

'Which is what?' asked Rex. 'What did you mean about her being over a century old?'

'Oh, you won't believe it,' said Watson, grinning nervously. 'Apparently, they used to go cruising together.'

'We don't have time for explanations.' Quist turned to the black candles on the altar, pondered for a moment, then broke off a lump of melted wax and handed it to Watson. 'You have to take one of those cars and go now.'

'What am I supposed to do with this?' he asked.

'Hopefully nothing, but it's best to be prudent. Keep it in your pocket.' The detective glanced at Elva. 'Am I right?'

The girl looked scared, but nodded.

'The sun has set,' pointed out Rex. 'I could stay and help you.'

'No, go with Watson,' said Quist. 'If you want to help, protect him.'

The teenager looked dubiously at Rex.

Quist gripped Elva by her shoulders. 'Listen to me, you really need to get away from here too.'

The girl shook her head emphatically and signed to Watson.

'Sorry, Guv.' He shrugged. 'She says she won't leave Ligeia.'

'Please, Elva. If you go with them, I promise I'll help your friend and…'

Elva signed again and hurried away, leaving silently through the chapel door.

'She trusts you, Guv,' said Watson. 'But she's staying to protect Ligeia. The Colonel is a bad woman and she's going back to

192

the house.'

'Very well,' sighed Quist, following the girl to the door. 'We have to hurry. They took Watson's phone and I assume you don't have one either, Rex? They can't track you, so get away from here, find somewhere safe and lie low. You need to wait a couple of hours before ringing the police. I want some time with Adler before the authorities arrive.'

'You really should come with us,' said Rex. 'These people are mercenaries. They're cold-blooded killers and you've no idea what they're capable of.'

'Sorry, but there's too much at stake.' Quist eased open the chapel door and checked the route was clear. 'Remember the moon, Rex. Use your music to overcome any dark urges as I've taught you.'

'Er, yeah, no problem.' Rex had been trying and, so far, the technique had been as useful as a chocolate ironing board. He decided not to mention this, but there was one thing he *definitely* ought to mention and it involved biting a psychopath. 'Er, listen…'

'By the way…' Quist closed the door and narrowed his eyes. 'Why did Adler load her weapons with silver? How does she know about our little secret?'

'Oh, *that*.' Rex cleared his throat. 'The voodoo guy did some ritual on my blood and he found out. Then last night I changed and, er, Adler saw me.'

'How discreet,' snapped Quist, angrily. 'What the hell have I told you about transforming during the full moon?'

'I was kidnapped,' said Rex, defensively. *This might not be the best time to bring up the lupine bite.* 'I wasn't thinking straight.'

'Well think straight *now*,' hissed Quist, opening the door again. 'Come on, it's time to go.'

* * * *

Watson parted the bushes at the edge of the car park and looked around. 'It seems to be all clear,' he whispered, trembling.

'Let's move.'

Scurrying across the gravel and staying low, Rex followed to the nearest car, a black Range Rover. He eased open the door, grimacing as the internal light winked on, but Watson jumped in the driving seat and quickly reached to switch it off. The keys were in the ignition as Quist had said and he started the engine. Leaving the headlights off for concealment, they turned out of the parking area and onto the drive, picking up speed on entering the trees.

'The voodoo barrier thing was somewhere back there,' said Rex. 'Hey, we crossed it and I didn't feel a thing.'

'Great.' Watson squinted into the darkness ahead and let out a dry laugh, the fear tightening his throat. 'To be honest, I'm more concerned with the feeling of bullets tearing through the car.'

He switched on the lights as the gates appeared. A security guard walked out from the gatehouse, shielding his eyes from the blinding beams, and realised the approaching vehicle had no intention of stopping.

'You know what?' said Watson. 'I've seen this in so many films and I've always wanted to do it.'

The guard dived into the safety of his shelter as the Range Rover smashed through the gates, ripping them from the stone pillars and launching twisted metal across the road ahead. Watson skidded into a tight turn and headed up the lane.

'Nice one,' laughed Rex. 'That's fucked their lovely front entrance.'

'Yeah.' Watson pointed to the steam gushing over the bonnet. 'Er, but both headlights are smashed and it doesn't seem to have done our radiator any favours.'

* * * *

Chapter 28

Adler stood at the library window looking out over the moat as she spoke with the gate personnel on her phone. She thumbed off the mobile and tugged up her sleeve to check where Rex had sunk his teeth. *The forearm bite marks had virtually vanished, which meant her plan had worked – it had actually worked. This was incredible.* Her heart beat faster, excitement coursing through her lithe frame.

'Remarkable,' she murmured, fingering the fading redness. *Grant had given her the supernatural power and abilities she craved.* 'Truly amazing.'

According to the guards on the gate, the prisoners had crashed their way through in a stolen car. The Colonel and her team were vacating Charlington Hall after tonight's concert, but she now debated whether it had been an oversight to dismiss the extra security personnel so soon. She smiled cruelly and rolled down her sleeve. *It didn't matter too much. The trio would soon be brought back and disposed of and, besides, the most important thing was that the werewolf bite had worked.*

Ligeia burst into the library and ran up to the Colonel. 'You lied to me,' she snapped. 'Why did you say that Rex had gone? Elva says he's in the zoo.'

'No, he *was* in the zoo,' said Adler, calmly. 'We discussed this, didn't we? Like I told you, he was with your lovely tiger, but then he left to see your concert. Elva is mistaken.'

'She says you hurt her.'

'It was an accident. Why on earth would I hurt you sweet young ladies? I take care of you and give you everything you want. You know that.'

Ligeia looked puzzled. 'So Elva was wrong?'

'Of course, my dear,' soothed Adler. 'It's soon time for your concert and a wonderful helicopter ride. You know how you like to see cities all lit up at night.'

'Oh yes,' said Ligeia. 'Yes, I do.'

Unbelievable, thought Adler, cuddling her and smirking. *If only all people were as childish and easily manipulated as this.*

Stroking her back, the Colonel gazed through the huge window. This side of the building descended directly into the moat, with the lily-covered water twelve feet below. Twilight was turning into night, but she could see perfectly well. *Her eyesight and hearing seemed clearer, but that could be imagination and wishful thinking rather than any supernatural augmentation. The disappearance of the bite, however, was another matter entirely.*

'Ah, I see I'll have to reprimand my security team,' said Adler, her smile tightening as the French doors opened and Quist walked in from the terrace. 'Well, you appear to have vacated the guest room and I hear your friends have just left in one of my vehicles. I assumed you were with them. I take it the accommodation wasn't to your liking?'

'I've had better,' said Quist.

'There you are.' Ligeia's face lit up and she ran to the detective, wrapping her arms around his tweed jacket and squeezing. 'It's been so long, but I want to say thank you for what you did that night.'

'I can't believe you still remember,' said Quist, holding her shoulders.

'What do you mean?' asked Adler, suspiciously. 'When did this man help you?'

Ligeia kissed his cheek. 'A long time ago on the boat.'

'Is that so?' The Colonel leant against the wall by the moat window and slid her right hand into her jacket. 'I have something here in my pocket, Mister Quist. I won't produce it, as it might scare Ligeia, but you can doubtless guess what it is?'

'Absolutely.' Quist gave a sarcastic grimace. 'I'm rather good at guesswork.'

'The contents are silver,' she continued. 'I'm not sure if that's necessary, but it's best to be safe, isn't it? My Padre doesn't care for your vibrations.'

'He dislikes my vibrations? You can give a person a complex, you know?'

'I've just taken a phone call from the main gate. The other two just left somewhat dramatically, but they won't get far. I'm curious as to why you didn't accompany them.'

'You told me we'd have a chat later,' said Quist. 'Here I am.'

'I wanted to know who you were and your connection with Grant. I detained you because you were searching for him and you could have posed a threat, but things have changed and I no longer care.'

'I'm afraid we still need to talk.'

'Unfortunately I don't have time. A helicopter will be arriving soon to transport us to the O2 for a night concert.'

'The helicopter.' Ligeia clapped her hands and sat on the couch.

'Believe me,' said Quist, 'you'll have enough time for *this*. It's something you definitely need to hear. Are you aware of what Ligeia is?'

Adler regarded him curiously. 'I'm aware she has a talent for making money.'

'You know she has a rather unique power? You know her voice is supernatural?'

'Yes, of course,' said Adler, moving closer. 'It only works when she's happy and content. The Padre has always known. He senses that she's very different to us.'

'Far more *different* than you can imagine,' said Quist. 'Ligeia, how old are you?'

The girl smiled and shrugged.

'What does that matter?' asked Adler.

'You don't know, do you?' asked Quist, eyeing the petite singer. 'Do you remember showing Elva around that club in Edinburgh the other night? Did you once sing there?'

'Yes, many times.' Ligeia sat up, excited. 'I showed her the stage where I sang.'

Quist nodded. 'And you showed Elva an old poster on the wall?'

'Yes, someone had drawn a picture of me. I looked funny.'

'What are you talking about?' asked Adler, shaking her head irritably. 'When did you sing there, my dear?'

'Indulge me, Colonel.' Quist gestured to a computer terminal by one of the bookcases. 'Use your search engine and look up Scottish music hall acts around 1910.'

'I'll keep my hand warm,' said Adler, pointing the concealed gun. 'You can do the searching.'

Quist sat at the terminal, thankful that Watson had shown him how to do this. He tapped at the keyboard, negotiating several websites before finally finding what he was looking for. He gestured to the screen.

'Sally Songbird?' Adler peered over his shoulder at the page of old photographs. 'Who's that and what the hell are you supposed to be showing me?'

'Look closer,' said Quist, enlarging one of the shots.

The Colonel stared at the girl in the picture, the caption informing her this was a famous Glasgow music hall act from 1911. Adler's single eye widened as recognition suddenly hit home and she wrestled with confusion. Sally's dress was Victorian, she wore too much make-up and her blonde hair was piled high, but there was no doubting who it was.

'Incredible,' whispered Adler, turning aghast to Ligeia on the couch. 'If this website is genuine, it makes you over a century old.'

'Quite a bit over a century,' murmured Quist, staring at the girl.

'That would explain certain things,' said Adler. 'You told me you'd lived with small groups of people in the past. Inuit people in Canada, you said. Berbers in Morocco and North American Indians. I wondered how that could be possible for one so young.'

'There was a Scotsman,' said Quist, scrolling through the information on Sally Songbird. 'He *managed* her back then as you do now. Ah, here we are – Lenny Logan.'

'I remember Lenny,' said Ligeia. 'He was nice. He used to do magic tricks for me.'

'Which made you happy.' Quist nodded. 'Just like the Colonel keeps you happy. Lenny realised you sang when you were feeling happy and people would pay to hear you. He took you to that Edinburgh music hall, didn't he?'

The girl nodded. 'He didn't like my name. He told me no one would like Ligeia, so he called me Sarah.'

'Which he changed to Sally for your stage appearances.'

'Yes, he called me Sally Songbird. I liked that. He liked my hair blonde too and he dyed it for me. He used to do magic for me.'

Quist gestured to the website text. 'It says record amounts of money were charged for your shows and the audience famously threw money onto the stage for the encore. It says…'

'I'm sorry,' said Ligeia suddenly.

'Whatever for?' asked Quist.

'It was so very cold the night we met. I could feel you were like me, but I wasn't able to talk to you. You saved me, but I couldn't save you. People do what I ask, but that bad man in the boat wouldn't let you in when I told him to. It was too cold and I couldn't use my voice properly.'

'Don't worry about that,' said Quist. 'After all, I suspect that, like me, your body would have shut down, but you wouldn't have drowned.'

'What the hell are you talking about?' asked Adler.

Elva entered the library and ran to Ligeia's side. The two girls kissed and Elva glared icily at Adler who gave her a cynical smile.

Ligeia turned back to Quist. 'You saved me,' she said. 'But I never even knew your name.'

'Bernard,' said Quist. 'My friends call me Bernie. Now I wonder if you and Elva would like to leave the Colonel and I alone for a while? I need to speak with her.'

'Good idea,' said Adler. 'You need to get ready for your concert. Wear your silver dress, my dear.'

'I will.' Ligeia gave Quist another kiss. 'Thank you, Bernie.'

Elva scowled at Adler again and then left arm-in-arm with Ligeia.

With the need for concealment gone, the Colonel produced her handgun. 'She claims you saved her?' she said. 'Tell me about it and when was this?'

'It was a long time ago and it doesn't concern you,' said Quist. 'What *should* concern you is this information verifying her somewhat advanced years. So you indulge her every whim to maintain the unique power in her voice?'

'It only works when she's content,' confirmed Adler. 'If Ligeia is unhappy, she sounds like any mundane female vocalist. The Scottish gentleman mentioned on the Internet obviously discovered this, if that website is genuine.'

'Of course it's genuine,' snapped Quist. 'I'm showing you this to explain what you're dealing with.'

'I know what I'm dealing with; the billions in my foreign accounts prove it. As for the website, you could have uploaded that yourself. I've seen sites which prove the British Royal family are reptiles. Why should this be any different?'

'But you concede she has supernatural abilities,' said Quist. 'Why doesn't her song affect you?'

200

'It isn't just her song,' said Adler. 'Her speaking voice is mesmerising when she needs it to be.'

'I suspected as much.'

'Once you're aware of her ability, you can fight it, but it takes effort and I employ technology instead. My team use tiny ear implants.'

'Combatting the supernatural with science.'

'Yes, I had someone reprimanded yesterday for removing them and leaving himself susceptible to her instructions.'

'I assume this is why her interview with the Edinburgh police only lasted a few minutes?'

Adler grinned. 'She told them they had enough information and it was time for her to leave. They happily opened the door for her.'

'Incredible,' said Quist.

'I tried to discover how her voice works and employed a scientist from the Cambridge Institute of Acoustics. He's the doctor who manufactured the audio implants. He's been analysing her voice and filtering the sonic levels, but he doesn't understand much. Apparently the sound works on a different wavelength and stimulates the brain and nervous system directly, much like a drug.'

'So she asks for something in a certain way, and people magically obey?'

'Exactly. I had her lyrics written to work on that: *Years roll by, my music keeps me sane, my love...*' Adler laughed. 'The fans hear *buy my music*. The songs are filled with subliminal commands.'

'Very clever.' Quist nodded. 'So you use acoustic implants. Odysseus used wax.'

'Odysseus?'

'He's sometimes called Ulysses; it depends which book you read.' Quist typed *Lamarai* into the computer and smiled grimly as a website of ancient Sumerian history appeared. 'Ah, this is what I'm looking for. Mesopotamia, the land between the Euphrates and Tigris rivers. That's now Iraq, isn't it?'

'Correct,' said Adler, reading over his shoulder. 'What are you looking at that for and what does Lamarai mean?'

Quist took a deep breath. 'The Lamarai are mythical demons,' he said. 'Water scream demons and Ligeia is one of them. The Greeks named them Sirens.'

* * * *

Chapter 29

The black Range Rover limped along a dark woodland lane, steam pouring from the radiator and a disconcerting grinding noise coming from the engine. Watson drove past a pub and a jumble of cottages. With the lights completely smashed, the streetlamps provided welcome illumination.

'Nice work,' said Rex, leaning over from the passenger seat to check the oil temperature. The needle was fully into the red and strained to climb further. 'You've really buggered it.'

'Hey, you don't say?' Watson laughed sarcastically. 'Maybe I should have stopped and asked them to open the gates?'

'Bad idea. They wouldn't have let us out.'

The teenager shot him an incredulous glance. Quist accused his assistant of sometimes missing irony, but Rex had probably never even heard of it. 'We haven't got very far,' said Watson, 'and from the sound of the motor, we're not going much further.'

'We should ditch this car anyway,' said Rex. 'I've driven enough decent motors to know they're usually fitted with tracking devices. In any case, that bunch will definitely be following us by now and they can't be far behind.'

'You're right.' Spotting a track off the lane, Watson turned the car onto it and parked in the trees away from the street lights. 'We'll be safer on foot.'

'I spotted a sign for the Richmond Golf Club back there,' said Rex. 'We must be near Richmond Park.' Walking back to the lane, he pointed to a tiny railway station on the opposite side. 'Hey, we don't have to walk anywhere. I've heard of this Foxglove Line. It's a little steam train that operates for the tourists and goes along the edge of the park to Wimbledon Common.'

'That sounds good. It'll get us well away from the car if they *are* tracking it.'

'Better than that. It connects with a main line station near

Wimbledon and we can travel into London from there. I have friends where we can stay.'

'Unless they watch the news.' Watson gave him a rueful smile. 'Remember you're wanted for murder.'

'I know a girl who won't believe that crap. She's a model and she believes anything I tell her. We'll be okay at Merlot's apartment.'

They crossed the road to the pretty redbrick building, hurrying through an archway onto the platform where a small steam engine and three old-fashioned carriages stood ready to leave. The disused station had been renovated by railway enthusiasts and entering the place was like stepping back into the 1950s. Watson spotted the price list by the ticket office and saw that fares had risen a little since then. Not that it mattered, as he didn't even have the 1950s fare.

'Do you have any money?' he asked.

'Er, no.' Rex grimaced. 'How about you?'

Watson shook his head.

'Shit.' Rex looked around furtively. 'Let's just jump on board.'

'No, they'll probably see us and ring the cops. That won't be good, especially for you.'

'Adler isn't an amateur. From what I've seen of her and her military outfit, she probably monitors the police radio channels. Maybe using the train is a bit risky. Why don't we steal another car?'

'What?' Watson peered at him. 'How?'

'I don't know. Hot wire it or whatever it is you lot do?'

'*My* lot?' snapped Watson. 'Listen, you racist twat, I may be a black teenager, but I've no idea how to steal cars.'

'I didn't mean *black*. I thought that maybe you might…'

'Not since they fitted decent immobilisers anyway. No, it has to be the train.'

The youth noticed a length of white plastic pipe outside the toilet block where a plumbing repair had been carried out. 'Wait a minute.' He narrowed his eyes thoughtfully. 'It says on the noticeboard that disabled folk travel free.'

Rex nodded slowly. 'You want me to break your legs?'

'I have a better idea with less pain.' He grabbed the slender pipe and pulled him into the male toilet. It was small empty room with a urinal trough and two cubicles, one of which had been cordoned off with white tape and bore an *out of order* sign. 'Perfect. Okay, you need to change.'

'Into what?' Rex looked down at his shirt. 'You mean swap clothes?'

'I mean *change* change.'

'Oh, right.' Rex hesitated. 'Er, why?'

'Hurry. We don't have time for me to explain.' Watson tore lengths of tape from the broken toilet. 'That train's about to leave.'

'Your boss always said never to risk it on the full moon.' Rex quickly disrobed. 'Still, I transformed last night and I was fine, so what does he know? This will be okay.'

Praying that no one came in to relieve themselves, the naked man gripped the edge of the washbasin and arched his back. His spine crackled, fur sprouted and he grew in height. Watson stepped back as Rex grunted and snarled his way through the swift transformation and a terrifying black wolf stood in his place.

'I've never seen you do that before.' Watson cleared his throat and licked his bone-dry lips. He was already stressed, but the temperature drop had him shivering. 'You're different to old Cyrano. Kind of sleeker.'

'Yeah, well I'm younger and fitter.' Rex grinned proudly and flexed his furry chest muscles in the bathroom mirror. 'I keep myself in shape'

'Oh, very droll.' Watson gave an uneasy laugh. 'Shape.'

'Sorry?'

'You're a shapeshifter. I thought you were making a joke to relieve the tension.'

'No.'

'Whatever.' Watson shoved Rex's shoes and clothes up his T shirt, slipped on his sunglasses and picked up the white tube. 'Right, you need to be down on all fours.'

The wolf dropped into position and Watson nervously wrapped the tape around its chest like a harness, gathering the ends together as makeshift reins. 'Come on.'

The pair headed back onto the platform, Watson tapping the ground ahead with his improvised blind man's cane as he walked to the ticket office.

'Good evening.' An elderly man in period uniform smiled at Watson through the cubicle window. 'This is the last train of the night, so you've only just made it. Just the one, is it?'

'Yeah, but it says disabled travel free.' The youth faked blindness, peering into space over the man's shoulder and tapping the counter with his white stick. 'Do I just get on?'

'No, you don't pay anything, but you need a ticket so we know how many are on board...' The man peered down at the wolf. 'What the...' He stepped back. 'What the fuck is *that* thing?'

'You mean Rex?' Watson adjusted his sunglasses and patted the huge furry head. 'Rex is my guide dog.'

'Guide dog? What the hell kind of *dog* is it supposed to be?'

'Er, a Labrador.'

'Are you out of your mind?' gasped the old man. The wolf peered at him with glowing amber eyes and he clenched his buttocks as his bowel threatened evacuation. 'That's no Labrador.'

'What do you mean?' Watson groped Rex's face, clumsily poking him in the eye. 'What have they given me here? No wonder people pay for private health care.'

The man threw the ticket across the counter and slammed

the window shut.

'Thanks.' Watson pretended to fumble for it and hurriedly led the wolf to the train. 'Come on, Rexy. There's a good boy.'

They headed to the first carriage behind the engine, climbed the step and slammed the door, Watson quickly walking the wolf along the central aisle. The carriage was fairly empty for this late hour on a Friday evening and he chose a vacant seat well away from his fellow passengers.

'We made it,' he whispered, stroking Rex.

The wolf eyed him curiously. 'What are you doing?' he growled quietly through clenched razor teeth.

'Trying to blend in,' he murmured. 'Some of the passengers almost shat themselves when you walked past. I'm proving you're a nice guide doggie. Just a big softie.'

The screeching of tyres drew him to the window. Range Rovers had pulled up outside the little station and Gruner ran through the entrance arch. Two of his security team accompanied him, followed by Lafont and a pair of grey-suited men in bowler hats.

'Well...' drawled Watson, turning from the carriage window. 'I'm sitting here stroking a werewolf, but this shit has now officially entered the *Twilight Zone.* Laurel and Hardy are about to board the train.'

* * * *

Chapter 30

Colonel Adler kept her automatic trained on Quist as she poured two whiskies. 'So you're telling me Ligeia is a Siren?' she said, incredulous. 'Some mythical creature from Greek legend?'

'Hardly mythical,' said Quist. He sat at the computer reading about the Lamarai, his eyes widening as he arrived at a paragraph on the legendary Mesopotamian race named the Askari. 'Elva mentioned this name and I remembered what they were.'

'I take it she mentioned this when she released you? I should have had her watched, but I viewed her as an empty-headed mute. It seems even *I* make mistakes.'

'You should be thankful she *did* let us out and I was able to learn this. I knew I'd read about the Lamarai before and here are all the details.'

'Ancient scream demons?' said Adler, offering him a glass of single malt and reading the screen. 'This is ludicrous. You honestly think she's some immortal creature that's existed through the centuries?'

'I'm certain she's descended from them, so who knows how old she truly is?' Quist sipped the drink. 'I'm sure it can't be *too* difficult to believe. After all, your silver bullets suggest that you're quite comfortable with the idea of werewolves.'

Laughing quietly, Adler tugged up her sleeve to check her arm. The bite wound had completely vanished.

'Problem?' asked Quist.

'Oh, no.' Adler raised her drink in a triumphant toast. 'No problem whatsoever. I know Rex Grant is a werewolf. The Padre tells me he picks up identical feelings from you, so I assume you are too?'

'We're discussing a different supernatural creature,' said Quist, tartly. 'One which is far more pertinent right now. Sirens were misunderstood. They weren't evil, as portrayed in the ancient myths, and they didn't intentionally draw sailors to their deaths. They simply sang and people were attracted. Unfortunately, they had a love of water and a habit of sitting on rocks beside it, which wasn't particularly good news for passing boats.'

'She certainly has an affinity with water.' Adler looked down onto the moat through the huge window, then gesturing to the couch, she settled herself in an armchair. 'Come and sit.'

Quist nodded to the gun. 'How could I refuse such hospitality?'

'Ligeia seems unaware of what you're telling me, so I don't want her hearing it. Such things could upset her and she needs to concentrate on tonight and the week ahead.'

'But you don't realise the danger,' said Quist, sitting on the couch. 'Fortunately, I remembered the legends and that website confirms it. Sirens had *two* vocal abilities. The one you're familiar with, which enchants, but there's another voice which they use for defence. They have a much darker vocal power that harms humans. They're able to kill.'

The Colonel shrugged. 'If that's true, she's never used such an ability.'

'Then, so far, you've been lucky. If Ligeia feels threatened, the risk to the people around her is very real, especially her audience at these concerts. Can you imagine what she could do with a microphone and amplification system?'

'I've seen no evidence of this lethal voice and I certainly won't be altering any plans based on the word of a stranger and some mythology website.'

'Is money all you care about?'

'Money and power.' A surge of exhilaration flowed through Adler at the thought of her newly acquired lupine potential. 'I've always enjoyed power. I acquired a taste for it in the military and I'm starting to like it even more.'

'You said you were in the German army and that

surname…'

'My parents were German, but I was born and educated in Brazil.'

'Germans living in Brazil? Looking at you, I'd say you were born in the seventies. That suggests certain things to me.'

'I'm sure it does.' The Colonel smiled. 'Adler is my mother's name. My father's name carries a certain amount of…' She paused, searching for the correct word, 'baggage.'

'Your father's name?'

'Mengele.'

'Ah!' Quist raised his eyebrows. 'Not *the* Mengele? Doctor Joseph Mengele, the universally despised monster of Auschwitz? The twisted scientist who performed unspeakable experiments on people and became known as the Angel of Death?'

'You know him.' Taking a sip of whisky, Adler brightened and crossed her legs. 'I'm afraid I don't have my father's scientific brain.'

'I imagine he must be a difficult role model to measure up to.'

She grinned at the sarcastic tone. 'I've made up for it in other ways. My time in the military taught me a great deal about man management and I've always had a shrewd business sense. I believe my father would be proud of my accomplishments.'

'If I remember my history, Mengele had two wives, didn't he?'

'He divorced and married his brother's wife, but my mother appeared much later, a few years before his untimely death. She was a German doctor of biochemistry researching South American toxins and she assisted in his experiments. With her help, he perfected techniques for changing facial features using Paraguayan fish, poisonous frogs and jungle plants. The plan was to alter his appearance and that of his German friends living out there, but in 1979 he accidentally drowned. A great loss as he was a brilliant

210

man.'

'Yes.' Quist gave a sham whistle of respect. 'And to think history has labelled him a monster.'

Again, Adler ignored the sarcasm. 'My mother took me back to Germany. I have all his research and we have a physician here who puts it to good use. Doctor Roylott could do wonders with that large nose of yours.'

'I rather doubt it.'

Since the werewolf bite, Quist had stayed exactly the same. Fortunately he'd shaved that particular day, otherwise, apart from the occasional brief period when fashion decreed that men should sport designer stubble, he'd have looked remarkably scruffy over the past two centuries.

'I brought in people to keep Ligeia happy,' said Adler. 'The mute girl Elva, for example, but Doctor Roylott helped with the other additions to our entourage. Ligeia likes Laurel and Hardy and Roylott saw a resemblance to Hardy in Alistair Ramson. The police caught him in France and we intercepted the officers who were returning him to Britain. Ramson was only too willing to exchange a fugitive life for luxury as our unorthodox look-alike.'

'I met him briefly. He called on us in the menagerie. Stan Laurel was with him.'

'That's right. I had Roylott search through prison computer records for a Laurel and Sebastian Moran was perfect.'

'Ah, is that who it was? Moran, the cannibal murderer.'

'It's important to get the correct bone structure to ensure no surgery is needed. Just our revolutionary procedure using drug injections. We sprang Moran on his prison journey to Broadmoor.'

'Laurel and Hardy.' Quist nodded slowly. 'Ligeia must be overjoyed.'

'Indeed.' Adler smiled at his obvious disgust. 'We might give her a set of Marx Brothers next.'

'I understand Ramson cuts a letter R into his victims?'

'Yes, with a blade weapon he devised himself.'

'Why did he kill Charlotte Michie in Edinburgh?'

'He's a killer, Mister Quist. They aren't exactly stable. Two of our cleaning staff here met with the same fate.'

'So you cover up these inconvenient murders?' snarled Quist. 'You allowed Rex to take the blame for the Edinburgh death and kidnapped him to appease Ligeia. How long do you expect to get away with all this?'

'I haven't done too badly so far. You'd be surprised at the sort of things you can get away with when enormous amounts of money are involved. Anyone can be bought and paid to look the other way, including the police.'

Quist glared at the woman. 'So how did you come to be Ligeia's...' He paused. 'I was going to say *manager*, but *owner* would be more appropriate, wouldn't it?'

'Perhaps so.' Adler laughed. 'I was the head of *Red Globe Security* and we were in the Balkans assisting with the unrest there last year. We saw her singing in a bar and the audience were entranced; so were my men. I ordered them away, but they refused. I even punched one and broke his nose and they still didn't move. That's when I realised she was special and...'

'And you could profit from her.'

'Absolutely. A man had brought her to the town from one of the hill villages where she'd been living. We had an enlightening chat with him and he confirmed she had some sort of power. My Padre confirmed it was supernatural.'

'This will be your voodoo practitioner?'

She nodded and turned to the door as her Entertainment Manager walked in,

'Oh, er, right,' said Guevara, seeing the Colonel's gun trained on Quist. 'If this is a bad time, I can come back when...'

'Not at all,' said Adler. 'Shane, this is Bernard Quist. Shane Guevara here sees to the commercial side of the business.'

'*Shane Guevara*?' repeated Quist, frowning.

'It turns out Ligeia is a Siren,' said Adler. 'You know, like in the Greek myths.'

Guevara laughed. '*What*?'

'She's unbelievably dangerous,' said Quist. 'If this woman won't listen to my warnings, then maybe *you* will. Sirens have two songs. The one that enchants and another that harms people.'

'But we have the ear implants…' began Guevara.

'The audience don't,' snapped Quist. 'If anything should go wrong…'

'It won't,' said Adler. 'And if it does, believe me, I can live with the guilt.'

'I believe you,' said Quist, fuming.

* * * *

Chapter 31

The little steam engine pulled out of the station and headed into the woodland of Richmond Park, chugging slowly along the western edge of the vast expanse.

'Shit,' stammered Watson. Frightened and shaking, he turned from the train window and stashed his sunglasses in a pocket. 'Three of them got on the last carriage: Laurel and Hardy and some black guy. They're obviously searching the train. What the hell are we going to do?'

'The black one is the witchdoctor Lafont,' whispered Rex, keeping his head low behind the seat to spare fellow passengers the bizarre sight of a talking wolf. 'There are only three carriages, so it isn't going to take them long.'

'The lavatory,' hissed Watson, jumping up and tugging at Rex's makeshift guide dog harness. 'Come on, quick. There's nowhere else to hide.'

The toilet was situated at the end of the car in the entrance area just behind the steam engine. Watson closed the aisle door behind them as Lafont opened the door at the opposite end.

'Fuck, they're here already.' The teenager ducked into the cubicle with the huge wolf and locked the door, gazing in horror at the razor fangs close-up. He gave a nervous grin. 'This is the second time tonight we've been alone in a public toilet. We really have to stop this.'

'How the hell did they know we're on board?' growled the wolf.

'They must have tracked the car. They probably don't know we're here, but they're making sure.'

'Well, they're bound to check in here.' Rex slid open the window and shoved out his head, looking around. 'We have to hurry.'

'What are you doing?' Watson watched the wolf climb out,

digging its talons into the carriage coachwork for purchase. 'It isn't going too fast. We could maybe jump into the bushes and…'

His words ended in a terrified whimper as a clawed hand reached in and dragged him out, hoisting him up onto the carriage roof. Two seconds later, the toilet door was kicked in and they heard the sound of someone looking through the window.

'Empty,' announced a male voice. 'If there was anyone in here, they must have jumped.'

'The door was locked,' said Lafont's voice. '*Someone* must have been inside, but they're no longer on the train. I'll radio it in.'

The window was slammed shut and Watson sighed with relief.

'Climbing up here was a brilliant idea,' he whispered. 'We seem to be okay for now, but let's hope there are no low bridges.'

'That was Oliver Hardy at the window,' growled Rex. He dug his talons into the roof's metal sheeting to ensure he didn't slide off and the teenager clung to his furry bulk. 'I recognised the voice. That's the fat bastard who murdered Charlotte in Scotland.'

'We met Laurel and Hardy earlier,' said Watson. 'Cyrano reckons Hardy is some fugitive serial killer called Alistair Ramson.'

'He's right.' Trembling with anger, the wolf bared its teeth. 'Laurel is an escaped killer too and Adler altered their faces. Hardy has a long blade on a spring hidden up his sleeve. Believe me, it's really sharp; he stabbed me with it. He also used it on my friend and he's going to pay for that. He's going to fucking *pay*.'

'Er, okay.' Watson eyed the glistening fangs and wished he had something to hold onto that was a little less volatile and lethal. 'Cyrano was telling me you have a special tune that you concentrate on to keep your…' He coughed nervously. 'Your dark lupine urges at bay. What is it?'

'That's kind of personal,' snarled the wolf. 'It's *my* song.'

'Whatever.' The teenager glanced up at the full moon. 'I just hope you're singing it in your head when I'm around.'

The slow train reduced speed even more on a sharp bend where the line curled to run parallel with the A308 through the edge of the parkland. A man walked his dog on a leash in the trees, both owner and spaniel staring open-mouthed at the moonlit wolf and black youth sitting on the carriage roof. Watson smiled sheepishly and Rex raised his paw in an embarrassed wave. Mesmerised, the man waved back dazedly as the dog defecated on his shoes.

'When the train stops, Adler's men will get off,' said Watson. 'We can't be sitting out in the open when that happens.'

'No, we'll jump down before the station,' said Rex. 'Then we'll hide until they've gone, cross over to the main line and grab the first train into the city. It'll be safe enough when we reach my friend's apartment and I can ring McNulty in Edinburgh from there. His brother is in the police and he knows me. I'll explain everything about Ramson, Adler and the kidnap and he'll be able to pull the right strings and sort this out.'

The train vanished under a road, chugging through a tunnel that connected Richmond Park to Wimbledon Common.

'We met Gordon McNulty,' said Watson. 'We headed straight to Edinburgh to help you as soon as we found out about the murder and your disappearance.'

'Really?' the wolf wagged its tail. 'Hey, thanks.'

'What are friends for?'

'You didn't initially suspect I might have killed her? I mean, it *was* the full moon, so it can't have looked good when you heard about…'

'Are you kidding? Not even for a second.' Watson recalled how he'd pictured a savaged corpse with a blood-soaked furry fuckwit in sunglasses standing over it. 'No, we both knew there wasn't a chance in hell of that.'

'Well, that's really heart-warming to know. Thanks again.'

'McNulty's brother sounds like a brilliant idea. It's pointless trying to talk to the local cops. They'd take some convincing that a pop star's management team were capable of murder and kidnap.'

Rex gritted his huge teeth, wondering how the story of Charlotte's death and the goings on at Charlington Hall would play out with the authorities. *If his bite had worked on Adler, she wouldn't be mentioning his lycanthropy secret to anyone. They now shared the same hairy skeleton in the closet and she'd probably flee from any police investigation and vanish somewhere with her wealth. The problem was, there was a good chance he'd turned a powerful sociopathic mercenary into a supernatural monster and he was responsible for anyone she killed. Knowing this crazy bitch, she wouldn't be sticking to any vegan diets and humming Barry Manilow songs when she felt tetchy.* A surge of fury shook his body and he made a futile effort to concentrate on his personal melody.

The train crossed Wimbledon Common and Putney Heath, the line entering a steep-sided cutting as suburban streets took over from the woodland. Large houses stood on either side, with gardens backing onto the railway, and a station appeared ahead.

'Come on,' said Rex, bounding along the roof on all fours. 'We need to get to the back.'

Watson followed him, precariously jumping from car to car, and relieved that the train was moving slowly. Movie actors made this look simple – they usually paused to have a fight on the roof – but in reality it was bloody terrifying. Reaching the last carriage, Rex climbed over the rear, grabbed Watson's arm and lowered him onto the railway sleepers as the steam engine braked to ponderously cover the final fifty feet into the station. The wolf leapt down and the pair darted into the shadow of bushes at the side of the track. Watson noticed Rex's amber eyes glowing in the dark and swallowed uncomfortably.

'Are you going to change back?' he asked.

The wolf shook its large furry head. 'No, if we're going to get another train into London, we'll try the blind man and guide dog

217

trick again.'

The teenager patted his pocket to ensure the sunglasses were there, but realised he'd lost his *blind man's cane* when they escaped through the toilet window. *Then again, no one would notice such things with the wolf around. No one would notice if he'd lost his trousers.*

A road bridge crossed the line between the station and their hiding spot, and they crouched low behind the hawthorn bushes as two black Range Rovers hurtled over it.

'They looked like the Colonel's cars,' said Rex. 'They'll have driven from the Richmond Park station to pick up the three who searched the train.'

'No problem,' said Watson. 'We'll just hang around here until they piss off.'

Five minutes ticked by.

'By the way,' whispered Watson. 'Happy birthday.'

The wolf gave him an incredulous look. 'Thanks, but I've had better.' He turned back to the station. 'I can't see any more movement. The train must have emptied by now.'

'Yeah, Adler's men will have left.' The teenager nodded. 'Come on.'

They ran quietly along the dark track and watched for a while before climbing onto the platform beside the carriages. Apart from the driver tending to his hissing engine, the little station was now deserted. Descending steps and hurrying through a tiled tunnel beneath a road, they emerged in a larger *real* station through which ran the main line into the city. Thankfully, this platform was also empty and Watson peered along the tracks to see the lights of a distant express train heading towards them.

'This one isn't stopping,' said Rex, sitting dog-fashion beside the youth. 'We need to wait for a sprinter train into London and then…'

A tranquiliser dart hit the wolf's flank and he whipped

around snarling. Watson leapt backwards in fright, straight into the arms of Oliver Hardy. The fat man grinned with delight and his blade sprang out, glinting in the moonlight.

Lafont, Gruner and Stan Laurel stepped out of the darkness of the empty waiting room.

'Retract the knife,' snapped Gruner, pointing his dart gun at Rex. 'How many times do I have to tell you? You only use it when I say so.'

'Good advice,' stammered Watson.

'You're probably wondering how we found you,' said Lafont walking up to the drugged wolf. 'I used a magical technique known as psychometry.' He held up a crude wolf puppet. 'I knew you were on the train. I can sense you and home in on you using this.'

'The Padre used your blood to make that,' said Gruner, grinning. 'Think of it as a voodoo GPS tracker.'

'Think whatever you like,' said Lafont, proudly waving the puppet in front of the wolf's panting face. 'But know that my magic never fails.'

'This magic of yours...' said Rex, fury welling inside. 'Does it allow you to see into the future?'

'I'm afraid not.'

'Shame.' The wolf's rear leg kicked out hard. 'That would have been handy for you.'

The paw slammed into the Padre's midriff, launching him backwards off the platform and onto the tracks. Lafont sat up and opened his mouth, but didn't have time to make any sound as the express train hit him.

'*Fuck*,' hissed Gruner, wiping a hot splatter of brain from his cheek. The train braked hard, a deafening metallic squeal filling the station. The Sergeant fired another dart into Rex's flank and turned to Laurel and Hardy. 'Pick him up. Get them into the vehicles before that train stops. Move.'

Rex couldn't believe he'd done it. *He'd actually killed someone and he felt good about it.* He looked up at the full moon and snarled gleefully as the tranquiliser drained away his consciousness.

* * * *

Chapter 32

The black Range Rovers sped through the smashed gateway of Charlington Hall, one following the drive to the mansion, where a large AgustaWestland helicopter stood on the lawn, the other heading for the animal enclosures by the river. Gruner pulled up outside the menagerie building and Laurel and Hardy dragged out the unconscious Rex, carrying his naked body into the large end room. The Sergeant clicked on the fluorescent lights and Mister Tigsy lunged at the bars of his indoor cage, snarling furiously with ears pinned back and tail lashing. The tiger detested the sight and unmistakable scent of its Serbian tormentor, but cowered and moved back warily on sensing the supernatural wolf presence.

'Dump him there by the cage door,' ordered Gruner, fuming with anger and pointing to the tiles. 'Okay, you two had better get up to the house. The chopper will be leaving for the concert.'

'You're not coming?' asked Laurel.

'There isn't room for everyone and the pilot is making two journeys. I'm waiting for the second flight.' Gruner glared at the tranquilised man as he began to stir. 'I intend to have some fun first.'

'Sounds interesting.' Hardy grinned. 'Well, Mister Rex, here's another nice mess you've got yourself into.'

The Sergeant waited until the pair had left before taking out his phone and ringing Adler. 'The team are on their way to you with the black kid, Ma'am.' He hesitated. 'I'm afraid the Padre is dead. The shapeshifter killed him.'

'Damn!' Adler gritted her teeth, then regained her composure. 'Tell me you have him. Tell me you have Grant?'

'Oh, yes.' Gruner pointed his gun at Rex as he sat up groggily. 'He's here with me in the menagerie.'

'We're leaving for the concert,' said Adler, lowering her voice to an icy whisper. 'I'll send the chopper back for Laurel and Hardy and yourself. As for your captive there, he's served his purpose and he's definitely earned himself a silver bullet. I'll tell Ligeia he'll be meeting her in America.'

'Understood, Ma'am.'

'Do it now,' growled Adler. 'I want him dead.'

'Bad news,' said Gruner, thumbing off the phone and training his gun on Rex. 'You really upset the Colonel by killing her Padre.'

'Oh, dear.' Rex shook his head to clear the last effects of the tranquiliser darts. He climbed unsteadily to his feet, realising he was naked and that this was the large tiger room where he'd been brought after Hardy stabbed him. 'I suppose I'd better apologise and buy her a box of chocolates or something.'

Gruner laughed. 'Something tells me that's not going to do it. No, I'm afraid she wants you dead. She told me to shoot you, but I have a much better idea.' He pointed the gun at Rex's stomach. 'This isn't a tranquiliser gun and it's loaded with silver bullets. Open the cage door behind you.'

'What?' Rex glanced at the huge growling tiger. 'You're joking?'

'Not at all. People are coming from a zoo to take the cat to his new home tomorrow morning. Let's give Mister Tigsy a last bit of fun before he goes.'

'Are you out of your fucking mind? I'm not going in there with…'

'Get in, or I'll shoot you in the stomach and then shove you in. You choose.'

Rex stared at the pistol and turned to the cage where Mister Tigsy crouched hissing and spitting in the corner. The last time he'd been this close to a big cat, things hadn't gone particularly well. Gulping uneasily, he slid back the bolt, eased open the barred gate and walked in.

'Thank you.' Gruner hurried forward to secure the bolt behind him. 'I used to enjoy dog fighting and bear baiting in my country. A tiger and a wolf will be far better entertainment.'

* * * *

Quist sat on the library couch eyeing the pistols that Adler and Guevara held. Both had recently been fitted with silencers, which wasn't a good sign. It suggested they intended to use them and he knew the lethal ammunition they contained. He turned to the opening French doors as one of the Colonel's men arrived and roughly shoved in Watson.

'I can't say as I'm glad to see you,' said Quist. 'I was hoping you'd be well away from this place.'

'Bloody hell, Guv,' stammered the teenager. He backed up to the huge side window overlooking the moat. 'You won't believe what happened. One thing's for sure, there won't be any more voodoo.'

'The team are all back, Ma'am,' said Adler's guard. 'They're boarding the chopper with Doctor Roylott. I'll be piloting.'

'Very good,' said the Colonel. 'You'll be flying directly to the O2 and then returning for Gruner and Laurel and Hardy. Everything relevant has been sent on ahead to the States, so the Sergeant will finish off here and close up. After the concert, you'll transport us across the river to the London City Airport for the Miami flight.'

Quist listened, still watching the guns. 'Florida will be lovely at this time of the year,' he said, standing up and joining Watson at the window. 'Are you alright?' he asked. 'They didn't hurt you?'

'I'm fine,' said Watson, also staring at the silenced pistols. 'But I don't know for how long.'

'How about Rex?'

'I shouldn't worry about him,' said Adler. 'My Sergeant is looking after him.'

'Yes,' said Quist. 'You kept your voice low, but I have exceptional hearing and I heard you speaking on the phone.'

Ligeia and Elva walked into the library, both wearing silver mini dresses. Elva's anger hadn't diminished and she stared at Adler with open loathing, her sprained arm still aching from the earlier torture.

'Ah, you're ready,' said Adler. Quickly folding her jacket over the silenced handgun to conceal it, she kept the weapon trained on Quist and nodded at Guevara for him to do the same. 'Come along, ladies, it's time to leave.'

'We're going to fly in the helicopter,' giggled Ligeia. 'I love flying.'

'That's right.' The Colonel slipped her free arm around the singer's shoulders and walked her back to the door. 'You'll see the city all lit up below you; won't that be beautiful? You and Elva can go with Shane here. Get on the helicopter for your nice flight and I'll join you shortly.'

Glowering at Adler, Elva signed to Ligeia.

'Yes, I'll ask,' said Ligeia. 'Where's Rex? I want him to watch me singing.'

Adler smiled tightly. *Something would definitely have to be done about the mute bitch. The Padre had been right and she was now a liability.* 'He will,' she said. 'As I told you, Rex drove on ahead. He'll be in the audience and he can't wait to see you perform.'

'I want Bernie to come too.'

'That's a good idea,' said Quist. 'I'd love to watch Ligeia.'

'Bernie and his young friend will be on the next flight,' said Adler, waving for Guevara and her mercenary to escort the girls out. 'This one will be full when I'm on board. We're going to send the pilot back for them and for your friends Laurel and Hardy.

Come along now or we'll be late.'

Guevara led Ligeia and Elva across the terrace. Bringing out the gun, Adler waited until they reached the large helicopter on the lawn. They climbed on board and she turned to the two men standing at the side window.

'I now know what Ligeia is,' she said. 'Thank you for explaining about her. I still find it difficult to accept, but I'm especially grateful for the information about her *other* voice. I'll be sure to remember the dangers as I make money from her.'

'There's still time to stop all this…' began Quist.

'The chopper is ready to go,' she said, ignoring him. 'As I pointed out to Ligeia, there's no room on board for you two.'

'There's a surprise,' said Watson.

I never had time to discover how you know Rex Grant and why you were looking for him, but I don't see as it matters any more. He's gone and, now that Ligeia is safely out of the way, I can say goodbye to you too.'

'Hey, wait a minute…' began Watson, his eyes widening with fear.

The Colonel shot the detective in his chest and turned the silenced gun on Watson. Quist snatched the teenager with unbelievable speed and twisted around to use his body as a shield. Wrapping him in his arms and clasping a hand over his face, he launched them both through the huge window as another bullet tore through his shoulder. The glass exploded, falling in shards around Quist as he flipped over on the descent, allowing his assistant to fall on top of him. They hit the moat twelve feet below and vanished into the black depths, three more silver bullets cutting through the lily pads.

'Goodbye,' shouted Adler. No one surfaced and, realising she couldn't see a thing in the dark water, she slipped on her jacket and left. 'It was nice meeting you both.'

* * * *

Chapter 33

Rex wasn't sure if being torn to shreds by a big cat would prove fatal, but he knew the silver bullets in Gruner's gun would definitely do the trick. The Sergeant kept the pistol trained on him as he stood naked and trembling inside the tiger enclosure by the bolted door. Seething and snarling in the opposite corner, its body quivering in a tense crouch, the frightened animal could sense the supernatural aura and wasn't attacking. This didn't instil any confidence. If tigers were anything like women, decided Rex, it could change its mind at any moment and his chances would be significantly higher in lupine form.

Gruner watched eagerly, his breath coming in short excited gasps, as Rex bent double, grunting, gasping and quickly transforming. The temperature plummeted, human bones splintering and black fur sprouting, as the huge wolf appeared.

'Yes,' shouted the Sergeant, grinning crazily. 'Now do it. Let me see you fight it.'

The tiger hissed like the air brakes on a truck and pressed itself against the bars, its ears flattened against its skull and tail lashing wildly. Clearly terrified, the cat had no intention of going near this creature.

'No surrender here,' laughed Gruner, snatching his long cattle prod. 'You're fighting, pussy, and this is a fight to the death.'

The mercenary crackled the electrified prongs on the tiger's rump and, snarling in pain, it leapt forward involuntarily. Rex swung a high-speed fist, punching the animal's jaw, and it slumped onto its side unconscious.

'*What the fuck?*' Gruner's mouth fell open in shock. This wasn't the spectacular battle of titans he'd hoped for. 'What have you done?' He dropped into a squat to look through the bars at the twitching animal and assess the injury.

The wolf stooped too, swiftly grabbing a handful of fresh

tiger droppings.

'Ah, it's only stunned.' The Sergeant chuckled and adjusted the voltage on his prod. 'A poke with this should wake…'

Rex flung the soft dung through the bars, splattering Gruner's face and blinding him. He fired off several wild shots as Rex kicked open the door and snapped the bolt. Rubbing at his eyes, Gruner fired three more times before the werewolf rolled across the concrete and knocked the pistol from his hand.

'Oh, very good.' Gruner cleared his eyes and stared in horror as the creature circled him. 'So what now? You're going to kill me, are you? Do you think I'm scared of you? Come on. I'm not scared of you.'

'You look scared,' growled Rex, saliva drooling from his jaws. 'You sound and smell scared too, but no, I can't kill you. I can't take human life when I'm like this.' He headed for the door. 'But there's something you ought to know.'

'What's that?'

'I don't like hurting animals.' Rex looked over the Sergeant's shoulder. 'So I didn't punch too hard.'

Gruner twisted and froze to see the stunned cat was back on its feet and pacing slowly through the open door of the enclosure. The supernatural aura of the werewolf was still present, but it no longer concerned the tiger. The sight of Gruner without a cattle prod and without bars between them eclipsed all such sensations. The Sergeant spotted his gun ten feet away by the crush cage and, diving across the floor onto his belly, he snatched it, flipped over onto his back and pulled the trigger.

'Fuck,' he whispered. Firing at Rex had emptied the magazine.

With the most recent of several violations still fresh in its memory, the tiger pounced and pinned him to the concrete. The hot breath on Gruner's face triggered a bizarre childhood memory: he'd once grabbed a neighbour's cat to throw to a pack of dogs for fun.

The startled pet had clamped his hand with its front paws and whirled its rear legs in a blur of motion. After snapping its neck, he'd wondered why it did this, but now realised it was an instinctive scratching action common to all species of feline. It was a highly efficient method of disembowelling prey. He realised this as his shredded bladder and several feet of intestine shot across the floor like sloppy scarlet snakes.

Rex was unaware of the intimate moments shared by these two in the veterinary crush, but it was obvious this would be their last. The wolf winced and closed the door as Mister Tigsy began to devour the screaming Sergeant alive.

* * * *

Watson splashed and struggled at the edge of the moat, coughing up water and digging in his heels to heave Quist's shoulders onto the sloping grass bank. He looked up as the bright navigation lights of the helicopter passed overhead, the AgustaWestland thundering deafeningly as it headed for central London. Straining, he pulled again, dragging the limp detective half out of the lily pads.

'I can't get you any further up the bank,' whimpered Watson. 'You're clothes are piss-wet through and you're too heavy to...'

'Doesn't matter,' croaked Quist, shivering and groaning. 'Dig it out. The bullet, Watson. You have to get the bullet out of me.'

'*Dig it out?*' The youth was terrified. '*How?* With what?'

'Oh, here's an idea...' Quist coughed blood. 'How about that stupid SAS knife you're constantly playing with? One bullet went clean through my shoulder, but the other is in my chest. Get it out, NOW.'

Watson pulled the knife from his sock, his trembling hand almost dropping it in the water. He managed to open the main blade.

'Poison.' Quist coughed again and groaned in agony. 'You need to be quick; the silver is poisoning me. The flesh will heal around the cuts you make, but you have to work fast. Do it now.'

'I once took a dog to the vet,' stammered Watson, ripping open the detective's shirt to expose the bullet hole. 'I had to hold it for the examination, but he hurt it and it bit him. You won't bite me if I hurt you and…'

'*Do it*,' snarled Quist, slipping into unconsciousness.

Taking a deep breath, Watson shoved the shaking knife into the hole, cringing as blood poured out to gush over Quist's chest, glossy black in the moonlight. Gagging and retching, he twisted and dug deeper, then shoved his fingers into the hot gore and located the lump of silver. Trying his best not to vomit or faint, he pulled it out and tossed it in the water.

'Ugh, there we go. As easy as…' The words turned into a desperate moan as he realised the wound wasn't closing. Even worse, Quist's face had turned white, his glassy eyes stared at the night sky and he was no longer breathing. 'Hey, no, come on, Guv.' Shoving the knife in his jeans pocket, he pinched the detective's nose, blew air into his mouth and slapped his face hard. He rechecked his amateur surgery, silently willing the lacerations to supernaturally vanish, but the gaping hole remained. 'Jesus, Guv, no.' The teenager's eyes filled up. 'Please don't tell me you're dead.'

'Oh, I think he is,' chuckled a mocking voice.

Watson twisted around, his stomach turning to ice to see Laurel and Hardy standing at the top of the bank.

Hardy tipped his bowler hat politely and pointed. 'Look, Stanley, that's what we call a corpse. See how the eyes are open and glazed.' The fat man slid down the slope, grabbed the kneeling youth by the scruff of his collar and booted Quist's shoulder, the kick slithering the body back into the water.

'Gee, Ollie, so that's a corpse?' Laurel watched the

229

detective vanish beneath the surface and pointed to Watson. 'And what do we call *that*?'

'This, Stanley, is a loose end.' The titanium blade snapped out from the cuff of Hardy's suit. 'And the best way to deal with loose ends is to cut them off with a...'

Watson didn't wait to find out. Shrugging himself out of his wet jacket and darting away, he left Hardy holding the collar.

'Yes, run,' shouted Laurel, excitedly watching him scurry along the edge of the moat and up the banking. 'Get yourself hot and sweaty. I love it when young boys sweat.'

The petrified teenager raced through shrubbery with Laurel close on his tail and burst from the foliage into the funfair. The closest building was a Chinese pagoda and, dodging into the darkness inside, he looked around frantically for somewhere to hide. The place appeared to be a fairground hall of mirrors, but he didn't get the chance to view his distorted reflection. Sinewy arms grabbed him from behind and locked tightly around his torso.

'Got you,' hissed Laurel, his tongue licking greedily at Watson's neck. 'Yes, your sweat tastes good.'

'Oh, fuck,' he moaned. *The boss was dead and he was about to join him.*

Hardy followed them in, panting heavily from the exertion, and switched on the lights. Mirrors were everywhere, but every one showed Watson something he didn't want to see: a fat lunatic slowly approaching with a lengthy shining blade.

'Oh, fuck,' he repeated, absolute terror having limited his vocabulary.

With his right arm still gripping the struggling youth's midriff, Laurel wrapped his left forearm around his throat and squeezed. Writhing and perspiring, Watson reached into his jeans pocket.

'Well...' Hardy moved in front of them, theatrically slashing the air in rapid swishes. 'Here's another nice mess you've got yourself into.'

'You're loving the part, aren't you?' whimpered the teenager. Sliding out his SAS knife, he blindly thumbed open one of the blades and silently prayed. *Please don't let it be the fucking bottle opener.* 'You were crackpot serial killers and now you're budding actors.'

The obese man laughed cruelly and drew back his arm.

Watson stabbed upwards into Laurel's elbow and, grunting, he released the youth's neck. The spiked tool was for repairing sails, but it appeared to be just as efficient when disabling psychopaths. His head free, Watson ducked low and jerked his assailant forward. Hardy's sweeping weapon missed its intended target and sliced instead across his partner's throat. The wound opened in a wide scarlet smile, bubbling horrifically as Laurel attempted to cry out.

'No,' snarled Hardy. 'What the hell did you...'

Free of the dying man's grip and gibbering in fright, Watson pushed Hardy backwards, dodged a knife slash, and tore out of the exit. He raced into the ghost train building next door, his eyes bulging and heart pounding as he searched for a hiding place.

'Oh God,' he stammered, his voice choked. His spinning mind replayed the sweeping blade. *Death had claimed the boss and it had almost taken him back there.* 'Oh, my God.'

He spotted the control lever with GHOST TRAIN ON and GHOST TRAIN OFF printed either side. Praying the mechanical noise would hide his movement and frantic panting, he threw the switch. Recorded screams and sinister laughter poured from concealed speakers and the empty carriage rattled away on its journey through the complex. *There was a desk he could hide behind, but the best place would be in the dark tunnel.*

It was too late to hide anywhere. Watson squealed as Hardy leapt on him from behind, knocking him from his feet.

'Ligeia isn't going to be pleased,' hissed the overweight

killer, pinning him down. 'She wanted Laurel and Hardy, not just Hardy.'

Watson laughed like a maniac. 'You're the one who cut his throat, you mad bastard.'

'But it was your fault.' Hardy clamped a hand on the youth's neck. 'And you're the one who's going to pay for it.'

'Your breath,' gargled Watson.

'What's that?' Hardy grinned. 'Your windpipe appears to be restricted and I can't understand you.'

'I can see your breath.'

He blew, clouding the air. 'What the hell are you talking about?'

'Your breath is showing. Mine too. It means the temperature has fallen and do you know what that means?'

The fat man frowned slightly.

'It means you're screwed.'

The rumbling growl behind Hardy suggested Bernard Quist wasn't quite as dead as everyone had believed. The wounded wolf yanked the killer from Watson and stumbled weakly to the floor with his weight. Leaping up, the teenager fled into the dark tunnel following the train carriage as Hardy slashed at Quist with his blade, tearing open his furry chest. Physically drained and in debilitating pain, the wolf writhed on its back whining as the knife stabbed three times into its torso. Laughing as the creature shuddered and lay still, Hardy left it and ran along the train tracks after the teenager.

Watson had groped his way around two pitch-black corners, frantically freed himself from the cotton strands of a giant spider's web, and now stood hiding in the dark behind a luminous dangling skeleton, the pocket knife clutched in a shivering fist. Elation at seeing Quist wrestled with the terror.

The boss wasn't dead. Cyrano was still alive, but he looked to be in a bad way and where the hell was he? Why wasn't he here

232

helping?

Hearing footsteps, he peeped around the glowing skull hoping to see a wolf, but the fat shape approaching in the darkness wore a bowler hat.

Shit, shit, shit, shit. Watson gritted his teeth to prevent them chattering. *He wouldn't be seen in the blackness. Surely he couldn't possibly be seen.*

A burst of strobe lighting suddenly clicked on and Hardy's face lit up too.

'Look what we have here.' The killer chuckled and tore down the skeleton to expose the youth. He drew back his blade arm as Watson raised his own shaking knife. 'Ah, you still have your weapon and I have mine. We'll have a duel and I think I know who the winner will...'

The injured wolf slammed into the fat man, knocking him onto his back.

'You're still weak, aren't you?' laughed Hardy, crouching on the train tracks. 'There was no power in that attack. I don't think you have the strength to...'

The ghost train carriage hit him hard from behind, trundling over his body as it continued on its never-ending circuit. Still waving the SAS knife, the teenager watched open-mouthed in the flickering strobe as the bowler hat appeared from beneath the car and rolled across the floor. Hardy's legs twitched and Watson saw that his head had been completely crushed, the splatter of brains resembling steaming raspberry jam.

'Well...' croaked Watson. 'That's *definitely* a nice mess you've got yourself into.'

The werewolf collapsed gasping and he knelt beside it. 'This is brilliant. You're alive, Guv.'

'Evidently,' groaned Quist.

'It was horrible. I thought you were dead.'

'For a short while I *was*. The silver in my bloodstream

poisoned me. I'm still very weak; look how slowly these cuts and stab wounds are taking to heal.' Trembling, he gestured to Watson's knife. 'Speaking of which, I see you're still playing about with that.'

'Hey, it just saved my life back there.' Watson shoved the knife in his pocket. 'It saved yours at the moat too.'

'Only just. You took your time digging the bullet out.' The wolf shot him a sarcastic look. 'Perhaps you should have used that tool for repairing sails.'

'Funnily enough, that's what I used to stab Stan Laurel.' Watson grinned. 'I thought I'd lost you. It's really great to have you back.'

A second black wolf bounded along the ghost train track and rose on its rear legs, frowning to see Hardy's crushed head. 'Shit!' growled Rex.

'Absolutely,' said Watson. 'This place might have a *real* ghost now.'

'Ah, the cavalry has arrived,' said Quist, shivering. 'Are any of Adler's people still here?'

'Only her Sergeant,' said Rex. 'But he's in a worse state than Oliver Hardy.'

'You didn't kill in wolf form?' Quist's eyes widened. 'Please tell me you didn't bite or claw...'

'No, but the tiger didn't seem too concerned about biting and clawing.'

Watson grabbed Rex's furry arm, pulling him off the track as the ghost train carriage trundled by again.

'Rex and I need clothes,' said Quist, climbing unsteadily to his feet and leaning against the wall. 'Then we have to follow them to the London Docklands.'

'Greenwich will be faster along the river,' said Watson. 'Less traffic. Hey, can I drive the boat?'

* * * *

234

Chapter 34

The Thames curled in meandering loops as it flowed east towards the city, the black water reflecting streetlights and illuminated buildings along the banks. Quist sat at the wheel of the small motor launch with Rex and Watson beside him. They travelled as fast as the engine would allow, but the river was tidal here and luckily the tide was outbound and carrying them with it. London looked very different from the water, but certain locations were recognisable as they passed – the Royal Botanic Gardens at Kew and the Craven Cottage football stadium – and the detective saw they were nearing Putney Bridge. All three wore black clothing, pieced together from the leftover uniforms of Adler's defunct security squad. Quist had also found a wad of money on Stan Laurel's corpse which might prove useful once they reached North Greenwich.

'So Ligeia is a Siren?' Watson shook his head in amazement. 'A Siren from the ancient Greek legends? Cool.'

'I find it mind-blowing,' gasped Rex. 'They're using a mythological creature to make a shit load of money and it doesn't seem to faze you one bit.'

'Mate, I'm in a speedboat with two werewolves.' The teenager let out a dry laugh. 'It takes quite a bit to surprise me these days.'

'Sirens go by many names,' said Quist. 'The correct term is Lamarai, a race of supernatural beings from ancient Mesopotamia.'

'You claim it's impossible to tell her age?' said Rex. *He normally only slept with good-looking girls under thirty, but fate appeared to have stepped in to break his sexist rule.* 'If she's centuries old, you'd expect her to be wise and sophisticated, yet most of the time she acts like a child.'

'She's more a nature spirit than what we think of as a person,' said Quist. 'Apparently, she can sense other supernatural beings like us. I remember how she seemed interested in me on the Titanic and that's why she was drawn to you in Edinburgh.'

'Well, you say that…' Rex considered this. 'No, I'm pretty sure it was the sexy Rex Grant persona that attracted her, not the supernatural thing.'

'So you can't sense other creatures?' asked Watson.

'Evidently not.' Quist massaged his tender chest. The bullet holes, Watson's DIY surgery and Hardy's attack had all healed, but he was still feeling weak from the silver poisoning. 'I can't even sense other werewolves. The Siren song doesn't affect Rex or myself and that's why we both view Ligeia as a mediocre performer. I also have certain suspicions about Elva. I'm not sure about her.'

'You think she's a Siren too?' quizzed Watson. 'If so, she's a pretty quiet one.'

'No, but she's also childlike, extremely close to Ligeia and they look very similar. When we met Elva, she said I was like Rex, suggesting she could sense me, and her lack of voice intrigues me.'

'Incredible,' murmured Watson. 'You say Adler and her men use some sort of ear implants to protect against the enchantment?'

'Yes, and speaking of which, do you still have that wax?'

The youth reached into his pocket for the lump of black candle wax Quist had given him in Lafont's voodoo temple.

'Very good. Break it into two small pieces and look after them. I'm really hoping it won't be necessary, but if I tell you to use them, you need to cram the wax into your ears immediately and without any questions.'

'I've been listening to Ligeia for months,' said Watson. 'I hardly need protection from her songs.'

'It isn't her singing that concerns me,' said Quist. 'By the way, her name isn't a marketing fabrication, as I assumed. You can find references to a Siren named Ligeia in mythology.'

'You're supposed to be clever,' said Rex. 'Why didn't you realise that when you heard the name?'

'Peculiar names are commonplace today.' Quist shrugged and nodded to his assistant. 'Watson has had girlfriends called Andromeda and Chlamydia.'

'True,' conceded Watson. He opened a river map he'd found under the seat. 'Although Chlamy's mum was pretty thick and she was thinking of the flower Clematis.'

The boat sped beneath a railway bridge as they approached Battersea Park. A brightly-lit train passed overhead and Watson inspected the chart. He estimated the river to be over two-hundred metres across now and it was much wider in the city centre ahead. The floodlit chimneys of Battersea Power Station appeared on the right bank and the teenager followed the Thames with his finger to check their destination on the map.

The Isle of Dogs wasn't an island, apparently, but an elliptical peninsula formed by the river looping around Limehouse and Greenwich. Here on the chart, it looked like an inflamed uvula dangling in the rear of a mouth and the neighbouring peninsula resembled a raised thumb with the dome for a thumbnail. Watson knew the docks and factories there were long gone, replaced by luxury hotels, chic apartment blocks and skyscrapers owned by banks. Where cockneys once ate jellied eels and sang of *bulls and bushes*, the gleaming towers of Canary Wharf now soar hundreds of feet above London's East End.

The youth folded his map and turned to Rex. 'Well, you're off the hook for the Edinburgh murder,' he said. 'When the police hear about Charlington Hall, they'll find the bodies of those two wanted killers and the weapon used on Charlotte Michie. They might look like Laurel and Hardy, but the DNA and fingerprints both belong to psychos.'

'That's right,' said Quist. 'You can tell them the truth to a point. Adler's friend Alistair Ramson killed the girl and then kidnapped you from the Balmoral Hotel.'

Rex nodded. 'We should have rung my friend McNulty back there at the house. His police brother would have spoken to the right people and I'd be in the clear by now.'

'We can't alert them yet,' said Quist. 'Now we know the truth about Ligeia, we can't have the authorities descending upon the concert to arrest Adler's people. If Ligeia feels threatened, it could be hazardous for everyone around her including the police. A Siren has two songs, remember. One that enchants and a harmful one for protection.'

'So what's the plan?' asked Watson.

'First we have to get Ligeia away from Adler and end this dangerous exploitation. If she were ever to use her darker voice over a stage amplification system, the effects on the audience wouldn't bear thinking about. I warned the Colonel, but she doesn't care. As soon as Ligeia is safely out of the way, we can bring in the police.'

'Prison is too good for that one-eyed bastard,' snarled Rex, clenching his fists. 'She should be dead like Charlotte Michie.'

'Rex, listen to me...' Quist glanced up at the moon. 'However angry you feel, you have to control yourself. You mustn't kill anyone tonight, do you hear me?'

'Good advice, but a bit late,' said Watson. 'He's already wasted one of them.'

'What?' Quist stiffened. 'How?'

'Er...' Rex looked sheepish. 'It was Lafont, the one they called the Padre. I sort of lost my temper and accidentally kicked him under a train.'

'Alright, that's bad,' said Quist, relieved. 'But thankfully not *too* bad.'

'I reckon the voodoo guy would disagree,' pointed out Watson. 'Well, he'd disagree if he had a head and he wasn't in several pieces. Anyway, you can't blame Rex when you did the

238

same thing to save me in the ghost train.'

'True,' agreed Quist. 'But you mustn't use your teeth and claws, Rex. No matter how angry you get tonight, do *not* transform and attack anyone. Do you understand?'

'Yeah, right.' Rex thought about mentioning how he'd bitten a certain one-eyed woman earlier, but this didn't feel like the right moment. 'No problem.'

* * * *

Chapter 35

Standing at the very tip of the Greenwich Peninsula and soaring two-hundred feet above the looping Thames, the London Dome was practically surrounded by water. Quist, Watson and Rex stood outside the busy North Greenwich station, gazing up at this enormous white blister. Twelve support towers jutted from the exterior at angles, which reminded Watson of a giant pin cushion. He'd heard how £790 million had been spent to erect this place back in 1999 – a fairly high sum, he decided, for what was basically a temporary tent to house the Milenium exhibition. The rdiculous price had forced the planners into preserving the Dome as a permanent structure and the O2 Arena was built inside. This had proved to be a lucrative move and it quickly became a top venue for international stars.

The concert audience were already inside and the last stragglers were hurrying along the glass-covered causeway from the railway platforms and bus terminals in the transport hub.

'It's almost ten,' said Quist, spotting the station digital clock. 'Ligeia will be on stage soon and we need to find a way in.'

'The Dome itself is no problem,' said Rex, heading for the doors. 'It's full of public bars and restaurants, but the O2 is a separate structure inside. I've been to concerts here before and the security is always tight.'

'How many entrances into the stadium?' asked Watson.

'Just the one,' said Rex. 'Once you're through that, there's a walkway around the interior with entrances to the various seating tiers.'

'How are we doing?' enquired an East European voice behind them. 'This concert sold out ages ago, but if you guys want tickets, it's your lucky night.'

The trio turned to find a stocky Polish man with a shaven head.

'Are you a ticket tout?' asked Watson.

'Hey, no one likes that name.' The man chuckled, showing his gold teeth. 'I sell dreams to people who have a desire to turn dreams into reality.' Upright advertising frames of illuminated posters stood every few metres along the covered walkway. He gestured for them to follow him behind the closest where their conversation would be more private. 'The show's about to start,' he said. 'If you want tickets, you'd better be quick or you'll miss her entrance.'

'One moment, please.' Quist turned to Rex and Watson and lowered his voice. 'This is obviously our easiest way in. We can use the money I found on Stan Laurel's corpse.'

'That isn't a sentence I ever expected to hear,' said Watson.

'How much?' asked Quist.

The tout grinned with delight. 'Three-hundred each.'

'Jesus,' gasped Watson. 'Do you sell many?'

Sighing, Quist reached into his pocket and the man raised his eyebrows to see the wad of cash. 'Er, sorry, I meant four-hundred each.'

Snatching the tout's shirt, Rex dragged him close, his eyes glowing amber. His wolf muzzle extended in a crackle of facial bones. 'Give me the tickets,' he snarled, licking the man's cheek. 'Give them to me now, or I'll eat your fucking face.'

'Rex, calm down.' Quist grabbed his arm, but was unable to break the grip, the silver poisoning still leaving him weak. 'Change your features before someone sees.'

'Take them.' A urine pool appeared around the tout's feet as he quickly handed over three tickets. 'Just take them and let me go.'

'Thank you,' said Quist. 'You know this is illegal? You really ought to consider a new profession.' He watched the terrified man scurry away as Rex released him. 'What were you thinking?' he hissed. 'Rex, you need to control these violent urges before you...'

'I can control them just fine,' snapped Rex, his face transforming back to normal.

'The moon is causing you to act rashly.'

'No it isn't.'

'Yes, it's making you angry and argumentative...'

'No it isn't.'

'Yes, it is.'

'No, it isn't.'

Sighing, the detective rubbed his eyes wearily, wondering how long this ludicrous exchange might continue if he allowed it. Probably quite a while, he decided.

'Come on,' said Watson. 'We need to get in there.'

They followed the causeway through the glass entrance and paused to look around the colosal interior of the dome. Ultra-modern sculptures were suspended overhead and, rising to the curved ceiling, the enormous music venue virtually filled the structure. An indoor street known as the Avenue ran around the outside, throbbing with lively bars, cinemas, bowling alleys and countless restaurants. The O2 doors were straight ahead and, showing their tickets to the security team, the trio were ushered inside. From the music and deafening cheers, the show had obviously begun and they hurried throught the foyer area and access tunnel to appear between the lower seating tiers. Watson spotted the tiny figure on the stage at the opposite end of the arena and caught his breath.

'Shit,' he shouted, above the noise. 'We've missed the start.'

'We aren't here for the concert,' shouted Quist, testily.

Illuminated by banks of coloured light and surrounded by a carpet of dry-ice fog, Ligeia sang in her silver mini dress. A huge television screen backdrop allowed the crowd to watch her in close-up and Watson found it difficult to tear his eyes from the sight.

A vast oval filled with twenty-thousand people, the stadium was full and the detective looked around, attempting to work out some sort of strategy. The lighting was dim and the crowd resembled a starry night sky. It took a few seconds for him to realise the impression was caused by thousands of phone screens. Blocks of seating rose in two sloping tiers, the upper soaring into the roof of the dome. A packed standing area had been created between the sound mixing desks and the stage, and Quist saw the chances of reaching Ligeia from there were impossible. The audience were seperated from the stage by a chest-high fence and a no-man's-land populated tonight by roving cameramen. The line of burly O2 security staff didn't help matters.

'We should split up,' said Quist, leaning close to Rex's ear to be heard above the music. 'We need to somehow find a way backstage. She's quite childlike, so if one of us could get her alone during the interval, we could make up an excuse and convince her to leave with us.'

'If I can reach her, I can get her to come.' Rex winked. 'I'll just switch on the famous Grant charm'

Quist tugged at Watson's arm and they headed for the left side of the arena, leaving Rex to make his way to the right side of the stage.

'So do we have a clever plan, Guv?' asked the youth.

'We've had better,' admitted Quist. 'I'm making this particular clever plan up as I go along.'

The detective skirted the standing crowd and led Watson between two of the seating blocks. They entered a walkway beneath the lower tier and Quist noticed the fire exit doors spaced at intervals along the wall. Security staff were also positioned on the walkway, but they'd congregated in groups where they could view the stage and he smiled to see their glazed expressions. *These men worked for the O2, not Adler, and none would be using ear implants. Whilever Ligeia was singing, they'd be entranced like the audience and wouldn't notice what he was doing.*

'How long does this song last?' he asked, moving to the closest fire exit.

Watson smiled like a drunken simpleton and, sighing, the detective slapped him hard across the face.

'Shit!' spluttered the youth. 'What the…'

'Ths song,' repeated Quist. 'How long before it ends?'

'*Oceans of Love?*' Watson blinked a couple of times. 'Er, she's halfway through.'

Quist quickly checked the exit and saw the electronic sensor plates at the top, one fixed to the frame and the other to the door itself. If anyone operated the push-bar and opened this, the sensors would seperate and a host of alarms would sound. Glancing around and seeing that no one was watching, he gripped the unit and carefully peeled it from the woodwork with his strength, ensuring the plates remained together. Screws fell to the floor and, leaving the intact unit dangling by its wires, he pushed down the panic bar and eased open the door.

'Come on.' He pulled Watson through and closed it. 'Quick.'

The teenager saw they were in a tunnel. 'This looks as if it runs all around the arena,' he whispered.

'Yes, it's an emergency corridor,' said Quist. 'Any fires or bomb threats and the crowds will be herded into this to make their way out. The stage is this way, so let's follow it and see where it takes us.'

They hurried past several doors and muffled applause and cheering told them the current number had ended.

'We need to be careful,' murmured Quist, walking in front. 'The security staff here will be enchanted during her songs, but whenever she isn't singing, they'll be…'

'Guv,' said Watson, his voice a frightened stammer. 'It isn't the O2 staff we need to worry about.'

244

Quist turned and saw the muscular arm wrapped around the teenager's throat and the pistol pressed to his temple. A door behind them had silently opened as they'd passed by and one of Adler's team had stepped quietly out. The Colonel followed and peered curiously at Quist.

'Take them to the green room,' she said. 'I have to admit, I'm surprised to see you, Mister Quist. It seems the silver bullets didn't work. Your resilience is to be commended, but I'm sure your young assistant here won't be so lucky if my man fires one through his brain.'

'I'm sure you're right,' whimpered Watson. 'So let's not trust to luck, eh?'

* * * *

Chapter 36

Rex pushed and squeezed his way through the heaving crowd to reach the right side of the O2 stage. It wasn't easy, as the entire standing audience swayed in time to the song *Oceans of Love*, the majority waving phones with their screens showing a candle flame. He knew this App was a modern alternative to the old tradition of holding cigarette lighters aloft and he tutted at such nonsense. Most of the Apps on Rex's phone had comical functions that revolved around making girls giggle after picking them up. One or two rated female looks and sexual performance. *He'd never dream of downloading something as juvenile and shallow as a virtual candle flame.*

At any other concert, the audience might have turned nasty if someone brusquely pushed past them to reach the front, but this lot were enthralled by the love song and stared at the stage with glazed eyes and open mouths. Rex waved a hand in front of an unresponsive face. Pickpockets would have a great time here, he realised, except they'd be too enchanted to steal. He elbowed his way onwards and smiled grimly. *Picking pockets was exactly what Irana Adler was doing, albeit on a slightly different scale.* Rex now knew that Ligeia's voice was supernatural, but still found it difficult to comprehend. This mediocre singing was the best thing these people had ever heard and in many ways he envied them. *How truly wonderful must this Siren song sound to enchanted ears?*

Rex made it to the front of the throng and saw Ligeia stiffen on sensing his presence, her excited eyes searching the swaying masses as she sang. She spotted him at the crowd control fence on the far right of the stage and gave a warm smile. Rex waved and, still singing into her microphone headset, Ligeia turned to look down the rear steps that she'd climb to reach the stage. Elva stood watching the concert in the sunken area below and Ligeia signed to her. Sixty seconds later, the mute girl opened a security door on Rex's right and beckoned to him. He carefully eased between the mesmerised security personnel and darted through into the emergency corridor.

'It's great to see you again,' he said, as Elva squeezed and kissed him. 'I saw Ligeia signing to someone and I knew it had to be you. Were you backstage?'

She nodded and took his arm, leading him along the passage and around a corner.

'Were you alone back there?' asked Rex. 'Are any of the Colonel's men…'

The uniformed giant guarding the door around the next corner answered his unfinished question. The man reached into his jacket for a weapon. 'Where do you think you're going…'

Rex punched him hard and stepped over his unconscious body. 'I'm going backstage,' he said. 'Any objections?'

He opened the door and found *under stage* would be a more accurate description, as the acts climbed the stairs from here to emerge in front of the crowd. He also found two more of the Colonel's team on sentry duty. The mercenaries grabbed him and, tensing himself to fight them off, he suddenly hit upon an idea. *Adler claimed the enchantment in Ligeia's voice only worked when she was happy. Well, why not put that to the test?* Rex head-butted one of the men, but not too hard; just enough to anger him. The pair attacked savagely and wrestled him to the floor as another two rushed through the door to assist.

'Ligeia,' shouted Rex. 'Look down here.'

The singer turned and saw him at the bottom of the steps. Her eyes widened in alarm as she also saw the Colonel's men booting him violently in the stomach and ribs.

Great, decided Rex. *As experiments went, this was a fucking painful one.*

Elva ran to help, but received a vicious backhand smack

247

across her face. Ligeia gasped to see her friend fall to the floor, where she spat blood and trembled furiously. Shocked and frightened, Ligeia still sang as she watched the violence, but the Siren song instantly changed and a visible shudder ran through the audience like a wave, the crowd glancing at one another in confusion. The personnel on the sound mixing desk worked frantically at their controls, wondering what the hell could have happened to her voice; it had turned into something amateur and awful. Unable to sing any longer and bursting into tears, Ligeia ran off the stage and down the stairs where one of the guards snatched her.

'You need to get back out there,' he snapped. 'The Colonel won't be pleased and you can't let your fans down. Come on. Get back on that stage now.'

Elva crouched on the floor, seething furiously and fighting down the primal urges she was experiencing. Rex was way beyond fighting urges. Seeing Elva's split lip and Ligeia struggling in the guard's grip, he lost control, the lupine desire to kill his attackers taking over. He knew it was the full moon, but he also knew he didn't care anymore. Growling, he extended his talons as the metal base of a fire extinguisher slammed into the back of his head. The makeshift weapon cracked his skull on the second brutal strike and the wolf claws vanished with his consciousness.

* * * *

The Green Room adjoined the O2 Arena via a security tunnel, a luxurious VIP lounge with a well-stocked cocktail bar and plush white leather seating where the acts and their entourages could relax before and after shows. A private area with subdued lighting, white columns and a polished wood floor, the Green Room could accommodate 150 guests and Adler's team barely filled the corner by the bar. Doctor Roylott and Shane Guevara sat on a semi-circular couch with the sobbing Ligeia. Elva cuddled the distressed singer, trying to comfort her, and Adler paced angrily. Rex's limp

248

body had been dumped on the carpet, where Quist and Watson knelt examining him. Four of the Colonel's men stood guard over them clutching automatic pistols, and the remaining seven leant on the bar.

'Guv,' whispered Watson, glancing nervously at the guns. 'I have to say, this doesn't look too good.'

'It's going to be alright,' murmured Quist.

'Really?' snapped Adler, overhearing the exchange. 'Because I honestly don't think it *will* be alright.' She turned to one of her men. 'Are the doors locked?'

The guard nodded. 'Yes, Ma'am.'

The Colonel glared at Quist. 'The Green Room has superb soundproofing. Gunshots can't be heard by anyone outside.'

'Is Rex alright? Asked Ligeia, tears rolling down her face. 'Why did your friends hurt him?'

'They were playing.' Adler took a deep breath, attempting to control the rage building inside. 'It looked as if they were fighting, but it was all playacting.'

'Then why isn't he moving?' sobbed Ligeia.

'Yeah.' Watson gave Adler a sarcastic smile. 'Answer that, Sweetheart.'

'Shut up,' hissed the Colonel. She noticed Elva signing to Ligeia. 'And you can stop that. Stop it NOW, you dumb little fucker.'

Regaining her composure and sweeping back her dark hair, Adler strode to the bar and poured herself a whisky. *Why did she kept losing her temper? She was normally icy cool and this behaviour was way out of character. Why was she feeling so furious?*

Rex sucked in air and sat up as consciousness returned.

'Are you okay, mate?' asked Watson.

'Yeah.' He gingerly fingered the back of his head. 'They hit me with something and cracked my skull open.'

'The damage has healed,' said Quist. 'Let's hope no brains spilled out.'

'I don't think so,' said Rex, without a trace of irony. 'I can remember everything.' He turned to Adler. 'I can certainly remember *this* one-eyed lunatic.'

'I've been waiting for you to wake,' said the Colonel. 'I wouldn't want to do anything to you without you being fully aware.' She finished her drink in one gulp and slammed down the glass. 'What the hell are you doing here? By showing up backstage like that, you upset Ligeia.'

Rex grunted. 'I think it was your men kicking the shit out of me that upset her.'

'Do you know how much you've just cost me by ruining the concert? Ligeia was too distressed to go back on and nothing I say will soothe her. I didn't expect to see you again. I gave instructions to my Sergeant, but evidently he didn't comply. He isn't answering his phone either. Would you know anything about that?'

'I'm not surprised,' said Rex, climbing onto his knees on the carpet. 'If the phone was in his pocket, it'll be inside the tiger now.'

Adler smiled tightly. 'Gruner was my best man.'

'Oh, by the way,' added Rex. 'Your pet psychopaths Laurel and Hardy won't be moving any more pianos.'

'Is that so?' She seethed silently for several seconds. 'So some of my team now have to stay behind and remove the evidence from Charlington Hall. I really did *not* need this.'

'The news has gone viral,' said Guevara, checking his digital tablet. 'The social media sites are talking about how Ligeia's singing changed and how awful her voice sounded before she rushed off.'

'This can be remedied once we reach the States,' said Adler. 'Bad press surrounding one concert won't matter when the album goes on sale and her American tour begins…'

'I don't want to sing for you again,' stammered Ligeia, tears pouring down her face. 'Your friends hurt Elva and Rex. Elva told me you hurt her earlier too. You tried to break her arm and you lied to me about it. I don't like you anymore.'

Adler stared at the girl's cuddling each other on the couch and realised she wouldn't be able to placate her tonight and certainly not with Elva around. *After this debacle, it would take time and huge amounts of charm to render Ligeia submissive and cooperative again. She needed to get her safely onto the American flight, but first she had to finish up here and it no longer mattered if she upset the stupid bitch further.* The Colonel took a pistol from one of her men and walked towards Quist.

'So the silver bullets didn't kill you?' she said. 'Let's try again, but this time we'll see if one in the brain works.'

'Don't you dare hurt him,' shouted Ligeia, jumping to her feet. She snatched Adler's arm and took a deep breath.

'No you don't.' Adler swiped the gun across the girl's jaw, stunning her. She smirked as Ligeia collapsed on the carpet and turned again to Quist. 'Thank you for warning me about her dangerous abilities – how she's able to use a harmful voice when angry. It's going to be difficult to sweet-talk her around after all this, but I'll drug her and deal with that problem when she wakes in Miami.'

Elva stared at her unconscious friend and trembled with fury. Quist stiffened as she stood up from the couch and signed to Watson.

The teenager turned to Rex. 'Elva says she's sorry about earlier, but she couldn't help when they were hurting you below the stage because the audience might have heard her.'

'What the hell is that supposed to mean?' snarled Adler.

'She says there's no audience here now,' continued Watson, glancing uneasily at Quist. 'She asked me if I still have

251

that wax from the chapel.'

The detective gazed at Elva, his colour draining. 'Askari?'

She nodded, furious.

'I'll ask again,' said Adler. 'What the fuck is she talking about?'

'The wax,' whispered Quist, to his assistant. '*Now*.'

The suspicious guards pointed their guns as the youth reached into his pocket and stuffed the black beeswax deep in his ears.'

'What are you doing?' The Colonel raised her pistol too. 'Don't move.'

Elva took a deep breath and Quist clapped his hands over Watson's ears a second before she screamed. Light bulbs burst and glasses shattered behind the bar, but the Green Room damage bill was the least of Adler's problems. The Colonel and her men convulsed as if electrified and crumpled to the floor twitching with blood pouring from ears, eyes and noses. Roylott rolled off the couch dead and Guevara's right ear exploded, his brains splattering Ligeia's dress.

The scream ended and silence descended.

'I should have guessed earlier,' whispered Quist. He tore his eyes from the horror to gaze warily at Elva. 'You're Askari.'

Elva nodded. Still fuming with anger, she knelt over Ligeia, cuddling her as she awoke from Adler's blow.

'What the fuck *was* that?' stammered Rex, gaping at the corpses. 'She's what?'

'Askari,' said Quist, examining Watson. He was relieved to find him unconscious and not dead. 'You'll know her more familiar name. Elva is a Banshee.'

* * * *

Chapter 37

Watson tried to stand and stumbled drunkenly against the cocktail bar. He felt someone grab his shoulders to steady him and saw it was Quist. The detective's lips seemed to be moving, but he couldn't hear the words.

'Remove the wax,' shouted Quist. 'It might help.'

Clutching the counter to balance himself, the dazed teenager cleaned out his ears and looked around the Green Room as his blurred vision returned. '*What the...*' he mouthed silently.

Watson was aware of the rock bands who had performed at the O2 over the years. He guessed this VIP lounge must have played host to some fairly messy scenes involving booze, coke and semen, but he doubted it had ever witnessed this kind of devastation. Doctor Roylott, Shane Guevara and Adler's mercenaries were all dead. Their twitching bodies littered the carpet around the bar, pools of urine forming beneath them and their ears oozing blood and brain matter. He turned to see the Colonel's corpse slumped against one of the couches, blood running from the corner of her single glazed eye like a grisly teardrop.

'I must have blacked out,' stammered Watson. The last time he'd experienced a ringing in the ears like this was following a heavy metal concert when he'd been stupid enough to stand in front of the speaker tower. 'What *is* this? What the fuck happened here?'

'Elva screamed,' said Quist, grimly. 'She's a creature very similar to Ligeia. Mythology refers to her kind as Banshees.'

'Sorry, but I seem to have a fire alarm going off in both ears. Maybe I didn't hear you right, but it sounded like...'

'A Banshee.' Quist gestured to the dead mercenaries. 'Her voice killed them.'

'Too right it did,' muttered Rex, pouring himself a whisky behind the bar and downing it.

'I don't like to see things like this,' said Ligeia, trembling.

253

She gazed at the bodies with wide eyes, her voice quavering. 'I don't like it.'

'I don't think they liked it either,' said Rex, gulping down a second drink.

'Come this way.' Quist took her arm, leading her around the other side of the bar and out of sight of the carnage. 'You don't need to look at it.'

Watson and Elva followed, the latter signing.

'She says she had to do it,' translated the youth. 'We were about to be murdered and she couldn't let that happen. When the Colonel hit Ligeia, she lost her temper and stopped them.'

'She certainly did.' Quist smiled tightly at Elva. 'I find it difficult to condone killing, but those people were killers themselves and they left you with no other option. Thank you for your intervention and for warning Watson to use the wax.'

'This is all so confusing,' said Ligeia, staring in horror as Roylott's brains ran down her silver dress and onto her dusky legs. 'I don't understand everything that happened, but I don't like this blood. I have to clean myself and change my clothes.'

They watched her leave for the changing room and the detective gave Elva's shoulder a gentle squeeze.

'In a way, the two of you are related, aren't you?' he said. 'She's Lamarai and you're Askari. A Siren has two voices – the one that enchants and the one that harms – but the Askari are limited to just one. That's why you never speak. Your voice is highly dangerous to humans and your Banshee scream is lethal.'

She nodded glumly and turned to Watson.

'She says you're right,' said the teenager, translating as she signed. 'She loves Ligeia and sees her as a sister. She thought the Colonel was nice, but today she saw her for the bad person she really was. Ligeia had always been happy and she likes to see her happy. She went along with the way they exploited her, but that all changed today and she couldn't allow us to be harmed.'

'Did you know Elva was a Banshee?' asked Rex.

'I suspected something, as I mentioned on the boat, but I wasn't sure. I could see the close bond and how alike the girls were and I deduced she was similar to Ligeia. I read about the Askari on the Colonel's computer and Elva's lack of voice hinted that she might be one of these creatures. She confirmed it just before she screamed.'

'Well, the wax did the trick,' said Watson, rubbing his ringing ears. 'Cheers, Guv.'

Quist nodded. 'Adler's team used those audio implants to combat Ligeia's enchantment, but they were useless against a Banshee scream. Not only does beeswax safeguard the hearing in the normal sense, but it appears to have inherent supernatural properties which protect against such creatures. It worked in the classics like *Ulysses*. Apparently the ancients knew these things.'

Elva nodded and signed.

'That's right,' translated Watson. 'She remembered you giving me the wax and she knew her voice would only stun me if I used it. Adler said this room was soundproof, so her scream wouldn't hurt anyone outside.'

Quist smiled at Elva. 'When you met me, you could sense I was like Rex. You knew your voice wouldn't affect supernatural beings like Ligeia, Rex and myself, but everyone else within earshot would be...'

'Er...' Rex narrowed his eyes.

'Yes?' asked Quist, noticing his guilty expression.

'I think you ought to know...' He gulped. 'I er... I bit the Colonel earlier today. She forced me to do it.'

'Ah.' Closing his eyes, the detective ran a weary hand over his face. 'You might have said.'

'Shit,' whispered Watson.

'I was going to tell you, but the time was never right.'

Quist ran around the cocktail bar to the sprawling bodies.

'Damn!' he hissed, seeing that the Colonel's *corpse* had vanished. 'This way, quickly.'

Rex, Watson and Elva followed as he raced into the changing room, but it was too late. Ligeia was gone and the fire exit door stood ajar.

'*Wonderful*,' drawled Watson. 'You're telling me that crazy cow is a werewolf and she's out there somewhere on the full moon?'

* * * *

Quist and Elva ran out of the London Dome with Rex and Watson following close behind. The girl was frantic and the detective held her wrist to prevent her running away to look for her friend.

'It's alright,' he said, smiling reassuringly. 'Trust me. We'll find her.'

Rex arrived at the riverbank fence, looking across the black water from North Greenwich to the sparkling lights of the buildings a kilometre away.

'She has to be taking Ligeia to the London City Airport,' said Quist. 'The concert was supposed to end at eleven-thirty and Adler's jet is there ready for the flight to America. How far is it?'

'I'm not sure,' said Rex. 'Around three-thousand miles.'

'Not to America,' said Quist, as patiently as possible. 'How far is the airport?'

'It's on the other side of the Thames.' Rex pointed to a plane taking off to the east, its navigation lights winking as it soared overhead. 'Look, the airport is just past the ExCel Exhibition Centre over there.'

'How's she going to get across the river?' asked Watson, looking for bridges.

'She needs to go under the Thames through the Blackwall Tunnel,' said Rex. 'She must have cars here to transport her team. If we can find where they're parked, we might find Ligeia.'

Quist looked up at the red lights that dangled across the sky like a gigantic string of Christmas decorations. An illuminated pylon towered above the water to his right and another stood on the opposite riverbank. A cable stretched between them, over three-hundred feet in the air, with dozens of spherical passenger gondolas slowly crossing from Greenwich to the Royal Victoria Dock and the ExCel centre on the distant quay. The red aircraft warning lights were fitted above the cars, leaving the interiors in darkness, but squinting, the detective's enhanced eyesight made out a familiar female face peering down from one of them.

'Not *under* the Thames,' snapped Quist. '*Over* it. There she is.'

Elva saw Ligeia too. She jumped up and down frenziedly, unsure of what to do.

'They've taken the Air Line,' said Rex.

Quist spotted the Air Line cable car station across the car park to his right. 'Rex, come with me,' he said, thrusting a handful of cash into his assistant's hand. 'Watson, you need to look after Elva. Use this money to get a taxi and go with her through the tunnel to the airport. We'll meet you there.'

'Er, okay, Guv.' The teenager took the girl's hand and glanced uneasily at her. 'Let's just hope she doesn't stub her toe and accidentally cry out, eh?'

* * * *

Chapter 38

Quist and Rex ran into the Air Line boarding station, the detective paying for two tickets at the desk and racing up the stairs. Resembling glass bubbles, the futuristic cable cars could seat ten passengers, but they found an empty one and jumped in. The twin doors closed automatically as it reached the open end of the building, the gondola swaying gently as it floated out and began its steep ascent to the first cable support pylon.

'How far in front do you suppose they are?' asked Rex, anxiously. He peered up at the line of thirty-six cars that stretched for almost a mile across the night sky ahead. 'Can you tell which one Adler is in?'

'No,' said Quist, squinting at the red roof lights. 'When I first spotted Ligeia at the window, their car was rising to the first pylon like this. That means they must be quite a way across the river by now.' He turned to gaze thoughtfully at Rex. 'Now that we have the time, I have to ask – why on earth did you bite her?'

Rex cringed at the reminder. 'It all happened so fast,' he sighed. 'She was twisting Elva's arm. She was going to break it if I didn't do as she said and she didn't give me time to think. It wasn't my fault. I know it probably wasn't a wise move, but we don't know for certain that the bite worked.'

'The way Adler survived the Banshee scream would suggest it worked admirably.'

'It wasn't my fault,' shouted Rex, anger rising. 'She was torturing that girl and I wasn't thinking straight.'

'I know, I know,' said Quist, soothingly. 'Listen, you have to calm down and…'

'I don't *have* to do anything.' The gondola shuddered and Rex jumped to his feet. 'What the hell was that?'

'We just crossed over the first pylon tower which made the cable shake slightly. Now will you please sit down and control

258

yourself?'

'How slow is this thing?' Still standing, Rex cupped his hands against the glass and peered at the black water three-hundred feet below. 'We're never going to get across the river at this rate.'

'Rex, the moon is influencing you...'

'No it isn't.'

'Yes, it...' Quist recalled a similar pointless argument from earlier. 'Let's try your song. You know how it calms you when...'

'No, I'm getting sick of humming that stupid tune.' For the third time since leaving the station, their gondola came to a steady halt. 'Oh, this is ludicrous. Why does it keep stopping like this?'

'To let people on and off in the stations. Come and sit beside me.'

Rex narrowed his eyes, staring at the illuminated Air Line station on the quayside way ahead. His wolf vision was able to make out the distant passengers leaving the building. Adler was amongst them, tugging at Ligeia's arm and heading east at a fast pace towards the airport.

'There they are,' he snarled. 'They're already on the ground and we're stuck up here, swinging about like the dick on a dancing donkey.'

The detective cleared his throat, wondering where this peculiar phrase had come from and slightly unsettled by the mental image that had just been conjured up.

'Well, I'm sick of this.' Rex shrugged off his jacket and began to undo his trousers.

'What on earth are you doing?' asked Quist, his eyes wide.

'This is all my fault. I bit Adler and now she's getting away. I'm going to stop her. I have to put things right.'

'You're not thinking straight. You need to...'

Utilising lupine strength, Rex wrenched open the sliding doors and leapt out.

'Oh, for crying out loud...' hissed Quist, gripping the seat as the gondola swung precariously. 'I don't believe this.'

He peered down to see a white splash in the dark water. Seconds passed before a wolf broke the surface and began swimming towards the far bank. Knowing the Air Line probably wouldn't operate if the safety system sensed a door was open, he pulled it closed with difficulty, the silver poisoning still leaving him weak.

'I really do *not* believe this,' muttered Quist.

* * * *

The Royal Victoria Dock has changed dramatically since its 1855 opening. Gone are the masses of industry and shipping and the huge expanse of water is now given over to pleasure craft and water sports. Preserved cranes line the quayside by the modern buildings, their metal booms raised high in a poignant salute to their hectic past life.

'Come on,' snapped Adler, slipping off her stilettos to move faster in bare feet. She hurried along the edge of the water dragging Ligeia by her arm. 'Kick off your shoes like me.'

'I don't want to go with you,' sobbed the tiny singer.

Reaching down, Adler wrenched them from her feet, then continued at a brisker pace.

'Stop now,' said Ligeia. 'STOP and let me GO.'

The Colonel laughed. 'So that's your *other* voice, I take it? Your supposedly harmful voice? There's a tickling in my ears, so I can sense you're trying to do something with it, but you're wasting your time. It won't work on me and that's no longer down to my implants. I'm different now.'

Couples and small groups strolled along the dock between the chic waterfront bars and restaurants, some of the closer ones turning to look with uneasy frowns. Most assumed it was a gay couple quarrelling, but one bunch of inebriated young men didn't like what they saw.

'What's going on?' asked one of the four, standing in the

Colonel's way. 'Are you alright, luv?'

'This doesn't concern you,' hissed Adler, pushing past. 'Walk away, now.'

'She's crying. Why don't you stop crushing her arm and then I might leave.' He moved close behind, tapping Adler's shoulder. 'Hey, I'm talking to you, Sweetheart.'

'Wow!' One of his friends followed him. 'Do you know who that bird is? I don't believe this, but...'

Adler turned, slamming the heel of her palm into the first man's face, breaking his nose and propelling him ten feet backwards. She gasped at her new strength, before landing a swift karate kick on his friend's chin. His boots left the ground, he fell unconscious, and their shocked companions stepped back shaking their heads. Adler tugged at Ligeia and walked faster towards the ExCel and the airport.

'I want to be with Elva,' moaned Ligeia. 'I don't want to go with you. Why did you take me away from her?'

'You know what?' said Adler. 'I'm starting to wonder that myself. Why *did* I take you? I'm beginning to think I should just snap your neck and leave you here.'

The Colonel yanked her close, gripping her throat as she hurried past a wide square planted with lines of trees. *Why not do it? Why not break the stupid slut's neck?* She gazed at the dusky skin and felt the terrified pulse hammering beneath her fingers. *Better still, why not bite into her soft throat and tear out her windpipe? Why not eat her throat?*

Adler shook herself. *This was insane. Why was she allowing primal emotions to take over in this way? It was obviously something to do with the werewolf bite and she needed to control it.*

Everything had changed. God alone knew what Elva had done, but the Padre had been correct with his warnings. Elva was obviously a supernatural creature like Ligeia. The little bitch had wiped out her entire team and would have killed her too had it not been for Grant's bite. Thanks to those interfering bastards back there, the authorities would be investigating Charlington Hall, they'd find Moran and Ramson and this lucrative venture was finished. She needed to get away now, alter her plans and begin afresh. The Colonel had grabbed Ligeia in the O2 without thinking, but the more she debated, the more she realised there wasn't any point in taking her along. She had enough money and, more importantly, she had this incredible new power.

With her hearing accentuated, Adler picked up a distant splash. She twisted around, gazing at the wide dock and then up at the Air Line where she could make out the tiny figure of Quist closing the gondola doors. *She was being pursued and someone must have jumped from the cable car – probably that idiot Rex.*

'Run,' snapped the Colonel. 'Run now.'

A huge wolf climbed a boat ladder from the water and bounded along the quay after them. Adler ran past the Royal Victoria footbridge and along the narrow walkway between the vast bulk of the ExCel exhibition centre and the water's edge. Looking back she saw the black wolf closing on them. Four legs were swifter than two and Rex didn't have a struggling girl to drag. People leapt aside in horror as Rex raced past, all wondering what this creature could be and most wishing they'd had the foresight to photograph it on their phones.

'Please stop,' said Ligeia. 'I can't run any further…'

'No need to run.' Adler looked around to ensure there was no one nearby. The evening revellers were much further back near the hotels and bars they'd passed and this section of the quay was empty. 'I'm ending this right now.'

Still gripping her captive's wrist, Adler closed her eyes and concentrated. *How were you supposed to do this? How did you embrace the lycanthropy and change?* She felt an alien darkness rise within, bones lengthened and she bent double, grunting in pain as her entire frame began to transform. *Ah, apparently it wasn't too difficult.* Designer clothing tore apart and fell away, black fur sprouted and her wolf muzzle extended as Ligeia stared in terror.

'What are you doing?' she whimpered. 'You're frightening me.'

The Colonel no longer held Ligeia's arm. In her place, a huge she wolf stood on two legs, gripping her wrist with hairy talons and gazing malevolently with a burning red eye. The eye patch remained, with the elastic stretched tight around the creature's head. Ligeia opened her mouth to scream, then toppled stunned and bleeding as a paw smacked across her face. Adler fell to the ground too as Rex reached them and slammed into her from behind.

The Colonel flipped onto her back, slashing his chest with her claws. 'Following me was a stupid move,' she growled. 'Attacking was even more stupid. I'm trained in combat and, now I have this power and strength, do you honestly think you can best me?'

'I don't know,' said Rex. He buried his fangs into her shoulder and twisted his jaws, wrenching at the flesh. 'Let's give it a try.'

An ExCel fire exit opened and one of the evening cleaning staff emerged, a chubby man hoping for a quick smoke as he emptied his mop bucket. He tutted to see the writhing mass of fur, threw the soapy water over it, and the animals parted. The cleaner had assumed they were stray dogs fighting and had tossed the bucket without allowing himself the time to notice their size. He'd doused dog fights on occasions before, but as the creatures turned to scowl at him, he realised he'd never seen dogs that looked anything like *this*. Baring his fangs, Rex growled and the man soiled himself before bolting back indoors.

Still sprawling on her back, Adler took the opportunity to lift her knees and slam both feet into Rex's midriff, the kick launching him across the walkway and over the edge of the quay.

He smashed his head on the side of a boat and plunged into the icy water between the vessel and the dock. Adler turned to Ligeia and saw she was still unconscious from the swiping blow. Hesitating and making up her mind, she left her and darted away. This girl was nothing but a hindrance now and she didn't need her anymore. *She'd made enough profit from her and now she had the exhilarating power to do anything.*

Rex floated face-down in the dock, ten seconds passing before his head wound healed and he roused himself. He grabbed the boat ladder beside him, raging furiously and coughing up water as he climbed. His amber eyes turned to the deep red of glowing coals as he hauled himself onto the quay and he knew he had to kill Adler. *No matter what, he was going to tear this woman apart.*

'Rex, is that you?' asked a frightened voice. 'Rex, she hurt me. She hit me.'

He turned to see Ligeia awake and climbing unsteadily to her feet. The urge to help the girl momentarily wrestled with the darker homicidal compulsions. Like a bizarre traffic signal, his eyes changed from red to amber, and then back to red. Ignoring the girl, he raced after Adler, growling and snarling.

* * * *

Chapter 39

Watson sat with Elva in the rear of a taxi on Victoria Dock Road heading for the airport along the northern side of the ExCel exhibition centre. Turning to the girl, he saw how distressed she was and squeezed her hand reassuringly. Hopefully, she wouldn't forget herself and ask the driver to go faster.

'Hey, it's okay.' He smiled. 'Don't worry. We'll find her.'

Elva nodded, but didn't look too sure.

'How long have you known her?' he asked.

'Not long,' signed Elva. 'I lived in a place called Ireland for a very long time, but then I met a man who took me to a city called Prague. He was a driver and he hid me in his lorry. We had lots of sex and I thought he liked me, but when we got there he knew some very bad men and he tried to sell me. I escaped and met Ligeia. After all that time, it was wonderful to meet someone like myself at last – a sister.'

'Yeah, I'll bet.' Watson wondered how many years, or even centuries, she'd been in Ireland. He lowered his voice so the driver wouldn't hear. 'So you're er, you're a Banshee, eh? Don't they have fairy stories about you lot – legends about how your scream causes death? That's one myth that seems to have a grain of truth to it.'

'I'm never able to speak,' signed Elva. 'I only use my voice when bad people hurt me, like the ones in Prague…' Suddenly stiffening, she pulled at Watson's arm and pointed right, signing frantically.

'You can sense Ligeia?' Watson peered through the window. 'She's over there? Are you sure?'

She nodded excitedly.

He leant forward and spoke to the driver. 'Take your next right, please. We need to get into that big car park over there.'

The driver negotiated a roundabout and took them along

265

Lynx Way down into the ExCel parking area. Elva bounced giddily on the seat to see Ligeia in her crumpled mini dress walking across the tarmac, barefoot and dazed.

'The girl there in the silver dress,' said Watson. 'We have to pick her up.'

The taxi drew up beside the weeping Ligeia and Elva leapt out to embrace her. Watson looked around for Quist and Rex, but there was no sign of them. Fortunately, there was no sign of Adler either. With the full moon beaming down, she was the last person he wanted to meet in a deserted car park right now.

'Hey, that's amazing.' The driver grinned as they climbed in. 'You look just like that famous singer.'

'She gets that a lot,' said Watson. 'Okay, straight to the airport now, please.'

'Yeah, you've definitely got her looks,' said the driver, glancing in his mirror and chuckling. 'I bet you wish you had her cash.'

Watson watched the girls cuddling and kissing. 'Are you okay?' he asked, feeling slightly aroused. 'No need for tears; you're safe now. What happened to the boss and Rex? Where's the bastard who took you?'

'I don't know,' mumbled Ligeia, wiping her eyes. 'The Colonel was really nasty to me and then she turned into a big bad wolf. Rex had a fight with her, but then she left me and ran away. Rex left me too and chased her, but he was different. He was a bad wolf too.'

'No, Rex is okay,' said Watson. 'He's a good wolf.'

'He's bad now. His eyes turned red and I could feel he was bad.'

Realising the driver was listening, Watson glanced and saw his incredulous face in the mirror. Once upon a time, this kind of talk would get people burnt at the stake, but these days there were plenty of recreational drugs to blame.

266

The taxi sped across Connaught Bridge, which separates the Royal Victoria Dock from the Royal Albert, and the London City Airport appeared on their left. A compact facility, the single airstrip ran along the entire southern side of the latter dock and catered for propeller aircraft and small jets. The driver glanced warily in the mirror again. From the conversation, he was now wondering about the mental health of his passengers and, more importantly, whether these young nutters had any money for the fare.

'Nearly there,' he said. 'Er, you don't have any bags, so I'm guessing you're not flying. Are you meeting someone from a flight?'

'We're supposed to be meeting *someone*,' said Watson. He turned to Elva. 'The boss said to come to the airport, but then what? We've got your friend back, but where's Adler?'

'Rex is here,' gasped Ligeia, grabbing the youth and gesturing to her left. 'He crossed this bridge a few moments ago and now he's just over there. I can feel him.'

'*Oh, boy*,' muttered the driver.

'That's the end of the runway,' said Watson, peering into the blackness through the fence. The taxi turned left onto Connaught Road and he spotted an airport entrance off the roundabout just ahead. 'Turn in here, would you?'

'You aren't allowed in there,' said the driver. 'I think it's a service road or something. The public entrance to the terminal is a little further away on Hartmann Road.'

'No, this will do. Pull in here.'

'Okay, mate.' The taxi driver was glad to be rid of them. 'Whatever you say.'

'Thanks.' The teenager jumped out and paid the fare. He waited until the car had sped away before walking towards the security booth with the girls. A guard appeared and Watson turned to Ligeia. 'Get ready,' he whispered. 'I think you'll need to do the enchantment thing with your voice.'

'Sorry.' The guard held up a hand. 'You're not allowed past this point.'

'Tell him to let us through,' said Watson. 'Then tell him to forget about us.'

The girl repeated his words and the man stepped aside.

'Certainly, Miss.' He smiled politely. 'Have a nice night.'

'Hey, that was brilliant.' The teenager spotted an airport buggy parked behind the security booth similar to those used on golf courses. It was dark and hopefully no one would see them if he left the lights off. The guard returned to his post, oblivious to their presence. 'Come on. Jump in this thing with me.'

Ligeia and Elva climbed in the electronic vehicle, holding on to each other, and he drove across the grass towards the aircraft turning point at the end of the runway.

'So that's how your voice works, eh?' Watson laughed nervously. 'It's like using the force. *These are not the droids you're looking for.*'

Ligeia frowned. 'I'm sorry?'

'Not to worry.' He laughed again, but fear knotted his stomach muscles. 'I'm just quoting the classics.'

* * * *

There was no pedestrian walkway over Connaught Bridge, but the traffic was light this Friday evening and Adler crouched behind shrubbery waiting for a break in the flow of vehicles before running across unseen. The she wolf jumped the roadside barrier to land in bushes beside the airfield perimeter fence. This western end of the London City Airport was devoid of infrastructure. The enormous Royal Albert Dock was on her left, the terminal buildings stood some distance away to her right and, in front of her, an expanse of grass surrounded the end of the runway with its wide turning area. Taking a step back, she launched herself over the razor wire to land on the turf. *This was amazing. She was stronger and more alert than she'd ever felt in her life.*

Shrouded by darkness, Adler ran to the edge of the airstrip by the water and gazed around, sniffing the air and picking up vague scents which had always been indiscernible to her human nose: vegetation, rabbits and foxes, aviation fuel and oil. An aircraft taxied slowly towards her to turn and take off into the breeze. The front spotlight illuminated the tarmac and grass, but she stood outside its bright beam by the dock. One of the mid-range airliners which used this airport countless times per day, Adler recognised it as an ATR42, a French twin turboprop. *So where was her Gulfstream?* The wolf looked around and smiled. *There it was, parked on the right side of the runway with several other planes.*

Hearing a distant thud behind her, she turned and bristled to see glowing red eyes; Rex had jumped the fence and was bounding towards her on all fours. '*You,*' she snarled. 'Why the hell did you follow me? Why can't you just...'

Obviously not in the mood for questions, Rex attacked ferociously, pouncing on the she wolf and ripping into it with fangs and claws. Adler locked her jaws on his shoulder, gouging at his chest with taloned fingers and attempting to get her muzzle past his chomping teeth to tear into his neck. All reasoning had vanished and animal savagery had taken over. She had to kill this creature right now and she instinctively knew that decapitation would end her opponent's life.

Rex broke away from her as another wolf ran across the grass to appear beside them. The pair turned, panting and growling, to glare ferociously at Quist. The detective had transformed in the shadows after leaving the Air Line and had followed their scent trails. He raised himself on two legs and nodded grimly to see that Adler's single eye burned red. His heart sank as he noticed Rex's eyes were the same colour.

'Rex,' he yelled. The aircraft was turning some thirty feet away and he shouted above the noise of the twin propeller engines.

269

'Listen to me. Your eyes have changed and you need to calm down.'

Rex reared on his hind legs, drooling and glowering at the new arrival. Vague recognition registered, but the beast had taken over and this was just another wolf – another threat that needed to be disposed of.

The Colonel had lost all control and lashed out at Quist, tearing open the side of his neck in four deep gouges and splattering Rex's face in hot arterial gore. It wasn't the wisest move she'd ever made. Rex howled with fury, the tiny part of his mind that was still human recognising that his friend had been hurt. He leapt upon Adler, raking his talons through her face and ripping out her single red eye. The blinded she wolf screamed and, grabbing an arm and leg, Rex lifted her from the ground, swinging her furry bulk in circles before launching her into the closest aircraft propeller. The whirling blades chopped into the screeching creature and catapulted it into the dock.

Clutching his torn neck, Quist watched Adler hit the water in several pieces followed by a string of intestine and bowel. 'Goodbye, Colonel,' he growled.

Oblivious to the dismembered werewolf, the pilot briefly debated the shudder on his starboard engine, then completed his turn and sped away down the runway to take off into the night sky.

'Rex…' croaked Quist, grasping his wound. 'Calm yourself and listen to my voice…'

Turning to him, Rex saw the hot blood pumping over Quist's fingers and licked his lips, his eyes blazing scarlet. One adversary was dead and here was another invading his personal space. *He had to tear this wolf apart and then kill something else. He had to kill and continue killing.*

'Rex, I know part of you can hear me. You have to fight the dark urges and come back to me.'

The wolves circled each other, the sleeker one snarling and

salivating. Quist still felt weak from the silver bullets and was all too aware that when Rex attacked, it would be impossible to wrestle him off. There was a good chance his head would be torn from his body. Clearing his throat quietly, he began to sing.

'By the light, of the silvery moon...'

Rex stopped abruptly, but continued his loud snarling.

'I want to spoon. To my honey I'll croon love's tune...'

Furry pointed ears pricked up and Rex cocked his head to one side.

'Honeymoon keep a shining in June...'

Unable to help himself, Rex joined in, growling the lyrics through razor fangs. 'Your silvery beams will bring love dreams, we'll be cuddling soon...'

'By the light of the moon,' warbled Quist, moving towards him.

The wolves sang in unison. 'By the light of the silvery moon...'

Rex began to calm down, his eyes changing from bright red to dull red, then to glowing amber. Quist released his healing neck to take hold of his friend's muscular arms, slowly dancing as he sang. The younger wolf trembled and began to transform back into human shape.

'Keep singing,' murmured Quist, transforming too. 'It's working. By the light of the silvery moon, I want to spoon, to my honey I'll croon love's tune...'

Watson arrived on the electronic buggy with Ligeia and Elva to find the two naked men dancing and singing to each other.

'Well, that's something you don't see every day,' he said. 'Hey, nice song, Guv.'

'Yes,' agreed Quist. 'An odd choice, as I mentioned, but rather appropriate, wouldn't you say?'

* * * *

Chapter 40

Adler's Gulfstream jet stood near the terminal buildings with the pilot making his final instrument checks. He looked around as Quist opened the cabin door. Like Rex, the detective wore a baggage handler's outfit found in one of the airfield storerooms.

'What's going on?' demanded the pilot. 'Where's the Colonel? Where are the team?'

Quist realised this must be the last of Adler's men. His military piloting skills meant he'd been posted here, a fortunate turn of fate which had saved him from a nasty sonic death in the London Dome. *Speaking of which, he'd doubtless be protected from Ligeia's voice.*

'Last minute change of plan,' said Quist, his features transforming and muzzle extending. 'You're wearing ear implants. Remove them NOW.'

The whimpering man did as ordered, frantically digging out the tiny devices with his fingernails. *A difficult task*, Quist decided, *when your hands are shaking and you're attempting to get as far back as possible by climbing onto the aircraft instrument panel.* The audio implants were tossed onto the carpet and, returning his face to normal, the detective brought Ligeia to the cockpit doorway.

'Tell this man to calm himself,' he said. 'Tell him no one else is coming and he's to do everything you say.'

'Calm down,' she said, smiling sweetly. 'No one else is coming and you'll do everything I tell you.'

The pilot relaxed and nodded.

'Thank you' said Quist. 'Now please repeat the following. He'll take off shortly with you and Elva. His flight plan is for Miami, but he'll bypass Florida and land in Cuba instead. He'll tell the Cuban air traffic control that he has engine trouble and he has to make an emergency landing there. He'll also forget that you're a famous singer, everything about you and everything about his time

272

with Colonel Adler.'

Ligeia began speaking to the pilot and Quist turned to Elva who stood in the cabin with Rex and Watson. 'You seem to be more... *mature*,' he said. 'Mature isn't the correct word, but I believe you understand things better than Ligeia does. The pair of you were under Adler's influence, but now you're both free to live your lives. You need to take care of her, but you have to go somewhere where no one knows her. She's probably never had anyone like you to help her before.'

Elva signed to Watson.

'She'll look after her,' said the youth. 'She'll make sure no one exploits her again.'

'That's good,' said Quist. 'Remember you have to be anonymous. You have no passports or paperwork, but if you get Ligeia to speak to the right people in the Cuban airport, her voice will get you through. It will also secure you a boat passage from Cuba to the South American coast. There are many beautiful places there where you can live happily in obscurity.'

'This might help,' said Rex. 'Look what I've found.' He'd been searching Adler's luggage and twisted one of the open cases around to show it was filled with American dollars and gold Krugerrand coins.

'Excellent.' Quist turned back to Ligeia. 'Tell the pilot to make his final checks and let the tower know he's ready to take off.' He waited until she'd finished speaking. 'Everyone knows the name Ligeia, so you can't call yourself that anymore. Do you recall Lenny Logan's name for you – Sally? Why not adopt that instead? You can say Elva is your sister, Elva Logan.'

'I like that,' said Ligeia. 'Yes, Sally and Elva Logan.'

'By the way, before you reach your destination, tell the pilot to stop working as a mercenary soldier and to find alternative employment, maybe in a bar. It will be far healthier for him.' He picked up the pilot's phone from the seat beside him. 'Ask him to be a good chap and to unlock this, would you?'

He watched as Ligeia's instructions were followed and he took the man's cigarettes and lighter from the seat. 'Tell him to stop smoking too. It's bad for him.'

'Thinking about his health?' said Watson. 'Hey, you're all heart, Guv.'

A radio voice from the control tower informed the jet that it was clear to begin taxiing to the runway for take-off.

'Well, it looks like this is goodbye,' said Rex, sighing. 'You have to leave now or they'll want to know what the delay is.'

'Come with us,' said Ligeia, wrapping her arms around him and nuzzling her face into his neck. 'You're like us and we'll have such fun together. The three of us could have sex every day by the ocean.'

Watson swallowed uncomfortably, wondering if he'd get the same offer and how he'd explain it to his mum.

'I'm sorry,' said Rex. 'It would be nice, but I really can't. We might meet again one day, but my life is here and, believe me, you're going to be okay with Elva.'

Elva nodded vigorously.

Siling sadly, Ligeia embraced Quist. 'Thank you,' she whispered, a tear rolling down her face. 'I'm so grateful for this and for how you helped me all those years ago.' She kissed him and turned to hug Watson. 'Thank you.'

The teenager stiffened as both Ligeia and Elva kissed him long and hard.

'Wow!' He raised his eyebrows and grinned at Rex. 'Tongue.'

* * * *

The three men watched the small jet take off and climb above East London, its twinkling lights eventually vanishing amongst the stars. Quist turned from the night sky to peer at the dark expanse of water beyond the airport runway.

'I wonder…' he murmured, staring thoughtfully at the Royal Albert Dock. 'Did that propeller kill Adler? She was chopped into pieces and almost certainly decapitated, but the speed made it impossible to say for sure.'

'Don't ask me.' Rex shrugged. 'I wasn't exactly thinking straight at the time.'

'I got a kiss from Ligeia,' said Watson, still lightheaded from the earlier embrace. 'An amazing kiss.'

Quist held up the pilot's phone. 'We need to alert the police to Charlington Hall and the bizarre kidnapping by Alistair Ramson. Rex is in the clear, but we'll have to work on our stories before we're interviewed.'

'A kiss from Ligeia,' repeated Watson. 'She actually licked my tonsils.'

'You don't say?' Rex gave him a smug look. 'I got a little more than a kiss in Scotland.'

'Oh, lucky you.' The youth grinned sarcastically. 'Yeah, you probably do a little better than me with the girls, but I can stroke dogs and cats without them shitting themselves in terror.'

'Whatever.'

'By the light of the silvery moon?' snorted Watson. 'You're a werewolf and out of all the songs you could pick to calm yourself down, you chose *that*?'

'It works for me,' said Rex, defensively. 'My grandmother has an old music box that plays it. I used to listen to it with her when I was a little kid.'

'If you're going to dance naked with men, maybe a nice Barbara Streisand song or something by Abba would be more appropriate?'

'Yeah? Maybe *go fuck yourself* would be more appropriate?'

'The song by Shaggy? Yes, wolves are shaggy, so that would work too.'

Quist lit two of the pilot's cigarettes and handed one to Rex. 'Ah, my two best friends are bickering like childish idiots.' He gave a lopsided smile. 'It's good to have a happy ending with everything back to normal.'

* * * *

It was three in the morning and the dark quayside along the northern edge of the Royal Albert Dock was deserted. The full moon reflected on the black surface as Irana Adler emerged from the depths and slowly hauled herself onto the side. She vomited water before sprawling naked on her back, trembling and groaning.

'*Fuck*,' she hissed, sputtering up more fluid.

The aircraft hadn't sliced off her head, the profanity was proof of that, but her left arm was missing and most of her right leg. Incredibly, both appeared to be slowly growing back and the propeller gouges had virtually vanished. By dawn, the unbelievable regenerative process would be complete. Her stomach was healing too, which was fairly surprising as she'd been agonisingly disembowelled.

This was astounding, but she had to learn more about her lycanthropy. The wolf had taken over earlier and she needed to master discipline and control before transforming again – before making people pay for crossing her. With her martial arts and combat skills, no one could ever hope to best her once she was in control.

The majority of her blood must have drained away in the dock, but like her limbs, it was renewing itself. *The lack of blood was probably behind this overpowering compulsion to eat meat.; her body obviously required iron. Surely there couldn't be any other reason? A rare steak would feed the cravings, but any meat would suffice and the rarer the better.*

Adler let out a manic laugh. 'Meat,' she growled. 'Where can a girl find meat at this time in the morning?'

End

Also from Ian Jarvis

A contemporary Sherlock Holmes, the eccentric Bernie Quist is a consultant detective in the city of York. Christmas is days away and once again the reclusive sleuth will be quietly celebrating alone. His assistant Watson, a teenager from the Grimpen housing estate, has other ideas, mostly involving parties, girls and beer. Yuletide plans are halted when three chemists die and the fiancé of one hires them to look into her apparent suicide. After discovering the chemist wasn't engaged, they're drawn into the mystery when their employer is killed.

About The Author

Ian was born in the north of England, where he worked for three hectic decades as a firefighter with West Yorkshire Fire and Rescue. He lives in a village near Selby, where he writes humorous detective novels chronicling the exploits of private investigator Bernie Quist. Ian travels regularly, usually through Asia and the Americas. His interests include walking the North York Moors and Yorkshire Dales, natural history with an emphasis on birds, real ale, and ridding the world of all known evils. He also feels decidedly peculiar speaking in the third person and may have to do this in the future using a sinister ventriloquist's doll.

You can visit a digital Ian at www.ianjarviswriter.com

Or lurking on Facebook at

https://www.facebook.com/ian.jarvis.165

MX Publishing is the world's largest specialist Sherlock Holmes publisher, with over a hundred titles and fifty authors creating the latest in Sherlock Holmes fiction and non-fiction.

From traditional short stories and novels to travel guides and quiz books, MX Publishing cater for all Holmes fans.

The collection includes leading titles such as *Benedict Cumberbatch In Transition* and *The Norwood Author* which won the 2011 Howlett Award (Sherlock Holmes Book of the Year).

MX Publishing also has one of the largest communities of Holmes fans on Facebook with regular contributions from dozens of authors.

www.mxpublishing.com

Also from MX Publishing

When the papal apartments are burgled in 1901, Sherlock Holmes is summoned to Rome by Pope Leo XII. After learning from the pontiff that several priceless cameos that could prove compromising to the church, and perhaps determine the future of the newly unified Italy, have been stolen, Holmes is asked to recover them. In a parallel story, Michelangelo, the toast of Rome in 1501 after the unveiling of his Pieta, is commissioned by Pope Alexander VI, the last of the Borgia pontiffs, with creating the cameos that will bedevil Holmes and the papacy four centuries later. For fans of Conan Doyle's immortal detective, the game is always afoot. However, the great detective has never encountered an adversary quite like the one with whom he crosses swords in "The Vatican Cameos.."

"An extravagantly imagined and beautifully written Holmes story"
(Lee Child, NY Times Bestselling author, Jack Reacher series)

Also from MX Publishing

"Phil Growick's, 'The Secret Journal of Dr Watson', is an adventure which takes place in the latter part of Holmes and Watson's lives. They are entrusted by HM Government (although not officially) and the King no less to undertake a rescue mission to save the Romanovs, Russia's Royal family from a grisly end at the hand of the Bolsheviks. There is a wealth of detail in the story but not so much as would detract us from the enjoyment of the story. Espionage, counterespionage, the ace of spies himself, double-agents, doublecrossers...all these flit across the pages in a realistic and exciting way. All the characters are extremely well-drawn and Mr Growick, most importantly, does not falter with a very good ear for Holmesian dialogue indeed. Highly recommended. A five-star effort."
The Baker Street Society

Also from MX Publishing

The Missing Authors Series

Sherlock Holmes and The Adventure of The Grinning Cat
Sherlock Holmes and The Nautilus Adventure
Sherlock Holmes and The Round Table Adventure

"Joseph Svec, III is brilliant in entwining two endearing and enduring classics of literature, blending the factual with the fantastical; the playful with the pensive; and the mischievous with the mysterious. We shall, all of us young and old, benefit with a cup of tea, a tranquil afternoon, and a copy of Sherlock Holmes, The Adventure of the Grinning Cat."
Amador County Holmes Hounds Sherlockian Society

www.mxpublishing.com

Also from MX Publishing

The Detective and The Woman Series

The Detective and The Woman
The Detective, The Woman and The Winking Tree
The Detective, The Woman and The Silent Hive

"The book is entertaining, puzzling and a lot of fun. I believe the author has hit on the only type of long-term relationship possible for Sherlock Holmes and Irene Adler. The details of the narrative only add force to the romantic defects we expect in both of them and their growth and development are truly marvelous to watch. This is not a love story. Instead, it is a coming-of-age tale starring two of our favorite characters."
Philip K Jones

www.mxpublishing.com

Also from MX Publishing

The Sherlock Holmes and Enoch Hale Series

The Amateur Executioner
The Poisoned Penman
The Egyptian Curse

"The Amateur Executioner: Enoch Hale Meets Sherlock Holmes", the first collaboration between Dan Andriacco and Kieran McMullen, concerns the possibility of a Fenian attack in London. Hale, a native Bostonian, is a reporter for London's Central News Syndicate - where, in 1920, Horace Harker is still a familiar figure, though far from revered. "The Amateur Executioner" takes us into an ambiguous and murky world where right and wrong aren't always distinguishable. I look forward to reading more about Enoch Hale."
Sherlock Holmes Society of London

www.mxpublishing.com

Also from MX Publishing

The American Literati Series

 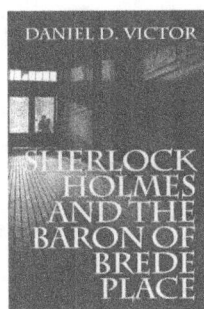 

The Final Page of Baker Street
The Baron of Brede Place
Seventeen Minutes To Baker Street

"The really amazing thing about this book is the author's ability to call up the 'essence' of both the Baker Street 'digs' of Holmes and Watson as well as that of the 'mean streets' of Marlowe's Los Angeles. Although none of the action takes place in either place, Holmes and Watson share a sense of camaraderie and self-confidence in facing threats and problems that also pervades many of the later tales in the Canon. Following their conversations and banter is a return to Edwardian England and its certainties and hope for the future. This is definitely the world before The Great War."
Philip K Jones

www.mxpublishing.com